THE CLOCKWORK SOLUTION

THE CLOCKWORK CHRONICLES BOOK II

Michelle D. Sonnier

eBooks
Pennsville, NJ

PUBLISHED BY
eSpec Books LLC
Danielle McPhail, Publisher
PO Box 242,
Pennsville, New Jersey 08070
www.especbooks.com

ISBN: 978-1-949691-35-1
ISBN (ebook): 978-1-949691-34-4

Interior Design: Danielle McPhail
Sidhe na Daire Multimedia
www.sidhenadaire.com

Cover Design: Mike McPhail, McP Digital Graphics

Illustrations: Ed Coutts
Art Credits - www.Shutterstock.com
Steampunk Clock © By Atelier Sommerland
Steampunk Owl © By renikca

For everyone who encouraged me
to keep going after the first one,
this is all your fault.

CHAPTER I

The Story Begins Anew with Danger Close at Hand

ARABELLA HELENE LEYDEN ALIGHTED FROM A HANSOM CAB TWO blocks from her father's house. The summer sun still hung above the horizon despite it being well past the hour for supper. She had hoped for a breath of air to clear her head, but the hot and sticky late afternoon air wasn't much better than the stuffy confines of the cab. Regardless, she walked the remaining distance. She brushed wayward strands of her dark brown hair from her sweaty forehead with a sigh, trying not to think of the oppressive heat.

She had quite enjoyed High Tea with Julian Pattersby, the cerebral young man who'd caught her eye. Even the company of his dour maiden aunt as chaperone hadn't put a damper on their enjoyment. Between bites and exciting conversation about the optimal number of teeth on a cog for various applications, Arabella watched a curious family drama play out between Julian and his impoverished aunt.

Aunt Adelaide's frown had deepened each time Julian ordered another pot of tea, but she said not a word. Julian pretended not to notice his aunt slipping part of her meal into the small carpet bag in her lap. No plate left the table with a single scrap of food upon it, and several linen napkins seemed to go missing. Julian paid the exorbitant bill without either concern or complaint.

After tea, while Aunt Adelaide was distracted by a spectacular example of pelargoniums on their garden stroll, Julian whispered in Arabella's ear that his uncle from his mother's side forbade him from giving money to his father's side of the family but never argued over extravagant dining expenses.

Deep in thought, Arabella strolled down the sidewalk toward her father's house, a dreamy smile on her lips. Even in the midst of a prickly and potentially embarrassing family matter, Julian showed himself to be kind and generous, a gentle soul. He was an eminently suitable young man. For just a moment, she allowed herself to forget about the dangers and political machinations of the witching world and pondered the romantic possibilities of a young heart.

It was in that moment that the perils she sought to distract herself from reinserted themselves.

Arabella cried out as heat from something flew past her cheek, missing her by inches. Yanked out of her woolgathering, she saw a witch a few feet ahead of her on the sidewalk. The witch held her flame-wreathed hands away from her body. Arabella gasped. Footsteps sounded on the pavement behind her. Another woman, dressed in the dowdy clothes of a washerwoman, leapt in front of Arabella. The washerwoman's hands twisted in an arcane shape, and the next blast from the snarling fire witch slid over a hastily erected shield. The flame shot up into the sky and dissipated harmlessly. The fire witch shrieked in rage.

"Get into the house!" Arabella's savior hissed over her shoulder even as she kept her eyes on the fire witch. "I'll hold her off."

"But? What?" Arabella stammered. "Who are you?"

"That doesn't matter," she growled through gritted teeth. "Get to the house. You'll be safe behind the wards."

The fire witch threw another fire ball, and the unknown witch projected her shield out and around it. The fire suffocated in the bubble.

"Tabitha!" Arabella's defender called out. "You don't have to do this."

"Lies! She cannot be allowed to live!" Tabitha screeched. She hurled another fireball. The mystery witch caught it and snuffed it out again, her movements sure, but she panted from the strain.

Tabitha was in between Arabella and her father's house. With a quick glance over her shoulder to make sure no carriages were coming, Arabella dashed across the street. She pelted up the sidewalk, dodging screaming people running for cover. Her unknown savior had Tabitha completely distracted, but who knew how long that would last.

Once she was past Tabitha, Arabella hurried back across the street again. *Almost home*, she thought. She gasped when she saw another woman by her father's front gate. She stood transfixed by the battling witches down the street and seemed not to have noticed Arabella yet. She could be a mundane woman; she could be a witch. If she was a witch, she could be here to either hurt her or protect her. Arabella had no way of knowing. Not wanting to risk it, Arabella darted into the alley and hurried to the back garden gate.

Tiny Fae faces peered from the foliage as Arabella dashed through the garden. Curious whispers followed her the whole way. She yanked open the kitchen door and threw herself inside. Arabella slammed the door shut and leaned against it, panting.

Safe. But for how long?

Arabella struggled to calm her racing heart and slow her breathing. She strained to hear if the battle still raged between the witches even as she knew it was useless. She would never hear anything this far away, through so much stone and brick. She shuddered to think about the conflict coming close enough to hear.

Her breathing restored nearly to normal, she stepped back from the door, staring at it. She wrapped her arms around her middle and bit her lip. Who was her savior? Which House did she have to thank? And her would-be assassin… *Tabitha*. Which House did she have to blame?

Would there ever be a time Arabella would be accepted enough to leave her home without risking her life? She briefly considered venturing back out to check on her benefactor, maybe help her, but she swiftly rejected the idea. Without training in the more violent magical arts, she was a hindrance, not a help. Arabella closed her eyes and tried to fix the visage of the brave witch in her mind. She would question her sisters when she got to Blackstone House, after the Investiture ceremony, to see if they knew who she was. Then she could offer proper gratitude to her rescuer.

Arabella sighed. She listened to the creaks of the house, trying to discern if her father or brothers were home. She thought she heard someone tinkering in the lab. Father? Henry? Upstairs seemed quiet. She expected John would be out late with his friends tonight. They were all to leave early in the morning to head for Blackstone Manor and her Investiture. John said something about a "last hurrah."

Arabella thought about poking her head into the lab, but she changed her mind and wandered toward the stove. There was no point in telling her father or her brothers about the attack. It was over, and she remained unscathed. They couldn't do anything about it, and it would only upset them. With an absent flick of her wrist and a bit of technomancy, Arabella turned up the gas lamp in the kitchen. She shook the kettle on the stove, relieved to hear water sloshing. A cup of tea would be just the thing to soothe her jangled nerves. After her Investiture things would be better, Arabella told herself. After her Investiture, every member of the English Council of Witches would have to accept her. There would, of course, still be the sly dance of passive-aggressive political maneuvering, but the outright assassination attempts would surely cease. Or so she hoped.

Snapping her fingers, Arabella lit the gas under the kettle on the integrated striker her father had invented for the stove. His little invention sold quite well and had become an integral part of the family's financial fortunes. The little device was easy enough to use the mundane way, but by using her magic, Arabella avoided streaks of ash on her hand.

Arabella bustled around the kitchen, preparing the leaves while the water boiled. Her eyes fell on the curling burgundy, black, and pearl ribbons of her Investiture invitation lying on the kitchen table. She frowned. It felt odd to be invited to one's own party, but she supposed it really couldn't be helped since she didn't live under Mother's roof anymore. It was Mother's own fault, really. She was the one who had disowned Arabella in the front hall of this very house when she refused to come to heel.

Of course, Mother *had* addressed the invitation 'Arabella Helene *Sortilege.*' Was the gesture a sweet treat offered in apology? Or was it a lure to trap her now that Arabella could be useful?

She found either prospect infuriating. Briefly, Arabella contemplated tossing the invitation into the stove's flame and watching it burn to ash, but she just shoved it out of the way and started the tea to steep. She could puzzle over Mother's motivations later. For now, Arabella must focus on her last-minute arrangements before they left this treacherous city for Blackstone Manor in the morning.

CHAPTER II

The Bonds of Brotherly Love

ARABELLA DOZED RESTLESSLY IN HER FATHER'S CARRIAGE AS THEY SPED westward to her mother's ancestral home. The second day traveling to Boscastle was always the worst. The excitement of leaving on the journey began to wear thin, and everyone grew a bit peevish. It did not help that the air hung still in the stuffy confines. She'd tried to sweep her dark brown hair up that morning in the small roadside inn where they'd spent the night, but she was not as cunning with hairpins as her sisters, and escaped curls clung to the back of her sweaty neck. She hunched against the carriage wall trying to put some space between herself and her brother John with little success. He had a habit of sprawling out in his sleep, which along with his snoring, made him a tiresome traveling companion.

Arabella sat up straight with a huff and fanned herself with the letters she clutched in her lap. "Can't we open a window?" she grumped to her father and older brother, Henry, sitting across from her. "It's unbearable in here."

"I don't think that would be a good idea," Henry muttered, without looking up from the book he was reading. His superior tone, along with his coloring—auburn hair and rich brown eyes—echoed their mother so clearly that Arabella transferred some of her irritation to him.

"We're out of the city, brother dear," Arabella retorted. "We have been for quite a while. I hardly think we need to worry about the miasmas and smells at this point."

"And I suppose you'd rather be covered in dust from the road when we arrive then?" Henry finally looked up from his book and arched one brow. "I'm sure that would make a stellar impression on the luminaries of the witching world, who I am sure Mother has invited to this occasion."

Arabella tightened her jaw. "Why, such tender concern! I didn't think you cared about the opinions of witches." A peevish tone entered her voice.

"I'm only trying to look out for my baby sister," Henry simpered. "For so many years, I've been deprived of the opportunity to attend to my brotherly duties."

Arabella snorted and crossed her arms over her chest. She opened her mouth to speak.

"Children!" Father barked as he snapped his own book shut. John started up mid-snore and scanned the carriage interior with bleary blue eyes.

"I understand you are not used to being in close quarters with each other," Father continued. He ran his hand through his thick gray hair, blue eyes blazing. "But for goodness sake, please try to be civilized and not snarl at each other like beasts."

"It's just so frightfully warm, Father," Arabella frowned. "And Henry is not being amicable about opening a window."

Henry grimaced as he turned to their father. "If Arabella has her way, everything in this carriage will be covered in dust before we're another mile down the road!" He held up the book in his hand. "This is a rare edition borrowed from the Club's library. I'm responsible for the condition I return it in."

"Why would you bring a rare book, which doesn't even belong to you, on a trip to the country?" Arabella's voice rose. "You should have left it at home, or at least packed it in your trunk so you could carefully read it after we arrive!"

"I am in the midst of important research that can't be stopped for some little witchy garden party!" Henry's voice rose to match Arabella's.

Color rose into Arabella's cheeks. "My Investiture is not just some little garden party!"

"Enough!" Father roared. He pinned his daughter with his gaze. "Arabella, you may open the window near you, but just a bit. We don't want too much road dust." He turned his gimlet eyes to his oldest son. "Henry, stop antagonizing your sister. You borrowed the book, and you are responsible for it. Arabella is right. If it is so fragile, you should have planned better for its care." He swept his gaze around the carriage. "There will be no more bickering today, *children*. Have I made myself clear?"

"But I didn't do anything," John protested. "I was asleep!"

Arabella leaned into the small stream of fresh air at the window and let her eyes flutter shut. "Your snoring is loud enough to be considered part of the argument."

"On that, I will agree," Henry grumbled as he tucked his borrowed book into his worn leather satchel.

"Two against one is hardly fair," John said as he adjusted his waistcoat.

"Don't whine," Father griped as he turned back to his book. "It's unbecoming of a gentleman."

John took a breath to say something, then clamped his jaw shut and settled back into his seat as he shook his head. Arabella held up her letters to shield her face from Father and Henry. She stuck out her tongue at John with a twinkle in her eye.

John chuckled as he reached out and tried to snatch the ribbon-wrapped packet from Arabella. "And what are you reading, sister dear?"

Arabella gave a theatrical gasp as she held them out of the way. "These are personal!"

Henry *harrumph*ed as he pulled out a portfolio to peruse from his bag. "You delivered most of them, John. You already know they are from Julian Pattersby." He rolled his eyes. "I don't understand why the two of you must insist on playing such juvenile games while we are in close quarters."

"Because we're hopelessly bored, and it's hours before we'll arrive at Mother's," John replied to his brother matter-of-factly.

He turned back to Arabella. "So, I only delivered *most* of them, did I? I wasn't your only secret postmaster? I'm wounded… Then there must be some I haven't read!" He tried harder to get them from Arabella. She giggled and tucked them behind her back.

"Children…" Father cautioned without looking up from his book.

John and Arabella settled back with a sigh, companionably leaning against each other.

"I really haven't read any of your letters," John said after a moment.

"I know," Arabella said with a little smile. "I'd have turned you into a toad if you had."

John looked at his sister from the corner of his eyes. "Can you really do that?" he whispered.

"Not yet," Arabella giggled. "But I'm still learning."

John laid his hand over his heart. "Please don't scare me like that."

"But a reasonable fear of witches improves your sociability so much, brother dear." Arabella put her hand over her mouth to stifle another giggle. Father and Henry sighed in unison but didn't say anything else.

John drummed his fingers on his knee and peered at the country fields outside his window. Arabella fanned herself with her letters and sighed.

"I don't suppose you want to tell me about anything in those letters," John murmured.

Arabella suppressed a smile. "That sounds suspiciously like digging for gossip."

John looked abashed. "I'm not looking for gossip. A good traveling companion holds up his end of a pleasant conversation."

Arabella shifted to face him and raised one eyebrow.

"Alright, I'm also out of my mind with boredom. Hearing you swoon over Julian Pattersby is bound to be more interesting than watching the countryside go by."

Arabella tilted her head to the side and raised her other eyebrow.

"Fine," John growled. "I am actually at least slightly interested in your feelings for the man. You might wind up married, and then I'll be stuck with him, so I might as well try to take his measure."

Chuckling, Arabella nodded. "I see… How amazing! My brother does actually care about someone other than himself."

"I thought I'd already proven that," John grumbled as he crossed his arms across his chest. "Fine. I'll just watch the countryside since you have no interest in conversation." He turned his head firmly to the window.

"John…" Arabella's kept her voice soft as she reached for his hand. "I was just teasing you." She leaned forward to try to get a good look at this face. "Can't a sister tease her brother?"

John turned back to Arabella and considered her a moment. Then he pulled his face into a mock pout. "Wounded again!" He placed the back of his hand on his forehead. "The outrageous treatment I suffer at the hands of my cruel, cruel sister!"

Henry snorted and turned another page in his portfolio.

John glanced at Henry and smirked, then caught Arabella's hands up in his own.

"Now that you know how grievously you've injured me, you simply must tell me every juicy detail. It's the only way to make it up to me." John grinned.

Arabella broke out into a full-throated laugh. "Johnathan Ambrose Leyden, you are absolutely ridiculous. But I still love you."

He settled back and tugged the lapels of his waistcoat. "Not quite the groveling apology I was hoping for, but I'll take it." He folded his hands on his lap, eyes sparkling. "Now, do I deserve even a few crumbs of chitchat? Just a little taste?"

A dreamy smile spread over Arabella's face as she looked down at the letters in her lap and stroked them.

"Well, I supposed I do owe you at least a little something after the horrible way I've treated you."

John put his elbows on his knees, chin in his hands, and fluttered his eyelashes at Arabella.

"You're terrible," she giggled, rapping his shoulder with her fingertips. The dreamy smile returned, and she sighed. "He just seems so perfect. It hardly seems like he can be real."

Behind his portfolio, Henry turned an ear toward his siblings, but he didn't lower his papers.

"Go on..." John prompted.

Arabella blushed. "It's silly..." she paused. When John let the moment stretch on, she let her words out in a rush. "He just... He takes me seriously. He seems interested in what I think, the things I have to say." She bit her lip and looked sideways at John. He tilted his head, giving her an encouraging smile.

Arabella flushed deeper and fluttered her hand in the air. "I should just stop talking. I'm not even sure how I feel about him. Every little butterfly could just be because he's the first man outside my family to actually pay me any mind. And courting right now? Impossible! I barely survived the Trials, no thanks to Beatrice. If it hadn't been for Parthena's quick thinking, I'd be dead. Just a scorch mark on the floor..." Arabella gasped and stopped cold. All eyes in the carriage were on her, stunned. The carriage creaked and swayed, but no one said anything.

Arabella finally broke the silence. "Can all of you please forget I said that?" She searched their faces desperately. "I'm really not supposed to say anything about what goes on in the Council Chamber." She dropped her eyes and stared down at the letters in her lap. Her lips pressed into a thin white line. She'd almost revealed everything to them. Fortunately, she'd managed to stop herself before she spooked them with the recent attempt on her life. At least now they might believe the danger was left behind in the Council Chamber.

Father coughed gently. "Well, yes," he harrumphed. "I am quite familiar with that restriction given how long your mother and I lived together. I am also quite familiar with conveniently forgetting things I shouldn't have heard for the good of someone I love." He reached across the carriage and squeezed Arabella's hand. She gave him a small, weak smile. He glanced back and forth between his sons and said, "I'm sure Henry and John will be the respectable gentlemen I raised them to be and do the same."

"Of course, Father," John sputtered. "I would never say a word that might endanger Arabella."

The three turned to Henry, who regarded them all with narrowed eyes and pursed lips. When he still didn't say anything, Father raised an eyebrow and frowned.

Henry huffed. "I'm insulted you even think you need to say anything. I am always a gentleman."

The three let out the breaths they had been holding and settled back in their seats. Henry shook his head and returned to perusing his portfolio. Father leaned forward and patted Arabella's hand again before settling back into his book. Arabella and John fidgeted with their fingers in their laps.

"So," John said after a moment. "Is there anything else you would like to chat about? Anything that doesn't involve death and secrets?"

Arabella sighed. "Everything in my life seems to involve death and secrets these days."

"Hhmm… Perhaps a secret that only mortally wounds then? We could start small." John jostled his sister with his elbow. Arabella frowned as she tried to sidle away. John nudged her again. "Just a slightly poisonous secret? Surely you have at least one… You can turn me into a toad if I tell."

Arabella stifled a giggle and elbowed her brother back. "You know I don't know that spell yet." She sighed again, then looked thoughtful. "I have some decisions to make after my Investiture. Perhaps you could help me think through them?"

"Do I have to worry about Mother or one of my other beloved sisters turning me into a toad for it?"

Arabella's eyes twinkled. "Maybe. Probably not. I promise I won't tell them you're my secret advisor."

"Then, by all means, let's plan out your future."

Arabella pursed her lips together. "The decision that's weighing most heavily on me is what House I will claim allegiance to. If I do not claim Blackstone House, then the web of loyalties between me, my House of birth, my House of choice, and my blood family gets complicated. I could tie Houses together where there were no ties before or strengthen already existing bonds, but I could also cause one House to become beholden to another, owing a debt they did not wish to incur. That would cause a bit of friction."

"Aren't you already of Blackstone House?" John's voice rose in confusion.

"Not since I was disowned," Arabella said with a bitter smile. "Besides, a witch may choose another House at her Investiture, as long as the House will have her. It's a bit like a marriage in that way. Some Houses will no doubt court me, while others will avoid me like spoiled meat left in the sun."

"I would think that your magical strength and potential ties to Blackstone House would make you attractive to all of the Houses," John said.

"And here is one of the things I don't think you understand," Arabella said with a wry half-smile and tilt of her head. "There are many in the Sisterhood who do not like change and who like technology even less. Since my power is centered around technology, they see me as a perversion of witchery, an abomination they'd just as soon see dead."

Henry dropped his portfolio to his lap and blinked in shock. "That's just ludicrous! Change is part of life. You are a natural and expected adaptation to the world around us."

Father snapped his book shut. He raised his finger as if about to pontificate. Arabella burst out laughing, silencing them all.

"Did *you* expect me to turn out the way I did?" She looked at each of them in turn with her eyebrows raised expectantly.

The men blushed and dropped their eyes. Arabella smiled at them fondly.

"I appreciate the support from all three of you, but I am quite aware of the dangers of my position at this point."

"So, what are you going to do?" Father asked in a gentle voice.

"I'm joining the Sisterhood, and I'm enjoying the party. Perhaps I'll even make Mother stew a little before I declare a House." Arabella chuckled to herself. "If Mother wants me to declare my allegiance to Blackstone House, she shall have to court me along with the others."

CHAPTER III

Wherein the Leydens Arrive and Sisters are Reunited

Arabella alighted on the brickwork in front of Blackstone Manor in Boscastle, joining her father and brothers, her back sore from hours in the carriage. Father's driver did not have as smooth a hand with the horses as Mother's driver Jeanette did, nor did his carriage have the same enchantments her Mother's had to even out the bumps of the road.

John pulled a large brown paper-wrapped package off the seat of the carriage and held it out to her as he directed the Boscastle servants to the rest of the luggage. Arabella smoothed down the skirt of her second-best dress and hoped the hunter green silk wasn't getting too wrinkled in her trunk.

"Mustn't forget this," he said.

"Are you certain it's alright for me to be here?" Alexander Leyden asked as he fiddled with his tie.

"Yes, Father, it's fine," Arabella said with gentle exasperation. "The invitation was very specific that the entire household was invited, even you. New witch celebrations are taken very seriously, especially in Blackstone House."

The front door opened, and Rowena flew down the steps to embrace Arabella, her brown eyes sparkling and auburn hair streaming behind her. "Welcome, Sister," she said breathlessly, tears in her eyes. Arabella relaxed into her sister's embrace, letting go of her stress and worry for just a few moments.

The sisters pulled apart, smiling, then Rowena turned her attention to the men. "Hello, Father, Henry, John," she said as she pecked each of them on the cheek in turn.

"The official ceremony will be in Mother's rose garden, and then we'll have the party in the back gardens." Rowena's voice bubbled with excitement as the sisters linked arms and headed into the house. The Leyden men trailed behind them, looking lost. "You only have a few hours before we start; we've been waiting for you. You must unpack right away."

"I thought we'd have more time to settle in," Arabella gasped. "I thought the date on the invitation was the arrival date, and we wouldn't gather for the ceremony until tomorrow! My dress is going to be a disaster without enough time to air it out!"

"Good thing for you I know the right spells to release the wrinkles," Rowena said with a giggle and a wink. "I'll make sure you look perfect."

Arabella squeezed her sister's arm and sighed. "I don't know what I'd do without you."

"Probably look like you'd just spent the night in the forest," Rowena teased as she reached up to smooth her sister's hair. "Really, Arabella, did you sleep on the side of the road last night?"

Arabella giggled and playfully batted Rowena's hand away as they arrived at the doorway of her room. Arabella's easy laughter trailed off as she looked around the room that had been hers since she'd been old enough to have a bedroom of her own. It was just as she'd left it, what seemed like forever ago, even though it had only been a few short months. She remembered her last time in this room, recovering from her first bout of spell sickness. The book of old Arthurian romance Rowena had read to her to pass the time still sat on her bedside table.

"We have quite a crowd," Rowena said, breaking into Arabella's reverie.

"Really? Who's here?" Arabella asked.

"Cecilia Kellar and Madeline Thurston, of course; Mother's best friends wouldn't miss her daughter's Investiture. Because of their early support, Charlotte Anwell and Selina Mortimer received invitations, and Theodosia Boscoe received one out of respect. Katharine Wardlow and Philomena Beedlebaugh received invitations too for voting yes on the technomancy question. And of course, all of their daughters and sisters, and even a few husbands and sons." Rowena ticked off the names on her fingers. "Oh, and Mother invited Parthena Luther since she was your examiner. The local Chapter House sent over a few Guardians, just in case. Mother had to cast quite a spell on the horses to get here with enough time to prepare for the party without killing them."

"Oh, my," Arabella said as she sank into the chair by her bedside, also still there from Rowena nursing her through ill health. "That is quite a crowd."

Behind the girls, John cleared his throat. "As much as the guest list is fascinating, where are we supposed to put our luggage and freshen up?"

"Your luggage will already be in your rooms," Rowena said. "Turn left and down the hall to the last three doors before the back stairs."

"By the servant's stairs?" Henry arched an eyebrow. "Is Mother cross with us?"

"Do you really want me to answer that question?" Rowena asked as she raised her own eyebrow back at him.

Father clapped his son on the shoulder. "She didn't put us in the garret with the servants, and we each have a private room, so she can't be that irritated. Let's leave the ladies to their preparations."

After the men trooped out of the room, Arabella turned to Rowena, her brows pinched with consternation. "There are certain names I didn't hear on the guest list."

"Yes," Rowena murmured as she fiddled with the button on her cuff. "Any House that did not support you in the technomancy question did not get an invitation."

"And what is supposed to be a great joy in my life becomes an exercise in politics without even so much as a consultation about my feelings on the matter..." Arabella sighed.

Rowena frowned. "Surely, you wouldn't want to have your party spoiled by the witches who tried to keep you from the Sisterhood?"

"Perhaps I wouldn't, but I would like to have been consulted," Arabella grumped as she lifted the lid of her traveling trunk and retrieved her best dress.

"How would Mother even have had the time?" Rowena shook her head. "You passed the Trials, and she had to have the invitations out the next morning. She was up all night planning the guest list and writing invitations."

Arabella turned and gave her sister a stunned look. "Mother actually wrote all of the invitations *herself?*"

"She did the same for all of us," Rowena said with a shrug as she helped Arabella hang her dress. "And you did startle Mother coming to the Trials without any warning. Usually, the family plans when a girl presents herself and has everything ready before she knocks on the door."

Arabella frowned. "Why does the Investiture have to happen so quickly anyway? If there's going to be so much pomp and frippery around it, they really should allow a girl's family more time to put it together."

"It has to do with making sure magic stays controlled," Rowena said. "We can't have witches running about with no allegiances just doing whatever they like."

Arabella sighed. "More politics."

"Not quite," Rowena shook her head. "I keep forgetting you haven't had access to some of the restricted texts. You'll be able to read them now. An unsworn witch is a dangerous thing." She shuddered. "Some of the old tales will disturb your sleep for weeks."

Arabella's sleep was already disturbed, thanks to the revelations of her Trial. It seemed each night since the Trial, she woke every other hour from nightmares. The three girls in the waiting room begged her over and over to save them. She tried to help them, but her hands always wound up covered in blood. Arabella shook her head to banish the intrusive thoughts. She picked up the book next to her bed, riffled the pages before tossing it onto the bed.

An uncomfortable silence stretched between the sisters. They looked anywhere but at each other, fidgeting with their hair and the cuffs of their sleeves. Rowena wandered to the window with a sigh.

"Do the rest of them do it?" Arabella's voice was soft.

"Do the rest of who do what?" Rowena murmured distractedly as she peered out at the hive of activity below.

"The Councils," Arabella said. "The other Witch Councils around the world. Do they also kill the girls who show no power at their Trials?"

Rowena let the curtain drop from her fingertips and turned to her sister, face pale.

"No," she whispered. "They used to, but they stopped. Most of them see us as barbaric for maintaining the practice."

"Well, aren't we?" Arabella's voice rose. "Aren't we barbaric for killing young girls for the sin of hope? Hope *we* gave them?"

"Not so loud," Rowena hissed. Her eyes flicked to the door.

"Why shouldn't I be loud?" Arabella refused to lower her voice. "I'm not the one killing innocent girls." Her eyes flashed defiantly.

Rowena took a few steps toward her sister but then lowered herself to the vanity bench with a sigh. She patted the seat next to her and gave Arabella a tremulous smile.

"Ari, come sit with me. Let me explain."

Arabella crossed her arms across her chest and frowned. "Don't take that tone, Rowena. I'm not a child to be patronized."

"I know you're not." Rowena's voice was weary, and her shoulders sagged. "But I have been swimming in these waters just a bit longer than you, and I would like to save you some trouble, if you'll let me. Please?"

Arabella considered her sister for a moment, then sighed and dropped to the seat next to Rowena. She clasped her hands into her lap but kept her back stiff and her gaze straight ahead.

"Well?" Arabella said in a brittle voice. "What can you tell me that makes killing innocent girls acceptable?"

"It's not acceptable," Rowena said.

"Then why are they doing it?" Arabella turned to face her sister. "Why are you not warning girls off? Why are you letting them die?"

Rowena took in a breath to speak and then paused, pinching her lips together. She looked down at her hands clenched in her lap. "I can't tell them," she whispered.

"Can't or won't?" Arabella's voice hissed out from gritted teeth.

"Can't." Rowena's voice trembled. "When you are sworn into the Sisterhood, as you are about to be, you are sworn to keep our secrets. It's a blood oath, blood magic. If you break your oath and reveal the secrets of the Sisterhood, you die."

Arabella swallowed hard and sprang, up pacing the room past the bed to the window and back.

"So, even more killing to keep their power and secrets?" she said in a strangled voice. "I won't take the oath then. I just won't swear, and then I can say whatever I want. I'll tell all the girls who come for the Trials, I'll stand on the steps every day if I have to." Her voice rose to a hysterical pitch, and she turned to Rowena with wild eyes. Fear and desperation washed through her like the icy Northern Sea.

Rowena shook her head sadly. "They won't let you."

Arabella lifted her chin. "I'm a grown woman and a full witch now. What can they do to stop me?"

"They can kill you," Rowena answered, her voice as soft as a dove's wing. "And they will. They will kill you at the ceremony if you refuse. If you run before the ceremony, the Council will send the Guardians to hunt you until they find you. When the Guardians find you, they may be kind and offer you the oath first instead of just striking you down. Perhaps."

"But…" Arabella protested, reaching out to steady herself on her bedpost.

"No," Rowena said as she stood. In two quick strides, she was almost nose to nose with Arabella. Her voice carried a hint of steel. "This is one thing that all the world's Councils agree on. No witch may remain unbound. A wild, unbound witch is too dangerous. She has no controls on her. You would find no safe harbor any-where."

Arabella pressed her forehead against the bedpost. "So, I must take the oath to save my life, and then I must remain silent to keep living?"

"Yes." Rowena nodded solemnly. She put a hand on Arabella's shoulder.

Arabella shook Rowena's hand off. "There must be some other way." She paced the room while Rowena settled on the foot on the bed and watched her with a furrowed brow. Frantic thoughts spiraled in Arabella's mind.

She stopped suddenly and whirled to face Rowena. "How did the other Councils manage to stop doing it?"

"They voted to discontinue the practice," Rowena said. "The terms of the blood oath can be altered by Council decision."

Arabella paused her pacing by the window with the view of the garden. "That's madness," she protested. "You're forced to swear an oath that can change terms at any time?"

Rowena snorted and gave her a wry half-smile. "Now you see why all of us are so obsessed with the Council sessions. Not every Council decision alters the blood oath. There's a particular cere-mony for that. We only alter the oath for occasions of the utmost importance."

Arabella clenched her eyes shut and shook her head from side to side. "I can't do it." Her voice came out in a strangled whisper. "I can't take that oath. It is abhorrent. I can't sacrifice innocent girls so I can live." Arabella's heart thudded in her chest. She turned away and leaned on the window sash.

Rowena remained quiet for a moment, then her eyes flew wide open. She gasped and smiled as she sprang up from the bed. "So, don't."

Arabella whirled around to face her sister, her mouth open in shock. "First, you tell me I must comply in order to live, and now you're telling me… What? To just lay down and die?"

Rowena's eyes took on a devilish sparkle. "No, I'm not telling you to lay down and die. I'm saying I've just had an idea that may save your life and soothe your conscience."

Arabella tilted her head and looked at her sister with narrowed eyes. "Go on…"

"You have a new kind of influence because of your power…" Rowena began.

Arabella scoffed. "I barely got out of the vote at my Trials alive, Ro. And there was an attempt on my life just before we left the city, a fire witch named Tabitha."

Rowena gasped. "What happened?"

Arabella shook her head. "She was waiting for me on the street near Father's house. She tried to throw fire at me, but another witch intervened so I could get safely behind the house's wards. I didn't dare go out afterward. I don't even know if they ran off or killed each other. I had planned to ask you and Amelia to help me figure out who they are after the Investiture ceremony." Arabella twisted her fingers and stared at the floor.

Rowena closed her eyes and sighed. "You really should have sent a crow as soon as it happened, Ari. But done is done. You're safe here at the Manor. We'll tell Mother after the ceremony and she'll get the Guardians on the case." Rowena shook her head. "But back to your leverage…"

"How much influence can I really have if so many witches would rather see me dead?" Arabella asked.

"No, no, think!" Rowena hissed. "What has the Council been so obsessed with for years? What has Mother been grumbling about over dinner since we were small?"

Arabella thought for a moment, tapping her chin with her forefinger. "Our waning power in the halls of mundane government…" she allowed slowly.

"Yes!" Rowena clapped her hands together. "And what do you have that those very men in the halls of government are eager to get their hands on?"

"My power over machines…" Arabella said with soft wonder as her eyes widened.

"So, you dangle the possibility of a return to political power for your sister witches, and you lure influential men with your magic. You could even try to convince the Council to go the way of the Continental witches and stop killing the girls. You hold the key!"

Arabella wished she could share her sister's enthusiasm. She wandered to the vanity and trailed her fingers over the familiar painted wood.

"This is a very dangerous game to play," she murmured. "I don't know if I'm up to it."

Rowena took her hand. "What other choice do you have?"

"Apparently none," Arabella said in a faraway voice.

"Then we are getting ready for your Investiture?" Rowena asked as she squeezed her sister's hand.

"Yes, I suppose we are." Arabella squared her shoulders and let Rowena gently turn her to the mirror.

"Now, let me see what I can do with that frightful hair of yours," Rowena said.

CHAPTER IV

On Arabella's Investiture and Renewed Hope for the Future

A S THEY STEPPED OUT INTO THE GARDEN, ARABELLA BLINKED AS SHE entered the bright sunlight, and shaded her eyes with her hands. Her mother's garden Fae had outdone themselves decorating the grounds. Every flower was in bloom, even those out of season, and bright-colored ribbons fluttered from every branch and stem. Tiny silver bells tied to the end of each ribbon tinkled lightly in the breeze. Extra servants dressed in the maroon, black, and pearl livery of Blackstone House—hired just for the occasion—circulated around the garden under the watchful eye of the regular household servants bearing trays of lemonade and finger sandwiches.

"My sweet chickadee," her mother, Minerva Sortilege, said as she walked toward Arabella with her arms outstretched, gathering her into a tight embrace. Arabella struggled not to stiffen, still not certain how she felt about her mother's abrupt change of heart.

Mother seemed wholly unaware as she held Arabella at arm's length. "Let me see you, all grown up." She smiled as she looked her daughter up and down. "But we must take you shopping, my dear. Your station certainly deserves better dresses than this."

Arabella blushed and looked down at her feet. "I'm sorry, Mother," she mumbled. "It's the best dress I have."

"Don't be sorry," Mother exclaimed as she lifted Arabella's chin with her finger. "Three days is certainly not enough time to have anything made. We just need to rectify that."

Arabella gave her mother a tremulous smile. "Really?"

"Of course, child," Mother said. "Now, come say hello to your sisters."

Mother stepped aside to reveal Vivienne standing in the pathway smiling beatifically at her baby sister, her hands resting lightly on her full-term belly. Nathaniel stood behind her, looking strained and concerned.

"Vivienne!" Arabella gasped, and her hands flew to her mouth. "You should be resting, not running about the garden in your condition."

Vivienne held out her hands and took Arabella's in both of hers. "I wouldn't miss this for the world, Arabella. Welcome, Sister," she said, kissing her on each cheek.

"Vivienne?" Their father stepped forward from behind Arabella. "You've changed quite a bit from last summer. John told me I was going to be a grandfather, but I didn't know you were this close."

Vivienne blushed and smiled. "She should be here any time now, Father."

"So, the Crones are saying it will be a girl then? That's very lucky for you," he said.

Everyone fell quiet for a moment, and then Amelia bustled up to embrace Arabella. "Welcome, Sister."

"Thank you, Sister," Arabella said, and she kissed Amelia on both cheeks.

Amelia turned to their father and kissed him on the cheek. "Hello, Father."

"It's good to see you, Amelia." Father looked over Amelia's head and caught Mother's eye. They both froze, the expressions on their faces warring between anger, hurt, and longing.

Father stepped around Amelia, closer to Mother. He clasped his hands behind his back and cleared his throat as he rocked from heel to toe.

"You're looking very well, Minerva," he said. He stopped rocking and raised his eyes to her, wide and pleading.

Mother shut her eyes and turned her head away, taking a breath before she spoke. "You're looking well too, Alexander." She opened her eyes and turned back to him, her mouth trembling ever so slightly.

He licked his lips and searched for something to say. "Did you ever manage to find a solution to that Irish issue?"

Mother's shoulders tensed a bit more. "Not yet. Things seem to be getting worse again, so we'll have to think of something."

"Perhaps we could have tea sometime," he said, his voice quivering. "It used to help when you and I could talk things through."

Their children looked from one to another with wide eyes, and Mother's mouth formed into a soft little 'o' as her eyes widened.

"Yes," she said, her shoulders relaxed. "Yes, I think that would be a lovely idea. Will you be staying after the party?"

"I'll make sure I stay for that," Father said, smiling. Mother also allowed herself a small smile before she broke eye contact and coughed slightly.

Just then, the twins, Jessamine and Josephine, came skipping up hand in hand. "Sister!" they cried in one voice, launching themselves at Arabella, nearly knocking her over as they wrapped their arms around her. Arabella laughed and hugged them back.

"I've even missed the two of you," she said as she kissed each one on the cheek.

"We knew you would," they said in unison before they turned and skipped away.

"Are you sure they aren't precognitive?" Father asked, looking sidewise at Mother. "They certainly seem odd enough to be."

Mother frowned. "They've never scored higher than the average witch on any precognitive tests, but you know how our twins are. You never quite know what they are hiding."

"Indeed," Father said with a sigh.

Mrs. Holly, the Housekeeper for Blackstone Manor, came up the path and curtsied to the family. "Everything is ready, ma'am. We can have the ceremony any time you wish."

"Thank you, Mrs. Holly," Mother said. "If you'll inform the guests, we'll begin."

Everyone gathered around a temporary altar set up in the middle of the largest grassy patch of the rose garden. The invited witches and their households stood shoulder to shoulder, jostling for position to ensure they got a good view. No one seemed to mind on this joyous occasion. The Fae gathered in the branches and on flower stems, their own whispered conversations adding to the general buzz. A half dozen Guardians sauntered around the edge of the crowd, their movement deceptively casual. No being, human or Fae, escaped their shrewd gazes. They wore no formal robes to encumber them, and their hands never strayed far from the tools of their trade hanging from their belts. Even if Minerva Sortilege had been inclined to invite any of the more treacherous witches from the Council, the chances of trouble were vanishingly small.

Mother donned her formal robes with Mr. Holly's help, then stepped up to the altar and raised her hands to the sky. The entire garden fell silent.

"Gods and Goddesses, Lord and Lady, we bring forth a new initiate," she began, turning and beckoning Arabella to join her at the altar. "What do you seek, Initiate?"

"I wish to dedicate myself to the Gods and the Goddesses, to their service, and to the Sisterhood of Witches," Arabella said.

"And do you come of your own free will, under no influence of others?"

Arabella bit back the sarcastic answer behind her lips and only said, "I do."

Mother picked up a small ceramic dish of anointing oil and, with her index finger, drew a circle with a cross inside it at the center of Arabella's brow. She dipped her finger again and drew a pentagram, point up, over her heart. "So mote it be," she intoned.

"Do you acknowledge the beauty of all life, that animal, vegetable, and mineral are all your brothers and sisters, and will you treat them with the respect they are due?" she asked.

"I will," Arabella said.

"Do you acknowledge the Sisterhood as your family, and will you defend your family against all challenges? Will you keep our secrets and protect us from harm?" Mother's eyes seemed to burn into Arabella's with potent meaning.

"I will." Arabella was only partially successful in keeping the tremor out of her voice. She tried not to think of the secrets she'd just promised to keep or the political maneuvering she'd just committed to. What if she couldn't do it? What if the Council turned her down cold? What in the Cosmos had she just bound herself to? Arabella swallowed hard. The only choice was to move forward and do her best. The life of a witch was long. Even if she lost the first skirmish to save the lives of innocents, she could continue the war in the years to come. They could force her to keep the secret, but she would not perpetuate it. That was a vow she whispered to herself in her own heart.

"Do you acknowledge the power of all the Gods and Goddesses, and will you pledge your life to them, serving them to the ends of your ability?"

"I will," Arabella said.

Mother set the anointing dish back on the altar and picked up a chalice filled with wine. It was the same chalice that had served in the Investiture of every witch of the Sortilege line for the last three hundred years. Mother held it up and chanted, "As the wine drains from this cup, let the blood drain from your body should you ever betray your vows to the Divine or your Sisters."

Arabella took the cup and drank. "So mote it be," she said as she handed it back to her mother, who drained the last of the wine and said, "So mote it be."

Mother picked up the athame and held out her hand for Arabella's. "And now we enter your blood into the Book."

Aster Abernathy, the witch of the Ledger, stepped forward with a book even older and larger than the smaller record book Arabella had seen at the Council during her Trials. It held the name and bloody thumbprint of every witch in Britain since the Dark Ages. Arabella laid her hand, palm up, in her mother's and took a deep breath.

Mother raised the athame and looked at Arabella, "Are you ready?"

Arabella nodded.

"Arabella Helene Sortilege, you are now of the Sisterhood." She began to bring down the blade, but Aster cried out.

"Wait!" she said, and Mother froze. "She was registered in the Trials as Arabella Helene *Leyden*. She must enter the Sisterhood under that name." Everyone in the garden gasped.

Mother frowned. "It was a clerical error. Surely we can correct it."

Aster pursed her lips. "Minerva, you know the power of names."

Mother sighed. "I'm sorry, chickadee, but we're going to have to register you as a Leyden."

Arabella nodded. "What about my House?"

"You will always be of Blackstone House," Mother said in a fierce whisper.

"What if I don't want to be of Blackstone House?" Arabella whispered back just as fiercely.

"You don't have to choose a house right now," Aster broke in, also whispering. "You can decide later. But you must declare by the Winter Solstice." A small smile played on her lips and she seemed oblivious to the tension between Arabella and her mother.

Mother fixed Arabella with a look filled with hurt and anger, which Arabella returned. "I haven't decided yet. Blackstone House is still in my heart, but I have reservations."

"Reservations?" Mother's face went even paler, pain twitching across her tight lips. She dropped her arm, holding the athame to her side in shock.

Arabella swallowed hard, full of fury and sorrow herself. "Certain events have caused me to wonder if Blackstone House is the best place for my talents. Perhaps I should venture to Wales and see if Mynydd House is suitable."

"You must certainly do what you think is right for yourself and your future daughters." Mother's voice came out in a strangled whisper. "I fully understand protecting yourself and daughters, even unborn ones, Arabella. You must know that no matter what has passed between us, you are still my daughter. I still want you to come home."

"Blackstone House will be in my heart always, Mother, but I cannot make such an important decision without careful thought. And I don't want to keep our guests waiting while I decide."

"I can accept that," her mother murmured.

They both took a deep breath, and Mother intoned, "Arabella Helene Leyden, you are now of the Sisterhood." She raised the athame again and pierced the pad of Arabella's thumb. A brilliant red dot of blood welled up, and Aster offered the Ledger for Arabella's imprint. As she pressed her thumb into the page next to her name, Arabella felt something click inside her. It was done. She was sworn to the English Council of Witches, for good or for ill, until the end of her days.

"Welcome, Sister," Aster said with a snaggle-toothed grin. The garden erupted with cheers and applause from the witches, Fae, and assembled men. Arabella and Mother turned to the crowd, smiling. Mrs. Holly quietly passed a small square of linen to Arabella for her to press against her thumb.

"I hope it will be alright, my dear," Mother said in a bright and cheery voice that sounded forced to Arabella's ears. "But I didn't have time to have new novice robes made for you, so I thought you might want to wear my old novice robes until we can have yours made."

"Oh, Mother, that is such a generous offer, but I already have robes," Arabella said, shocked to feel a bit of vicious glee in her heart as her mother's face fell a bit. She squashed it down and hoped it didn't show on her face.

Mother composed herself quickly. "You do?"

Arabella nodded and waved to John, who brought forth the package he'd taken from the carriage. He held it out for her to open. Arabella undid the string and pulled back the paper to reveal the thin brass wire, curling and looping around, dancing among gears in all types of metals, the robes that Juliann Pattersby had made for her. John helped her pull it from the package and settle it on her shoulders. The bronze and gold wire cascaded from her shoulders, tumbling down to a small train behind her. Arabella was grateful that formal witches' robes were sleeveless given the weight before her innate magic transformed them. Once again, bright light twisted and whirled up and down and around each bit of wire. The gears were still interlocked and began to spin on her lapels and back. As they rearranged themselves, more waves of light rippled over the robe, and the individual twists and links pulled together to form one thin, glowing, ethereal sheet. The golden radiance complimented Arabella's hunter green gown, which showed from the open front of the robes. Gasps and chatter spread throughout the garden. Arabella smiled and turned to her mother, lifting her chin.

"Well," Mother said with a sniff. "That is certainly impressive."

"Just one last thing," Aster said when she recovered her voice. "Are you declaring a magical specialty yet?"

"Yes, technomancy," Arabella said in a firm voice.

"Ah! You are the first," Aster said with a wink. She turned away and disappeared into the crowd, her quill pen scratching in the tome.

With the ceremony over, the guests crowded in on Arabella and her mother to give their congratulations. Then the party began in earnest. The flow of food and drink was impressive, even for a Blackstone House event. Such extravagance brought together on short notice must surely have cost a small fortune. Arabella wondered if the party was the beginning of her mother's efforts to make amends for everything without actually admitting fault or apologizing.

As usual, Arabella watched the party from the edges with a warming glass of lemonade in her hand when John and Rowena found her.

"We really must break you of this habit," Rowena said. "Witches are expected to be at least somewhat social. Especially at their own Investiture party..."

"Even I know that, and I'm not a witch," John said as he cast his sisters a wink.

Arabella looked down into her glass with a melancholy smile. "Thank you both, but I think I've been through a bit more than the average witch just before her Investiture. And not all of it is resolved. It just has me a bit pensive, and well, somewhat nervous. It's hard to enjoy something when the future is so uncertain."

"We've shared our secrets since you could talk, Ari," Rowena said as she caught her sister's hand in hers. "I hope that will continue."

"I hope I have also proved that I can keep a secret, even if I can't bluff at cards to save my life." John took another sip of his drink. "I guess we all have to have some sterling qualities somewhere."

His sisters laughed.

When the laughter subsided, Arabella sighed as she caught sight of their mother across the garden. "I still have some very important decisions to make, and it's quite possible they will make Mother furious."

"You mean picking a House?" John asked. Rowena looked at him in surprise. "What? I *can* actually pay attention sometimes."

Arabella favored him with a smile. "Yes, picking a House would be the most immediate political quagmire. But there are other things..."

"Council Chamber things you can't discuss with a mere man?" John guessed as he raised an eyebrow.

Arabella and Rowena exchanged glances. "Partially, yes..." Arabella allowed.

"Witches," John groaned with a shake of his head. "You're such a secretive lot." He paused. "What else? Council matters can't be the only thing making you skulk around the edges of your own party."

Arabella's face darkened, and her brows came together. "There is still the Westerfeld matter. He seems to blame me for all his misfortune because I uncovered his fraud with the Distinction Engine. And we know he's prone to violence since he's attacked me twice. Has anyone heard where he is?"

"I did ask a few friends at the club," John said, swirling his drink. "If rumor is to be trusted, he has decamped for the Continent since his prospects here are in such shambles. He may have managed to run off before anyone could commit him to an asylum, but one of my sources strongly hinted that it was a near thing. Perhaps you won't have to worry about him anymore."

"That would be lovely." Arabella sighed.

"Ari, you don't have to decide on your House until the Winter Solstice. We'll have more than enough time to work out your political problems between now and then." Rowena squeezed her sister's hand. "Let's enjoy your party and not worry about anything. Instead, let's think about the good things, like Amelia and Harlan's wedding and Vivienne's baby..."

Arabella whipped her head around to look at her sister. "Amelia and Harlan have set a date?"

Rowena sipped her lemonade with a twinkle in her eye. "As a matter of fact, they have. Our sweet sister will wed in the spring, May 26th, to be exact. These are the things you miss living in another house."

Arabella laughed and laid her head on Rowena's shoulder. "There are some lovely things on the horizon, aren't there?"

CHAPTER V

The Grande Dame Spars with Her Newest Witch

ARABELLA'S INVESTITURE CELEBRATION WENT ON WELL INTO THE NIGHT, and yet the dawn brought her a summons to attend her mother in her office at her earliest convenience. The formal words on the official stationery of the Grande Dame of the Witches Council sent Arabella's heart leaping into her throat. Mother had not invited her for a cozy family chat but rather had summoned Arabella, as the greenest member of the English Witches Council, in her official capacity.

Arabella paused in the open doorway of Mother's office, taking a deep breath to gather herself. She raised her knuckles to rap on the doorjamb, but Mother lifted her head from her paperwork and smiled at her youngest daughter before she was able.

"Arabella, my chickadee," Mother waved to the empty chair facing her desk. "Come. Sit. We have much to discuss."

"Thank you, Grande Dame," Arabella said as she sank into her seat and folded her hands into her lap.

Mother frowned and removed her spectacles with a sigh. "So, we are still not allowing a thaw in relations?"

"I'm not sure yet," Arabella murmured. She twisted her fingers together and fought to hold her mother's cool gaze without flinching away.

"Do you have a list of demands?" Mother said with a sarcastic twist of her lips.

"Not as such," Arabella said and lost her battle, dropping her eyes to her clenched hands in her lap. The silence between them grew.

Mother sighed again, more deeply, and rubbed her temples. "What am I going to do with you?" she murmured half to herself.

Arabella's jaw tightened, and her eyes flashed. "Perhaps you could begin by treating me as a grown witch instead of as a burdensome child," Arabella said in a flat voice.

"I see," Mother said as she arched an eyebrow. "I had hoped you might be a little more forgiving. The changes in your status have been rather abrupt. Anyone might be excused for needing a moment to adapt."

"That's quite a bit of gall, Mother," Arabella hissed through clenched teeth. "You've treated me as a disappointment and an embarrassment for most of my life, then you try to drown me, and failing that, you disowned me. If you had needed any more time to adapt, I might be dead!"

Mother's head jerked back, and she drew in a sharp breath. "You would do well to watch your tongue, young lady. If you will not respect me as the one who gave you life, then you *will* respect me as the Grande Dame of your Council and the Head of your House!"

"I will respect you as my Grande Dame, but I will remind you that I have not yet declared a House," Arabella bit off each word.

Mother ground her teeth, seething. "See that you do. There are consequences for disrespecting your Grande Dame."

The two women glared at each other in silence. Finally, Mother closed her eyes and let out a slow breath.

"Perhaps we should just discuss the Council business I called you here for and leave familial discussions for another time." Mother's tone was soft yet held a hint of menace.

"Yes. Perhaps that would be for the best."

Mother selected a sheet from the neat stacks on her desk and slid on her spectacles. She made a show of carefully perusing the contents. Without raising her eyes to Arabella, she began, "Even though you were quite sheltered from uncomfortable subjects while you were in my home, I'm sure you remember the concerning issues in Ireland." She looked over her spectacle rims at Arabella. "What do you recall of the situation?"

Arabella frowned and settled more deeply in her chair. "As I recall, there is a blight causing widespread famine. The poor have turned to religious zealots who believe the only good witch is a dead witch, making life extremely dangerous for our Sisters on the Isle."

"A simplified but essentially correct assessment." Mother nodded and returned her gaze to the paper in her hand.

"I also know that the troubles there have been going on for quite some time," Arabella continued in a rush. "I know our family has suffered losses because of it. It leads me to wonder whether the blight and famine caused the antipathy toward witches, or if the anti-witch sentiment already existed and the zealots seized upon the blight and famine to sway more desperate people to their cause."

Mother's eyes widened slightly as she looked up from the paper. "That is a philosophical question we've been debating over tea for quite some time. I'm not sure we will have any answer until we can gain the more dispassionate perspective of time," Mother said, her voice distant. She shook her head as if to clear it.

"It must be difficult to be dispassionate about the conflict given what you witnessed yourself," Arabella said.

Mother's gaze sharpened, and her voice dropped. "What can you know about what I have witnessed?"

"Father told me about your mission over there," Arabella said, her eyes locked on her mother's. "He told me about what happened to Aunt Lenore and Aunt Lorena and how you had to make your way home."

The paper in her mother's hand crumpled as she clenched her fist to suppress a tremble. "That's not something I ever wanted you to know," Mother let out in a strangled whisper.

"Why?" Arabella's voice rose. "Why would you not want me to know about my family history? They were my aunts!"

"They were my sisters!" Mother snapped.

"Do my sisters know?" Arabella lowered her voice to a whisper.

"Only Vivienne," Mother said. "The rest of your sisters know what you knew before your *father*," Mother spat the word, "decided to tell tales that weren't his to tell."

"Why keep it a secret? Why not share the story?" Arabella asked.

"It was my story," Mother whispered as she laid the crumpled paper on the desk and began to smooth it out with her hands. "It was terrifying and brutal and it was mine. I should be the person who decides when to tell it." She clasped her hands on the desk in front of her and lifted a defiant gaze to Arabella.

Arabella narrowed her eyes and tilted her head to the side to consider her mother.

"Thank you for your honesty," she said with a nod. "Perhaps if there had been a bit more honesty instead of secrecy in our household when I was growing up, things might be quite a bit different now."

"Does this change your current hostility toward me and Blackstone House?" Mother's gaze was predatory.

"I have nothing against Blackstone House," Arabella said with a sad shake of her head. "I never have. As for you…" Arabella paused and looked upon her mother with anguished eyes. "I have no hostility for you. I'm hurt. I'm angry. My trust is broken. I don't know what it will take for me to recover from that, or even if it is possible."

"Well, that was certainly blunt," Mother said as she pursed her lips. "It seems that as you gained your powers, you lost some of your manners along the way."

Arabella sagged back in her chair and pinched the bridge of her nose as she sighed. "Or perhaps I was hoping some candor would allow us to move forward more productively." She sighed again. "Shall we proceed with Council business then?"

"Very well," Mother said with a curt nod. "As you have no doubt observed over the years, we witches must earn our stipend from the Council, and now that you are a full witch, you must earn your way as well."

Arabella arched an eyebrow. "You are putting me to work rather swiftly, aren't you?"

"Putting you to work and also getting you out of harm's way. Rowena told me about the attempt on your life," Mother said. "I am not quite the monster you believe me to be."

"It seems that Father isn't the only one telling tales that aren't his to tell," Arabella grumbled. She straightened in her chair and folded her hands in her lap. "What would the Council have me do?"

"Returning to the subject of Ireland," Mother began. "We must at least make an attempt to resolve the issues on the Isle. You will travel to Dublin and return with a report on the current situation." Mother waved a hand over the numerous sheets of paper crowding her desk. "Although, if there isn't any new information, I don't know what more we can do. We've tried everything we know already." Her brow furrowed as one of the older reports caught her attention. She traced her fingers over the lines of script.

Arabella's jaw dropped open. "That is your idea of sending me out of harm's way? To send me to one of the most dangerous countries for witches on a fool's errand?"

Mother looked up and frowned. "Well, I'm not sending you alone. You'll have a Guardian assigned to you, of course."

"Who am I supposed to talk to while I am there? Where do I even start to solve the riddle that has stumped the most talented witches of our age?" Arabella threw her hands up into the air. Fear and fury warred in her belly.

"Arabella, don't be melodramatic." Mother rolled her eyes. "I don't really expect you to find anything of substance. I want to get you out of the reach of those on these shores who mean you harm, just until their ire cools and I can make them see reason. The blood oath now provides you some protection, but I'd rather not rely on it. Some witches can be as creative as the Fae when it comes to reinterpreting oaths and contracts, and there are ways to employ the services of others without technically violating their vow.

"And if you exhibit your usefulness to the Council, then you will make my job that much easier. Tour the countryside, take in the sights, find a quiet cottage and read a few novels. Whatever you fancy." Mother waved her hand dismissively. "Come back and tell me nothing has changed. The witches who are already disposed toward solving the problem will continue working on it, and we will find a better position for you."

Arabella's face flushed with rage. "You still don't think I'm capable of doing anything useful, do you?"

Her mother scrutinized her. "To be honest..." she paused. "Are we still being honest? I'm not sure what you are capable of. You could be the answer to the prophecy I'd always dreamed of, the one I gave up hope for. Or you could be dangerous, poised to destroy everything we know without even meaning to. I have no way of knowing. I've consulted the oracles, and they tell me everything around you and your future is nothing but murk and haze."

"But I..." Arabella protested.

"But you are my daughter," Mother continued as if she had not spoken. "So, I will hope you are not the destruction of all I hold dear, and I will do my best to put you in the most advantageous position I can, for both of our sakes."

"I see," Arabella murmured as her anger seeped from her. She took a steadying breath and straightened her back. "I will need more than just a Guardian to protect me on this mission. I'd like to have Rowena come with me. I imagine she'll need a Guardian of her own. And I'll need more details on the history of the situation and what's been done so far. If I'm going to make a good show of it, I'll need to at least appear knowledgeable. Who knows, I may even bring you the key that unlocks the answer." Arabella's eyes flashed.

"Indeed." Mother gave her a half-smile.

"And if I do bring you the answer, then I would ask a boon of you." Arabella ran her palms over her skirt.

Mother snorted a little. "I knew we would eventually come to the list of demands. Very well, what is it?"

"If I bring you the solution to the Irish issue," Arabella started and then swallowed a lump in her throat. "The Council must stop killing unsuccessful applicants to the Trials."

Mother went completely still, so still that the very air around them seemed to pause with her. "What did you say?" her voice came in a dangerous whisper.

Arabella swallowed hard. It took everything she had to not drop to her knees and beg Mother to forget what she'd just said. "It's a barbaric practice. All the other Witches Councils think so, don't they?"

"The practices of other Councils are not in your purview at this time," Minerva hissed.

"But the practices of *my* Council are in my purview, isn't that so?" Arabella's fingers twisted in her lap. "Killing innocent girls just looking for a better life is a horror!"

"You think I don't know that?" Minerva growled. "Do you think I enjoy sending a death witch to take a terrified young girl's life?"

"I didn't think…" Arabella began.

"Of course, you didn't think." Minerva's voice remained controlled and tight. "You young girls believe you are the first to have ever noticed injustice when really you don't notice the things that bind our hands. We thought we were protecting ourselves by making magic seem so dangerous. We were fighting to survive. And now…" Mother let out a deep breath. "Now it has been going on so long, how would we explain that magic suddenly isn't dangerous enough to kill? The entire country would rise up against us for the girls who are already gone."

"But if something changed…" Arabella began. She tapped her finger on her chin. "If something changed about how magic works, then the Council can joyously announce that all applicants can be safe now, that no one has to die!"

"Magic hasn't changed in millennia, Arabella."

"But magic *has* changed," Arabella said with a sly grin. The anxiety boiling in her stomach began to ease. "It changed with me."

Realization dawned on Mother's face.

"Yes, yes… That could work. We'll temporarily suspend the Trials, give them some story about fluctuations in the magical sphere. Then when we resume, we'll announce the happy news." She turned to Arabella with a look of wonderment.

"Perhaps now you can think of me as somewhat useful?" Arabella raised an eyebrow. Mother chuckled and shook her head. "And perhaps since the boon I wanted for solving the Irish problem is really a boon for you, then perhaps I can ask for something else?"

Mother put her chin on her clasped hands, her eyes twinkling just a bit. "Oh, indeed? I thought you didn't have a list of demands?"

Arabella gave her mother a little smile. "I thought that maybe you could tell me about some of my other aunts?"

The mirth drained from Mother's eyes and she stiffened her back. "Some things cannot be bargained for, child. You would do well to remember that." She turned back to her paperwork and flipped her hand at Arabella. "Go find your sister and see if she will agree to go with you. That must be her decision."

CHAPTER VI

*Wherein Sortilege House Gathers
to Greet its Newest Member*

ARABELLA LEFT HER MOTHER'S OFFICE FEELING A BIT DAZED. SHE paused in the hallway, placing one hand on the wooden balustrade of the stairs leading up to the bedrooms and the other on her heart. Had she really won a victory of sorts over her mother? Would the English Council of Witches truly become a more modern and civilized governing body because of her? It seemed too easy. Not five months ago, she had been an embarrassment and a burden to the family, and now this sudden reversal of fortune gave her the power to make demands, significant demands. Arabella could hardly believe it. There had to be some hidden impediment.

She sighed and let her forehead rest on the artfully carved baluster beneath her hand. The swirls and dips of stylized ivy wrapping up each spindle brought back memories of gathering on the stairs with her sisters. They had peered down on the parties and meetings their mother hosted, feeling vaguely naughty that they'd given their nannies the slip so they could spy on the excitement below. She closed her eyes and inhaled the familiar and comforting scent of the wax polish the housemaids used.

Arabella let her mind wander. She felt pulled to the great clock ticking in the hall. With her third eye, she saw the black streamers of nature-based magic already beginning to bind the mechanisms. As she idly teased the wooly bits from the gears, she remembered the afternoon she'd freed the clock from its seventeen-year slumber. It seemed like a lifetime ago, rather than just a few months.

She plucked another bit of magical flotsam from a clock spring and let it float away on the metaphysical winds. Her brow furrowed as she worked her mental fingers a little deeper to dislodge a particularly stubborn bit. As it came free, a memory buried deep in her psyche jolted her.

Shining golden bands that had been swaddled under the magical roving, the words inscribed along them…

Bravery.

Compassion.

Sisterhood.

Strange symbols she couldn't read, yet they thrummed against her soul…

War.

Evolution.

Balance.

And then there came the voice that spoke to her from some otherwhen… A voice as familiar to her as her own, and yet she could not name it.

Be ready.

What was she supposed to be ready for? Sweat beaded on Arabella's forehead as she remembered the bands and how hard she'd had to strain to remove the deeper ones. She'd strained so much she had nearly killed herself in her effort to prove to her mother that she had magic in her blood. Then the bands and their messages got mislaid among her muddled memories during her spell sickness that followed and then her desperate bid to survive the Trials.

What did all those words mean? What message should she have taken from them? Arabella's heart sank toward her stomach as she wondered whether she should have removed all of the bands at once. The last ones had been so difficult. Perhaps she should have waited until she learned more and increased her strength? But if she had not pried them free right then, would her mother have ever let her leave the house? Would she ever have gotten access to the Trials and the somewhat fickle protection passing them brought? The questions roamed through her mind in search of answers, of which she had none. Her heart began to race, and she wondered again what she was supposed to be ready for. What was coming wrapped in ominous words like war and evolution, or the symbols she could not decode?

Footsteps thundering down the staircase yanked Arabella from her reverie. Her eyes flew open. She jerked her head around to see one of the housemaids scurrying down toward Arabella with her skirts hiked up in a most unladylike manner.

"It's time! It's time!" the maid puffed as she skidded around the newel post, almost slipping on the slick marble floor. She dashed past Arabella, heading in the direction of her mother's office. "Ms. Vivienne's time is upon her! The babe is coming!"

Arabella gasped and bolted up the stairs. She sprinted into her bedroom to unlock and crack all of the windows. Nothing could be left to chance; the wee babe's soul mustn't have any obstacles to finding her way. Arabella almost collided with another housemaid dashing into her room with an armload of sheets to cover all of the mirrors. They both laughed with genuine delight. The very air crackled with excitement. Arabella helped her drape each mirror to ensure that the babe's soul didn't get trapped on her journey earthside. The two young women hugged each other and giggled before racing off in different directions, the housemaid to cover more mirrors and Arabella to tend her sister.

Arabella arrived in Vivienne's room flushed and out of breath. Her sister paced the length of the room with fierce strides, huffing and puffing, her white cotton nightgown billowing around her. Amelia scurried in her wake, waving a hairbrush in her extended hand. Two housemaids dawdled at the edge of the room with clean towels stacked in their arms and amused smiles on their faces.

"Just let me take your braid out," Amelia huffed. "Knots are bad luck for a newborn babe!"

"It's a braid, not a knot, featherhead," Vivienne growled. "I can't stand the hair on my neck. It's too hot in here! Aren't the windows open? The windows are supposed to be open!" Vivienne's voice took on a whining tone Arabella was sure she had never heard out of her eldest sister in her entire life.

Arabella scurried to the nearest window and opened it further. "It's open, sweetheart," she sang out. "I can check the others."

"Don't open them too far," Amelia chided. "We don't want a room full of drafts when the baby gets here!"

"Open them all the way! It's sweltering in here!" Vivienne roared.

"Of course, we can open them as far as you like, darling," Mother soothed as she sailed into the room. "But this will help you more." With a twirl of her fingers, she drew a tiny whirlwind across Vivienne's sweaty neck and bright red cheeks. Vivienne's shoulders immediately relaxed and she sighed with relief. Then a contraction rippled through her belly, and she doubled over and moaned.

Mother supported her on one side and Amelia on the other, rubbing her back and murmuring encouragement and reminders to breathe.

After the spasm passed, she leaned heavily on her mother and whimpered, "Momma, it hurts. Is it supposed to hurt so much?"

"There, there, darling," Mother murmured against her daughter's hair. "I know it hurts, but at the end of it, you'll have a beautiful new babe and it will all be worth it. You are a strong witch; I know you can do this."

"Can I?" Vivienne lifted her face from her mother's shoulder. "I don't know if I can. I've only had a few pains, and this is supposed to go on for hours. How did you do this nine times?" Vivienne's eyes were wild.

Mother chuckled and guided Vivienne to her vanity bench, helping her ease her way down. She clucked her tongue at Amelia. "How did you let her keep this in so long?" she chided as she began to pick apart the braid. She held out her hand to Amelia for the hairbrush. "I know I taught you knots are bad luck around a newborn babe."

"But I…" Amelia protested.

"Perhaps you could go fetch your sisters and grandmother," Mother murmured absently as she drew the brush through Vivienne's hair, lifting the mass of dark strands every other stroke and directing a puff of breeze across Vivienne's neck.

Amelia dropped her eyes and turned her face away to try to hide her burning cheeks. "Yes, Mother."

"What can I do, Mother?" Arabella asked. Mother looked slightly startled that Arabella was already in the room. She recovered quickly and crooned to Vivienne. "How are your feet, my chickadee? My feet and ankles always ached so with each one of you."

"They do throb a bit," Vivienne pouted.

"Arabella," Mother called. "Come here and rub your sister's feet."

Arabella sank to her knees in front of Vivienne and pulled her bare feet into her lap.

"You're so swollen!" she exclaimed. "How do…"

Mother hissed at Arabella and silenced her with a glare. Arabella blushed and returned to her task.

Mother glanced over at the housemaids waiting on their next orders. "As soon the rest of the family gets here, you may go. Make sure Mrs. Holly has the oatmeal on. Oh, and check on the men. They get so flummoxed when it's birthing time. They have no idea what to do with themselves."

"Yes, ma'am," the girls chorused together as they both bobbed up and down in curtsies.

"Why can't Nathaniel come see me, Momma?" Vivienne murmured as she leaned into her mother's brushstrokes. "He only wants to be sure I'm alright."

"I know he has the best of intentions, darling, but you know the traditions. Men are not allowed to be present at all, and as much as possible, only your family should tend you. Lucky girl that I gave you so many sisters so we'd have plenty of hands to help!" Mother laughed and squeezed Vivienne's shoulders.

Arabella looked up at the sound of scampering feet. Rowena hurried into the room, her eyes alight with joy, with Jessamine and Josephine close on her heels.

"Oh, Vivienne!" Rowena gushed as she sat next to their sister and pulled her into a fierce hug. "I'm so excited for you!"

Vivienne smiled wanly and placed her hand on her swollen belly. "Thank you, but I don't feel so well. Breakfast isn't agreeing with me."

Jessamine startled Mother and Vivienne as she popped up next to them with a small washbasin. "You won't need this," she chirped. "But it will make you feel better."

"Thank you?" Vivienne said as she accepted the basin from her sister.

"Amelia should be here any moment with Grandmother," Rowena said as she patted Vivienne's hand. "We met her in the hall on the way."

"What about Elizabeth?" Mother said with a frown. "We should all be here for the first child of our next generation."

"Yes, we should." Rowena looked away and caught Arabella's gaze. "I haven't seen her since Arabella's party. She left early and said something about not liking the way one of the Guardians was looking at her. I assume she's sulking in her room."

"Well, one of you is going to have to go fetch her," Mother said as she placed the hairbrush on the dressing table.

"She won't come," chorused Jessamine and Josephine together.

Mother started to question the twins on their assertion, but Vivienne moaned as another contraction hit her, and she dropped the basin on Arabella's knees. Chanting together in hushed tones, the women all guided Vivienne through her breathing.

"I have to walk! I have to walk!" she cried after the contraction ended, struggling to push her bulk up off the bench. Rowena and Mother grabbed her flailing arms and helped her up.

"Of course, darling," Mother crooned. "Walking in the early stages helps the baby drop."

"I'll walk to London and back if it will get this over with sooner," Vivienne grumbled as she waddled around the room.

No one noticed when Grandmother Eleanor crept in until she settled on the floor next to Arabella with a grunt.

"You've made a poor choice for comfort, but this does seem to be in the thick of it." Grandmother smiled at Arabella and gave her a conspiratorial wink. "We'll probably want to get up at some point soon, though, it's going to be a while, and I don't think my back will tolerate sitting on the floor that long." Arabella smiled, wondering what silly things Grandmother might do to lighten the mood during a long labor.

"It's going to be a while?" Vivienne wailed. "How long am I going to be laboring, Grandmother?"

"I've seen different things, sweetling," Grandmother said in a pleasant conversational tone. "But trust me, you want to have the long labor. Whenever you have a short one, it kills you." She nodded emphatically, then started to dig about in her reticule. "I thought I had some sweets," she muttered to herself.

"A long labor it is," murmured a startled Vivienne. She turned to her mother and said in a wheedling voice, "Can't you do something about the pains, Mama? Please?"

"You've read the histories," Mother said with gentle reproach.

"Yes, yes," Vivienne groaned and rolled her eyes. "Unpredictable effects on a girl's magic!" Her eyes flicked to Arabella and then away. Vivienne pouted. "Sometimes I wish I was having a boy."

"Hush, now," Mother soothed, patting her shoulder. "You don't really want a boy, chickadee."

"Why do you keep calling us that?" Vivienne exploded as she shrugged her mother's hand away. "Those blasted birds aren't even on this continent!" She turned to glare at Mother, who looked shocked, her fingers to her lips.

"Those little birds did sing so sweetly when we visited those nice witches in Appalachia, didn't they, Minerva?" Grandmother said. "Oh, a sweet!" she crowed as she finally dug one out of the bottom of her bag.

"Yes, I enjoyed their song very much." Minerva wrapped her arms around herself. Her voice was soft. "It was the last trip we were all together, before…" she swallowed. "Before Helene left us…" She paused again to wipe the tears gathering on her cheeks. "Their song was so joyful, and I was happy. So, I call you girls that because it reminds me of more innocent days."

"Oh, Momma…" Vivienne gathered her mother in an embrace and began to cry herself. "I'm so sorry. I had no idea."

Arabella perked up at the sound of her middle name. "Who is Helene?"

"She was my sixth daughter," Grandmother said, her voice distant and her face creased with pain. "I couldn't stop her. I tried to." She looked to Arabella with pleading eyes. "You know that I tried to keep her safe, don't you? I really did." Grandmother's voice cracked.

Amelia dashed into the room, huffing and puffing. "The midwife is gathering her tools," she gasped out. "I can't find Elizabeth at all. Her door is locked, and she won't answer. She's nowhere in the rest of the house." She threw her arms up in exasperation.

Mother shook her head to clear it and lifted her chin. "Well, then she will just have to miss this momentous occasion. We can't coddle her temper when there are more important things at hand." She caressed Vivienne's cheek. Vivienne leaned into her hand with a soft smile.

Amelia bounded up to Vivienne and kissed her on the cheek. "That was from Nathaniel." Amelia kissed her other cheek. "And that is from Father. They are playing cards in the solarium with Henry and John. John is beating them all rather handily because they're so distracted."

CHAPTER VII

Wherein Blessings and Betrayal Mingle on a Joyous Day

WHEN ALICE THEW, THE MIDWIFE, CAME TO ATTEND VIVIENNE, EVEN Mother and Grandmother showed her deference and a bit of fear. In addition to her midwifery knowledge, Alice was a death witch, as all the best midwives were. It was true that she had the power to deal death with the simple touch of her hand, but that same hand held the power to cast death away. A midwife equipped with this power could coax the breath into a newborn babe, so long as her soul had already perched in her body. If a mother's heart failed, a death witch could hold her soul close and keep her on the mortal plane long enough to repair the damage to her body so she could live. Birthing a child was a dangerous time in any woman's life. Having a helper who could stand between her and death was a great comfort. Even mundane women offered large sums of money to tempt midwives with the death touch to attend their births, fear them as they may.

But as the long labor Grandmother predicted wore on, the women of Blackstone House relaxed in Alice's presence. The sun had tracked across the sky, the moon rose and fell, and the dawn heralded the day again before Alice lifted her head from examining Vivienne's progress and pronounced it time for her to push her babe into the world. The birthing room became suspended out of time because of sleep deprivation and everyday tasks left beyond the threshold of the closed door. The women took turns mopping Vivienne's brow, squeezing her hands, and exhorting her to be strong. The sun had just fully cleared the horizon when the tiny little girl began to emerge.

"She's coming now! I can see her head!" Alice crowed from between Vivienne's knees. "Just a few more pushes; you're almost there."

She whimpered, but she still pushed herself up on her elbows and gathered herself for another round of pushing.

"Minerva, if you want to be the one to catch your granddaughter, you need to come here," Alice said. Rowena slid into the bed beside Vivienne to take their mother's place. As Mother positioned herself at Alice's shoulder, Arabella passed her a creamy white blanket to wrap around the newest Sortilege daughter.

"Alright, push now," Alice cried out. Vivienne roared as she bore down, Amelia and Rowena propped up her shoulders.

"Almost there! I have her shoulders! One more!"

Vivienne sobbed and bore down again, gritting her teeth.

"She's here!" Mother caroled as her first grandchild slid into her hands. "She's beautiful!"

The little girl's chest hitched as she drew her first breath and wailed to protest the cold air.

"How is she? How is she?" Vivienne's voice was frantic.

Mother sniffled, gazing down at the infant in her arms. "She's perfect."

"Now, lay her on Vivienne," Alice said, gently guiding Mother's hands. "A new babe needs her mother, and you need to cut the cord."

Vivienne sobbed with joy as her mother laid her daughter on her chest. Tears rolled down her cheeks as she regarded the howling child with awe and wonder. Alice helped Mother maneuver around Vivienne and guided her hands as she cut the cord with a blessed silver athame.

The older women took a step back to watch with bemused exhaustion as Vivienne lost herself in the joyful regard of her child, and her sisters clustered around her shoulders to coo at their newborn niece.

Arabella glanced up just in time to see a melancholy cloud pass over her mother's face as she murmured to herself, "I wish my sisters would have been there for me."

Arabella remembered how her mother immediately closed off the day before when she'd asked about her other aunts, and now this. Why hadn't her aunts supported her mother at her births? Then the baby sneezed, drawing Arabella's attention back into the present. Let her mother have her secrets, for now.

"Alright, ladies," Alice called everyone to attention briskly. "We'll let Vivienne nurse the babe a bit, and then we can have the bath. Has anyone called for the oatmeal or the Fae yet?"

"No, not yet." Mother rubbed her eyes and sighed. "I'll have to…"

"I took care of it," Grandmother said as she joined them. "I don't have the energy you young ones do to handle all of this." She flapped her hand at the bed and the exhausted women falling in love with the tiny new arrival. "The least I can do is help orchestrate the others."

Rowena and Arabella lifted the heavy, silver bath onto a waiting bench next to Vivienne's bed. Josephine filled it with sacred spring water she'd gathered herself by the moonlight while Vivienne labored. She winked at Vivienne and blew across the water, bringing the temperature up just slightly so it wouldn't be too chilly for the baby. Next to her, Jessamine applied just a smidge of her fire magic to the towels in her arms so they would be toasty warm after the bath.

"Let's have our little treasure," Mother said and held out her arms. Vivienne pulled the sleepy baby closer for a moment, then sighed and handed the child over to her mother. The baby's brow furrowed. Her lip quivered as Mother pulled the blankets back.

"Oh no, sweetheart, no fussing," she murmured to her grand-daughter. "We'll have this over with and you'll be back with your mother in the rustle of a raven's wing." Grandmother hovered over Mother's shoulder as she lowered the baby into the bath. As soon as the water touched her new skin, the baby began to squall.

"Should I warm the water more?" Josephine asked, wringing her hands.

"No, it's perfect," Mother said as she accepted a washcloth from Alice. "Our little darling just doesn't like having her world change." With gentle and sure strokes, she washed the last of the vernix from the baby's skin, cooing all the while. The baby's fussing grew more fitful as she grew used to the water. She turned her face to Mother's voice.

When she was done, she lifted the dripping child and laid her in Jessamine's arms, who gently blotted her niece dry with the warmed, fluffy towel. Jessamine passed the girl to Rowena, who diapered her and passed her on to Arabella, who then dressed her in a soft cotton gown with trembling fingers while Alice murmured advice and encouragement. With a wistful sigh, Arabella laid the clean baby into Vivienne's arms.

"Hello there, dear one," Arabella crooned, her fingers trailing on the gown. "Welcome earthside."

Vivienne kissed her daughter on the forehead and stared at her in adoration, tracing her cheeks and tiny hands with her fingertips.

Just then, the door of Vivienne's door flew open and Elizabeth stomped in, her face as dark as a storm cloud.

"Fine, I'm here. Are you happy now?" She stopped at the foot of Vivienne's bed, crossing her arms over her chest and pouting.

"Only a whole day late," Arabella leaned in and whispered into Rowena's ear.

Mother drew herself up and fixed an icy gaze on her prodigal daughter.

"And what, pray tell, finally convinced you to bestir yourself to your familial duty?"

"Amelia could tell you," Elizabeth growled and narrowed her eyes.

"I only asked the gentlemen to send you to us if they happened to see you," Amelia sighed and rolled her eyes.

"They sat outside my door for hours singing ridiculous songs about pirates and drinking," Elizabeth sniveled as she dropped her arms and stamped her foot.

Amelia began to giggle, then blushed and slapped her hands over her mouth. Arabella, Rowena, and the twins continued their own quiet amusement behind her.

"Some of the verses were quite scandalous!" Elizabeth stamped her foot again.

"Girls," cautioned Mother even as a small smile played on her lips. "Elizabeth, we will discuss your atrocious behavior later. For now, we are celebrating your sister's good fortune to have a healthy daughter. You will join in the festivities and behave as befits a member of Blackstone House. Do I make myself clear, young lady?"

Elizabeth lifted her chin and held her mother's cool gaze for a moment, but in the end, she could not win. She dropped her eyes.

"Yes, Mother," she grumbled.

Mother nodded and turned her attention back to Vivienne.

"Have you settled on a name?" she asked as she perched herself on the bed next to Vivienne and tenderly stroked the top of the child's head.

"Yes," Vivienne whispered. "She will be Adella Anne."

Mother looked at her eldest daughter sharply. "Anne? Such a plain name! That means your first granddaughter will be Anne, and probably a mousy thing with a dishwater name like that."

Vivienne glared at her mother and sidled away from her, clutching the baby closer.

"It's a fine and honorable name," she said through gritted teeth, her eyes glittered as she continued. "I also considered Adella Jane."

Mother stiffened and sniffed. "I suppose Anne is better than Jane."

"Oh, Mother, dear," Elizabeth began in a syrupy sweet voice, a wicked grin on her face. "Perhaps you can educate me on something. I thought witches used their middle name for their firstborn, like our Vivienne Adella just did. It was how we could have some tracking of our generations while we still hid from the patriarchy so long ago, wasn't it?" Her eyes flashed, and she brought up her left hand and began to twist it. Mother flinched, and her brow furrowed with pain. "Why is it that you have Grandmother's middle name as your given name even though you are the seventh daughter, not the first?"

Grandmother smacked Elizabeth's upraised hand and Mother relaxed immediately.

"Stop that," Grandmother Eleanor chided. "It's just rude to force someone to reveal a family trouble before she's ready."

Elizabeth cradled her stinging fingers against her chest. "I was just curious," she whined. Her eyes darted frantically from face to face as she took two steps back.

"It does seem to be the time for family secrets coming to light," Mother sighed and rubbed her temples as she glanced at Arabella.

"It seems so," Grandmother said as she nodded. "My first daughter was Minerva Sophia, but she died in a childhood accident before your mother was born. My mother was quite put out that I didn't name my very next daughter Minerva, but I couldn't bring myself to, not until I had your mother."

"What happened to Minerva Sophia?" Arabella asked in a soft voice.

Grandmother blinked tears from her eyes and shook her head. "It was a common enough thing. She climbed a tree to pick an apple for Frances. She misjudged a branch and fell. Her neck was broken and her spirit fled before we could get to her. Such a mundane accident…"

The momentary silence of the birthing room was broken by the light rapping of knuckles on the doorjamb. Eliza Josolyne, one of the Guardians who had attended the Investiture, stood framed in the doorway with the house fae gathered around her skirts.

"I am so sorry to interrupt," she murmured, clasping her hands in front of her. "This is certainly not what I expected to find when I followed the disturbance."

Mother motioned her to enter the room. "A disturbance?"

Eliza strode in with a confident air. The fae scampered in upon her heels and went straight to the bed. They perched on the headboard and the footboard and all around Vivienne. They gazed at little Adella with unabashed wonder. Elizabeth drew back further into the room regarding Eliza with narrowed eyes. Arabella wondered what she was up to.

"What kind of disturbance?" Mother asked, her voice strained. "The child is very vulnerable right now, as you well know. We must ensure she is protected."

"It was one of those… specific… kinds of magical impulses my Sister Guardians and I are trained to look for." Eliza frowned. "It was brief, and it's over now. But it was strong enough that I was concerned."

"I appreciate your concern very much," Vivienne broke in from the bed, where she clutched her infant tighter. "What can we do to ensure my daughter's safety before her Saining?"

Eliza inclined her head. "I'm afraid there's not much beyond the usual protections, the amulets and fae blessings. If it would make you feel more comfortable, I can call one of my Sister Guardians from the Chapter House to stay with you until the child has her Saining and the full protection of her blessed name."

"Yes, please, call one of your Sisters, Guardian Josolyne," Mother said. Vivienne nodded vigorously.

"Of course, Grande Dame," Eliza said. "Until our Sister can arrive, Guardian Gardner and I will take turns standing watch. A witch babe is precious. We must not allow any harm to come to her."

Mother inclined her head with reverence. "The dedication of the Guardians always inspires such deep admiration in my heart. What would we do without your stalwart protection?"

"You are too kind, Grande Dame." Eliza allowed herself a small smile. "We are only doing our part, just as every other witch does."

In the corner, Elizabeth snorted and rolled her eyes. Everyone in the room, witch and fae, turned to stare at her. Elizabeth's eyes grew wide as her skin paled. Her frightened gaze shot left and right.

"It's these curtains," Elizabeth squeaked, pointing to her right. "They're dusty. I was trying to keep from sneezing. Around the baby." She put her hands on her hips and huffed. "Really, Mother, we need to encourage some higher standards in the house staff."

The house fae gathered around Vivienne grunted and rolled their eyes this time, then began to murmur among themselves. Eliza lifted her chin and regarded Elizabeth with keen interest.

"Look, the oatmeal is here!" Elizabeth pointed to the door to turn everyone's interest.

Indeed, Mrs. Holly bustled in with a massive tureen of steaming oatmeal with three girls behind her carrying stacks of linen napkins and silver spoons.

"Such a fine day! A wonderful day!" Mrs. Holly warbled. "A precious little fledgling in our nest again!" She beamed down at Vivienne and her sweet bundle.

Her eyes lighted on Arabella where she stood next to the bed. She reached over patted Arabella's cheek. "You were the last babe in the house, and look at you now, all grown." With a happy sigh, she turned her attention back to Vivienne and the baby.

"We'll have our ceremonial oatmeal, and then I'll go prepare whatever your heart desires, Ms. Vivienne," Mrs. Holly said. "We must keep your strength up so you can provide enough milk for our little darling." Mrs. Holly turned to her girls and nodded. One whisked away the lid to the tureen while another passed out spoons to every woman in the room.

"Perhaps even the female fae should eat," Eliza proposed. "The extra luck couldn't hurt."

Mother nodded her approval. One of the motherly-looking kitchen fae, looking rather like a miniature version of Mrs. Holly, accepted a spoon from the housemaid.

"We'll only need the one for all of us," she chirped.

Mrs. Holly and the housemaids circulated with the tureen of oatmeal, beginning with Vivienne, and each woman ate three spoonfuls to fortify the new babe and bring her luck. As Mrs. Holly progressed around the room, the house fae began to hum and sway in their circle around Vivienne and the child. The air of the bedroom filled with the scent of earth and green growing things as the garden fae arrived and joined their house cousins. The female fae passed the heaping spoon of oatmeal among themselves, each taking three delicate bites.

When the oatmeal was done, Mrs. Holly and the housemaids withdrew against the walls to watch the fae and their ceremony. A hob representing the house fae and a pixie representing the garden fae climbed onto opposite ends of the footboard, both holding the bedpost for balance. The humming grew louder, and the hob began to sing.

"Hearth and home, blood and bone."

"Hearth and home, blood and bone," the pixie echoed.

The female fae of both house and garden sang, "hearth and home."

The male fae responded, "blood and bone."

Then all the fae sang together as one voice:

Hearth and home,
Blood and bone,
This child we claim as one o' our own.
The awaited one,
She brings the sun.
The promised one,
Her path's begun.
We give our hearts of our free will,
Long may she dance upon the hills.

Arabella felt tears welling up at the emotion of the moment. The fae had sung the same blessing and binding to her and all of her sisters when they were born, and to her mother and aunts and grandmother, back up the Sortilege line for generations. The fae of the house and the lands watched over them all while they were within the bounds of Blackstone Manor and the grounds.

Arabella felt a shiver ripple up her spine, remembering the nursery stories about the great Sidhe Wars. Not all fae bound themselves to witches. Five hundred years ago, even before witches were revealed to the mundane world, the witches of the world found themselves in the middle of a vicious war between factions of the fae. Some believed in aligning with the witches, while another faction believed that path led to bondage and the destruction of all the fae held dear. There was another small faction that took a middle ground, believing temporary alliances with humans could be beneficial, but that lifetime bonding was unwise. They were cast aside by the louder, extreme factions.

The devastation in the Faery Realm had been immense, and each side blamed the other completely. In the end, those who wished to be independent did manage to banish the fae who wished to bind themselves to witches from the Faery Realm. There began hundreds of years of cold détente. Those who bound themselves to the witches always swore they would one day reclaim their home realm.

The fae blessing song drew to a close, all of the voices singing together in ethereal harmony:

> *Hearth and home,*
> *Blood and bone,*
> *Hearth and home,*
> *Blood and bone,*
> *This child we claim as one o' our own.*

Mrs. Holly dabbed her eyes with the corner of her apron as she balanced the empty tureen on her hip. "Ah, that was lovely."

"Indeed." Vivienne chuckled as a moor sprite hovered over Adella and captured her attention with a sprig of heather. "I am grateful to the Fair Folk for their kindness and protection."

"'Tis our honor to protect the babe, Mistress," piped up one of the gentleman gnomes. "Did I hear right as I came in? Is the babe under some sort of extra threat, beyond the usual perils of being without a proper name?"

Eliza stepped forward and spoke. "There is some concern, good sir. I felt some disturbances, and we don't want to take risks with the child. I'm sure you understand."

The gnome tugged his wee beard. "I do see… We shall be exceptionally vigilant then. No child of Blackstone House will be harmed under our watch." He turned to confer with some of the more wizened fae. "Is it urgent enough that we should call the redcaps? We don't like to call on them unless it's necessary, but if it is needful we won't hesitate."

Mother frowned and touched her fingers to her chin. "Calling upon the redcaps would indeed be serious. Would you and your kin be able to control them once they are within our bounds?"

"Aye, that we could, Mistress," the gnome responded. "There is a small band in the wilds nearby. We'd not allow them to go marauding willy-nilly in the Manor nor on the grounds."

Mother nodded. "Then we should…"

"Mother, I don't think inviting redcaps into our home is a good idea," Elizabeth interrupted. Arabella's eyes widened as she caught a flicker of Elizabeth's fingers twisting in complex shapes in the shadows of her skirts. She tried to speak, but her breath caught in her throat.

"Redcaps are vicious little creatures," Elizabeth continued. "I don't think the danger to the baby is that great."

Eliza's head snapped around. Her mouth set in a grim line, she leapt for Elizabeth. Elizabeth cried out and took a step back. Eliza's hand shot forward like a striking snake. She struck Elizabeth on the forehead with two fingers, right on her third eye. As her fingers made contact, Eliza breathed a word of power that made every witch in the room cringe and groan. Arabella sucked in a deep breath and sagged against the bedpost. The fae gathered in a tight knot around Vivienne and her child, facing out. They balled their fists and produced garden tools and needles from nowhere, faces grim and ready to fight.

Elizabeth collapsed to the floor, clutching her throat. She glared up at Eliza with a feral grimace. She opened her mouth to speak, but no sound came. She clamped her jaw shut, hunching forward with her shoulders rounded in. Then she tilted her head back on a silent scream. She pounded the carpet with her fists and kept up her soundless scream until her face was bright red. She collapsed, her shoulders heaving as she panted.

Eliza frowned and clasped her hands behind her back. "I believe we have found the source of the disturbance."

Rowena gasped. "What do you mean? Elizabeth?"

"Yes," Eliza said. "Your sister was the source of the disturbance I felt earlier." Her glance flicked across the room to Mother. "How long have you known? And why didn't you tell the nearest Chapter House sooner? It's late to begin her training."

"Known what?" Mother sputtered.

Eliza tore her eyes from Elizabeth and stared at Mother in shock. "You didn't know?" Eliza shook her head. "She must be quite powerful if she kept it veiled from you this long." She turned her thoughtful gaze back to Elizabeth. "Training her may not be possible since she's been feral so long. We may only be able to contain her."

"Speak plainly!" Mother's voice cracked like a whip. The baby began to wail.

Eliza dragged Elizabeth to her feet. "This seems to be a bit of a shock to you, but please don't be dense. You know what kind of magic we Guardians traffic in. We have our warriors, our trackers, and our restrainers. But the most useful, and dangerous, skill we wield is mind manipulation. Your daughter is very good at it; she'd have to be to keep it from a houseful of powerful witches for years."

Elizabeth screamed with no sound again and tried to yank her arm out of Eliza's grip to no avail.

"Good Master Gnome," Eliza grunted as she began to drag the struggling Elizabeth toward the door. "I don't believe we will need the extra precaution of the redcaps at this time."

Eliza paused in front of Minerva. She nodded gravely and said, "I'll take her to the Chapter House. We'll do what we can to bring her to heel. But after this long without proper discipline, it will be difficult to mold her into a suitable Guardian."

"What happens if she can't be made into a Guardian?" Arabella's whisper seemed loud in the hushed room.

"Then we will have to ensure she is contained," Eliza said.

Elizabeth screamed silently the rest of the way out of the room.

CHAPTER VIII

Wherein Agreements and Fraught Travel Plans are Made

A RABELLA FOUND ROWENA IN THE SOLARIUM TAKING TEA WITH Henry, John, and their father. The aroma of the Darjeeling wafted enticingly, and the scones looked fresh and delectable. Arabella's stomach reminded her that she'd slept through breakfast in her exhaustion after the birthing.

"Arabella, darling," Rowena beckoned her to join them. "Come join us. Henry and Father were just telling us how their transmutation experiments are going." With a flick of her wrist, Rowena summoned an extra chair from behind an exotic potted palm. Henry's eyes widened a bit to see the chair sailing through the air, seemingly on its own. Arabella took the seat with a grateful smile.

"What Rowena won't tell you is that she's only pretending interest to be polite, and I'm bored to tears," John leaned over and stage-whispered. Arabella giggled behind her hand and felt some of the tension start to melt from her shoulders.

"Oh, John, you scamp," Rowena teased with sparkling eyes as she batted at his shoulder with a cloth napkin. Father looked on them with an indulgent smile, and Henry looked only mildly scandalized.

"Are you hungry? Would you like tea?" Rowena asked Arabella. "I've already called to Mrs. Holly for an extra place setting."

"It's still a bit unsettling to think about you talking to people who aren't even in the room," Henry grumbled, but with good humor.

"You'll eventually get used to it," Arabella shrugged. One of the housemaids arrived in the doorway to the Solarium and levitated the place setting into place with consummate grace. Henry pressed his lips into a thin white line as the saucer and cup settled with only the slightest rattle. "Yes, tea would be lovely," Arabella said. "Are those scones as delicious as they look?"

"Indeed, they are," Father said merrily as he helped himself to another. "And do not deprive yourself of the currant jam. I've quite missed the food that comes out of your mother's kitchens. She is extremely talented in choosing the right people."

Rowena looked sidewise at Henry with an impish grin as she poured tea for Arabella. "If you came to visit more often, you might not find such simple displays of magic so unsettling."

"Yes, old boy," John nudged his brother's shoulder with his own. "There certainly wouldn't be any harm in availing ourselves of these delicious morsels more often." He also helped himself to another scone and the dish of fresh, creamy butter.

"My, but everyone does seem to be in a good mood." Arabella began to dab the recommended currant jam on her scone.

"New babies will do that," Father chuckled as he saluted the table with his cup. "Even your mother has been positively sweet, if a bit distracted." Half to himself, he said, "Something is on her mind, I'd wager. Something other than the baby..."

"I just hope what I have to say won't spoil the mood," Arabella said. She nibbled her lip.

"Oh, dear." Rowena sighed and took a sip of her tea. "Are you sure we need to discuss it now?"

Arabella echoed her sister's sigh. "I'm afraid there is no help for it. Mother spoke to me before Vivienne went into labor, and then the situation with Elizabeth..." Arabella trailed off, glancing at the gentlemen. "We've all been a bit distracted since, haven't we? But first..." She paused to take a delicate bite and let her eyes flutter nearly shut with pleasure. "The jam really is absolutely delightful, Father. You might be able to convince Mrs. Holly to send a few jars home with you. She always did like you."

Father flushed, but his eyes twinkled with pleasure as he nodded and busied himself with his plate. "Yes, that would be very nice. I shall try to remember to speak with her."

John frowned. "Situation with Elizabeth? Is this secret witch business? Do we need to excuse ourselves?"

Arabella shook her head and shared a glance with Rowena. "Yes and no. What I need to discuss with Rowena does concern our official duties, but there is nothing secret we need to discuss. We'll save the secret witch business for later," she said with a wink, hoping she'd distracted them from the mention of Elizabeth.

John rolled his eyes and chortled.

Henry narrowed his gaze and frowned. "What does all this have to do with Elizabeth? I haven't seen her since..."

"Well?" Rowena interrupted as she fiddled with the napkin in her lap. "Are you going to keep me in suspense?"

"We need to leave on an official Council mission," Arabella began. "That is if you'll agree to the assignment. Mother said I must go, but you may choose whether or not you join me. But I'd really like you with me. It would be so much easier to have my best friend along when I attempt my first official Council business," Arabella babbled, her hands fluttering absently over her place setting.

"Of course, I'll come with you." Rowena chuckled. "Where are we going?"

Arabella's hands stilled. "Ireland." Everything around the table stopped as all eyes turned to her, wide with shock. The color drained from Rowena's face.

John swallowed hard. "Isn't that rather dangerous? For a witch, I mean."

"I know I don't have an official voice in Council matters," Father began, his voice trembling. "But as your father, I would like to make my reservations known. The last time our family went to that benighted country, we suffered severe losses." His eyes locked on Arabella's.

"Yes, Father, I know." Arabella nodded, then turned back to Rowena. "Mother said we'd each have a personal Guardian to protect us there. And we're to come home immediately if anything goes too wrong."

"If anything goes too wrong?" Rowena's voice came out in a strangled whisper. "Don't you think we're a little past too wrong after what happened to Aunt Lenore and Aunt Lorena?"

Arabella sighed and closed her eyes for a moment. "You don't have to come if you don't want to." She pressed her lips together and pushed her plate away. Of course, it had been ridiculous to expect Rowena would be thrilled to leap into the basilisk's lair with her. All the same, Arabella felt the disappointment rise in her throat while her stomach clenched in fear.

"Arabella," Rowena wheedled with a tilt of her head. "Be reasonable. You've caught me completely unawares and asked me to go to a terribly dangerous place. Did you expect I would be excited about the prospect of journeying to a country in turmoil, where our own aunts were viciously murdered?"

"Murder, what?" Henry choked out. John spat out his tea and looked to their father, who shook his head and mouthed, "Later."

Arabella's shoulders sagged. Tears started to well in her eyes. "You're right, Ro. I'm sorry, I shouldn't have even asked."

"No, darling." Rowena reached out and took Arabella's hand. "You just have to give me a moment to digest things, to voice my shock a little." Rowena squeezed her hand. "Of course, I'll go. I just wanted to be a bit dramatic about it first."

Arabella squeezed her hand back. Her stomach unclenched in relief. "Be as dramatic as you like, Ro. As long as you're coming, I'll put up with any histrionics you'd like." She tittered. "But I do reserve the right to tease you mercilessly about it."

Henry cleared his throat. "Pardon me? Our aunts were viciously murdered?"

"Are you going to explain that shocking little morsel of information?" John frowned.

"I can fill in that knowledge gap," Father said, glaring at his sons. "We'll talk later. Perhaps we can take Nathaniel out on a hunt, so I don't have to repeat the story."

Henry turned to his father with wide eyes. "This is something you knew?"

"Yes, well…" Father fiddled with his teacup. "Your mother wanted to keep the story to herself and she forbade me to tell any of you children. But now that Arabella knows, and apparently Rowena, it seems the vow of silence is broken."

"Mother was quite put out with you for telling me," Arabella said and sipped her tea. "Then she was upset with me for telling Rowena."

Father *harrumph*ed. "Since I'm already in trouble, I may as well unburden my conscience fully. But perhaps it would be best to leave Nathaniel out of it for now as he's only bound to the family by marriage." He looked to Arabella with questioning eyes. "Does Vivienne know?"

Arabella nodded. "Until you told me, she was the only one."

John shook his head in amazement and picked up his teacup. "This must be quite a story."

"It is," Rowena said. "But for right now, we need to focus on the present." She turned to Arabella. "What did Mother say about our mission? What are our goals?"

"To hear her tell it our goal is to keep me out of harm's way," Arabella said with a wry twist of her lips.

"Out of harm's way by going somewhere dangerous?" Henry huffed. "That's quite a logical twist."

"And it may be a shrewd twist depending on the level of danger here at home, *especially in the city*." Rowena raised her eyebrows at her sister.

"Yes, that was her line of thought once she took into consideration the new information *you* gave her." Arabella frowned at her sister, then shook her head. She was still upset with Rowena for tattling on her, but now was not the time to air those feelings, not in front of the gentlemen. Arabella sighed. "She'll use me to make a show of trying to help the Irish witches and curry favor there, while also getting me away from those who would wish me particular harm here until Mother can bring them under control."

Rowena nodded. "So, we're not expected to really do anything then? Just make a show of touring some of the less dangerous places and perhaps listen to a few Irish witches to placate them and make them feel like they've been heard?"

"Yes," Arabella grumbled, resentment rising in her throat. "I'm just meant to be shuttled around like a pawn and not really do anything useful."

"Perhaps I can help," John said.

Rowena chortled. "You? Help? With something that doesn't involve a game of cards?"

John rolled his eyes. "Yes, yes, I know it's quite unusual for me to be able to help with something useful. But in this case, I can indeed help." He paused. "Or rather, I know someone who can."

Rowena suppressed a giggle, her eyes sparkling.

"Who is it?" Arabella asked. Which powerful person did John know? Perhaps someone he played cards with…

"I think you're rather familiar with him," John said with a smile. "Julian Pattersby."

"Oh!" Arabella blushed, and her heart fluttered like an eager sparrow.

"Julian has a widower uncle in Ireland," John said with a chuckle. "He has no children of his own blood and he is fond of Julian's technologist pursuits, so Julian is set to inherit. In fact, I think Lord Sampson Plunkett-Nelson, the Baron of Louth, would be quite fascinated with you and your recently discovered talents. His manor may even be the safest place for you if you have to go to Ireland."

"Thank you, John," Arabella said with clear relief. This Lord Plunkett-Nelson must be the uncle he'd mentioned the last time they had tea. "That is indeed very useful. I trust you can arrange the introduction?"

"Indeed," John said, hiding his smile with his teacup.

"Plunkett-Nelson?" Father's eyebrow quirked up. "Any relation to Vice-Admiral Horatio Nelson?"

"I believe so," John said. "On his paternal grandmother's side. It's a bit distant, but they're understandably proud of the connection."

Henry narrowed his eyes. "But what if you could actually solve the Irish issue?"

Arabella clasped her hands in her lap and leaned forward. "You have my attention, brother dear. What did you have in mind?"

Henry smirked as he took a moment to adjust the seam on his trousers and brush off a non-existent crumb. "Mother, and indeed all the witches I've met, have been dreadfully focused on solving the issue with magic." He sat back and crossed his arms over his chest, his grin growing wider.

"You look like the cat who's gotten into the cream, Henry." Arabella tilted her head. "Perhaps you'd like to let it out and share your little secret with the rest of us?"

Henry chuckled and leaned forward. "Most of the world doesn't have magic to solve their problems. Perhaps the Irish issue doesn't have a magical solution, but rather a mundane one."

"Are you offering to come with us?" Arabella asked.

"Oh, good lord, no!" Henry guffawed. "I have no desire to put myself in that sort of danger. But if you would bring back some samples of the soil and the diseased plants, then perhaps Father and I could find the solution in our lab. There are other gentlemen in the club who are more horticulturally inclined. We could tap their expertise."

Arabella and Rowena exchanged glances. Arabella bit her lip.

"Finally solving this issue might bring around some of the witches against me…" Arabella murmured.

Henry threw his hands up and crowed. "And it would give us more clout among the captains of industry. Sensible witches working with sensible men!"

"Give *us* more clout?" Rowena pursed her lips.

"I meant you! You would get more clout. This could be the beginning of healing the rift between the witches and the technologists." Henry stammered. John looked at him sidewise.

"It seems Mother isn't the only chess player in the family," Arabella said with an acid tongue.

Henry frowned, twisting his napkin in his lap. "I'm only trying to help."

"I don't doubt that you're trying to help, Henry." Arabella straightened her back and regarded him with a cool gaze. "But I also don't doubt that you are all the more eager because of what you can gain from the arrangement."

Henry coughed and fumbled for his teacup.

"Regardless, I'll bring you your samples," Arabella said. "I do hope that you and your colleagues can find the answer." Arabella leaned in and fixed her brother with a gimlet stare. "But make no mistake, brother dear, I am learning to play chess because I have to. And I won't forget that you are also on the board."

CHAPTER IX

On the Delicate Dance of Tea and Treachery

ARABELLA LOOKED OUT THE WINDOW AT THE SERVANTS READYING the garden for guests. "Is this really necessary?" she sighed.

Rowena glanced into her dressing table mirror and patted her hair. "It is if you want to play the political games and secure the changes you desire."

Arabella made a sour face. "It's not that I want to. It's that I feel that I must."

Rowena turned to face her sister. "Then stop whining. The decision is made. Get on with it."

Arabella raised both eyebrows, her jaw dropped open. How could Rowena speak to her like that?

"Enough!" Rowena stood and threw up her hands. "I love you, darling, but all this dithering and moaning is getting tiresome. You know what you must do, now you must do so to the best of your ability." Rowena crossed the room and took Arabella by the shoulders. "You are not a stupid girl. You can play this game and play it well, if you'd just stop complaining and get on with it."

Arabella pouted. "Well, that's rather harsh."

Rowena crossed her arms as she tilted her head to the side. "In this case, I think you deserved it, don't you?" Arabella frowned, and they locked gazes for a moment. She hated to admit it, but Rowena was right. Arabella stuck out her tongue.

"See, you agree with me, even if you refuse to say it aloud." Rowena nodded emphatically.

A knock at the door interrupted them.

"Come in," Rowena called.

Jessamine and Josephine skipped in, holding hands. "Mother wishes us to assemble in the garden before the guests arrive," they chorused.

Arabella closed her eyes and blew out a long breath. Just the thought of going to swim in such cunning seas made her want to hide until the danger had passed, forever if necessary. She shoved the mutinous thought away. When she opened her eyes again, she murmured, "I suppose it's time to get this over with."

The twins giggled and skipped back out the door. Rowena threaded her arm through Arabella's. Together they made their way to the garden.

"Just think of the ways this afternoon can advance your cause," Rowena encouraged.

"Don't forget how new I am to this game," Arabella sighed. "Will you help me think of those things?"

Rowena chuckled, shaking her head. "It's not obvious?"

"Obvious perhaps to someone who has been playing the game for years, like you..." Arabella trailed off.

Rowena squeezed her arm. "You still haven't declared a House. With your bloodlines and the interest in your new kind of power, there will be more than one House courting you."

Arabella bit her lower lip and glanced sideways at her sister. A little hope blossomed in her chest. "Do you really think so?"

"Indeed," Rowena responded. "I don't think all of the Houses will court you, but there should be at least enough interest for you to gain some leverage with Mother. That is... if you would still consider Blackstone House." Rowena snuck a sideways glance at Arabella.

"Of course, I am," Arabella huffed. "How could I not consider the House of my birth?"

Rowena stopped and stared at Arabella. "There are many reasons to not consider Blackstone House. Or have you put your dunking in the basement out of your mind?"

Arabella shuddered. "That's not something I can ever forget."

"Mother has never treated you well..." Rowena began.

"She had her reasons!" Arabella interrupted.

"We all have reasons for everything we do," Rowena snapped. "That doesn't mean they are good reasons."

Arabella pulled away from Rowena and narrowed her eyes. Rowena was trying awfully hard to put Blackstone House in a poor light. "You sound like you don't want me to be part of Blackstone House. All this talk of political games... Do you think I'm some sort of threat to you? Do you want me out of the way?"

Rowena gasped and put her hands over her mouth. "No! Ari, no!" She reached out and snatched up Arabella's hands. "Of course, I want you to be part of Blackstone House. But I also want you to do what is in your best interest, even if it would break my heart to lose my favorite sister to another House."

"Your favorite?" Arabella whispered.

Rowena winked at her, then tugged on her hands and they continued on their way.

As Arabella and Rowena joined their mother and sisters in the rose garden, Mother was lashing the servants with her sharp tongue as they finished the last of the preparations for the farewell tea. Dark circles under her eyes spoke to her recent lack of sleep. Vivienne sat to the side on a bench nursing little Adella, deep in hushed conversation with Amelia. Jessamine and Josephine were quiet, for once, observing the swirl of activity with dark, curious eyes as they casually leaned on each other.

"Good, you're finally here," Mother snapped, stepping away from the hubbub. She swept her six daughters with her gaze. She clutched her hands together, and her mouth flattened into a hard line. "Before our guests arrive, we must speak of what happened with Elizabeth. No one outside of our household can know the truth yet."

"How is she?" Vivienne broke in as she lifted Adella to her shoulder to burp her. "Have the Guardians said anything?"

Mother looked away and clenched her hands so hard her knuckles turned white. "They have not seen fit to give me a full report. All the Head of the Chapter House will say is that she is alive and healthy."

Amelia gasped. "Why wouldn't she be alive and healthy?"

"Don't be dense," Rowena sighed. "You were there when she was removed, and you know just as well as the rest of us that mind-warping magic cannot go unchecked." Her voice dropped to a whisper. "And you know as well as I the penalties that apply to those resistant to being checked."

Amelia blanched and bit her lip.

"You must tell me what those penalties are when you have a moment," Arabella murmured into Rowena's ear. Elizabeth had never been her favorite sister, but she would not want to see her suffer.

"Might we return to the concern at hand?" Mother bit off each word. "We need to ensure that we all tell the same story of Elizabeth's absence. Cecilia Kellar, in particular, will not believe that I would tolerate her refusal to attend."

Vivienne frowned. "I had assumed we would all delicately indicate she is ill and then change the subject."

"Yes, yes," Mother nodded and twisted her hands together. "But is that enough? Do we need more detail?"

Vivienne cocked her head to the side. "It would be quite rude for anyone to ask for more detail about Elizabeth's illness." She paused. "Mother, are you feeling alright?"

Mother stilled her hands with obvious effort and gave her eldest daughter a wild-eyed look. "Of course, I'm alright. Why wouldn't I be alright?" Her voice trembled.

Vivienne nodded slowly and glanced at Amelia. "Perhaps you should tell Nathaniel and the rest of the gentlemen what to say about Elizabeth, Mother? You know they aren't as well-versed with House politics. They'll likely need some guidance." She gave her mother a gentle smile.

"Splendid idea." Mother nodded emphatically. She scanned the garden. "I think I see your father over there; I'll start with him." She hurried across the lawn without another word.

Arabella let out her breath. "I have never seen Mother this agitated. It's very concerning." Arabella turned to Vivienne. "Aren't you concerned?"

"Of course, I'm concerned," Vivienne said smoothly as she bounced Adella and tickled her chin. "Mother has quite a bit resting on her shoulders. Lesser witches would have shown the strain long before now." Vivienne looked at each sister in turn. "I have seen Mother like this before. It is one of my earliest memories. I was two." She looked hard at Arabella and Rowena. "I believe you both know of what I am speaking?"

Arabella swallowed hard. "Her return after the difficulty in Ireland?"

"Yes, that would be the time." Vivienne nodded.

"What difficulty in Ireland?" Amelia piped up. "Do you mean what happened with Aunt Lorena and Aunt Lenore?"

Vivienne silenced her with a flick of her hand. "I'll explain later. For now, we need to focus on the moment. Any woman would be upset by the prospect that someone could have been manipulating her very thoughts. And for it to be your own child makes it doubly upsetting. Mother has reason to be distressed."

Amelia shook her head. "How did she not see it? She's supposed to be the strongest witch in the Isles…"

Vivienne hissed and turned on her sister with narrowed eyes. The baby began to fuss.

"Do not even breathe such traitorous words," Vivienne said as she rose from her seat. "Mother is a strong witch, but even she has limits. None of us are children anymore, and it is our responsibility to our mother and to our House that we provide her the support she needs until she comes back to herself."

"The broken vessel may be mended, so long as children are well-tended," Jessamine and Josephine chorused in a single voice.

The Sortilege sisters all stared at the twins, then exchanged bewildered glances.

"Right then," Vivienne said with an exasperated sigh and a shake of her head. "So, ladies, we are agreed? Elizabeth is ill and not taking visitors. Mother is simply tired from the excitement of adding both a new witch and a new baby to the household in such close order. Not to mention the early stages of wedding planning for her second daughter…" She fixed each of them with a hard glare in turn.

"Yes, Vivienne," each sister murmured.

"Good," she said with a fierce nod. "We always protect our own."

Vivienne glanced at the sun. "Guests should be arriving at any time now. We mustn't gather all in one spot as that will make Elizabeth's absence more obvious. Off with you all," Vivienne said, motioning for her sisters to disperse. "But don't you dare use it as an excuse to disappear entirely!" She called after Jessamine and Josephine.

Amelia joined Rowena and Arabella as they strolled deeper into the rose garden to inspect the impressive array of finger sandwiches and sweets laid out for the party.

"Vivienne is certainly being overbearing," Amelia pouted. She stole sideways glances at her sisters. "It's not as if she knows everything."

Rowena turned to her with a little snort. "Who are you, and what have you done with my sister?"

Amelia pursed her lips and crossed her arms over her chest. "What?"

"Amelia, you've always been Vivienne's shadow, parroting back everything she says." Arabella chuckled. "And now you are going to call her overbearing because she sensibly calls for us to show a united front in a time of family crisis?"

"I have not been Vivienne's shadow!" Amelia gasped. "I am my own witch! I am about to be married and, Goddess willing, a mother soon after. I can think for myself."

Arabella and Rowena smirked at each other.

"I just think she could have handled it better, perhaps asked some of our opinions." Amelia pursed her lips.

Rowena raised an eyebrow. "My opinion is that Vivienne is right. We protect our own, and her plan is sensible."

"Neither of you has ever taken me seriously, and that is very hurtful." Amelia *harrumph*ed and marched away.

"It's hard to take her seriously when she acts like a spoiled brat," Arabella muttered.

"At least we're spared from hearing her natter on about the wedding for the afternoon," Rowena chirped. "Our respite might even last until tomorrow!"

"You're terrible," Arabella laughed. "And I love you."

"Oh, thank goodness, someone does."

The girls were still giggling when Mother found them.

"There you are," she said, her voice full of exasperation. She turned Arabella to face her and looked her up and down. "Better than usual," she muttered. "It will do." Arabella felt the indignity of her mother's continued low opinion. She struggled to keep the mortification off her face.

"Arabella, you'll need to come with me to greet the guests with Vivienne," she said briskly. "Rowena, you should mingle, perhaps get to know Sarah Gardener since she will be your Guardian on your trip."

"Yes, Mother." Rowena kept her voice meek and curtseyed. When Arabella glanced back over her shoulder, Rowena gave her a small wave.

Vivienne waited for them on a stone bench in the shade of an arbor near the entrance to the rose garden. Humming and swaying in her seat, Vivienne gazed down on her daughter. Adella napped peacefully in her arms.

As Mother and Arabella approached, she murmured just loudly enough for them to hear. "Mrs. Holly said Cecilia Kellar and Madeline Thurston just arrived. They shared a carriage."

"Ah good," Minerva nodded. "Have you decided which one of them will serve as Adella's Gramuin Mother? Of course, you'll ask Theodosia Boscoe to serve as Gramuin Crone. She's served the role well for you and all of your sisters. That only leaves Gramuin Maiden… Although that role has much less impact on the child, perhaps a new witch in one of the other Houses to increase our reach?"

Vivienne frowned. "I thought perhaps I'll place emphasis on true kinship for Adella's Gramuins. Select ladies who will truly care and guide rather than let politics steer my choice…"

"That hardly seems wise," Mother huffed. "A properly executed ritual ensures that any witch accepting a Gramuin role is bound to guide and protect the child. A politically advantageous choice is beneficial to the whole House, not just your daughter."

Vivienne sighed. "Do we need the help, Mother? We are already the most powerful House in the Isles. Other witches beg us to serve as Gramuin to their daughters. Does Adella really need to be playing politics before she can even crawl?" Arabella squirmed internally as Vivienne and their mother bickered. She longed to turn on her heel and disappear into the depths of the gardens.

"If we wish to continue to be the most powerful House in the Isles, yes, she does," Mother retorted. She drew her breath to say something more but held her tongue when she caught sight of Cecilia and Madeline coming down the garden path. "We will discuss this further later," she hissed.

Mother's face changed in an instant from a haughty snarl to a warm welcome. Arabella clenched her hands in the folds of her skirts for a moment. She reminded herself that Mother's volatility would pass. She would return to her frosty, calculating, but predictable self. One could hope, anyway.

An hour later, Arabella's head felt stuffed full introductions and bland pleasantries. She despaired of remembering even half the names. She backed away from yet another banal conversation that masked yet more political sparring. Fossdrum House's position was much weakened since Beatrice Paskin, their former Head, attacked Arabella in the Council Chambers just as she completed the Trials. Beatrice had lost her standing even among the witches who did not back Arabella and her new powers. Infighting and devious machinations were certainly expected in the Council Chamber, but an outright physical attack was gauche. Such things were not done by well-bred witches. Beatrice's immediate removal as Head of House mitigated some of the damage, but her behavior was still a stain on Fossdrum House.

"You always did prefer to watch from a distance, even as a little girl."

Arabella jumped at the voice behind her. Her heart fluttered in her chest.

Cecelia Kellar laughed and handed Arabella one of the two cups of tea she carried.

"It's quite sensible of you, really. Careful observation can show you a person's true intent." Cecelia sipped her tea.

"Yes, well, I…" Arabella stuttered. She never quite knew what to say to this woman, the most intimidating witch she knew outside of her mother. Her cup clattered against the saucer as she fumbled with the handle. "I'm afraid I wasn't thinking that shrewdly, Aunt… I mean, Dame Kellar."

Cecelia chuckled and laid a gentle hand on Arabella's arm. "You can still call me Aunt Cecelia, darling. I am your Gramuin Mother, after all."

Arabella flushed, dropping her gaze. "I thought the binding of that ritual had passed, now that I am a woman and full-fledged witch."

Cecelia chuckled again, but it had a more forced quality to it. "Oh, that technicality…" Cecelia waved her hand through the air as if shooing away a fly. Arabella raised her head. She felt her stomach tighten. Cecelia was never this friendly to her.

"Some witches may find it a relief to be free of the onus of guiding and protecting their Gramuin charge, but I never felt that way about you." Cecelia laid her hand over Arabella's.

Arabella felt a shiver she could not explain roll down her spine.

"I have and always will consider you as close to my heart as one of my blood daughters," Cecelia continued. "I hope you will always remember that." Cecelia smiled, but her eyes maintained a calculating glitter.

"Yes, of course." Arabella returned her smile as Rowena's words about playing the game echoed in the back of her mind. "That is a very comforting thought." She pretended to sip her tea and turned her attention to the reserved reveling of the farewell gathering among the rose garden. Arabella forced herself to sigh and fake clatter her cup against her saucer again. Better to let Cecelia think she was still a naive little lamb who might be easily herded along.

"Would it be improper to seek your advice?" Arabella dropped her voice to a whisper. "About something I don't feel I can ask Mother?"

Cecelia stepped closer, a satisfied gleam in her eyes. "Sweetling, you can ask me anything." She kept her voice gentle and even. "I've only ever wanted to help you blossom into the remarkable witch I knew you could become."

Arabella looked up, fluttering her eyelashes as if trying to blink away tears. "What should I do about declaring a House? I know Mother expects me to declare for Blackstone House. She's all but demanded it. But after certain events…" Arabella turned her head away and sniffed.

"Oh, my darling…" Cecelia put one arm around Arabella's shoulders. "It pains me so to see your heart wounded like this. I know your mother better than most. After all, we've been best friends for as long as I can remember. It doesn't surprise me that she's been a bit… harsh… with you. Your mother never could stand not to have things her way, even as a little girl."

"You don't think it's my fault?" Arabella sniffed and made sure her eyes were wide when she looked up at Cecelia. Could something as mundane as a little playacting really work so well to trick Cecelia?

"Of course not, child!" Cecelia said, squeezing Arabella closer for a moment before releasing her. "Your mother is a difficult woman. No one would blame you if you wanted to strike out on your own, away from her shadow."

Arabella put her fingertips to her lips and gasped. "You don't think I could…."

"Thornfire House would welcome you with open arms, my girl," Cecelia whispered into her ear as she laid a hand on her shoulder. "Now, I must return to the party or risk your mother's ire." She winked at Arabella and drifted back toward the rose garden.

Arabella took a deep breath and a gulp of tea as she traced Cecelia's progress, noticing Guardian Josolyne standing discretely nearby. She really should get to know the woman better since they would be in close quarters as they traveled.

"For someone who said she doesn't know how to play the game, you certainly seemed to do well there," Rowena said as she stepped out from behind a rosebush, her own teacup in hand.

"How much did you hear?" Arabella asked without taking her eyes from the crowd.

"All of it," Rowena said. "I saw her making her way toward you. I followed because I thought you might need rescuing."

Arabella nodded. "What do you think?"

"Of your performance or her offer?" Rowena murmured.

Arabella glanced sideways at her sister. "Both?"

"You'll need to hone your skills for people who will see you as a serious adversary, but since Aunt Cecelia doesn't see you as anything but a little girl hungry for love and approval, you did just fine." Rowena sipped her tea again. "As for her offer, you could do worse and you could do better. Thornfire House is well positioned, but if you think the politics in our household are daunting, you might not want to enter that battlefield."

"Should I seek out other offers?" Arabella whispered half to herself. Her mind whirled with the possibilities.

"It certainly wouldn't hurt to see if there is a more advantageous position for you, but you should be careful. If you seem too eager, then you will look desperate, and no one will want you. When a House Head pursues you, she needs to think it was her idea." Rowena looked at her sister. Arabella caught her gaze and smiled. There was some fun to be had with this game, it seemed.

Arabella was more prepared when Madeline Thurston, the Head of Hazelrood House, sidled up to her.

"Such lovely weather," Madeline said, sipping her tea. "I hope it holds well for your journey."

"That would be a kindness," Arabella murmured. She glanced around, taking note that Madeline had approached her when there was no one close. This was indeed meant to be a private conversation.

"Has your mother provided you your instructions yet?" Madeline asked.

"Only a general outline." Arabella favored her old family friend with a small smile. "I'm sure she will provide more specifics before we go."

Madeline forced a little chuckle. "Ah, so like Minerva, to hold everything so close until the very last minute. She's been like that since she was a girl."

"Has she?" Arabella raised an eyebrow and took a sip from her cup.

"Oh, yes," Madeline said as she laid a hand on Arabella's arm. "Your mother has always been quite secretive, but I'm sure you're aware of that."

"Indeed." Arabella nodded. She waited for Madeline to offer more information.

The older witch looked away and theatrically sniffed into a handkerchief. "Oh, how I wish I were officially one of your Gramuins so I could give you advice!" She turned back to Arabella with wide eyes. "I've always felt you were like one of my own. More than your sisters..." Madeline sighed theatrically.

Arabella patted her hand. This was almost too easy. "There is nothing that says you cannot take me under your wing," she soothed. Arabella glanced down then and looked up through her lashes at Madeline. "I'm afraid I've felt so lost lately. A familiar guiding hand would be quite welcome... Aunt Madeline."

The Head of Hazelrood House broke out into a grin. "I'm so glad to hear you say that, my dear girl." She looked around them to ensure there was still no one paying attention to them. "I must caution you that your mother is likely to hide information from you." Madeline sighed theatrically again. "I do so dislike speaking ill of her. She is one of my dearest friends, after all. It's just that..." She bit her lip. "It's just that Minerva has been so damaged, I'm not quite sure she can help herself. But I don't want to see her... struggles cause you any pain. I really only want what is best for you."

"But of course, Aunt Madeline." Arabella caught her hand in her own. She decided now was the time to offer something irresistible. "I trust you."

"You don't know how much it pleases me to hear that," she gasped, her eyes twinkling.

Arabella squeezed her hand. "So, what else would you advise me?"

"You should make good use of your travel time," Madeline said with an emphatic nod. "It does give you time to think, and it would be a shame to waste the opportunity."

"Just think?" Arabella asked. That wasn't what she'd expected. "Not practicing spellcraft? Rowena will be along, so she could help me."

"Practice is always valuable, of course." Madeline flipped her hand through the air as if to wave the idea away. "But deep thought will serve you better at this juncture." She paused, her mien serious. Her eyes bored into Arabella. "Working within the Council is much like playing chess, except you are playing multiple games at the same time. Sometimes even multiple games with the same person… You would do well to think carefully about the best seat to play from, the one that would be most advantageous for your gambits." She leaned in close and whispered into Arabella's ear. "Hazelrood House will always welcome you."

"Madeline!" Mother cried, approaching from behind them. "There you are! I've been looking all over for you. You simply must come fuss over my first granddaughter." She threaded her arm through Madeline's and drew her away.

"But of course!" Minerva's old friend enthused. "The first of us to have daughters and now the first to have a granddaughter… You are so blessed."

As they began to stroll away, Madeline paused and glanced back over her shoulder at Arabella. "You'll think about what I said?"

"Yes, Aunt Madeline," Arabella said as she bobbed a curtsy.

She sighed deeply as she watched them go. This playacting and gamesmanship was exhausting. She jumped when yet another voice rose from behind her.

"She was rather blatant, wasn't she?" said Parthena Luther, Arabella's Examiner from the Trials. "Did she actually think you would swallow that performance?" She shook her head. "I certainly hope her spellcraft is better than her acting."

Arabella put a hand to her chest and muttered to herself, "I do wish people would stop sneaking up on me."

Parthena's thin lips lifted, and her eyes twinkled. "Perhaps you'd like to show me some of the deeper gardens so we can speak privately?"

Arabella felt torn. Parthena had left the House of her birth to join Birchwold House, giving her unique insight into the game Arabella was playing. But all the politically motivated conversational sparring had left her exhausted already. She honestly just wanted to hide.

"Or we could walk together and not talk?" Parthena tilted her head to the side.

Arabella's eyes widened. "That would be..."

"A relief?" Parthena finished her thought and laughed.

"Yes, that." Arabella laughed with her. "That would be delightful."

The women walked in companionable silence deeper into the garden. Birds flitted among the topiary bushes while softly buzzing bees visited every flower. They paused their stroll to admire a pair of jewel-winged butterflies fluttering past. The murmur of the party began to fade in the distance.

Arabella broke the silence.

"How did you know declaring for Birchwold House was the right thing to do?" she asked the question sitting on her tongue.

Parthena smirked. "I didn't."

Arabella's jaw dropped open. "But... What... How?"

Parthena tilted back her head and laughed. "Did you think once you were past the Trials that you would be granted some miraculous wisdom that would make the correct choice for every decision obvious?"

"Well, when you put it like that, it just sounds silly." Arabella pouted. Would the ground never stop moving under her feet? "Everyone else always seems so sure. Mother, Vivienne..."

"Arabella," Parthena said gently. "There's no way to be sure about everything. Even the most crystal-clear prophecy can be interpreted wrong, and we don't have prophecy to guide us for many things." She shrugged. "Most of us are very good at pretending we know what we are doing because not knowing is weakness."

"More politics?" Arabella groaned.

Parthena chuckled. "You'll get used to it after a while. It just starts to become part of the air you breathe."

Arabella sighed. "So, everything is just blind guesswork?"

Parthena shook her head. "Only some things. You make the best decision you can with the information you have."

"I was hoping for an easy answer."

"Some answers are easy, and some are not," Parthena said.

"That's not helpful." Arabella squinted at Parthena. "I thought you wanted to help me."

"I do. Why don't you talk things through with me? Which Houses are you considering? What are their benefits and drawbacks? Sometimes saying it aloud makes things a bit clearer."

Arabella looked thoughtful. "Well…"

"There you are!" Amelia rushed up, all out of breath. "This is your sendoff party, and you've gone and disappeared. Some of the guests want to leave. You must say farewell." Amelia grabbed Arabella's hand and began to pull her away up the manicured path. "Mother is quite cross with you, you know," she grumbled.

"How did you decide in the end?" Arabella called over her shoulder to Parthena.

Parthena's laughter followed them. "I flipped a coin."

CHAPTER X

A New Witch Ventures Forth

L IVERPOOL MOVED WITH A MORE DILIGENT PURPOSE. IN LONDON, Arabella was used to seeing the upper crust strutting and going about the business of seeing and being seen. The people who did the real work of tending beast and home, of making things, stayed out of sight where she traveled. But here in Liverpool, everyone she could see seemed to have the business of real work in their hands and purpose in their strides. Arabella shaded her eyes against the mid-afternoon sun as she leaned out the carriage window, trying to catch sight of the harbor. The excitement of finally venturing beyond her mother's rigid constraints tingled in her veins. The wonder of it nearly banished her worries of Council politics and potential attacks.

Rowena tugged at her sleeve. "Oh, do stop gawping! Everyone will think you're some kind of bumpkin."

"I've never seen the sea." Arabella pouted as she sat down hard. "The largest body of water I've ever seen is the Thames."

Her sister rolled her eyes. "It's just the Irish Sea. It's not like we're sailing across the whole of the Atlantic to the Americas."

"People may think I'm a bumpkin, but they'll certainly think you're putting on airs," Arabella sniffed. "You've hardly traveled much more than me, and I know you've never seen a sea this big."

Guardian Eliza Josolyne glanced at Guardian Sarah Gardner and tried to give her a little smile. Sarah frowned and pointedly turned to the carriage window. Arabella groaned inwardly. The two Guardians had been like this since they'd left Blackstone Manor. She dearly hoped it wouldn't continue for the entire trip.

Eliza forced a chuckle. "Your first sea is always impressive, even if it's one of the smaller ones." Arabella caught Sarah rolling her eyes.

The carriage rattled to a stop at King's Dock. Jeanette handed the reins to her assistant and hopped off the box, calling out to the stevedores loafing nearby to come handle the luggage. She opened the door with a flourish, ready to hand all the ladies out of the carriage. The Guardians ignored her offered hand and bounded to the ground with ease. Eliza held up her hand to stop Arabella and Rowena while she and Sarah scanned the area.

The Guardians were dressed for hard travel and trouble. They wore plain brown waistcoats over undyed linen shirts. Both waistcoats and shirts were cut with extra ease in the shoulders and arms so as not to inhibit movement. Their plain brown trousers were tucked neatly into sturdy brown leather boots. Wide leather belts supported their backs and held the accoutrements of their profession. At her right hip, each Guardian wore a carefully coiled length of braided silk rope impregnated with silver and spells and a small pouch full of hex bags and potion vials. On their left hips sat single-edged dirks. The twelve inches of steel were certainly not the delicate ritual athames most witches used; they were meant for a fight. But just like any good athame, they were layered with spells to make their work more effective. Eliza wore her dark brown hair swept back in a tight chignon at the nape of her neck, while Sarah kept her wheat blonde hair almost shorn to the scalp.

The stevedores who approached the carriage stopped dead in unison, then took a step back while they gulped and exchanged worried glances. The Guardians were indeed a formidable pair. They were trained to be able to take down men twice their size with ease. However, their true danger lay not in their physical prowess but rather with the spells at their lips that could lay the entire dockyard flat in the space of three breaths.

Eliza motioned for Sarah to stay close to the carriage. The Guardian clenched her jaw, but she crossed her arms and planted herself between the docks and her charges. Eliza strode with confident ease in the direction of the stevedores. She inspected each man in silence, then returned to the carriage.

"They may handle the luggage," she said to Jeanette. "Their auras aren't pristine, but there's no malice toward us." Jeanette beckoned the nervous men forward, but none of them moved. She rolled her eyes and jingled a heavy purse in the air.

"There's good, hard coin in it if you can find your backbones and load this luggage onto the *Kittiwake*."

The promise of good pay was enough to set their feet moving. The men swarmed the small pile of luggage tied to the roof of the carriage and made quick work of it.

Eliza nodded to Sarah, and they offered their hands to Arabella and Rowena. The stevedores were halfway down the dock with the luggage before they both had their feet on the ground.

"What did you mean by their auras aren't pristine? Are those men dangerous?" Arabella asked.

"Folk who have to live hand to mouth sometimes have to do unsavory things to survive," Eliza answered.

Sarah snorted and turned her attention down the dock.

Eliza frowned and turned back to the girls. "I'm sure any one of those men has done things they'd prefer a constable not find out about. But there's no malice in their hearts toward us."

Arabella and Rowena glanced at each other and swallowed hard.

"Sometimes I forget how sheltered you girls have been," Jeanette guffawed. "These boys may not be angels, but we're paying them, and that's all they need to think well of us. I guarantee they'll be blessing our names as they put real meat on the table for their families tonight." She shook her head and chuckled. "Folks who have never had to worry about where their next meal comes from forget too easy how much loyalty can be bought with a full stomach."

"Indeed," Eliza said. She turned to Arabella and Rowena. Her expression was as hard and sharp as the steel she carried. "Now, listen carefully. You two are our responsibility. Do not make our jobs any harder than they need to be. You will stay close to one or both of us at all times, and if we tell you to do something, you will do it without question. Have I made myself clear?"

"Yes, ma'am," the girls chorused without a second thought.

"Good." Eliza's expression softened, and she smiled. "As long as you listen and pay proper attention, we shouldn't have any trouble on this trip. We'll do some sightseeing and spend some quiet nights by the fire, then we'll come home once things are a bit more settled. I hope you brought some good books."

Snugged up to King's Dock, the *Kittiwake*, a sixty-foot sloop, waited for Arabella and her entourage. Arabella gave its whole length an appraising gaze, the single mast, the jib on the foredeck waiting to be hoisted, and the small deck house on the aft deck.

"It's not exactly luxurious, is it?" Rowena murmured.

"Well," Jeanette said as she deposited coins into stevedore hands. "When you're trying to find a boat leaving soon that still has room for passengers with luggage, there aren't a lot of choices."

"We'll only be aboard for one night," Arabella chirped. "By this time tomorrow, we'll be docking in Dublin. I'm sure we can arrange something much more comfortable on our return trip since we'll have more time."

"I suppose we should introduce ourselves to the captain," she said, squaring up her shoulders.

"*You'll* wait here until I check the boat," Eliza said. She flicked her hand at Sarah to keep her with Arabella and Rowena. Arabella noticed Sarah's hand clench by her side, but again the woman obeyed without a word. Eliza leapt over the railing and prowled around the boat. The sailors paused in their preparations to watch her in bemused wonder. One bearded and tanned gentleman in striped blue trousers came to the railing to greet Arabella.

"Ahoy," he called. "You'll be my new passengers, I presume?"

"Yes, sir." Arabella smiled and shaded her eyes. "Arabella Leyden and Rowena Sortilege, of the English Council of Witches. This is Guardian Sarah Gardner." Arabella gestured to her left. "And that would be Guardian Eliza Josolyne." She pointed to Eliza just as she disappeared below decks.

"Captain Harry Midstock, at your service, ma'am," he said, tipping his cap.

"You'll have to excuse Guardian Josolyne. She's dedicated to her job and quite thorough." Arabella said with an apologetic tilt of her head.

Captain Midstock shrugged. "It makes no never mind to me if she wants to interview the ship's cat just to be sure he's not a threat, ma'am. The Witches' Council paid me some fine coin to make sure you make it to Dublin as quickly and safely as possible." He snorted. "I hired us the best wind witch in Liverpool, and there's still more coin in my pocket than I usually get for three runs to Dublin. All of you can be just as odd as you want, and I'll still be the first one offering to take you the next time you want to sail."

Arabella laughed. "Oh my! Well, I'm certainly pleased this voyage has been so profitable for you."

Eliza slipped up next to the captain's shoulder and murmured into his ear. "We have a problem."

Captain Midstock frowned. "What sort of problem?"

"One of your crew is a danger to my charges," Eliza continued, her hands clasped behind her back. "We cannot sail with you if he is present. His aura shows significant malice."

The captain grunted and nodded. "Which one?"

Eliza jerked her head toward the bow. "The one with the dark hair, bent over, coiling the line."

"Evans!" Captain Midstock bellowed. "Grab your gear and shove off! You'll not be going on this run."

The tall, thickly muscled man straightened to his full height, glowering. He threw the line on the deck in a haphazard pile.

"You can't do this to me, Harry!" he roared back. "I need the money! I'll tell Ma…" He curled his lip and raised his fists.

"I'll pay you anyway, boy!" Midstock yelled. "Put yer damn hands down. And there's no need to tell yer Ma."

Evans relaxed his stance and lowered his fists. "You'll pay the full amount? No cheating?"

"No cheating," the captain snarled. "Just get yer things and get off my damn boat."

Grumbling the whole way, Evans went below and emerged with a small sea bag moments later. He stopped in front of Captain Midstock and thrust out his hand.

"You don't get paid until we get back, same as always. Don't spend it all on gin before I give it to you," Midstock said with a growl.

A barely banked heat of rage rolled off Evans as he ambled away across the deck, not taking his eyes off Captain Midstock until he vaulted over the railing onto the dock. He looked Arabella and Rowena up and down.

"Damn witches," he said, sneering. "Don't know your proper place."

A shiver ran down Arabella's spine as he turned and slunk off into the crowd.

"Sorry about that," the captain huffed as he tilted back his cap and scratched his head. "He's my wife's boy from a youthful mistake. She loves him more than he deserves, and sometimes she pushes me to take him on for a cruise when he can't find other work."

Eliza nodded. "Do you need to find a replacement?"

The captain shook his head. "He's mostly useless. The rest of the crew can handle things just fine. See," he jerked his thumb to another crew member who had already deftly coiled the line Evans had left behind. "Once you ladies are on board, all we're waiting for is the wind witch."

"Has she been cleared by the Council?" Eliza raised her eyebrow.

"Aye, and I'll vouch for her myself. Bathsheba is the best there is. Keeps her word, works hard, and can pull a gale out of the doldrums if you need her to. We got lucky that she was available."

Eliza beckoned to Arabella, Rowena, and Sarah. "Well, let's get settled then and hope that Bathsheba is as punctual as you say she is."

"I am always precisely where and when I say I will be," a rich, mellow voice rose from behind Arabella.

Arabella turned and set her eyes on Bathsheba. The wind witch's dark brown eyes sparkled back with amusement. She was tall for a woman. She wore a modest dress of olive-green linen, and a saffron-yellow scarf completely covered her hair, tied above her brow with an artful knot. Both colors complimented her deep umber-colored skin. She had a small canvas sea bag slung over her shoulder. Arabella tried not to stare at the scar snaking from Bathsheba's temple down her left cheek, ending just at her chin and dragging the left side of her lips down ever so slightly. The vivid pink against the witch's deep brown skin kept drawing her eye.

"Hail, my queen of the wind," Captain Midstock bellowed as he whipped his cap off and bowed low before straightening and covering his head once more. "My humble thanks for taking this job on such short notice, Mistress Bathsheba."

Bathsheba's rich laugh resonated with real mirth. "You're paying me well, and the Council was very… *encouraging*." She considered Arabella and Rowena closely. "So, which one of you is the Grande Dame's precious cargo?"

"I suppose that would be both of us. This is my sister Rowena Sortilege, and I am Arabella Leyden, at your service." Arabella curtseyed to Bathsheba.

"Oh ho!" Bathsheba chuckled. "The new little mechanical witch that has everyone in the high seats in such an uproar? We'll have to trade stories once I get the wind running right."

She then turned back to the boat and said, "Permission to come aboard, Captain?"

"You hardly need to ask, Miss Bathsheba." The captain waved one of his deckhands over to assist her over the rail.

Bathsheba nodded her thanks to the deckhand as she dropped lightly to the deck. "Manners are important, my dear captain. Where would we be without a civil society?"

"You'll be sharing the deckhouse with our passengers. If you want to put your things away," Captain Midstock said. He turned to Eliza. "If you're satisfied, we can get your charges on board and be underway with the tide."

Eliza gave him a nod. "I'm pleased with the rest of the crew."

Sarah and two deckhands helped Rowena and Arabella over the rail. As soon as she had her feet on the deck, Arabella stumbled, and Rowena put out her arms to find her balance.

"Oh my," Arabella cried. "I didn't expect it would be so unsteady."

The crew stifled snickers, hiding their grins behind their hands as they readied the ship to get underway.

"We're still at the dock," Bathsheba noted. "This is as steady as it gets."

"Oh, dear," Rowena murmured as she took a few wavering steps.

The captain motioned over to the aft deckhouse with his thumb. "Perhaps you'd be more comfortable sitting in there." As he turned away to check on the crew, Arabella heard him mutter, "And it would keep you out from underfoot."

The four of them made their careful way to the aft deckhouse huddled close to the port side of the deck. As she pushed the door open, Arabella noticed the wood wasn't as weathered as the rest of the boat.

"This is certainly… cozy," she remarked as she took in the confined space. There were two sets of stacked bunks, one on the port wall and one on the starboard, and a round table with three spindle-back chairs took up the rest of the cramped cabin. Despite a small window on the aft wall letting in some afternoon sunlight, shadows hugged the corners of the chamber. What she could only presume were bespelled lamps bolted to the walls would, however, provide golden light once the sun went down. *A smart move on the captain's part to use magic instead of open flame on board a boat,* Arabella thought.

"There aren't even enough beds," Rowena complained. "There are five ladies on board. Does the captain expect one of us to sleep under the table?"

"Four bunks will serve," Eliza said. "Sarah and I will use the same bunk. One of us must always be on guard."

"But what about dressing? There's hardly enough room to turn around in here, let alone change into a proper nightgown when it's time for bed." Rowena threw up her arms.

Arabella raised an eyebrow. "Well, aren't you just the little hothouse flower?"

"You can't possibly find this comfortable!" Rowena said, her fists on her hips.

"Comfort needed to be sacrificed for speed." Eliza snapped, her eyes blazing. "Neither of you seem to be truly aware of how much danger Arabella is in." She turned to Arabella as she crossed her arms across her chest. "Did you know a Guardian watched over your father's house every hour of every day after you left the Trials? That a pair of Guardians followed you from London to Boscastle? That I waited at Blackstone Manor to take up the duty of keeping you alive until cooler heads prevail?"

"I had no idea," Arabella murmured. "I never saw any of you until I came to Blackstone Manor."

"Then you probably have no idea that we stopped an attempt on your life, did you?" Eliza said in a husky whisper.

Arabella's stomach dropped as the memory of the witch throwing fire at her flashed through her mind. In a barely audible voice, she whispered, "When?" though she already knew.

"In London, after you met Julian Pattersby for tea, you left the safety of your cab to walk the last few blocks," Eliza said, her expression grim. "Guardian Waterman was on duty. She stopped Beatrice Paskin's younger sister, Tabitha, from burning you alive. The Paskin line does seem to favor fire magic for offense…"

Arabella nodded. "I didn't know her name, the one who rescued me. Is Guardian Waterman… alright?"

Eliza paused. "Guardian Waterman survived and managed to subdue Tabitha, but she suffered serious burns. She has already returned to duty. Her scars are minimal."

Arabella sighed in relief and closed her eyes for a moment. "I thought it was an isolated incident and that the witch who protected me was just… there by chance." Arabella swallowed hard. Her voice trembled. "Were there more?"

Eliza's mouth thinned to a hard line. "Yes. But we were able to stop them before they got too close."

"Did Mother know it was this bad?"

"Yes."

"But why didn't *I* know?" Arabella's voice came out in a strangled cry.

The tightness in Eliza's face eased. She glanced at Sarah, who leaned against the port wall. Sarah gave her a curt nod.

"Your mother thought it best to keep you unaware of how dire the situation is, for your nerves." Eliza held up her hand to stop Arabella's sputtering attempt to interrupt. "I wasn't in agreement. But I could not gainsay my Grande Dame in her own house about her own daughter."

"And now?" Despite her effort to remain composed, Arabella's voice squawked.

"I am authorized to do whatever I must to keep you and your sister alive," Eliza said. "And I believe I can do my job more effectively if you are aware of the extent of the danger."

Arabella trembled and wrapped her arms around herself, barely noticing as Rowena's arms enfolded her as well.

"What now?" Rowena murmured.

"You listen to me and you listen to Sarah," Eliza said. "And we will be honest with you about any further threats."

"The man you threw off the boat?" Arabella's voice shook.

"Non-magical threat," Eliza said briskly. "He is a dangerous man, but likely no more dangerous to you than he is to any other woman. I would just as soon not to have to deal with mundane threats while I'm also trying to fend off magical ones."

Arabella nodded and laid her head on Rowena's shoulder.

"I had no idea things were that perilous," Arabella whispered. She pulled away from her sister's embrace and sat at the tiny table. In the silence of the cabin, it was easy to hear the sailors shouting to each other, the *thunk* of heavy lines cast off, and the flap of the sails as Bathsheba fed them wind.

"Why?" Arabella asked in a low voice. "Why so much trouble over me? Is it because I am the Grande Dame's daughter?"

"We let her think that," Sarah said. Eliza's head snapped around, her eyes sharp and glittering. Arabella and Rowena stared at her with round eyes. This was the first time they'd heard Sarah speak. They hadn't been sure that she could. Sarah lifted her chin, returning Eliza's glare with defiant eyes. Eliza dropped her gaze first.

"We Guardians deal in more than just the martial magics. We also have witches capable of scrying and farseeing," Sarah began. "There is something special about you, Arabella, something beyond your oh so unusual capabilities. Something about you is vital to keeping balance in this world."

"Why me?" Arabella sighed and rubbed her temples. It all felt a bit too much. She had already upended the magical world with her new abilities. It seemed likely she was the fulfillment of the Cagliostro prophecy her mother had been chasing for decades, and now there was another shadowy prophecy laid on her shoulders. Or perhaps this new prediction was an extension of the powerful vision that struck all of House Cagliostro at once? The weight of it all felt so heavy.

"We don't know. It's still too shrouded." Sarah glanced at Eliza, who glared back. "But we've been waiting for you for almost a year now."

"Enough!" Eliza snapped.

"I thought we were being honest about the gravity of the situation?" Sarah scoffed.

"A murky prophecy from casual seers isn't helpful," Eliza growled. "It's just as likely to be the effects of bad digestion as it is to be a true prophecy."

Sarah sneered. "You hold such little regard for your Sisters."

"I like you better when you're silent."

"I like you better when you're not pretending to be superior to everyone else."

Arabella and Rowena shrank back as the air nearly crackled between the two Guardians.

"I am here to complete my mission…" Eliza started.

"As am I!" Sarah interrupted. "I took the same vows you did."

The women continued to glare at each other. Finally, Sarah tore her eyes away and gave a snort.

"Have your way, Lady High and Mighty," she jeered. "I'll hold my tongue, just try to keep your loathing of me to a minimum. I'm just as capable as you."

"I know you're capable!"

Sarah made a rude gesture. "I couldn't tell from how you treat me."

"I haven't…"

"I know I can't trace my lineage back hundreds of years, but I still laid you flat on your back in battle training," Sarah snarled.

Bathsheba entered the cabin and tossed her sea bag onto the starboard-side lower bunk. She paused and looked at the Guardians, facing each other like territorial alley cats.

"Do I need to deploy a shield spell? Or can the two of you," she wagged her finger back and forth between them, "resolve this without hurting anyone else?"

Eliza drew herself up and straightened her waistcoat. "We are in perfect control of our tempers. We would never allow anyone to be injured accidentally."

Rolling her eyes, Sarah snorted and returned to leaning against the wall.

"See that you don't injure anyone *at all*," Bathsheba said crisply. "I work with the gentlemen on this boat regularly, and I've become rather fond of them." Her gaze swept over Arabella and Rowena. "And these two naïve lambs don't seem like they deserve it either."

"I'll thank you to keep your tongue civil and not take that tone with me," Eliza snapped.

Bathsheba's eyes blazed. "And I'll thank you to remember the Council believes I am vital to the success of this little adventure." She dropped her voice. "And the wind is not all I command. You may wish to take care of your tone with *me*."

Eliza's eyes widened, and her nostrils flared, but she didn't move. Sarah stifled a giggle behind her hand.

Bathsheba took a deep breath to compose herself and turned to Arabella and Rowena. "We are making our way out of the harbor, and that can be quite a stirring sight. If you ladies would like to venture out onto the deck, I can show you where to stand so you will not be in the way."

"That sounds lovely," Arabella chirped with false cheerfulness as she leapt out of her chair. She snatched up Rowena's hand, casting a nervous glance over her shoulder as they followed Bathsheba out of the cabin. "Why don't we leave Guardians Josolyne and Gardner to their strategy session. I'm sure they have much to discuss."

Later that evening, Arabella, Rowena, and their Guardians gathered in the cramped cabin for the meager dinner the ship's cook sent up for them. Bathsheba declined to dine with them and instead took her meal with the sailors. They lounged about on the deck rather than try to jam themselves into the tiny galley below. The weather was fine enough for it. The thin cabin walls did little to muffle the raucous laughter and jaunty sea shanties the sailors shared.

Rowena, Arabella, and Eliza shared the small table while Sarah perched on the edge of her bunk. She shoveled down her dinner efficiently while she stared at the wall without seeing it. Arabella nudged her beans and salt pork around the tin plate with her spoon. The slice of dense, dark bread the cook put on the side wasn't quite stale, but it was close to it. The tea in their tin cups was bitter and strong. Arabella sighed and wondered how little she could get away with eating. Her stomach growled. Rowena's eyes jumped around from person to person. She examined them all over the rim of her cup as she sipped her tea. The silence was well past uncomfortable.

"Have you traveled much, Guardian Josolyne?" Arabella asked Eliza, trying to keep her voice casual.

"I have been to the Continent once or twice as a girl, but my duties keep me on the soil of the Empire most of the time," Eliza said. "And please, call me Eliza. It's a long journey, and we're going to be in close quarters much of the time."

"And you, Guardian Gardner?" Rowena asked Sarah.

"Sarah," she mumbled around a mouthful of beans. She swallowed and took a gulp of tea. "I'm always just Sarah among my Sisters. I'm not one to put on airs." She stole a pointed glance at Eliza. Eliza rolled her eyes.

"As for travel," Sarah continued. "This will be as far as I've ever been from home. I didn't come from a rich family. We couldn't afford trips to *The Continent*."

"My family is not rich!" Eliza tossed her spoon onto her plate with a clatter.

"I'm one of those low-class girls that comes to the Trials not expecting to survive. All I hoped was to get my family some money and one less mouth to feed." She closed her eyes and sighed. "But my Da always taught me to do my best, no matter what. We may be poor, but we have our pride. So, I tried to move the feather in the vase with wind magic. Instead, I made the vase explode, and the Guardians claimed me."

Sarah scraped up the last of the beans from her plate and sopped up the pork fat with the last bit of her bread.

Rowena gaped at Sarah. Arabella felt absolutely wretched for disdaining the simple meal in front of her. She forced down another bite and reminded herself to be grateful.

"Do you still talk to them, your family?" Arabella asked as she set her spoon next to her plate. "After they sent you to die?"

Sarah's head jerked up. "Don't you dare speak ill of my family," she hissed. "I asked to go to the Trials. It was the best way I knew how to help them. Now I send money home every month, and my little brothers don't go hungry. We could even afford to call a real doctor last winter when Ma got sick. She might not have lived otherwise."

"I'm sorry. I didn't mean…"

Sarah waved away Arabella's attempt to apologize. "You don't know any better. You've been raised soft." She pinned Arabella to her chair with a hard stare. "But maybe now that you're grown, you need to start thinking about how hungry other people are for everything you've always had."

Sarah stood with her plate in her hand, turning for the cabin door.

"For what it's worth, I requested you for this assignment," Eliza blurted out.

Sarah turned slowly and looked at Eliza quizzically. "You requested *me*? The witch you've hated from the first day of training?"

"You're uncouth, and you have no manners. You're practically a barbarian." Eliza paused. She shook her head and sighed. "But you're still one of the finest Guardians I've ever seen. I couldn't do better than to have you watching my back."

"Well, I think you're a prissy little know-it-all with more breeding than good sense." Sarah grinned at the shocked look on Eliza's face. "But you're also a damn fine Guardian. We don't have to like each other; we just have to work together."

"Agreed." Eliza nodded emphatically. "Truce?"

"I still think you're a snot, but yeah. Truce." Sarah whistled a happy tune as she left the cabin while Eliza fumed.

CHAPTER XI

The Threat of Outside Influence

GOLDEN SUNLIGHT SLANTED ACROSS ARABELLA'S BEDROOM IN Blackstone Manor. It was late morning, perhaps? Had she missed breakfast? She sat up and stretched, luxuriating in feeling rested for the first time in a long time. Climbing from her bed, she splashed water on her face at the washbasin and rang the bell for Emmie to help her get dressed. While she waited, she sat down at her vanity, unbraided her hair, and set to brushing it. By the time her hair was soft and gleaming, Emmie still had not arrived.

Arabella frowned and rang the bell again. It sounded hollow.

She drifted to her window and peeked out her curtains. The gardens were empty. That was odd. Mother's roses alone demanded such care that the garden should be abuzz with gardeners, both human and fae, by midmorning. Arabella dressed herself and ventured from her room to find someone.

Stepping out into the hallway, Arabella was seized at once by the silence. The Manor was sometimes quiet, but it was never silent, not even in the darkest hours of the night. Servants cleaned and polished, laid fires, and mended clothes and linens at all hours of the day and night whenever they had a moment from the demands of the family. Even in the small hours of the night, one could hear the house fae scuttling around, going about their business. On the nights of the new moon and full moon, the house was nearly as busy at midnight as it was at noon. Lunar working amplified so many spells.

Cheerful, golden sunlight filled the hallway, and yet, there were no whispers of voices. No footsteps upon the stairs. No ticking from the reawakened clock. Only silence.

The creak of the first stair as Arabella put her foot down rang like a gong in the hush of the house. Arabella froze. In the stillness that followed, she heard the rustle of skirts coming from the hallway behind her. She whirled around to catch the flash of a hem disappearing through a doorway, one of the linen closets that kept fresh sheets and towels near at hand. Was that the sturdy gray wool of a housemaid's dress? Or her mother's favorite bluish-gray Italian wool dress? Arabella couldn't tell from her brief glimpse.

The tightness in Arabella's chest eased. The person belonging to the dress might be able to tell her where the rest of the household was. Arabella hurried forward to where the woman disappeared. The door hung open wide. Her momentary relief fled. The staff did not leave the inner workings of the house open to the family. It was just not done. The interior of the closet was deep and dark, far more than it should be. At least some of the midmorning light in the hall should filter past the doorjamb. Arabella's stomach gave a little flip.

Arabella paused on the threshold. Her breath caught in her throat. She inhaled the strong lavender scent from the sprigs Mrs. Holly tucked between the layers of fabric. There was a hint of cedar, too, from the blocks meant to discourage moths from feasting on their winter blankets. Arabella leaned in slightly, squinting as she tried to make anything out in the pitch black.

"Hello?" she called. Silence pressed down on her ears like muffling wads of wool at first.

Then another rustle of fabric answered from deeper in the closet. A light began to glow as if someone had uncovered an oil lamp. The light shone from much farther away than should be possible. The closet was simply not that deep. As Arabella took a step over the threshold, icy phantom fingers brushed up her spine. She looked behind her with a gasp, but there was no one there. Only the empty hallway full of midmorning light that seemed to have lasted for hours already.

"H-h-hello?" Arabella called again.

She heard the rustling again. This time she spied the back of a practical gray dress, similar to those the housemaids wore. The figure stood in the shadows, her back to Arabella, adjusting linens on the shelf.

"Oh, thank goodness!" Arabella laid her hand on her chest. Her shoulders sagged with relief. "Please, can you tell me where everyone is? What's happening?"

The figure gave no response and kept at her work with the linens. Fear trickled down Arabella's spine like ice water.

Arabella frowned. "Did you hear me?"

The figure maintained her silence and her back to Arabella.

"Please." Desperation began to creep into Arabella's voice. "Please, talk to me. Where is everyone? Are they alright?"

The figure's hands stilled. She remained silent and kept her back to Arabella. Arabella stepped forward and laid her hand on the figure's shoulder.

"What's happening? Please, can you tell me?" Arabella was near frantic. Her heart thudded in her chest.

The figure finally turned around. She had no face. No eyes, no nose, no mouth, just a smooth expanse of pale skin stretching from her hairline to her chin. The woman tilted her head to the side as if asking Arabella a question, but made no sound.

Arabella yanked back her hand and shrieked. She stumbled back two steps, then turned and fled the closet. Arabella raced for the grand staircase into the foyer.

But the faceless figure was already there, standing at the top of the staircase. The figure held out a hand to Arabella. Her cheeks flexed as if she smiled, though she had no mouth.

Arabella yelped. Stumbling, she scrambled to turn in the other direction. The servant's stairs at the back of the house. If she could get downstairs, she could exit the house. What she would do then, she couldn't be sure. But for now, escaping the faceless figure was enough to think about.

As Arabella thundered down the servants' stairs, her feet nearly slid out from under her on the worn wood. A soft voice in another corner of her mind advised her to have carpet installed to prevent the servants from falling when she became mistress of her own home. Arabella shook her head to dislodge the nuisance. Now was not the time to mull over the practical matters of housekeeping.

Arabella burst into the kitchen with a gasp. Mrs. Holly stood at the stove, stirring something in a tall pot. The smell was most unappetizing.

"Thank the Goddess, Mrs. Holly," Arabella panted. "What in Hera's name is going on around here? There's a housemaid upstairs with no face!"

Mrs. Holly stopped stirring and tapped the wooden spoon on the rim of the pot. She set the spoon aside, wiping her hands on her apron as she turned toward Arabella.

Mrs. Holly had no face. And she spoke.

"You can trust me." The voice seemed to come from Mrs. Holly. But she had no mouth, and the voice did not sound like her at all. It was flat but with a grating quality that set Arabella's teeth on edge.

Arabella shrieked and pelted out of the kitchen. The servants' sitting room was blessedly empty as she thundered through. She slammed her body into the green baize door and burst into the grand foyer. Not three steps in, she stumbled over her own feet and fell to her knees. Raising her head, she spied another figure by the grandfather clock, standing with its back to her. From her vantage point on the floor, the figure looked like it could be her mother. Her dark hair swept up off her neck, her favorite blue-gray Italian wool dress draping just so, the very set of her shoulders proclaiming her authority over all she surveyed… Arabella whimpered. The figure who seemed to be Minerva Sortilege turned.

She had no face.

The Mother figure reached out her hand, tilting her head to the side, blank cheeks flexing as if to smile… if she'd had lips.

"You can trust me," she said in the same grating, flat intonation.

Arabella heard a creak behind her. She whipped her head around to see the faceless housemaid descending the stairs with her hand extended.

"You can trust me."

Arabella felt more than heard the servants' door swish open behind her. She twisted her head around as the faceless Mrs. Holly emerged from the servants' quarters with her hand extended.

"You can trust me."

Arabella scrabbled across the slick marble floor, heading for the small hallway off the foyer that led past her mother's office and ended in a door out into the rose garden. The three followed.

"You can trust me," they said in grating unison.

Sobbing as she finally hauled herself to her feet, Arabella staggered down the hall, her heart pounding in her chest. If she could just reach the door to the garden, she might be safe. A hysterical giggle bubbled past her lips as she reached the door.

The knob would not turn. The door would not budge.

Arabella looked back over her shoulder. They were coming. All three of them with their arms outstretched.

"You can trust me." They said in unison.

Arabella wailed and hammered on the door with her fists. She closed her eyes and felt as if she were falling.

Arabella gasped, and her eyes flew open. She hung halfway out of her tiny lower bunk in the cramped cabin on the *Kittiwake*. Clutching the rough wood, she panted. Starlight shone through the small aft window. Waves slapped the hull. Rowena snored above her.

"Are you alright?" Eliza whispered from the upper bunk across from Arabella.

"Just a nightmare… I think." Arabella groaned as she levered herself into a sitting position. She'd loosened her corset to sleep, but the boning still pressed and rubbed in tender spots. She heard feet hit the floor. Suddenly, Eliza crouched in front of her.

"You think?" Her voice was sharp.

Arabella rubbed her eyes. "Yes." She paused. "Probably?"

The Guardian's fingers pressed against her forehead, cool and lovely. Inside her mind, she felt Eliza's metaphysical fingers probing. After a moment, she withdrew her hand. "I can't find any evidence of interference. It's hard to tell if someone has influenced you after the fact. She would have to be clumsy indeed to leave a mark behind."

Arabella shivered despite the heat in the stuffy little cabin. "Do you think someone would actually try to affect my mind?"

Eliza shrugged. "Anything is possible. What happened in the dream?"

"It was… there were…" Arabella gulped and took a breath to steady herself. "I was back at Blackstone Manor, and everyone was gone. Or at least I thought so… It was so quiet, very eerie. Then I did find people, well, I thought they were people at first. But they had no faces! One was dressed like a housemaid, and the other two looked like Mrs. Holly and my mother. Well, mostly looked like them since they didn't have faces." Arabella gulped again. Her voice trembled. "They kept offering me their hands, and they chased me. They kept saying, 'you can trust me' in this strange voice."

"Did any of the faceless figures actually touch you?" Eliza asked.

Arabella shook her head. "No. I woke up before they did. But it was close."

Eliza nodded and stood. "That is certainly an upsetting dream, but I think it's probably just an ordinary nightmare. The kind that any mundane woman might suffer while she's in a stressful situation."

"That's a relief." Arabella sighed.

"But if it happens again, tell me immediately," Eliza admonished. "Dream magic can be very subtle and hard to detect."

Arabella shuddered. "I promise."

As Eliza climbed back up into her bunk, Arabella leaned down to collect her shoes from the floor.

"I don't think I can go right back to sleep," she said as she laced them on. "I think I'll get a breath of air on the deck." She paused and looked up at Eliza. "Unless you think that would be unsafe?"

"We're in the middle of the sea." The Guardian yawned as she settled back down onto her pillow. "And Sarah is out on deck standing watch. You'll be fine." Eliza joined Rowena in snoring before Arabella opened the cabin door.

Arabella sighed with contentment as the sea air swept across her brow and cooled the sweaty back of her neck. As she stepped out, the deck creaked beneath her feet. She held her arms out to her side as she adjusted to the rolling and swaying of the ship under sail.

Sarah looked up from where she leaned on the starboard rail, puffing on a pipe. She nodded to Arabella and continued her contemplation of the night sea. The gentle wind Bathsheba used to fill the sails ruffled her close-cropped hair. Perched on the bow of the boat, the youngest member of the crew — a boy of eleven or twelve — scanned the horizon line and the sea for obstacles or dangers. Behind Arabella, far back on the aft deck, one of the sailors held the tiller in a soft hand. Bathsheba perched on the port rail, gazing up at the full sails. Every so often, her lips moved, or she twitched a finger. She held her body loose, rolling easily with the movement of the boat. Arabella's knees trembled as she stumbled to the rail a few feet from the wind witch, watching her for a long time.

"You know," Bathsheba said after a while. "Some people consider staring rather rude." She didn't take her eyes from the sails.

"Oh! Oh, I'm so sorry." Arabella blushed, glancing away and back. "I've just never met anyone quite like... you. I'm sorry," she repeated. "I'm just curious. I didn't mean to be rude."

"I see..." Bathsheba flicked her wrist, making the mainsail just a bit fuller. Down the deck, the tillerman made his own adjustment. He kept half an eye on the sails and half an eye on Bathsheba. "I'll assume that since you were raised by witches that it's not my particular skills that you are so fascinated by." She turned to Arabella and raised her eyebrow. Arabella dropped her gaze to the deck.

"No," she mumbled. "I've met other wind witches before."

"Hhhmmm..." Bathsheba made a show of tapping her forefinger on her lips. "What could it be about me that you find so unusual? Is it my skin? Or the scar on my face?" She fixed Arabella with a gimlet eye. "I know society usually discourages being direct. Some say that it is rude, but not so much as staring. I would rather you asked me your question. So, which is it? The scar, or the skin it's on?" Silence stretched between them.

"Both," Arabella whispered softly. Then the words came out in a rush. "My mother kept me quite sheltered. I've never had the opportunity to speak to anyone with your heritage. And that scar is rather eye-catching, don't you think? I mean, there has to be an interesting story behind how you got it." She paused, but Bathsheba declined the opening. "Isn't there? An interesting story, I mean." Arabella's belly tightened as she wondered if she'd overstepped the bounds of propriety, despite Bathsheba's invitation.

"Eye-catching? Interesting?" Bathsheba shook her head and chuckled to herself. "You ignorant little fools, always so wrapped up in yourselves, never thinking before you speak. You're not the first witchling to ask me about such personal things." She glared at Arabella. "Though I have to admit, you've been more polite than most."

"I'm so sorry," Arabella apologized again. "I just wanted to hear your story. As I said, I thought it might be interesting, and I couldn't sleep..."

"My life is not a bedtime story for you, little girl," Bathsheba snapped. She shook her head. "You don't own me, and I don't owe you anything. Your mother paid me to put wind in the sails, not entertain you."

Arabella's jaw dropped open. "Of course, I don't own you! People are not things or animals."

"Tell that to the white men in your former colonies," Bathsheba huffed.

"Oh, no." Arabella's stomach dropped as it dawned on her just what Bathsheba's history might be. "Please accept my deepest apologies. I didn't realize. I just assumed you'd always lived in Liverpool, that it was your home."

"Liverpool *is* my home," Bathsheba growled.

"There, I've done it again. I've gone and said the wrong thing and been perfectly awful to you," Arabella said as she chided herself in her head. The nightmare and short sleep had unsettled her, but that was no reason to be so boorish to a Sister witch. She clasped her hands to her breast and dipped her head down in respect, hoping that the ritual of contrition would smooth things over with Bathsheba. "I am profoundly and humbly sorry, Sister Bathsheba. I never meant to cause you a moment's discomfort. I shall go now." Arabella turned to go.

Bathsheba laughed. "Well, that was a pretty little apology. I could almost believe it was heartfelt."

Arabella winced. She turned back to Bathsheba and said, "I can assure you that I am most sincere. I wanted to hear your story, but you are right that you don't owe me anything, particularly after I asked in such a crude manner." Arabella turned to go again and was almost halfway back to the deckhouse when Bathsheba spoke.

"Are you interested in me as a person or as an amusement to pass the time because you're bored?"

Arabella whirled around, clutching her hands together in front of her. Relief loosened her throat. "As a person, most definitely as a person."

Bathsheba nodded and looked thoughtful. "A piece of advice, girl. If you want to learn about a person, it's better to start a conversation with them rather than demand that they entertain you with stories." She shook her head and looked up at the sky, mouthing something under her breath. She turned back to Arabella. "I must be bored." She clasped her hands in her lap and raised her eyebrows in expectation.

Arabella looked confused for a moment but then caught on. "Oh! Oh, yes." She scurried closer and bobbed a curtsy. "Good evening, Miss Bathsheba. How has the weather been this evening?"

Bathsheba's eyes twinkled. "The wind has been running mostly well. I haven't had to encourage it too terribly much."

Arabella nodded and bounced on her toes. "Did you enjoy your supper tonight?"

Bathsheba shrugged. "It kept heart and soul together, standard fare for the *Kittiwake*. And you?"

"I have to admit it was my first experience with salt pork and beans. Was this a good example of the dish?"

Bathsheba let out a full-throated peal of laughter. "You *are* trying hard to make up for treading on my toes, aren't you?"

Arabella blushed and ducked her head.

Bathsheba sighed. "I've met so many young girls like you, privileged little witchlings who think everything in the world is theirs for the taking." She tilted her head and gave Arabella a smile. "I'm sorry I was so prickly. I've just had a lot of poor experiences. You do seem to be an authentically nice, young witch."

"Thank you," Arabella murmured. They both fell quiet for a moment.

"My story is not the exciting adventure you may be hoping for." Bathsheba's voice was barely above a whisper. "My story is painful, not interesting. Do you still wish to hear it?"

"Yes, please, I do," Arabella breathed. "If you wish to tell me."

Bathsheba cast her eyes back to the sails, eyes tracing their curve and ensuring they were full. She did not look at Arabella as she began her story.

"I was not born free," she said, her voice strangely devoid of emotion. "My mother was a breeding slave on a plantation in Virginia, in the Americas." Without meaning to, Arabella gasped. Bathsheba's eyes flicked to her, then back to the sails. "Yes, she was treated no different than a sow or mare, bred to whatever stud her master saw fit. She worked in the household laundry too. The Master believed he was being kind by allowing her to lie in bed for three whole days after each birth before sending her back the dirty linens with an infant on her hip. As soon as each baby could eat solid food, he'd take her child away to dry up her milk and send her back to the breeding sheds every night after a hard day of washing."

Arabella sank against the railing. "That's appalling," she gasped.

"Of course it is, to any decent person with a heart," Bathsheba said. "The Master just thought it was business as usual. Are you sure you want me to continue?"

She pressed her lips together and nodded. "I asked for this."

Bathsheba turned her eyes back to the sails. "Mama couldn't remember how many pregnancies she'd had before me. She had a lot of miscarriages between healthy babies. I was her eighth child, the third girl. The Master liked that she kept giving him mostly boys. A healthy slave buck that can be sold for field work fetched a pretty penny. Mama never knew where all her children wound up. I'm sure the Master kept records, but Mama couldn't read anyway even if she'd found them." A soft smile broke across Bathsheba's face. "But Mama liked to tell me I was her favorite because the Master let her name me, and he let her keep me for a while. I was the only one he ever let her name. She picked Bathsheba because she'd heard him reading passages from the Bible, and she was a beautiful queen." The wind witch paused to throw a little more wind into the sails.

"The Master had decided that I was going to go to the breeding sheds, just like my Mama, as soon as I was old enough. I got my first period at thirteen, and Mama cried and cried. When she tried to hide it from the Master, he beat her for it." Bathsheba choked back a sob, but when she spoke again, her voice was matter of fact. "The Master gave me over to the master of the plantation next door for my first time. He said since he'd sired me, it wouldn't be good breeding to get a child on me himself." Bathsheba swallowed hard. She closed her eyes. "The neighbor master was not a gentle man. After he hurt me the first time, he came at me again because he wasn't satisfied. That's when my magic manifested. I just *couldn't* do it again." Her voice turned to a growl. "I blew the bastard through the wall of the breeding shed. I heard later the doctor pulled splinters out of his back for a week."

A choked sputter came from the starboard railing. "Good for you," Sarah called.

"I can't imagine…" Arabella breathed. "What happened next?"

"Next, my own Master came to beat the tar out of me," Bathsheba continued. "What he didn't know was that what I'd done had caused enough of a metaphysical ripple that every witch within fifty miles felt me. And felt my fear. The local witches were already on their way to fetch me. Still, horses can only run so fast. My back was bloody by the time they got there. The Master's whip slipped once and gave me this."

Bathsheba's fingers drifted up to the scar on her face. "I don't remember much about how they rescued me. I was delirious with pain by that time. But they took me. The witches nursed me back to health and tried to keep my wounds from scarring up too much. I heard later that the Master spent a few weeks recovering from what *they* did to him. After I was better, the American witches taught me to read and write, and how to control my power, but it wasn't good for me over there. I couldn't go pick daisies outside the house without a slave patrol trying to snatch me up. They knew the witches didn't own slaves, so anybody with any color to their skin on witch property had to be a runaway, in their opinion. I begged to go somewhere else, anywhere else, where I could make a living and have a life." Bathsheba blew out a deep breath.

"So here I am," she said. "Sworn to the English Council of Witches. I make a nice little living helping the sailors. I have a cottage of my own with a garden toward the eastern edge of town. I've even managed to make enough money to buy some of my family and bring them over here to freedom. My sister Emma and my half-brother Isaiah share a home with me. Emma takes in washing and mending and keeps our house. Isaiah goes out as a deckhand on whatever ship he can find. He's on a trip to Calais right now."

Arabella made a little strangled sound. "You had to *buy* your family?"

"Well, how else am I supposed to get them out of there?" Bathsheba asked. "It's not like I could start a war and win it from this side of the ocean." She shook her head. "If I knew who the Master sold the rest of my brothers and sisters to, I would buy them all. But Mama... He made it clear he'll never sell Mama to me."

"There aren't words for how horrific that is," Arabella murmured as she wiped a tear from her cheek. Her emotions tore at her. Her heart boiled with fury and ached with grief at the same time. No person deserved to be treated the way Bathsheba and her mother had been treated.

"No, there isn't, is there?" Bathsheba grimaced. She turned and looked Arabella right in the eye. "Promise me something?"

Arabella nodded hard as she wiped more tears from her cheeks.

"Promise me you'll remember how you feel right now, that tenderness in your heart for me and my kin," Bathsheba said. "There are people in this world who will try to make you believe that there are others who are less than you or they are. That these lowly people can be treated like animals or worse, and you don't have to feel sorry about it..." Bathsheba's voice turned fierce. "Never believe them."

"I won't," Arabella said with just as much ferocity.

"I hope I can trust you, little witchling," Bathsheba sighed. "Now, go back to bed." She turned her attention to the sails once more.

CHAPTER XII

*Wherein the Travellers First Spy
the Welcoming Shores of Ireland*

THE *KITTIWAKE* GLIDED INTO DUBLIN'S HARBOR IN THE MID-AFTERNOON the next day. The captain, Bathsheba, and the sailors performed the complex dance of dodging the larger ships as they made their way to their berth on Alexandra Quay, on the north side of the River Liffey. Arabella and her entourage stood at the rail, attempting to stay out of the way.

Arabella shaded her eyes with her hand and scanned the shoreline. "Where are we landing?"

"Wherever the captain secured us a berth." Sarah yawned as she stretched and swung her arms.

"I just want to know where to look," Arabella muttered.

"So, you can catch sight of Julian as soon as possible?" Rowena teased with a twinkle in her eye.

"Perhaps." Arabella pursed her lips and blushed a little. "It's just been so long since I've seen him." The words tumbled out. "Do you think he'll still find me attractive? Does my hair look alright?" she asked with a gasp as she fussed.

"That young man is so enamored of you," Rowena laughed. "I think you could walk off the boat in a burlap sack and your hair in knots and he would pronounce you the most elegant creature he'd ever seen."

Arabella took a deep breath and tried to calm her fretful stomach.

"Maybe so, but I'd rather not push my luck." Her hand crept up to her hair again. "Do I really look alright?"

Rowena grabbed her by the shoulders, pulling her around. She looked her up and down with a grave expression.

"To be honest," Rowena began. "I'd be embarrassed to take you for tea in one of the finer tea houses in London. You've slept in your clothes, and you've done only a passable job with your hair." Arabella squawked and tried to pull away from Rowena, but her sister held her tight.

"Of course, you're on the run from assassins with no access to a mirror, and sleeping in the most rudimentary conditions possible." She paused and leaned in close to Arabella. "You're fine. He's in love with you. Any rough aspects about your appearance will only enhance your air of mystery and make you even more desirable to him. You'll see." Rowena's eyes sparkled.

Arabella turned back to the railing, her cheeks reddening further. "I don't know that he's in *love* with me…" The very thought that Julian might love her scattered Arabella's thoughts like a flock of startled starlings.

Rowena rolled her eyes and threw up her hands. "You've only shared the most tame parts of his letters with me and *I* can tell he's madly in love with you. I dare say you need only to crook your little finger and he would go down on one knee. He'd probably offer you a twist of wire for an engagement ring, but it would be the shiniest bit of wire he had."

"Marriage!" Arabella gasped. "You don't really think…" She returned to scanning the horizon. Contemplating Julian asking her that oh so important question both thrilled and terrified her. Would she answer yes? No? What did she want to say? Did she even want him to ask…? Her thoughts tumbled over one another like pebbles in a stream during spring floods.

"I think he's about as sensible as a moonstruck owl, and it's more than possible that he's already daydreaming about taking you to wife." Rowena's face grew serious as she scanned the horizon herself. "Now, whether marrying him is a good idea or whether the two of you would be happy together is an entirely different matter."

"What do you mean?" Arabella turned to her sister with a frown. Her heart skipped a beat. Could she be misjudging Julian, or was her sister just jealous that Arabella hadn't spent as much time with her lately?

Rowena sighed. "It's obvious that the two of you care for each other a great deal. One might even say you share a mutual ardor. But you've only known him a few months, and you can't possibly tell if he would make an amiable companion over the years, or if the relationship would turn sour." Rowena paused. "After all, Mother and Father loved each other very much, and they still obviously care for one another. But for whatever reason, now they can hardly spend more than a few hours together."

"That's awfully harsh." Arabella's voice barely rose above a whisper. A tendril of fear uncoiled in her belly. What if Rowena was right? What if she and Julian really were in love but in the end that didn't matter at all? The notion that she might wind up like her mother, alone, without a companion to share the trials and tribulations of life, made the fresh sea air seem suddenly foul.

"I only want you to be careful, sister dear," Rowena cajoled. She slipped her arm around Arabella's shoulders. "The heart is such a delicate thing." Arabella gave her sister a tremulous smile.

Alexandra Quay soon came into clear view, thanks to Bathsheba's careful coaxing of the wind. Julian caught sight of Arabella before she caught sight of him. At least, he was waving furiously in the direction of the *Kittiwake* with a huge grin on his face by the time Arabella spotted him.

Rowena leaned over and whispered into Arabella's ear. "See? I told you he's absolutely besotted."

Arabella glanced down the rail at the Guardians, wondering what the more experienced women thought of the young man who sent her heart fluttering.

Eliza and Sarah stood shoulder to shoulder, hands clasped behind their backs. They surveyed the quay with the sharp eyes of raptors hunting for prey.

"Do we know anything about him?" Sarah murmured to her fellow Guardian.

"He's quite young, only nineteen years old. He's considered a bit of a genius prodigy and has apparently already accomplished a few things of note in the area of engineering. He's wholly focused on his pursuit of machines and absentminded about everything else. He's set to inherit his widowed uncle's position as the Baron of Louth." She glanced down the rail at Rowena and Arabella. "And as Rowena has noted, he seems completely captivated by our Arabella." Eliza caught Arabella's gaze for a moment. The girl dropped her eyes and blushed.

Sarah grunted. "Probably just fascinated with her, like some shiny new toy. Young men are highly distractible."

"Indeed." Eliza shrugged as she shifted her scrutiny back to the dock. "But we may be able to use it to our advantage for now. He's more likely to follow our rules for Arabella's safety so long as he is still entranced by her. Nothing we've found out about him so far indicates that he's dangerous, at least, not any more than any other… ahem… passionate young man."

Arabella approached the Guardians, coming close just in time to hear Eliza's calculated response. She clenched her jaw, all of her introspection and uncertainty coalesced into annoyance. Why should she trust their judgment over her own? She'd spent more time with Julian than any of them. She was so tired of shoving down her own feelings and accepting what others said as truth without question. She lifted her chin.

"All of you are so callous. Julian is honest and noble, steadfast and true. He's a brilliant man and completely honest with his affections. He's a true gentleman. *Hmph.*" Arabella crossed her arms over her chest.

Sarah, Eliza, and Rowena all exchanged glances and clearly tried to contain their amusement. Rowena turned to Arabella and laid a hand on her shoulder. Arabella stiffened and shook her sister's hand off.

"Ari, darling, we're not saying Julian is disagreeable in any way. He's a lovely young man," she coaxed. "I only suggest you be practical, and our Guardians must consider all potential threats." Rowena held up her hand to forestall any objection from Arabella. "A threat Julian may not even be aware he poses. Other unscrupulous people may try to take advantage of his proximity to you. Julian is a dear, but he's not exactly attuned to all the nuances of the social dance, is he?"

"Well, no…" Arabella allowed.

"Eliza and Sarah are just doing their jobs as our Guardians. And I am doing my job as your big sister." Rowena tilted her head to the side with a little smile. "We are not casting aspersions on your fair Julian."

The tension across Arabella's shoulders eased, and she dropped her arms. "I just don't want anyone to be unfair to him." Her voice took on a dreamy quality. She leaned forward with her hands on the rail. "He's such a gentle soul." She lifted her hand and waved back to Julian with enthusiasm.

By the time the sailors slid into a slip, Arabella bounced on her toes, trying not to pace the deck and get in the way. "Can't they move any faster?" she muttered as she clasped her hands together.

Behind her, Captain Midstock chuckled. "If I didn't know any better, I'd think you didn't enjoy my hospitality."

Arabella gasped. Her hand flew to her mouth. "I didn't mean…"

Captain Midstock threw back his head and roared with laughter. "You're right, Bathsheba! This one does get flustered easily!" He leaned in toward Arabella. "On this boat, we only tease the ones we like. You're a sweet little lamb, and I hope the wolves you're running from don't catch you." He nodded toward the railing. "We're all tied up now. You can go join that young man you're so eager to see."

Arabella blushed. "Thank you, Captain Midstock." She bobbed a curtsy. "Your hospitality was most generous. I will recommend the *Kittiwake* to anyone looking for a swift journey on the Irish Sea."

Captain Midstock tipped his cap to Arabella, then turned to go on about his business.

Eliza and Sarah were already on the dock giving the stevedores Julian brought with him the once over. Arabella couldn't take her eyes from her suitor even as a sailor helped her and Rowena over the rail and onto the dock.

Finally, they stood face to face. Neither of them spoke at first. They just stood there with silly grins on their faces.

"Good afternoon, Mr. Pattersby," Rowena said with a sigh. She thrust out her hand. Julian gripped her hand lightly and nodded over it, but he never took his eyes off Arabella.

"Good afternoon, Miss Sortilege," he said in a faraway voice. "I do hope your trip here was pleasant."

"If you could consider a sea monster attack pleasant," Rowena said. "I believe that kraken was twice the size of the *Kittiwake*."

"What?" Both Arabella and Julian snapped their heads around to Rowena, their eyes wide with shock.

"Now that I have your attention…" Rowena straightened the cuffs of her dress. "Perhaps the two of you could save the moony eyes for later. This is a public dock, and people are staring."

Julian's face flushed bright red. Arabella smiled and stifled a contented sigh. He was distracted, flustered… He obviously cared for her, and that soothed some of her anxiety.

"Yes, yes… quite right…" Julian murmured. He straightened his waistcoat. "I didn't think there were any krakens of any size in the Irish Sea," he said with a twinkle in his eyes as he caught on to the joke. He gave Arabella a wink.

"Well, of course!" Arabella bantered back. "That's what we found so surprising. They tend to breed in the Channel and prefer the open ocean for feeding." While Arabella and Julian chuckled, Rowena rolled her eyes.

Arabella wiped a tear of laughter from the corner of her eye. "Julian, this is Guardian Josolyne and Guardian Gardner," she gestured to where Eliza and Sarah oversaw the loading of the luggage. "They are here to chaperone us and see to our safety."

Julian made a grand bow. "I am delighted to make your acquaintance, both of you. Anyone who ensures the well-being of Arabella is an angel in my esteem."

Eliza and Sarah exchanged uncomfortable glances. Eliza trained her gaze past Julian's shoulder and frowned. She crooked her finger in an arcane gesture and made a twisting motion toward Sarah. Sarah's eyes flicked from Eliza to the throng of humanity at the top of the dock. She grimaced, then gave Eliza a barely perceptible nod.

"Yes, well… Just doing our jobs," Sarah muttered.

Eliza cleared her throat. "The stevedores Mr. Pattersby hired are safe enough, but it would be a good idea if we left the dock as soon as possible. We are far too exposed."

"Yes, the sun is quite strong today, is it not?" Julian looked up, shading his eyes with his hand.

Eliza frowned. "It's not the natural phenomena I am worried about, but if you will direct us to wherever you left your carriage, we can gather our things and be gone. I can explain more about our haste once we are on our way."

The tone of Eliza's voice broke through Arabella's infatuated fog. She turned her attention to the head of the pier, shocked to find so many hostile faces staring at them from the crowd. Men and women gathered in tight knots, muttering to each other. Their eyes went from the deck of the *Kittiwake*, where Bathsheba stood with the sailors in a protective ring around her, to Arabella and her entourage. Their expressions hardened when their eyes lighted on Eliza and Sarah with their weaponry and mannish garb.

With a basket of fish on her hip, one old woman stepped out of the thickening crowd and made the forked finger gesture against the evil eye at them. Eliza and Sarah slid smoothly in front of their charges, hands drifting toward their belts. The wizened biddy hobbled even closer, hawking and spitting on the ground at Sarah's feet. "Your kind aren't welcome here, witch," she hissed.

Arabella gasped.

Sarah held her hand out to placate the old woman. "We don't want any trouble. We'll be on our way as quickly as we can."

Snatching a fish from her basket, the granny slapped Sarah's hand away with it. "Don't even think of touching me, you foul thing! I don't want none of your pox!" She tossed the fish to the ground and spit on it.

Sarah shook her hand out and placed it on her dirk. Eliza's eyes narrowed as she readied her lips to fling a spell. Arabella shrank back and reached blindly for Rowena's hand. She couldn't tear her eyes from the angry throng.

A middle-aged man leapt out of the crowd and snatched the wrinkled grandmother back with an arm around her waist. "That's enough of that, Maude." He grunted as she struggled against him pulling her back. "You know what these creatures can do. Your boys need you."

Maude spat at the witches again and screeched incoherently as the gentleman dragged her back into the depths of the crowd. No one else made a move, but the mob's dark muttering grew louder.

"Get the luggage and the girls loaded now, if you please, Mr. Pattersby," Eliza barked. "We'll stand watch."

"You didn't tell us you were bringing witches to the Isle," growled the largest of the men Julian had hired.

Julian paled, but he kept his head. "I'll double your fee if we're all safely away with the luggage intact."

The man ground his teeth. "If my woman wasn't sick abed and in need of a doctor, I'd tell you to bugger off, ya pigeon-livered ratbag. Make it triple."

Julian swallowed hard. "Done." He gestured to the luggage. "Now, if you please."

Fortunately, the Irish stevedores were quite efficient, if surly, and the party was swiftly away.

Arabella was dismayed to find herself across the carriage from Julian rather than next to him. In the mad scramble to get away from the perilous crowd at the dock, there hadn't been much care given to seating arrangements. She was sandwiched between Rowena and Eliza, while Sarah shared the seat across from them with Julian. Julian snuck startled glances at Sarah's severe hairstyle. Arabella wished she could reach for his hand for comfort, to slow the terrified beating of her heart. She settled for clasping Rowena's trembling fingers. Her sister gave her a frightened glance. Eliza tilted her head back and closed her eyes for a moment. Every witch in the carriage, including Arabella, felt her disciplined release of the energy she'd been holding. Arabella's eyes widened. She wanted to ask a question, but the moment wasn't right, not with Julian present.

Eliza opened her eyes and rolled her shoulders. "Thank you for your alacrity concerning our needs, Mr. Pattersby," she said briskly as the carriage rolled through the city.

"Of course, of course…" Julian fidgeted with his hat in his lap. "Anything I can do to be of assistance." He paused. "Although John's letter didn't make mention of any sort of imminent danger. What happened just now… Well, that was quite a shock." He cast a longing gaze at Arabella. "Are you alright? You don't have to be stoic with me…"

"What happened on the dock is fairly customary for how witches are treated in this country, especially in the cities," Sarah retorted. "Surely you were aware?"

"I… I… I was not," Julian stuttered. "When I'm on the Isle, I tend to be in my workshop on my uncle's estate. And I've never had witches as guests here, or any guests really."

Eliza cleared her throat. "Whether you were aware or not is irrelevant. You are aware now, yes?" She raised her eyebrow and Julian nodded. "Mr. Leyden was not informed of everything. We thought it would be safer for him if he remained unaware."

Julian's eyes flew wide. "Oh my! More danger than what is... customary for the Isle?"

Eliza and Sarah shared a moment of silent communication. Eliza flicked a glance at Arabella, then returned her regard to Sarah.

Arabella looked back and forth between the Guardians. "I don't have any secrets from Julian," she said. "We should tell him." Sarah snorted and rolled her eyes. Rowena sighed and turned her attention to the city passing by the carriage window.

"You probably should have secrets," Eliza warned, her tone sharp. "Some things are too dangerous for mundane people to know."

"Didn't you say I was safer knowing? Wouldn't he be safer knowing?" Arabella frowned.

"We could just give him the high points," Sarah grumbled. "He could know that much without revealing any secrets."

"You shall all be the death of me," Eliza muttered under her breath. She closed her eyes and inhaled deeply.

"Fine," she said, loud enough to make everyone in the carriage jump. She pinned Julian to his seat with her glare. "There are certain factions in the witching world who wish to see Arabella dead."

Julian gasped so hard he choked.

"How could anyone..." he began. Eliza held up her palm to stop him.

"The motivations behind their actions are precisely what we cannot discuss with mundane people." She scowled at everyone on the carriage. "Arabella is in Ireland because it is marginally safer for her here. The danger presented by mundane means of harm is much easier to deal with than the injury magical means can deal, especially from witches who are determined to work around certain... safeguards. Guardian Gardner and I are here to protect her and her sister. All that we ask is that you allow us to perform our tasks. We need your full cooperation. Because of the nature of magical threats, there may be times we ask you to do things that seem odd to you. However, you must do what we ask without question if we are to protect Arabella and Rowena."

"Absolutely! There's no question! I would never want my dear Arabella to be harmed, not even in the smallest way." Julian reached out for Arabella, but the carriage was just a bit too large for their fingers to touch. They both settled back into their seats with a sigh.

"Julian, there's something I find a bit puzzling," Rowena said in a sharp voice as she turned away from the carriage window. "I was led to believe there is a famine raging here and yet," she glanced back toward the window, then back to Julian with a frown. "Most everyone seems so… plump. I don't see any more hungry people in the streets here than I might in London."

"The famine really only touches the rural areas," Julian said.

"Well, that's odd." Arabella frowned. "Aren't the farmers closer to the land and, therefore, the food? If your city dwellers are well-fed, then why wouldn't your farmers be as well?"

"Our grain is grown on the larger estate farms, and that's what feeds the cities. We grow enough that we export it all over England. The tenant farmers are only allowed what they can grow on the smaller plot their Lord grants them." He waved off Rowena as she tried to ask another question. Rowena narrowed her eyes but held her tongue. "I really don't want to discuss land use and farming practices right now. I am very concerned about Arabella's safety." He looked to Eliza. "Who wants to hurt Arabella and why?"

Eliza pursed her lips. "That is information that it would be safer for you not to know."

Julian frowned. "But how can I help protect Arabella if I don't know where the threat is coming from?"

"You can't help protect Arabella," Eliza said calmly.

"What do you mean? Of course, I can help," Julian sputtered. "I may be young, but I do have considerable resources at my disposal. I think you underestimate me, madam."

"I don't underestimate you at all," Eliza continued with icy composure. "In fact, my ability to protect Arabella depends on my skill in evaluating the resources I have available to me and using them efficiently. You are one of those resources, Mr. Pattersby. If I did not evaluate what you are capable of with clear eyes, I would not be doing my job properly. I *always* do my job properly." She paused, then tilted her head to the side. "If some witch threw a fire ball at Arabella, what would you do? Or if a weather witch called up a storm to sweep Arabella into a lake and drown her, what would you do? How would you protect her?"

"Well, I don't think I could protect her from magic. That is not in my expertise, but I do have other useful skills." Julian lifted his chin.

"I am quite aware of your talents, Mr. Pattersby, and they are indeed impressive," Eliza said. "They are remarkable feats of engineering in the mundane world. For your own safety, I cannot tell you who threatens Arabella, but I can tell you the greatest danger to her is through magic. And as remarkable as your abilities are, they will do nothing against the magical perils I am trained to protect her against."

Julian looked positively crestfallen. "I just want to help."

Arabella glared at Eliza. She'd wanted honesty for Julian, not barbed words to cut his spirit. Eliza raised an eyebrow at her, then sighed.

"I know you do." Eliza favored Julian with a gentle smile. "The best way you can help is to orchestrate the mundane details of our visit and let me and Guardian Gardner handle the life-threatening aspects."

"Yes, I suppose that would be for the best." Julian dropped his gaze. Silence filled the carriage, awkward and uncomfortable.

"Perhaps you could tell us a little about where we are going?" Arabella said, trying to keep her voice cheerful. "I've never ventured to Ireland."

Julian cleared his throat and gave her a grateful smile. "We'll be staying in my mother's ancestral home, Louth Hall. The oldest part is the gothic tower my family built somewhere around 1350. We've expanded on it quite a bit over the years, but the old arches in the original building have been my favorite since I was a boy. The village of Tallanstown is close by, but there's not much there. Ardee would be the nearest town of any size."

"It's so kind of your uncle to allow us the use of Louth Hall. I'll have to send a suitable thank you gift," Arabella said.

"But Uncle Sas is…"

"Uncle Sas?" Rowena chortled. Arabella scowled at her. Rowena pouted a bit. "I'm sorry," she said to Julian with a false smile. "But what a peculiar name."

It was Julian's turn to chuckle. "Oh no, it's my place to apologize here. I shouldn't have used my familiar name for him. It's just such a habit. When I was a small boy, I couldn't say Sampson, so I called him 'Uncle Sasson.' And that quickly became Uncle Sas." He sighed. "It's usually just the two of us rolling around that old house. I'm afraid we've fallen into the custom of using informal names. Frankly, I think he's grateful for your visit because he'll see more than just my face for a few weeks." Julian's shoulders seemed to relax.

"Oh, dear. Oh, dear. He's in residence?" Arabella looked down at her dress and brushed her hands down her skirts. How could she possibly meet a Baron, let alone Julian's uncle, in this state! "I am such a fright. I'm not fit to be received by a Baron!"

"Oh, you needn't worry!" The words tumbled out of Julian. "Uncle thought you would be tired and in need of some rest and privacy. He left this morning to inspect some of our distant holdings. He won't be home until late tomorrow morning. Then we'll have a formal supper that evening, and you can get to know him." Julian grinned.

"That's quite sensitive of him," Arabella said.

"Aunt Emmeline was very firm about manners and treating ladies well. Though she's since passed on, Uncle still follows her rules."

"I don't know about the rest of you ladies," Rowena said. "But I, for one, am looking forward to a hot bath and a good night's sleep in a proper bed."

The ladies all gave little groans of assent. The idea of washing away the salt from the sea and the weariness of the road was just delicious.

CHAPTER XIII

Introduction to the Baron

THE NEXT MORNING THE REFRESHED TRAVELERS MET JULIAN AT THE breakfast table in one of the more intimate dining rooms of Louth Hall.

"I trust you all slept well?" Julian asked as the servants brought forth steaming dishes and platters.

The staff of Louth Hall spread out a hearty country breakfast—thick sausages, rashers of bacon, eggs, baked beans, and soda bread with butter and marmalade. Arabella politely passed on the beans. She'd had quite enough aboard the *Kittiwake*, as they had been served for every meal. Although she had to admit, the Louth Hall beans smelled significantly better than those on the *Kittiwake*. Perhaps she would fancy them for breakfast another day.

"Our rooms are quite comfortable, thank you," Arabella said. "It was so kind of you to ensure we are close together. I imagine that makes things a bit easier on Guardian Josolyne and Guardian Gardner." She frowned at the array of dishes in front of her. "I thought you said food was scarcer in the country, Julian. Based on your table, there wouldn't seem to be a famine in the country at all."

"Yes, well..." Julian looked flustered.

"Arabella," Rowena chided. "We're going to be here for weeks, at least. There's no need to bring up uncomfortable topics over our first breakfast."

"Part of the reason we are here is to find a solution for the famine," Arabella huffed. "We might be able to go home sooner if we can present Mother with the key to ending it."

"I know you want to go home." Rowena reached for her hand over the table and squeezed it. "But we still need to give Mother the time to resolve those other… matters." Rowena raised her eyebrows and stared into Arabella's eyes. She squeezed her hand a little harder.

Arabella yanked her hand back. "Fine," she grumbled. "But we're going to have to at least make an attempt to look at the problem sooner or later."

Quiet descended on the table as everyone busied themselves with filling their plates.

"You need to have a carpenter in for the upper hall," grunted Sarah around a mouthful of sausage, breaking the silence. "The third floorboard from the wall between their bedrooms is a bit loose, squeaks horribly."

"Oh dear, thank you," Julian said. "I'll have that seen to right away."

"Or perhaps wait until we go," Eliza said as she stirred a spoonful of sugar into her tea. She took a deep swallow and sighed with contentment. "We know where it is and can avoid it. But it might give us some warning of someone with nefarious intentions."

"Oh my…" Julian coughed. "I know yesterday you were quite… adamant about the danger Arabella faces and that may follow her. And the incident at the dock was quite upsetting. But we're far out in the country here at the Hall. Surely you could relax your guard?"

Eliza set her teacup down gently. She clasped her hands on the table in front of her. "Mr. Pattersby, while I realize you are not used to women being as capable in the violent arts as Guardian Gardner and I are, I can assure you that our assessment of the risk to our charge is quite accurate. One of our number has already suffered severe injuries while on this assignment. We left certain dangers behind on British shores, but there are other unique hazards to this fair isle." Her gaze sharpened. "Do I need to offer you more education regarding the danger to witches in general here?"

Julian cleared his throat and tried to look anywhere but at Eliza. "I suppose… Yes. I hadn't thought about… those elements." He focused on the table in front of him and frowned.

Eliza picked up her tea again and settled back in her seat. "Perhaps it would be wise if we kept the young ladies to the Hall as much as possible."

"And not tell your neighbors witches have come to visit from England," Sarah added.

Julian perked up. He turned to Arabella. "I do have a project I was hoping to get your ideas on. It's quite complex, and I'm having a devil of a time making it behave. It could take weeks of concentrated effort from both of us. It could keep us here at the Hall for your entire visit." He dug back into his meal with gusto.

"Oh, how exciting…" Rowena muttered under her breath. Arabella kicked her ankle under the table without taking her eyes from Julian.

Arabella tilted her head to the side, her eyes gleaming with interest. "What is it?"

"You'll see." Julian gave her a mischievous grin. "If you would find it agreeable, we could visit my workshop as soon as we've finished eating."

After breakfast, the whole party traipsed to the other end of Louth Hall to Julian's workshop, which was housed in the more modern wing. It was merely a hundred years old. High, broad windows let in scads of natural light, illuminating a half-dozen long worktables covered with metal, tools, wire, gears, and all sorts of mechanical accoutrements. The whole room shimmered and twinkled with magical energy to Arabella's eyes.

In the far corner, Julian had set up a small reading area with two small, rickety bookshelves, a spindly end table, and a threadbare settee. It looked as if he had rescued the furniture when his aunt decided to redecorate the servant's quarters, which would have been hand-me-downs from the family's rooms.

Arabella surveyed the disarray of the room with bemusement. "Has someone robbed the place while you were gone?"

Julian scanned the room with a frown on his face. "No. No, every-thing seems in order. Though it's been entirely too long since I've done a proper inventory." He stepped up to the nearest worktable and began sorting through all the bits and bobs while muttering to himself.

"How can he even tell nothing is missing?" Rowena hissed in Arabella's ear. "This room is a disaster! How can you trust a man who can't even keep his workspace orderly?"

"Stop it!" Arabella hissed back. "Although I'll admit Father and Henry keep their workroom much more organized," Arabella murmured. "But at least there doesn't seem to be anything here that might explode." Rowena gave her a startled look.

Julian continued to putter, seemingly oblivious to Arabella and Rowena watching him and whispering. After a moment, Arabella cleared her throat. Julian jerked his head up and blinked owlishly at them.

"Oh! Right! Guests in the workshop…" he chastised himself.

Arabella gave him a tender smile. She turned her gaze to the room and her brow furrowed. "This does seem to be a rather large project. Which piece shall we start with?"

"All of this," Julian gestured broadly to the room. "Isn't one project. Each table has a project of its own, sometimes two, if the projects are small."

He grabbed her hand and led her down the length of the room to the worktable closest to the sitting area. Arabella's eyes widened a little at his familiarity, but she found the warmth of his palm against hers quite welcome. Two of the projects they passed were layered with dust, but everything on the worktable Julian stopped in front of gleamed. All hues of brass, copper, steel, and silver shone in the midmorning light. Julian gestured to the mass of springs and gears and small metal plates in the middle of the table. Arabella peered down at them, trying to make sense of what she saw. Rowena cocked her head to one side and furrowed her brow. Sarah nudged Eliza in the ribs and nodded her head toward the battered settee. The Guardians winced in tandem as the shabby little thing creaked when they gingerly settled their weight.

"You see," he said. "After you so delightfully altered my owl, I could not stop thinking about birds. The owl was designed more as an entertainment and proof that I could make something so small and complex work. But I kept wondering if there was something I could engineer in that vein that would be useful." He pointed to the most intricate pile of parts in the center of the table. "And there you have it."

Arabella raised her eyebrow. "There you have what?"

Julian chuckled. "Silly me." He gathered up the modest pile of metal. A fully articulated brass bird's foot flopped across his wrist. He slid three gentle fingers under a round, burnished piece, turning it to the side as he did so. Little facets of amethyst showed themselves to be eyes. As his nimble fingers rearranged all the pieces, a new metal bird, about the size of a dove, revealed itself. "I've been looking at it so long, it seems so familiar to me."

"It's another lovely piece of work," Arabella breathed. She saw the muted light of potential shine like a banked fire in Julian's hands. "You said you wanted it to be useful. What task did you intend for it?"

"Carrying messages," he said. He tapped a catch on the belly of the metal bird. It popped open to expose a small compartment. "Once I get the smaller birds worked out, I want to try to scale them up to something larger, to be able to send packages. Just small things, really, like a book."

"That's ingenious!" Arabella gasped.

"That's been done," Rowena said. She crossed her arms across her chest. "With real birds. Witches send crows and ravens all the time to deliver messages when it's too far for telepathy. I've seen the stronger birds carry small packages too."

"But what about non-witches?" Julian's eyes danced with sharp curiosity. "Can someone who is not a witch command these birds? How reliable are they?"

Rowena frowned. "They're very reliable, as long as they've been trained well. A bird that bonds fully with its witch can be trusted completely. But I don't know of them doing favors for mundane people, unless it was at the request of a witch."

"Ah-ha!" Julian crowed. "Then what I'm doing isn't useless!" He grinned. "Witches have enjoyed the services of their birds for generations. Now mundane people can enjoy the convenience and speed of avian messaging." Then his face fell as he gently laid the brass bird on its back on the worktable. "That is, if I can get it to work."

"What seems to be the trouble?" Arabella asked, leaning over the bird and prodding the wing with her finger.

"Power is one issue," he began. Julian leaned against the table on one hand, with the other on his hip. "I can work out the spring system to take it short distances, a few miles. But the longer I can make it fly, the more useful it would be." His face lit up with joy as he turned to

Arabella. "Can you imagine sending a letter to France in less than a day?"

"That would be very exciting," Arabella whispered. She flicked open the chest compartment to reveal the mechanical workings of the bird. She nudged one of the tiny gears. "This is much daintier work than the owl."

"It has to be," Julian said. "The lighter I can make the bird, the farther it can fly on a spring coil, or I could increase the weight it carries for a shorter flight."

"There's only one spring coil powering the bird?" Arabella asked. She leaned closer and peered deeper into the chest compartment. She opened her mind's eye to take in the magical potential, searching for where the flow might be blocked.

"Yes," Julian responded. "What are you thinking?"

Arabella looked up into Julian's eyes. "If we can place two spring coils next to each other and place them just so..." She paused for a moment and tapped her lip with her forefinger. "You trigger one coil when you release the bird, then as that one winds down, it can trigger the second, thereby doubling the flight radius."

"You're brilliant!" Julian shouted. "This is exactly why I wanted you to look in on the project!"

Arabella caught herself between blushing and beaming, not used to such effusive praise directed her way. She reached out and squeezed Julian's hand briefly. Rowena cleared her throat. She scowled when Arabella looked at her.

"It seems like an awful lot of work when magic would work just as well or better," Rowena pouted. "Honestly, if the Irish people would just treat witches with the respect they deserve, there would be no need for it."

"Rowena!" Arabella gasped. She turned to her sister and put her hands on her hips. This kind of snippy and confrontational behavior was so unlike her usually amiable sister. "What has gotten into you? Why are you determined to be as rude as possible today?"

"It's not just a solution for the Irish people. I'd hoped to expand..." Julian began.

Rowena cut him off. "I'm in a dangerous country. I won't apologize for being on my guard or questioning things that don't make any sense." She narrowed her eyes and tightened her jaw.

"Being rude to our host is not being on your guard, Rowena! If I had known you were going to behave like this, I would never have asked you to come." Arabella saw the shock and hurt on Rowena's face and immediately regretted her words.

"I'm sure everyone is just a bit tired and out of sorts from traveling," Julian placated. Both women glared at him.

"If I were you," Eliza called from her place on the settee. "I wouldn't get in between two arguing witches."

Julian's eyes widened. "Oh, yes... Well..." He snatched the mechanical bird off the workbench and took a step back.

"Really, Arabella." Rowena snorted. "You've been acting like you don't have the good sense Freya gave a flea. All you do is stare at Julian and flutter around him."

Arabella's cheeks flushed bright scarlet. Her regret over her own harsh words drained away in a flash. What had come over Rowena? "There's no need to be insulting," she said in a strangled voice.

"Ladies?" Julian cleared his throat. He clutched his precious experiment closer to his chest. "Perhaps you would like to take this discussion somewhere a little more private? Perhaps where there aren't quite so many breakable things?"

Arabella did not take her eyes off Rowena. "There's no need. We won't be continuing this discussion," she growled.

"We will talk about this eventually," Rowena huffed. Her eyes glittered with irritation. "We still have a job to do. I pray you don't forget your responsibilities or your other relationships in your distracted state."

Arabella spun back to the worktable. She closed her eyes briefly and took a deep breath. Forcing a smile, she said to Julian, "What other challenges have you encountered with the bird?"

Julian flicked a glance at Rowena, who stood behind Arabella in stony silence. He cleared his throat. "Err... I... Let's see..." He laid the bird back down on his workbench. The sight of the mechanics seemed to settle him. "Ensuring the payload gets to the correct person is an issue. I can set the bird to fly on a straight course, and that's all well and good. But it's a machine, and it doesn't know who is handling it. Any person who knows where the catch is could open it and retrieve the message. And what if there is a storm and it gets blown off course? It could keep flying but end up in the completely wrong place." Julian looked up into Arabella's eyes. "I had thought if I could convince the right people about the usefulness of this service that we could set up receiving stations, with trustworthy employees who would receive the birds and make sure that the messages or packages got to the right people. But that still doesn't solve the weather situation..." He trailed off, lost in her gaze. Arabella blushed.

Rowena scowled. "Yet another "problem" that's already been solved with the ravens and crows. A living bird can course correct in a high wind or shelter from a storm and continue when it's passed. And a living bird can obey instructions to only release a message to a certain person. Really," she clucked. "This is a solution to a problem that does not exist. These little machines, while amusing, are inferior in every way to live birds."

Julian's face fell. "Perhaps you are right."

"Rowena..." Arabella hissed at her sister. She turned back to the workbench. "You do have quite the set of challenges before you, Julian. But I'm sure if we work together that we can come up with something." He looked up from the workbench and gave Arabella a wan smile.

"You are quite correct that mundane people don't have ready access to avian delivery services," Arabella continued. She gave Rowena a sideways glare to silence any objections. "If we can find a way to make this work, I'm sure there are many who would avail themselves of this service. Why, you could build a whole network of delivery birds all over the Isles!"

Julian brightened. "That would be lovely," he murmured.

A light rapping on the doorjamb of the workroom interrupted them. Mr. Yates, the Louth Hall steward, stood patiently in the doorway.

"Yes, Yates," Julian called to him. "What is it?"

"His Lordship is home, sir," Mr. Yates intoned. "He would like you to join him for a private luncheon in his study to discuss the result of his inspection."

"Oh well, duty calls." Julian gave the bird on the bench a last fond look. "I'm sure you'll be able to arrange a suitable luncheon for the ladies while Uncle Sas and I are occupied, won't you, Yates?"

There was the briefest pause before Mr. Yates responded. "Of course, sir. If that is what you desire." His voice was flat.

Julian frowned with confusion. "Of course, it's what I desire. These ladies are my honored guests."

"Yes, sir," Mr. Yate said. He put a tight smile on his face and gave a short bow.

Julian turned back to Arabella and impulsively grabbed her hand. "Forgive me for having to cut our time short. I promise to give you my full attention again as soon as possible." He bent over, lightly brushing her knuckles with his lips. Arabella blushed. Rowena gasped and looked indignant. Julian nodded to the Guardians and left in Mr. Yates's wake.

"Arabella! How could you let him paw you like that!" Rowena exploded.

Sarah broke into giggles on the settee. Eliza still had her gaze fixed on the doorway where Mr. Yates had stood, a frown on her face.

"He was not pawing me! Kissing my hand is perfectly reasonable at this stage in our relationship!" Arabella knotted up her fists at her sides.

"There is nothing reasonable about the speed..." Rowena began.

"Right," Sarah interrupted as she hauled herself to her feet. She clapped her hands together. "Why don't we take this outside? There's a nice open field where you can both shout at each other to your heart's content. You probably won't even break anything."

"That's a brilliant idea," Eliza said. She stood in a smooth motion and straightened her waistcoat. "Let's go. Sarah, you and I must discuss that steward. There's something amiss bout him..."

Eliza and Sarah marched Arabella and Rowena out of Louth Hall and through the kitchen garden onto a sunny lawn. A couple of goats nibbled grass at the bottom of a rolling hill. The large bells around their necks clanked mournfully. Sarah flopped down in the grass. Eliza lowered herself to the ground with a bit more grace.

"Alright then, get to it," Eliza said. She flapped her hands at Arabella and Rowena. "Go get yourselves sorted out. We don't want to have to listen to you snipe at each other the whole time we're here. Just please, try not to kill each other."

"Can they make each other bleed?" Sarah asked with a playful smirk. "I wouldn't mind practicing my field dressing a bit."

"*Hhm*.... Yes." Eliza nodded to the girls. "Just nothing that scars. I don't want to have to explain that to your mother."

Eliza and Sarah grinned, broad and impish, as Arabella and Rowena *hmph*ed in unison, then turned and started to meander down the hill in flinty silence.

"So," Arabella finally broke the silence. "How long are you going to make me wait for an apology?"

"Apology?" Rowena yelped, stopping dead. Arabella kept walking. "I have done nothing that requires an apology."

Arabella stopped and turned around. "You most certainly have! You've been unforgivably rude to Julian and to me."

"The two of you have been absolutely insufferable since the first moment you laid eyes on each other," Rowena ranted. She clasped her hands next to her cheek and crossed her eyes. "Oh, Julian," she threw her voice into a high register. "You're the most amazing person ever to walk the earth. When you break wind, it smells like flowers!"

"I never said anything like that!"

"Maybe not exactly, but I'm not far off!" Rowena jammed her fists onto her hips. "It's like you've taken leave of your senses. He's just a person, not a god!"

Arabella's jaw worked up and down. She sputtered, trying without any luck to force out words.

"I just can't believe the way you idolize him. The first man to pay you any attention, and you act like a drooling idiot!" Rowena threw her hands up in the air.

"But, but…" Arabella shook her head in disbelief. "You liked it when I read parts of his letters to you. You dreamed with me!" She paused for a breath. "And I'm not an idiot!"

Rowena sniffed. "Hearing a few snippets of a romantic missive is quite different from seeing the two of you act out a treacly melodrama in front of me."

Arabella drew herself up straight. She tilted her head to the side and squinted. "You're jealous," she whispered.

"What?" Rowena furrowed her brow.

Arabella smirked. "You're jealous of me."

"*Feh*. You're not making any sense." Rowena flipped her hands dismissively. "Why would I be jealous that some awkward, *mundane* man fawns over you?"

"He pays attention to me, and you want him to pay attention to you," Arabella hissed.

"What!" Rowena's jaw dropped open.

"Yes, that must be it! You're jealous he fell in love with me and not you!" Arabella crossed her arms across her chest and scowled. "A true sister would be happy for me."

"This is absurd." Rowena turned her back and crossed her arms.

"What's absurd is that you can't be happy for me," Arabella retorted.

Rowena whirled around, dropping her arms. "Of course, I'm happy you found love! Why wouldn't I be happy about that? I'm thrilled for every joy that comes into your life!"

"Then why are you yelling at me and being rude to Julian?" Arabella shouted, panting loud in the silence that followed. Rowena looked befuddled and on the verge of tears.

"I'm not jealous of you," Rowena whispered. She sniffed. "I'm jealous of *him*. When he gets your attention, I get less of it." She paused to wipe a tear from the corner of her eye. "It was one thing to hear a few bits of his letters and giggle with you over them, but to see you get lost in him right in front of me…" Rowena held out her arms. "I just don't want to lose my sister."

"Oh, Ro…" Arabella grabbed her into a tight hug. "You'll never lose me. We'll always be sisters," she whispered fiercely.

Arabella held Rowena and let her cry on her shoulder for a few minutes. When her sobs faded to fitful sniffles, Arabella squeezed her shoulders. They stepped apart. Rowena fished a handkerchief from her pocket and began dabbing at her nose.

"I suppose I look frightful," she chuckled.

Arabella reached out to tuck some flyaway hair behind Rowena's ear. "We'll sneak you back into the house and have you looking fine in time for dinner."

"I'm so sorry that I've been perfectly awful." Rowena slid her arm through Arabella's.

"Nonsense. All is forgiven." Arabella squeezed Rowena's arm. "And once I'm sure you won't burst into tears, I'll start teasing you mercilessly about it until we're old and gray." The sisters put their heads together and laughed. They began to stroll back up the lawn to where Eliza and Sarah were enjoying the sun.

"So." Arabella patted Rowena's hand on her arm. "Now that I have Julian, we'll just have to find someone for you. I think his older brother is already married off, but maybe one of his friends…"

"Blech…" Rowena stuck out her tongue. "No, thank you. I do not want some awkward, mundane man making eyes at me."

Arabella giggled. "I'm sure we can find a more polished gentleman to suit your tastes."

"No. No men at all," Rowena said emphatically.

Arabella stopped and peered at her sister. "You would rather a lady of your own?" she whispered. "I think I heard Mildred Bowen's second daughter prefers the company of ladies as well. She's nice and very pretty."

Rowena blanched and shook her head. "No. No women either."

"Then what?" Arabella furrowed her brow.

"Then nothing," Rowena said firmly. "I like my life the way it is. I don't want anyone complicating it, man or woman."

Arabella gave her sister a puzzled look. "But what about..." she paused, groping for words. "Kisses... and other things?" she whispered.

"Arabella!" Rowena turned bright red. "I know we are close, but there are limits."

"I'm sorry." Arabella blushed and stared at her feet. "I was just wondering if I would need to... at some point... help you with finding private moments to enjoy things without attachments."

Rowena turned her head and stared resolutely at the goats. "You needn't worry about that," she murmured.

"What?"

"I have no interest in that, with a man or a woman." Rowena sighed. "I tried making myself think about it when I was entering womanhood. I'd always heard Vivienne and Amelia have those whispered conversations and I thought I was supposed to think about it and feel... things." She looked at Arabella with pleading eyes. "But I don't. I just don't feel anything."

Arabella hugged her sister. "You don't have to if you don't want to. You're perfectly fine just the way you are."

"You really think so?"

"Absolutely."

"I'm not broken?"

"Maybe in some other way, but not that way," Arabella teased. She tugged on Rowena's arm to get them moving again. "Now, let's get you back into the house. We need to do something about those puffy, red eyes of yours."

CHAPTER XIV

An Unexpected Visitor at Dinner

LORD SAMPSON PLUNKETT-NELSON RECEIVED ARABELLA AND HER entourage in the grand east dining room for dinner. A tall man with a lush beard and a jolly smile, he threw his arms open wide and bowed low.

"Welcome to my humble home," he boomed. "I do hope my nephew has been taking good care of you." He winked at Julian, who escorted Arabella on his arm. Julian blushed.

"He has been lovely, thank you," Arabella said as she sat while Julian held her chair. "Thank you so much for opening your home to us in this difficult time."

Lord Plunkett-Nelson waved away the thanks as he took his place at the head of the table. "It's only what any loyal subject of the crown should do. The powerful Blackstone House is one of our great assets. So, when Julian said one of the daughters of the House needed assistance, of course, I didn't hesitate." He leaned forward and grinned. "I have to say, I'm enjoying the consternation of my native neighbors. They think I'm positively mad for allowing witches into my house."

"We had hoped to keep our presence here rather more discrete," Eliza said with a frown. "Because of the challenges witches face in this country."

"Tosh!" Plunkett-Nelson waved away her concern. "My estate is secure, and none of the locals would dare cross me. They know you are under my protection."

"Let's hope that's enough," Sarah muttered. She exchanged concerned glances with Eliza.

Dinner began with a lovely leek and potato soup, but Arabella hardly noticed. She took advantage of the current conversation to broach the topic of her official duty in Ireland.

"Lord Plunkett-Nelson, perhaps you can help us with a different facet of our responsibilities here," Arabella said. Rowena stiffened by her side.

"Of course, of course," Baron Louth replied. "I shall do whatever is in my power to help you."

"I'm so glad to hear that." Arabella smiled brightly. "You see, the witches of Ireland have sent us several delegations to ask for assistance with a famine." Arabella jumped as Rowena kicked her ankle under the table, but she continued. "However, from our arrival in the port to these delectable meals at your table, I haven't seen any evidence of privation. Have we been misled?" Rowena kicked her under the table again, wincing as Arabella kicked her back. Rowena's spoon clattered against her bowl.

"Ah yes, such a regrettable situation." Lord Plunkett-Nelson blotted his lips with his napkin. "There are some people who are suffering at this time, but it can be attributed to their own mismanagement. You see, as a portion of their payment for working the land on the greater estates, the common folk are given their own allotment of land to work as they see fit. They are allowed to keep anything they grow on that portion. And if they cannot manage it properly…" He shook his head. "Most unfortunate."

Sarah leaned forward. "Is the land they are given fertile enough? Rocky soil would not yield much."

"Our whole island is fruitful," Lord Plunkett-Nelson reassured her. "Why my own estate provides enough wheat and beef that I send significant exports to England. This land supports me very well." He shook his head and sipped his soup.

"But witches are not receiving the proper tithes and supports." Eliza's voice was strident.

Lord Plunkett-Nelson set aside his spoon with a frown. "This conversation is not terribly conducive to good digestion."

"I'm so sorry, sir. Please excuse us," Arabella pleaded. "We were given a charge by my mother, the Grande Dame of the Isles herself, before we came. It pains her to see people suffer and for her Sister witches to be treated so roughly. She asked us to find the reason for the famine that we were led to believe ravaged the land. We are in search of solutions. My companions and I are only so dogged in our questioning because the suffering of others pains us so." Arabella gave the Lord her sweetest smile. She crossed her fingers in her lap, hoping they hadn't pushed his hospitality too far.

Lord Plunkett-Nelson seemed mollified. He chuckled to himself. "Yes, I can see that even with the differences between you, you witches are just as softhearted as any mundane woman. My dearly departed Emmeline used to weep when a hunting hound got a thorn in his paw. Such a gentle woman..."

"Aunt Emmeline was the epitome of kindness," Julian said. "I miss her."

"As do I, my boy." Lord Plunkett-Nelson grew misty-eyed for a moment. Then he gestured for the servants to clear the soup dishes and bring the next course. "I hope you ladies like oysters. I brought some in from the west coast for a treat."

The servants laid fresh oysters on the half shell before each diner.

"Now," Lord Plunkett-Nelson clapped his hands and eyed his plate with delight. "Perhaps we can change the subject to something more conducive to pleasant dining."

"Arabella helped me resolve one of the troubles with my messenger birds," Julian announced brightly.

Lord Plunkett-Nelson gave his nephew an indulgent smile. "You know I can listen to you for hours. I've been fascinated with your work since you were a small boy." He glanced around the table. "But as I understand it, witches aren't as comfortable with technology. Shouldn't we think of our guests?"

"Actually, Lord Plunkett-Nelson, I am a technomancer. The first of my kind," Arabella said. "I'd be quite happy to chat about machines, but," she smiled to the other ladies at the table. "You are correct that my Sisters may not find the conversation so fascinating."

Lord Plunkett-Nelson's eyebrows flew up. "A technomancer? Really?" He set the oyster he was about to eat back down. "I've never heard of such a thing!"

"Until a few months ago, uncle, no one had!" Julian's words fell over each other in his excitement. "You remember the brass robe I told you about? Arabella is the one I made it for." He turned to Arabella. "Did you bring it with you?" He turned back to his uncle. "She makes it look so magnificent, the way her magic influences the metal. Just stunning!"

"If we're willing to listen to him natter on about Arabella and machines, we won't have to say anything ourselves," Sarah muttered to her fellow Guardian. Eliza smirked.

"I did bring my formal robes," Arabella said. "I wasn't sure if I might have a meeting with the local Council."

Julian's uncle nodded. "Well, I shall certainly have to see it if it's the wonder Julian says it is. But we shouldn't interrupt dinner for that." He finally popped the oyster into his mouth. "This leap forward, Julian." He waved his fork in the air. "Tell me about it."

"Arabella came up with the idea of fitting the messenger bird with two power springs."

Lord Plunkett-Nelson looked thoughtful. "Does it make the wings flap faster or harder? Would the bird reach its destination sooner?"

"No, no, even better." Julian grinned. "If you put the springs next to each other just so, you start the release on one as you send the bird, then as the first spring runs down, it triggers the next spring! Thereby doubling the possible flight radius!"

Understanding dawned on Lord Plunkett-Nelson's face. He turned slowly to Arabella. "Why, that's almost brilliant in its simplicity."

"It *is* brilliant, Uncle Sas," Julian noted as he worked an oyster free of its shell. "I told you Arabella is special."

"Manners, boy. We mustn't be so familiar with guests at the dinner table," Lord Plunkett-Nelson murmured as he scrutinized Arabella with keen attention. He hardly acknowledged Julian's babbled apology. Arabella shrank a little under the intensity of his gaze.

"It just seemed like a logical addition to me," Arabella said.

"Does it add too much extra weight, Julian?" Lord Plunkett-Nelson drawled thoughtfully without taking his eyes from Arabella.

"It adds some," Julian said. "But the benefit is so great that it's worth it. I'll have to find another place to compensate."

"You could remove the eyes," Arabella said, her tone distracted as she focused on a stubborn oyster. When she noticed a silence had fallen over the table, she glanced up to discover everyone was staring at her. "I mean, the jewels. The jewels you're using in place of the eyes."

"I suppose…" Julian said, his brow furrowed in thought.

"Do they serve a purpose?" Arabella asked Julian.

Julian frowned. "Not a functional one. But people seem to feel uncomfortable if it doesn't have eyes."

Arabella shrugged. "Then etch the shape of eyes into the metal. It will save the weight, and people will still have the comfort of eyes to look at."

"Oh-ho!" Lord Plunkett-Nelson guffawed. "Another rational suggestion from a witch!" He signaled the staff to clear the oyster plates and bring the next course. The servants presented generous slices of roast beef laid over a bed of colcannon with a side of roasted carrots. As they ate, Lord Plunkett-Nelson queried his nephew again.

"Have you figured out the problem of making sure the bird gets to the correct person?"

Julian sighed. "Unfortunately, no. I'm completely stumped."

"I did have a thought while I was getting ready for dinner," Arabella said. Julian's eyes widened, and he leaned forward.

"By all means, my dear," Lord Plunkett-Nelson said. "Enlighten us. You have already brought such significant progress to the project. Just over dinner!"

Arabella blushed. "I was just thinking about something my brother said before we came here." She paused. Julian motioned for her to go on. "Well, we were talking about the potato blight, and he mentioned that we'd been trying so hard to solve it with magic with no success. He theorized that if we worked together with mundane horticulturalists that we might find the solution." She looked around the table enthusiastically.

"And?" Lord Plunkett-Nelson furrowed his brow.

"If we combine the magical and the mundane, we might be able to solve more problems," she responded. "That might be the solution here! If we combine Julian's engineering brilliance and my magic, we could create something marvelous!" Arabella's eyes shown with excitement. Eliza and Sarah looked bemused, while Rowena looked thoughtful.

"Stupendous! Yes!" Julian crowed. He started to rise from his seat and sat back down.

"Rowena." Arabella turned to her sister. "When you—or any witch really—send a message by crow or raven, how do you make sure the bird knows where to go?"

"We just tell it," Rowena said with a shrug.

"But *how* do you tell it?"

"We think it, I guess. It's like telepathy, putting an image of a person and place in the bird's mind." Rowena looked to Eliza and Sarah. "Doesn't the Guardian order use messenger birds frequently? And send them to places you aren't personally familiar with? I always have trouble getting a messenger bird to understand the idea of a place or person I don't know well."

Eliza nodded. "Some witches have more of a knack for it. We keep detailed sketches of places and people we send messages to frequently, but we, the human, have never personally met. I can use the sketch to build a more detailed picture in the messenger bird's mind."

"This is fascinating…" Julian breathed.

Arabella pursed her lips. "Do you think we could build a picture in the mechanical bird's mind?"

"I don't think I could," Rowena laughed. "I have no talent for technomancy. But you might be able to."

"Do you think we could try tomorrow?" Julian blurted out. "I have a test bird ready to fly. You could try to imprint it and send it on a short flight to the other end of the hall!"

"Oh, that sounds exciting!" Arabella enthused.

Just then, Mr. Yates entered the dining room, his expression dour. His gaze swept over the witches at the table, and his lip began to curl. Arabella met his gaze, and with a visible effort, he schooled his features to bland neutrality. She glanced over at Eliza. The Guardian's lips pressed together in a harsh line. She shook her head slightly, mouthing *not here*. Mr. Yates approached Lord Plunkett-Nelson and leaned over to whisper in his ear, laying his hand familiarly on the baron's shoulder. The baron nodded and waved the man back.

"It would seem we have any unexpected visitor," he said.

"Did Cauley come by with the gear works he wanted me to look at?" Julian looked up from his plate and blinked owlishly. "He's even worse than I am about the social graces, interrupting dinner…" Julian *tsk*ed as he cut himself another mouthful of beef. He blotted his mouth with his napkin, still chewing, and started to rise.

"No," Lord Plunkett-Nelson said. Blinking at his uncle, Julian sat back down. "Our visitor is here to see Miss Leyden." He raised his eyebrow at Arabella, then turned his regard back to Eliza. "I thought you said you were trying to keep your presence here undisclosed?"

"We are." Eliza slapped her hands on the table and stood up. Sarah stood as well, glowering. "The number of people we told about our location is limited. You, however, seem to have been a bit more free with the information."

Lord Plunkett-Nelson's head reared back. "Well, now," he huffed. "Yes, it would seem that I am the likely source, but there is no need to be rude!"

"The safety of my charge is more important to me than social graces," Eliza growled.

"Well, who is it?" Arabella burst out. "It's entirely possible the visitor is friendly, or at least offers me no ill will."

Eliza frowned. "Yes, I suppose that is a possibility, but I would still rather keep the knowledge of your temporary residency here more controlled."

Arabella sighed. "I don't think we can keep my existence a complete secret and still accomplish what Mother asked of us." She turned to Mr. Yates. "Well? Who is it?"

"There is a Miss Deirdre Iona Colman to see you, Miss Leyden." Mr. Yates held himself stiff.

Arabella searched her mind, but she could find no memory of anyone with that name. She cast questioning glances at the other witches in the room, but they all shook their heads.

"Did she say what she wanted?" Arabella asked, perplexed.

"Miss Colman is one of the local…" Mr. Yates paused and grimaced as if he'd swallowed a bone. "witches. Perhaps she wishes to speak to you about… those sort of things." His voice dripped with distaste. Eliza nudged Sarah surreptitiously with her elbow. Both Guardians locked intent gazes on the Louth Hall steward for a moment.

Breaking off their examination, Eliza and Sarah exchanged narrow-eyed glances.

Mr. Yates turned back to Lord Plunkett-Nelson. "Shall I send her away, sir?"

"Don't be ridiculous," Lord Plunkett-Nelson said. "We're almost done with dinner. Just make her comfortable in the drawing room, and we'll be along after we've finished dessert."

"Make her comfortable?" Mr. Yates scowled.

"Yes, yes, give her tea and such, let her rest her feet by the fire. She's likely had to come a long way." Lord Plunkett-Nelson's face lit up as he thought of something. "Her horse! Have we tended to her horse yet?"

Mr. Yates's mouth thinned into a tight line. "She walked here."

"She walked here? At night? What lady goes walking about at night?" Lord Plunkett-Nelson seemed genuinely confused.

"She's not a lady, she's a witch!" Mr. Yates snapped. He gasped, his eyes wide and fearful as he surveyed the shocked dinner guests. Eliza and Sarah stepped away from the table with matching glares. Arabella and Rowena stood and dropped their napkins on their chairs. Julian just sat with his mouth silently opening and closing.

"Good God, man! Where are your manners?" Lord Plunkett-Nelson barked.

"I am so sorry, my Lord," Mr. Yates stammered, his face pale. He bowed low to Lord Plunkett-Nelson. "I will watch my tongue with much more care in the future."

"Be sure that you do," Lord Plunkett-Nelson retorted. "I will not abide being humiliated in front of my guests." He turned his attention to the angry witches standing at his table. "Ladies, ladies," he kept his voice smooth and honeyed. "Please sit. I have such a lovely dessert planned. Please don't allow this momentary unpleasantness to spoil our evening."

"I'm afraid our evening is already spoiled," Arabella said, lifting her chin.

"Perhaps we should go meet with Miss Colman while you and Julian enjoy your dessert," Eliza said. "We wouldn't want to further disrupt your meal." The stiffness of her tone belied the sweetness of her words.

"Well, if you insist on cutting our dinner short," Lord Plunkett-Nelson grumbled. He sighed as he hauled himself to his feet. "I will always see to the comfort of my guests. Let us go see this Miss Colman." He wagged his finger and forced a laugh. "Tomorrow night, you must promise to stay at the table through dessert."

The ladies did not respond. They all regarded him with carefully neutral expressions. Julian jumped up from his place.

"This way, ladies." He bowed slightly and swept his arm toward the door. "I assume you took her to the drawing room, Mr. Yates?"

"She is waiting in the grand foyer," Mr. Yates grated.

"The grand foyer?" Julian clucked his tongue. "Poor thing, there's nowhere to sit down there!"

As he passed Mr. Yates, Lord Plunkett-Nelson hissed in his ear. "I would be having dessert right now if you could have minded your manners." Mr. Yates grimaced.

As they exited the dining room, Arabella heard Eliza whisper to Sarah behind her, "Did you see it this time?" Looking over her shoulder just in time to see Sarah give Eliza a grim nod. Arabella pursed her lips. It seemed she needed to have another conversation with her Guardians about openness and honesty.

One ostentatious crystal gaslamp chandelier provided buttery yellow light for the grand foyer. A tall woman waited near the front door, looking uncertain. She stood easily a head taller than Arabella, with grey eyes and orangey-red hair pulled back into a low chignon. She wore a plain brown dress, worn but clean and well-cared for. It hung on her lean frame like it had been made for a much plumper woman. Lord Plunkett-Nelson lengthened his stride so that he reached her before anyone else.

"Miss Colman," he boomed, extending his hand. "Welcome to my humble home."

"Actually, it's Mrs.," she said as she blinked at his extended hand. "May I see Arabella Leyden now? I have a very important message to deliver."

"I am Arabella Leyden," Arabella said, stepping forward. "How do you do?"

Deirdre bobbed a curtsey. "Good evening, Sister. My name is Deirdre Iona Colman, of House Realta and Clan Colla. I hope I am not disturbing you."

From his place hovering at Lord Plunkett-Nelson's shoulder, Mr. Yates snorted. "Your Clan still claims you?" he muttered.

Deirdre pulled herself up straighter. "Yes, they do." Her voice rang out. "Clan Colla is proud of her powerful daughters."

Mr. Yates started to say something, but he saw Eliza and Sarah glowering at him. He snapped his jaw shut.

"You're not disturbing me at all," Arabella reassured her, trying to soothe ruffled feathers. "I always have time for my Sisters. Would you care to have some tea? Perhaps a bite to eat? Mr. Yates said you had to walk; you must be tired."

Deirdre licked her lips, then cast her eyes down. "I wouldn't want to be a bother, ma'am. I am only here to deliver a message."

"I'm sure we can send you off with a little something after you've done your duty." Sarah stepped up next to Arabella. She gave Mr. Yates a hard look. Her voice took on a more menacing tone. "I'm sure we didn't eat all of the soda bread at breakfast, and there must be a bit of cheese or an apple? Or perhaps a bit of the beef we had for dinner? Surely there is some left?"

Mr. Yates made a sour face and drew in his breath to respond with vitriol, but until he caught sight of the Baron's warning countenance. He paused and said, "I will go to the kitchen and see what I can find." He turned sharply on his heel and took off.

"Make sure it's a substantial portion!" Lord Plunkett-Nelson called after Mr. Yates. He stole a sideways glance to make sure his guests had heard his order.

Deirdre's eyes went wide. She bobbed a curtsy to Sarah. "That's most generous of you, ma'am."

"I've been hungry too, Sister," Sarah murmured, her expression gentle. Her eyes flicked to Deirdre's prominent cheekbones. Deirdre blushed and nodded.

"It's lovely to meet a Sister from another Isle," Arabella stepped in to try to cover any of Deirdre's embarrassment. "I must say, I am rather surprised that someone would know to send me a message here. I did not think my destination was widely known."

"We've had birds watching for your arrival since the news circulated that your mother booked passage for you," Deirdre said. "Once your carriage left the main roads, it wasn't hard to know where you were going."

"Who is we?" Eliza broke in. She took up a place on Arabella's other shoulder.

"What is left of the Irish Council of Witches," Deirdre said. "And you have nothing to worry about from us, Guardian. We've heard the whispers about those who would wish Miss Leyden harm, but I can assure you, we are not among their ranks." She searched Eliza's face, then Arabella's. "May I be honest with you?"

"I would like that very much," Arabella said with a smile. "Honesty is a gift to be treasured."

Deirdre nodded, then took a deep breath. "There aren't many of us left here on the Isle. Some of our younger sisters have even taken to going back into hiding, as it was in the Dark Times." Her shoulders hitched up as she choked back a small sob. "We haven't gotten support from the main Council in London, and quite frankly, we're grasping for anything we can get. We don't want to damage our chances of gaining your support, Miss Leyden. In fact, we would do everything in our power to protect you."

"Oh, my!" Arabella put her hand to her mouth. "I don't know that I have the kind of power you imagine I have."

"Does your mother listen to you at all? About anything?" Deirdre's voice trembled. "Can you hold a conversation with her about any topic?"

"Well, yes…" Arabella began.

"Then you have more power than we do," Deirdre said. "We've tried for years to get her to just listen. We've begged… pleaded… And nothing but silence. She won't hear us." Deirdre turned her head away to blink the tears out of her eyes.

"I think I might know why Mother is so adamant against hearing you." Rowena joined the conversation.

"We already know!" Deirdre burst out. "Your mother may have treated the story like a great secret, but here on the Isle, every witch knows every horrifying detail about the deaths of the Sortilege twins and how your mother fled to protect herself and her unborn child." Deirdre looked beseechingly to Arabella. "She disappeared before we could find her. We would have helped her, protected her. We would have."

"You don't think Mother believes that whole ugly business was your fault?" Arabella's voice was shocked.

"What else are we to imagine?" Deirdre's shoulders fell in defeat. "She won't answer our letters. We can never get a hearing before the English Council of Witches. She won't even talk to us."

Arabella and Rowena exchanged glances.

"And you feel my sister can help you past this impasse?" Rowena asked.

Deirdre nodded. "If we could just get the Grand Dame to hear us, just once… I know your mother has a reputation for being a bit… unsympathetic at times, but surely even she can't refuse us help if she knew how dire our situation is."

"You mean the famine?" Arabella asked. "But we've seen no evidence of any famine since we got here. The land seems fertile."

"The land *is* fertile," Deirdre's voice dropped. She tightened her jaw as she looked at Lord Plunkett-Nelson with narrowed eyes. "Our people, the ones who work the land, are not allowed to keep any of the fruits of their efforts. And they are given no coin for their labor!"

"It's *my* land! Why should I give *my* crops away!" Lord Plunkett-Nelson exploded. "I allow everyone who works my land to live on my land, and they are each allowed to work a bit of their own to grow food for themselves. I can't help it if they cannot manage what I give them."

"Hovels! They live in hovels!" Deirdre shouted. "And the little patch you give them to work for themselves couldn't feed a flock of chickens, let alone a whole family."

"I will not be attacked and insulted in my own house! My people are none of your affair!" he roared.

Arabella stepped between them, holding up her hands. "Please! Please! Can we stop shouting at each other?"

Lord Plunkett-Nelson took a step back, fists balled at his sides. He glared daggers at Deirdre. Deirdre scowled right back, but she said nothing.

Arabella waited for a moment to ensure that no further eruptions were imminent. Then she turned to Deirdre and said, "Is that the message you came to deliver? That the remains of the Irish Witches Council desire my support?"

Deirdre tore her eyes away from Lord Plunkett-Nelson. "No. I came to tell you that Kiera Maeve Walsh, the Magistra of the Irish Council of Witches, kindly requests your presence for tea on the morrow. She would like to welcome you to our land and hopefully have a convivial discussion about our mutual concerns." Deirdre paused. "And if you are feeling at all reluctant, we do have an enticement for you to come have tea."

Arabella raised her eyebrow. "An enticement? My, but doesn't that sound mysterious."

"Magistra Walsh has some letters she thinks you will find very interesting," Deirdre said.

"I'll admit to being afire with curiosity now," Arabella said. "Can you tell me anything about these letters, or do you mean to keep their contents completely secret until I come for tea?"

"We don't know what the contents are, Miss Leyden," Dierdre said. "These letters were sent to your aunts, Leanore and Lorena, and your mother when they were last here in Ireland. They were delivered to the inn where they were staying a few days after… the incident. Magistra Walsh took possession of them from the witch who found them when she searched for your mother. She's been keeping them safe ever since. She never opened them. The wax seal is still intact."

Arabella and Rowena gasped.

"Where did the letters come from? Surely you can tell us that," Arabella said.

"They came from somewhere in France. That's all we know," Deirdre responded. "Somewhere in their travels, they got wet, and the ink smudged."

"Why didn't you tell Mother you had some of her personal correspondence?" Rowena huffed. "Surely that enticement would have worked better for her than for us."

"I can only assume she never read our letters to her, or she didn't care what her missed correspondence contained," Deirdre said with a shrug. "I can't know her mind. That's not where my talents lie."

"These letters are thirty years old," Rowena whispered to Arabella. "Can anything written in thirty-year-old letters still be relevant?"

Arabella shrugged. "We'll find out once we deliver them to Mother. I intended to have tea with Magistra Walsh anyway. Perhaps the letters will be dull things. Perhaps they will give us some insight into the Aunts we never met." Arabella reached out for her sister's hand and squeezed it.

"Splendid!" Deirdre broke out into a wide grin. "I'll inform Magistra Walsh you'll be joining her. I'll come pick you up around noontime tomorrow."

Rowena made a face. "Isn't that a bit early for tea?"

"We'll need the time to walk to my home for the tea," Deirdre said. She blushed and ducked her head. "I'm afraid the land near my cottage is a bit rough, and there aren't proper roads a carriage could traverse."

"I'm sure some fresh air would be good for our constitutions," Arabella said brightly as she nudged Rowena in the ribs with her elbow.

Mr. Yates emerged from the green baize door with a canvas-wrapped package in his hands. He thrust it at Deirdre with a scowl on his face. Deirdre pursed her lips, but she accepted it.

"Bread, cheese, apples, and a bit of beef, as requested," he growled. He threw a nasty look at Sarah.

"Well, then," Arabella said, trying to keep her voice light. "We'll see you at noon tomorrow. I hope I remembered to pack some walking shoes!" She forced a laugh.

After Deirdre left, the ladies said their goodnights to the gentlemen and retreated to their rooms. The air was just too unsettled for genial post-dinner conversation.

At the top of the stairs, Arabella laid a hand on Eliza's elbow. "Perhaps we should all gather in my room for a bit? Maybe you'd like to tell us about what you and Sarah saw regarding Mr. Yates…"

Eliza heaved a great sigh. "Yes, I suppose we need to have a chat about that."

"Indeed, especially since it was only a few days ago that you promised to be honest with me." Arabella worked hard to keep the frustration out of her voice.

"I have been honest with you," Eliza insisted as they shut the door behind them. "I just wasn't certain what I was seeing, and I wanted Sarah to have a look before I said anything."

Arabella watched as Eliza sank into one of the chairs by the empty fireplace then sat across from her. Intent on the Guardian, she barely noticed as Rowena took a seat on the vanity bench and Sarah perched herself on the foot of the bed.

"How good are you at reading auras, Rowena?" Eliza asked.

"Not very good, I'm afraid. Elizabeth has always been the best of us at that sort of thing," she paused. "Although you can never tell with the twins. They often seem to be hiding something."

"Then you wouldn't have caught it…" Eliza trailed off and stared into the distance.

"Caught what?" Arabella asked after a moment.

"The cloud around Mr. Yates," Sarah said as she watched her partner with concern.

Rowena started up as if someone had pinched her. "I remember reading something in a book about auras and clouds a long time ago. As I recall, it wasn't a good thing."

"No, it's not," Eliza murmured. She shook her head as if to clear it and turned her attention to Arabella. "Reading auras is one of my specialties. That is why I was assigned to protect you. I usually spot the people who mean my charge harm long before they can get close. That's how I knew the stevedores were safe and the one sailor might be a problem. I read Julian while we were in the carriage. He is exactly as he presents himself. Lord Plunkett-Nelson is a bit full of himself, but he is harmless enough. All the maids and cooks are good folk." She sighed and leaned back in her chair, staring into the empty fireplace.

"But Mr. Yates?" Arabella prompted softly.

"He's clouded," Eliza said distractedly. "A thick dark cloud. It's common enough for witches on clandestine tasks to cloud or otherwise obscure their auras. Some Grande Dames use the technique during delicate negotiations with the Grande Dames of other nations. But even the most deft hand at the technique cannot render an aura completely unreadable. Yet I cannot read Mr. Yates."

Arabella scowled. "How is that even possible? He's not even a witch!"

"Perhaps a witch cast a spell on him?" Sarah offered.

Eliza shook her head. "That makes no sense. It's obvious even without reading his aura that he hates witches. Why would a witch spend the energy for that kind of working on someone like him? It does him no harm but makes him a danger to witches who aren't as sensitive to auras as I am."

"He could have been cursed," Rowena offered. "Couldn't a curse do something like that?"

"It is technically possible. Those spells exist," Eliza said. "But again, why? Any spell that can achieve it is arduous, and the curse would never actually harm him. It would just confuse witches."

"What else can do something like that?" Arabella asked.

Eliza clenched her hands so tight her knuckles turned white. "There are two alternatives I can think of, and neither of them is very pleasant." She exchanged a glance with Sarah. "He could be possessed by a demon. Demons don't cast auras that humans can detect. A possession would cover his own aura."

Arabella gulped. "What's the other alternative?"

"He could be soulless," Eliza whispered. "A man without a soul cannot cast an aura."

CHAPTER XV

*Wherein the British Delegation Meets
with the Smallest Council*

BY THE TIME THEY REACHED DEIRDRE'S COTTAGE, TUCKED ON THE leeward side of a verdant grassy hill, Arabella felt like her legs would fail her. Rowena looked as though she might pass out, but Eliza and Sarah matched Deirdre's pace with ease. They were right at the edge of Lord Plunkett-Nelson's land. The cottage itself was about the size of two deckhouses on the *Kittiwake* put together, but it looked snug and well cared for. Wisps of smoke rose from the chimney. A nanny goat nibbled on grass growing up around the foundation stones by the front door. A small garden plot—surrounded by a picket fence to keep the goat out—extended to the right.

"Here we are," Deirdre chirped. "It may not be so grand as what you're used to, but it's mine, passed down through my mother, her mother, and her mother before her. Great-gran earned this property by saving his Lordship's Grandda from drowning." Deirdre frowned. "But since he took charge up at Hall, Mr. Yates has been trying to convince his Lordship to take it back from me. Claims Old Lord Plunkett only meant to lease it to Great-gran and that the lease is up, and I owe him money." She shook her head.

"Well, your garden looks lovely," Arabella said as she mopped her brow with a linen handkerchief. It didn't do any good since it was already saturated from the many times she'd mopped her brow on the march to the cottage.

"I'm no earth witch, but it grows well enough." Deirdre sighed. "But it's not sufficient. I can't feed everyone."

"Do you have a large family?" Arabella asked.

"Ach, no. Just me and my husband," Deirdre said. "Danu hasn't blessed us with any children yet."

"Then why…" Rowena trailed off.

Deirdre tilted her head to the side and regarded her in exasperation. "You don't listen well, do you? The people who work the Lord's lands are starving. The only thing they can grow enough of on the tiny plots the Lords allow them is potatoes, and the potatoes are rotting in the ground from the blight." She gestured to her garden. "Almost everything I grow I give to the workers. I'd rather go hungry myself than watch another wee babe starve."

"Oh yes, well…" Rowena stammered. Behind her, Sarah shook her head.

"Come inside," Deirdre sighed. "The Magistra is waiting. I'll put the kettle on, and we'll have a little tea."

Inside the cottage, there was a hearth for cooking and a stone sink with an attached countertop across the room for washing and food preparation. Above it hung a small cabinet for storage. A bucket full of water sat on the floor next to the sink. Across the room, a partially open threadbare curtain revealed a bed and a wardrobe. In between the sink and the hearth stood a plain wooden table with four chairs. One of the chairs was already occupied.

Kiera Maeve Walsh, Magistra of the Irish Council of Witches, was a tiny woman. Standing at her full height, she would have barely come to Arabella's shoulder. She was painfully thin, her cheekbones sharp against her face, her eyes sunken in. It was obvious that Deirdre was not the only witch going without eating to feed the people. The frailty of her body made her thick mane of black curls seem that much grander. She wore her hair loose and free in defiance of mundane rules for how a woman should groom herself. For all her lack of physical size, she radiated power Arabella could feel even with her lack of earth-based magic. Kiera's icy blue eyes commanded respect.

"Magistra," Arabella murmured as she dipped her head and curtsied. Rowena, Eliza, and Sarah followed suit. Deirdre gathered water from the bucket and put the kettle on the hob. She turned to the countertop and began preparing the food for tea.

Kiera inclined her head to Arabella but did not stand up. "Come, sit." She waved her hand to the other chairs. "We have much to discuss." Arabella sat across from Kiera. Rowena sat to Arabella's left. Eliza and Sarah took up sentry positions on either side of the door.

"If I may introduce my companions…" Arabella said.

"Your sister, Rowena Maude Sortilege," Kiera interrupted her. "Your Guardian, Elizabeth Victoria Josolyne, and the Guardian assigned to your sister, Sarah Gardner. I am not as interested in pleasantries as some of you city witches. When you live in the country, you have to be more practical and quick."

"I see," Arabella said as she folded her hands on the table.

Deirdre laid a plate in the middle of the table with slices of apple, cheese, and soda bread arrayed upon it. Arabella wondered if this was the same food Sarah had forced Mr. Yates to give Deirdre last night.

"The tea won't be but a minute," Deirdre said. "I don't have any sugar, but I do have milk from my nanny goat, Bess, if you'd like."

"Plain is fine, thank you, Sister," Kiera murmured. "Save Bess's best for Molly's little boy.'"

"I'll also have mine plain," Arabella said. Rowena nodded in agreement. Deirdre busied herself with measuring tea into the pot as the kettle on the fire began to sing.

Keira laced her fingers together on the table in front of her. "Deirdre said she'd spoken plainly with you last night when she delivered my invitation."

"Yes, ma'am," Arabella said. "But I'm still not sure how much assistance I can be." Deirdre laid out tin cups in front of the ladies.

"You need to rid yourself of your sorry self-image if you wish to be a help to anyone," Kiera snapped. Dierdre laid a hand on Kiera's shoulder.

"Sister, eat something," she admonished. "It does your temper no good to remain hungry. I checked what that bodach gave me. It's neither spoiled nor poisoned."

Kiera gave Dierdre a sour look.

"Fine," she muttered. She snatched a piece of apple from the plate and took an angry bite. She chewed slowly at first but then gnawed the rest of the piece in quick, savage bites.

"If that is the same cheese Lord Plunkett-Nelson served at his luncheon table," Arabella said. "I would recommend pairing it with the soda bread. The combination is quite lovely."

Kiera inclined her head to Arabella. She took some cheese and bread but ate them with slower, more measured bites. Deirdre smiled to herself as she poured the tea.

Arabella wrapped her hands around her tin mug. "Perhaps if you tell me what you think I can do for you, our conversation might be more efficient."

Kiera took a sip of tea to wash down her cheese and bread. "You could begin by talking to your mother for us. As Deirdre informed you last night, we've not had her ear for thirty years. As bad as circumstances were on her last visit, they've gotten worse."

"Deirdre said some of the young witches have gone back into hiding." Arabella's eyes widened as she leaned forward. "Is that true?"

Kiera nodded. "Mostly in the cities," she said. "It's harder to hide where you come from in the country where everyone knows everyone else and all their cousins. But you go into the city, and you can start a new life and tell whatever story you like."

"That's so distressing, having to leave family and House like that." Arabella's hands tightened on her mug.

"It's not just a sad thing." Kiera's voice grew tight. "It's a dangerous thing. We try to keep an eye on where everyone goes and what daughters are born, but there are so few of us left loyal to the Houses. We've already lost track of a few." She turned to Arabella, her gaze sharp. "It's fertile ground for undiscovered witches, unbound to any House or Council. Perhaps that will catch your mother's attention."

Rowena gasped. Arabella's cup trembled in her grip. Eliza and Sarah exchanged glances and nodded.

"I see what you Guardians are thinking," Kiera growled. "You'll send your secret little army here and drag frightened young girls from their homes. You'll put them in danger by revealing who they are before all their neighbors. It's a death sentence!"

Eliza kept her voice low and controlled. "Would you rather a young fire witch burn down a tenement and kill all the people in it when she loses her temper? Or have a death witch roaming unchecked with her death touch upon her and no one to teach her how to control it?" Arabella swallowed hard at the thought of the scenarios Eliza presented.

"Of course not," Kiera growled. "That's why I'm talking to you now, why I've been *trying* to get the Grande Dame's attention for years!" She snatched up another piece of bread and gnawed on it thoughtfully, gimlet eyes on the Guardians. "If the Grande Dame still refuses to hear us through her daughters, perhaps there is something the Guardians might do... covertly?"

Sarah nodded slowly. "Guardians have been known to quietly bring in wild witches, the ones not born to a House."

Eliza's mouth quirked up. "Huh, yes.... We call them our little surprises, just popping up in a bloodline with no witches."

"I'm a little surprise?" Sarah smirked at Eliza.

"A big pain more like..." Eliza shook her head and returned to the conversation. "Since they have no Houses, we'd have to bring them over to England for proper testing and training. We'd not be able to let them travel until they'd sworn themselves."

"But they might stay in England? Be safe?" Deirdre asked breathlessly.

"They would have a safe place if they wanted it," Sarah said with a decisive nod.

Kiera and Deirdre exchanged glances. "It certainly would help some of the younger girls..." Dierdre said. "They might even come back to help."

"Or Ireland might become a country with no witches," Kiera said sourly.

"Why is that such a problem here?" Arabella broke in. "We have people who don't care for witches in England, but we aren't in such fear for our lives that we go into hiding."

"The *Ilhexerai*," Keira spat.

"The what?" Arabella asked. A chill ran down her spine.

"The *Ilhexerai*," Kiera repeated. "They keep to the shadows and hide themselves, but they think witches are evil and should be destroyed."

"Some say they are descendants of those who burned witches before we rescued humanity from the Great Plague," Deirdre piped in.

"Wherever they came from, they work from the shadows and encourage the hatred of witches," Kiera said. "The Catholics used to tolerate us, but because of the incitement of the Ilhexerai, they don't anymore."

"And with the common people hungry and looking for food and someone to blame..." Deirdre sighed.

"It's the perfect storm to let a group like that get a foothold," Sarah murmured.

"I've never even heard of the *Ilhexerai*!" burst out Eliza.

"Another mistake of our dear Grande Dame," Keira smirked. "Keeping her little island kingdom isolated may keep it safe for a few decades, but eventually, the monsters out in the wide world will come howling at her door. And we will all be unprepared for the onslaught because she stuffed her fingers in her ears like a spoiled child."

"Now, see here!" Rowena snapped. "Our Grande Dame is the most powerful witch in the Isles, quite possibly the world. She may not be perfect, but she works very hard to ensure the safety and prosperity of all those in her sway. I will not stand to hear her judged so!"

The room fell quiet. Arabella's jaw hung open, while Deirdre shook her head. Kiera regarded Rowena with a raised eyebrow. After a moment, Kiera said, "Are you quite finished with your temper tantrum, little girl?"

"I am not a little girl!" Rowena replied hotly. She turned to her sister. "Are you going to sit there quietly and allow this stranger to insult our mother? Insult *me*?"

Arabella swirled her tea, staring down into the depths as if it had something to tell her.

"Tell me, Rowena," Arabella said in a soft voice. "Is our mother perfect?"

"Of course not! No one is."

"Has she not kept us sheltered from the world, carefully manipulating us, feeding us only what she wanted us to know?" Arabella's voice barely went over a whisper.

"When we were small, yes, but I've been sitting on the Council for years now. I listen carefully at every session." Rowena waved away the suggestion of her ignorance as if it were a gnat.

Arabella lifted her head and locked eyes with Rowena. "What's to say that Mother doesn't treat the Council like she treats her own daughters? How often have you heard a report from another Council about world events in our chambers?"

"I have… there had to be…" Rowena furrowed her brow in confusion. "I can't recall." She finished weakly.

Arabella took a slow sip of her tea. "Rowena, given recent events, ones that I'm sure you would rather I not speak of here, you must know that I do not trust our mother fully."

"But she's not evil!" Rowena retorted.

Arabella sighed. "I never said she was, and neither did the Magistra. Mother is, however, fallible. She puts on a good show of being cold and implacable, but given those recent events we're not speaking of, she seems to be more ruled by fear than a Grande Dame ought to be."

Rowena's shoulders sagged, and she bit her lip. She blinked tears out of her eyes. After a deep breath, she said, "I do apologize for my rude outburst, Magistra. It appears I spoke without thinking."

Kiera nodded. "I understand. We'd all like to believe our mothers are faultless goddesses. They seem so when we are small. It is not an easy thing to realize they too sometimes fail." She gave Rowena a small smile. "Unfortunately, your mother has so much power that her failures count much more than a spoiled dinner or a fizzled rain spell."

"Indeed," Arabella murmured.

Just then, the front door of the cottage bumped open. A wolf stood in the doorway with a rabbit hanging from his jaws. Keira did not move. She selected another slice of bread with cheese from the plate and bit into it with obvious pleasure. Eliza and Sarah, however, sprang away from the door and put themselves between the wolf and their charges. Their hands flew to their dirks on their belts, spells ready on their lips.

"Eliza! Sarah! Wait!" Deirdre cried.

"There's a wolf at your door, Deirdre," Eliza growled.

"Yes and no," Deirdre said. "Please, just let him be..." When Eliza and Sarah made no additional moves, Deirdre turned to speak to the wolf. "Be a dear and put it on the counter. I'll clean it after we're done with tea."

Casting wary glances at the Guardians, the wolf trotted across the cottage and laid the rabbit neatly on the counter next to the stone sink. With a loping stride, he headed into the bed alcove and pulled the shabby curtain shut behind him with his teeth.

"You live with a wolf?" Sarah hissed through her teeth.

"Yes and no," said Deirdre with a blush. A moment later, a tall, dark-haired man emerged from behind the curtain, tucking his shirt-tails into his trousers. He went to Deirdre and pecked her on the cheek.

"I'm sorry to interrupt, Dee," he said. "I just wanted to get the hunt in before you went to visit the families. Shall I go and milk Bess while you finish up?"

"Thank you, Tom. Yes, that would be lovely," Deirdre said.

He nodded to the rest of them. "Ladies," he murmured and headed out of the cottage to milk the goat.

The English witches all turned to the Irish witches with wide eyes and slack jaws.

"A witch married to a werewolf wasn't all that unusual once upon a time," Deirdre huffed.

Kiera rolled her eyes. "It's always been unusual, Deirdre. You've just tried to convince yourself otherwise," she groaned. "And I tried to talk you out of it, but you wouldn't listen."

"But it's turned out fine, hasn't it? He's been a good husband!" Deirdre crossed her arms across her chest and pouted.

"Yes, yes." Kiera flapped her hands. "He's been an attentive husband, and his pack protects you well. But when some Lord shoots him out on the moor, it's going to break your heart."

"I didn't think there were any wolves in the Isles," Arabella said.

Deirdre shook her head. "There are no more plain wolves in Ireland," she said. "The English Lords killed the last of them years ago. But the werewolf packs have grown a bit crowded on the Continent, so a few decided to try their luck here."

"This is a complication we didn't need," Eliza muttered as she pinched the bridge of her nose.

"Oh, you'll have no trouble with the packs here," Deirdre said. "The ones that came over are very peace-loving. They wanted to escape all the violence and bickering among the Continental packs."

"Did I hear him say that you were going to visit families?" Arabella interrupted. "Did you mean the families of the field workers?"

"Yes," Deirdre said. "As soon as we finished tea with you, we were going to take what we could to them. We like to go during the day when it's just the mothers and children. Some of the men can be... rather uncivilized."

"May we come with you?" Arabella asked. "We've been misled by so many people about the conditions of the famine. Perhaps we had better see it for ourselves?"

"Perhaps that is just what we need for you to become our passionate champions," Kiera agreed. She stood and nodded to Deirdre. "Let's gather what we have and go."

CHAPTER XVI

*Wherein Good Intentions Go Awry and
Arabella Learns of Harsh Reality*

ARABELLA REGARDED THE GATHERING STORM CLOUDS WITH CONCERN. They arrived, footsore, at a tiny, ramshackle stone cottage situated in the middle of a stretch of rocky field. The dirt footpath they followed wound past the cottage to another, perhaps fifty yards down the path, and another fifty yards past that. Spreading out behind each cottage was a small patch of cultivated land. In contrast to the verdant green grass all around, the cultivated patches were full of leaves thoroughly covered in black and brown spots.

"Dammit. The blight's gotten worse," Kiera murmured through gritted teeth.

"I know." Deirdre sighed. "I don't think they'll pull anything edible out of the ground this season."

Three emaciated women in raggedy dresses of indeterminate color gathered in front of the nearest cottage. One woman seated in a single chair rocked a tiny bundle in her lap. The eldest of the trio puffed on a pipe and watched the witches approach with a wary eye.

"Bridget, Nora, Molly!" Deirdre hailed them as the witches got close.

Nora, the eldest, nodded. "Dee. Who'd you bring with you this time?" Her craggy cheeks worked like bellows as she puffed on her pipe.

"You remember Kiera?" Deirdre gestured to her left. Then she gestured to her right. "This is Arabella, Rowena, Eliza, and Sarah, guests from England."

Bridget crossed her arms across her chest. "Witches dressed like men? Is that what witches in England are like?" she huffed. "You Irish witches are daft enough, now this?"

Deirdre smiled. "They just wanted to see the true nature of the famine."

"We're not beasts in a zoo," the seated woman croaked.

"I never thought you were, Molly." Deirdre's voice was gentle. "We're hoping that some powerful folks will listen to these ladies and help get some relief."

Bridget shook her head. "Like I said, daft is what you are. None of the high and mighties have cared a bit for me my whole life. Why would they start now? Because these little slips of girls bat their eyelashes at them?" She let out a mirthless laugh. "Stop trying to feed us fairy stories. Did you bring food this time?"

"Of course," Deirdre said as she slipped the basket from her hip and held it out. "There's some turnips and onions from my garden, a loaf of bread, some beef…"

"Beef!" Nora barked. "Where did you get beef? Did you steal it?"

Deirdre shook her head, then nodded in Sarah's direction. "Miss Sarah made Mr. Yates give me some when I went to deliver a message to the Lord's house last night. There's also some apples and cheese from that."

Nora gave Sarah a speculative look. "You may look like a refugee from God, but we're glad of your help just the same." She turned her attention back to Deirdre. "We'll make sure it gets parceled out fairly between us and the other families. Thank you for your kindness."

"There's goat's milk in there too. For your boy, Molly," Deirdre said. "How is he?"

Molly pulled back the tattered blanket from the pale baby in her lap. He barely stirred, limp and lethargic. "He doesn't cry anymore." Molly choked back tears. "I don't think God will let me keep him much longer."

Arabella clapped her hands over her mouth to hold in a sob. She blinked her eyes furiously against her tears. Rowena turned her face away and pulled a handkerchief from her sleeve. Keira took a step forward. She twisted her fingers together.

"Would you allow me to help him," She said in a husky voice.

Molly pulled her baby close. Her eyes went wide. "I'm thankful for the food, mum. But please, please don't touch my baby."

"I only want to help," Kiera whispered. She dropped her eyes.

Molly just shook her head and held her baby tighter. She refused to meet Kiera's eyes.

Kiera sighed. "If you ever change your mind, just call for me. I have the healing touch. I could help if you'd let me."

"She said no," Bridget growled. "Now, leave her be. Please."

Kiera nodded and stepped back, her face mournful.

Arabella took a deep breath and clasped her hands in front of her stomach. "How many families will be sharing this food?"

Nora glanced off into the distance, her lips moving as if counting. She shrugged. "Half a dozen. No, seven… seven families."

Arabella gasped. "That's not enough food to keep one family, let alone seven!"

Bridget shrugged this time. "It's more than we had, more than we had hope of before Deirdre came down the lane."

"I will get you more," Arabella said fiercely, clenching her hands together.

"T'would be lovely to have more. I can't remember what a full belly feels like. But you'll have to pardon me if I don't hold out too much hope." Nora said. "Hope is a painful thing in times like these."

Arabella flushed and cast her eyes to the ground, blinking away tears. Deirdre patted her shoulder.

"We should be off," Deirdre said briskly. "I know you have other things to tend to." She nodded to her party. "Come along, ladies."

The witches shuffled back down the path, their heads hanging low, each sunk in her own thoughts. Once they were well away from the cottages, Deirdre halted and turned to face Arabella.

"Well?" she asked. "Now that you've seen it for yourself, does that stir your heart any further?"

Arabella lifted her head. She dashed the tears from her eyes with the back of her hand. "We have to fix this," she said in a husky voice.

"But how?" Rowena asked, her voice trembling. "Our own aunts died from the strain of trying to end the potato blight, and they were very talented earth witches." She shook her head. "And then it's not just the blight. The landlords take too much from them and give too little back. Even if their potato crop was strong, how much could they grow in that little piece of rocky soil? Could they really feed their families well?"

"We can't stand by and do nothing," Arabella hissed. Fresh tears began to roll down her cheeks.

"Then what?" Rowena sighed. "What shall we do?"

Arabella bit her lip and thought for a moment. "First," her voice hitched. She took a deep breath. "First, we go get more food. Lord Plunkett-Nelson has a full larder and pantry. He'd not miss a few baskets."

"Alright," Rowena said. "That will help for a few days. Then what?"

"When we bring the food, we bring jars and vials and trowels," Arabella said. Her words came faster as the plan surfaced in her mind. "We need samples of the soil and all the parts of the blighted plants. Henry will need them for his experiments, to find out what's wrong and how to fix it. I think he was right; we've been too narrow in our thinking about where to find solutions. We need to work together, mundane and magical."

"Do you really think Henry can figure this out?" Rowena asked.

"If he fails, we're no worse off than we are now," Arabella said, wiping her cheeks. She frowned. "We'll need to get the samples to them faster than we can get there." She turned to Deirdre and Kiera. "Do you have messenger birds? They might take a whole day, maybe a little less?"

Keira nodded. "There are a couple of half-wild rooks we might be able to call on. We don't really have the time or energy for proper bonding or training, so they may refuse the message. Where do you want to send them?"

"To London, carrying the samples to my brother," Arabella said, her eyes bright as if with fever.

Keira shook her head. "They'll not go to someone who's not a witch, especially not that far."

Arabella's shoulders sagged.

"Maybe we can convince one to take a message to Vivienne," Rowena said. "You know how strong her earth magic is. And Boscastle isn't as far as London."

"That still doesn't get the samples to Henry…" Arabella's voice trailed off. She tapped her lip with her forefinger. Then she gasped, and her eyebrows shot up. "Julian's birds! We could send one of Julian's clockwork birds with the samples in its chest cavity." Her voice dropped to a murmur. "We might have to add another spring to fly that long... Maybe extend their wingspan so they could save energy while gliding..."

"Arabella..." Rowena tried to get her attention.

"Does he have anything bigger, like a raven or a gull? I must ask him..."

"Arabella!" Rowena grabbed Arabella by the shoulder and shook her. "We haven't done any of the tests with Julian's birds. We don't even know if you can imprint a destination on them."

"You're right, we haven't." Arabella pursed her lips. "But we have to try. If his clockwork birds don't work, we'll just have to carry the samples back ourselves. We'll book passage back right away. I'd rather not take that long to get the samples to Henry, but we'll do what we must."

In the distance, thunder rolled. The ladies looked to the sky to see the darkening clouds undulating across the horizon.

"You'd better hurry if you're going to make another food delivery today," Deirdre said. She pointed down another footpath branching off into the hills. "That's a more direct route to Louth Hall. If your Julian would let you borrow some horses, the trip back to the cottages would be much faster."

Arabella blushed. "He's not my Julian."

"Yes, he is," Rowena said with a playful shake of her head. "You've already got him wrapped around your finger. Come on," Rowena snatched up her hand and started to lead her down the footpath. Eliza and Sarah followed close on their heels. "We haven't a moment to lose if we're going to do this."

Arabella called back over her shoulder to Deirdre and Kiera, "We'll call on you again after we test Julian's birds. Get the rooks ready just in case!"

Arabella, Rowena, Eliza, and Sarah burst into the kitchen at Louth Hall, out of breath.

"We need food," Arabella panted. "Lots of it."

Mr. Yates looked up from his conversation with the cook. "I presume the hedge witch didn't feed you well over tea? Even after we were so generous with her?" he sneered.

Sarah stepped forward, her fists balled at her sides. "Stuff it, windbag. Children are starving, and we intend to help." Mr. Yates drew back with a look of horror on his face. Sarah turned to the cook. "How many baskets can you pack, and quickly?"

"What do you need, ma'am?" the cook stammered.

"Anything. Everything." Eliza gestured broadly. "Those poor cottars have nothing, and they'll be grateful for whatever you can spare."

"You want to take food to those lazy cottars?" Mr. Yates roared. "Absolutely out of the question! Those animals will not get one scrap from my kitchens!"

"*Whose* kitchens do you think these are?" came a sharp voice from behind them. Julian strode into the kitchen with a frown on his face. He bowed to Arabella. His voice softened. "I thought I saw you coming from across the fields and came to find you. What's going on?"

"Oh, Julian!" Arabella impulsively grabbed his hand. "The people in the cottages… They're really starving. And the potatoes are blighted. They have nothing to eat." Her voice dropped. "There's a baby who might not live if they do not get food." She put her other hand over her mouth to cover a sob.

Julian's face turned serious. "Then food they shall have. I can't bear to see you cry." He turned to the cook. "Mrs. Murphy, please pack the largest baskets you can, bread, beans, cabbages, the lot. I'll go have the chaise hitched up. We may not be able to take it all the way to the cottages, but maybe it will help us beat the storm."

"Your uncle would not allow this," Mr. Yates hissed.

Julian whirled on Mr. Yates, his face as dark as the gathering storm clouds outside. "Since the day I first toddled the halls of Louth Hall, hasn't my uncle always said I should have anything I want? That I should never be hungry?"

"Yes, of course…" Mr. Yates huffed.

"And hasn't my uncle always been explicit that any guests we have shouldn't know a moment of want?"

"I…" Mr. Yates tried to get in a word.

Julian cut him off. "I am suddenly ravenous, and I desire a picnic."

"I'm terribly hungry, too," Arabella chimed in.

"I'm starving," Rowena piped up.

"I could eat an entire roast by myself," Sarah said as she patted her belly with a wicked grin on her face.

"I'm famished," Eliza said. "I need at least a whole loaf of bread for each hand."

"Your uncle will hear about this," Mr. Yates seethed.

"Don't worry, I'll tell him myself," Julian said with an impish smirk.

The gray rain clouds looked ready to burst by the time Arabella arrived back at Molly's cottage with Julian, Rowena, Eliza, and Sarah. They had to walk the last half mile because the carriage couldn't manage the narrow, rocky path. Arabella's arms burned from the heavy basket she carried, but she refused to stop. She almost whimpered in relief when she saw the uneven thatch of Molly's roof appear over the crest of a hill.

"I had no idea they were tucked this far out of the way," Julian grunted as he shifted the balance of his basket.

"You mean, you've never visited your tenants?" Sarah's eyebrow twitched up.

"Technically, they are not my tenants. I have not inherited yet," Julian said. "But I daresay Uncle Sas has never been out here himself either. When he performs his inspections, he really only looks at the producing fields. He lets his middleman handle all the details regarding the cottars."

Sarah shook her head. "It's no wonder the conditions are so bad. It's easy to ignore suffering when you're an absentee landlord," she growled.

"So, I don't get any credit for being here now?" Julian huffed.

"We'll see," Sarah looked him over with narrowed eyes. "We'll see if this is a grand romantic gesture to catch your lady love's eye, or if you continue your support because you truly care for the people."

The chair outside Molly's cottage stood empty. Bridget and Nora were nowhere to be seen. But a thin tendril of smoke curled up out the chimney. Surely someone was home. Thunder rumbled in the distance as Arabella knocked timidly at the door. A moment later, the thin plank of wood squeaked open. Molly stood there with her silent baby on her shoulder. Her eyes widened, and her jaw dropped.

"You came back," she gasped.

"I said I would," Arabella said with a lopsided grin. She grunted with effort as she held up the basket. "We have more food."

Lightning flashed, and thunder cracked almost immediately after. The wind began to pick up. Molly looked to the threatening sky and blanched.

"I'm very glad of the food, but you need to go," her voice trembled.

"Go? But we don't mind getting wet. We were going to help carry the baskets to the other families. They are quite heavy, and we know you have the baby to manage." Arabella hoped her smile inspired trust.

Molly pressed her lips together. "That won't be necessary." She shook her head. "Nora and Bridget can help me. I really do appreciate your generosity, but you *must* go. Now."

"But we've also come to collect samples of the blighted potatoes and soil," Arabella explained. Julian held up the bag he had slung over his shoulder that held vials, jars, and trowels. "There's a man in London, my brother, who thinks he may be able to find a cure for the blight."

"Come back tomorrow if it's sunny." Molly's voice was frantic. "But please, go now."

Arabella forced a laugh. "We don't mind getting wet, really."

"It's not the rain!" Molly burst. "Well, it is... but it's not." She swallowed hard and looked up the road past Arabella's shoulder. The fear etched plainly on her face. "The men will be coming home from the Lord's fields because of the rain. They don't know that we get the extra food from witches."

"What's wrong with food from witches?" Julian asked, sounding genuinely puzzled.

"You daft boy," Molly spat. "You spend so much time over in England you have no idea what's happening here."

Eliza gave Julian a quelling look when he drew in his breath to speak again. "And this is why I didn't trust your assessment of danger. You don't listen when you're told the truth."

The color drained from Julian's face. His mouth flopped open.

"We, the ladies that is, we've gotten used to helpful witches," Molly said. "I can't say that I fully trust you lot. But no one has tried to curse me or poison me so far. And the food Deirdre and Kiera bring by has kept more than a few of us from death's door." Lightning tore the sky again, and the thunder clapped. It began to drizzle. Molly bit her lip. "But I can't say what my husband would do if he saw the lot of you. He's a true believer in the evilness of witches. Will you go now, please?"

Arabella paused for a moment, then nodded. She set her basket on the ground at Molly's feet. "We'll go. I don't want to cause any trouble for you." She motioned for the others to set their loads down as well. "We'll come back on the next sunny day for the samples. I promise you, we'll find a way to cure the blight."

The witches and Julian turned to leave, but it was already too late. A pack of filthy, sweaty men rounded the curve of the path, chattering among themselves. The man in the lead, tall and lean-muscled with a black beard, caught sight of them and stiffened. There was nowhere to hide. There was no time to run. Arabella hoped that they could find a way to make a graceful exit before any of the men discovered they were witches.

Eliza and Sarah widened their stances. Sarah rolled her shoulders. Both Guardians put their hands casually to the dirks on their belts. Julian stepped in front of the women, putting himself between them and the returning fieldworkers. The eight men came to a halt in front of Julian, blocking the path.

"Good afternoon, my Lord," the dark-haired man addressed Julian. "Is there something I can do to help you?"

"Ah, no. No, no, we're fine," Julian stammered. "We'll just be on our way. Wouldn't want to keep you from getting home and dry. We're off."

"Funny thing a young Lord coming to our homes while we're out," drawled a sandy-haired man from the back of the pack.

The dark-haired man frowned and crossed his arms across his chest. "You wouldn't be trying to lead our women astray, would you?" His eyes flicked from Julian to the baskets of food in front of his house, to Molly standing whey-faced in the doorway. "Is this where all the food has been coming from, woman?" he growled menacingly.

"Oh no, no, Jack," Molly said, her voice trembling. "It's nothing like that. He's never been here before. He didn't come inside."

"So why is he giving you food?" Jack's voice dropped a menacing octave. Molly flinched.

"We were just trying to help," Arabella said quickly, stepping forward to stand by Julian. "I'm here visiting, from England. One of my cousins brought me with her when she brought your Molly some turnips from her garden. I wanted to bring more, so here we are!" Arabella tried to keep her voice cheerful. She pulled her shawl tighter around her. "But goodness, this rain. We should be going and let you all get snug in your homes."

"Visiting your cousin, eh?" Jack raised his eyebrow. "Who's your blood? And how did the young Lord get involved with this?"

"My cousin? Oh yes, Deirdre, just around the way..." Arabella waved vaguely in the direction of Deirdre's cottage. Behind her, Molly choked back a gasp.

"Deirdre..." Jack snarled. "The witch over the hills? Witchery runs in bloodlines, doesn't it?" Arabella paled. Rowena wrapped her arms tight around herself. Eliza and Sarah took a step forward.

"Are you a witch?" Jack hissed.

"It's perfectly clear she's a witch," the sandy-haired man said. "You said it yourself, Jack. Witchery runs in the blood, and look at those two dressed like men and armed like villains. Abomination! Corruption!"

The men all balled up their fists as their mouths drew down in grimaces. They started muttering darkly among themselves. Jack held up his hand for silence.

"I want to hear it from her myself, Sean," Jack said. He fixed Arabella with a piercing gaze. "Are you a witch?"

Arabella stammered incoherently. She clasped her hands together, eyes flicking left and right. She took a step back. Cursing under her breath, Eliza slid in front of Arabella as Sarah slid in front of Rowena.

"That'll be enough, gentlemen," Eliza pitched her voice a little lower to give an air of authority. "The lady does not have to submit to your questions just because she came to provide food out of the kindness of her heart."

"Witch!" Sean hissed.

"Yes, I'm a witch," Eliza replied evenly. "And I'm a witch trained in violent spells so I can protect my charges." She put her hand on the hilt of her dirk. "Do any of you want to see how good I am at my job?"

"Filthy witch!" came the cry from another man.

"The only good witch is a dead witch!" yelled another.

"You've got a lot of nerve coming to my house and threatening me," Jack roared, putting his fists up in front of him.

"I bet they poisoned all that food," Sean hissed. "I bet that's what they've been doing all along, poisoning us and cursing us."

"That's enough!" Molly shrieked as she came barreling out of the house to stand in front of Jack. "Enough! Yes, the witches have been bringing us food. No, it hasn't been poisoned or cursed." She spat at Sean. She turned back to Jack. "Just stop it. They've only tried to help us."

"Woman!" Jack growled and raised his fist.

Molly screwed her eyes shut, steeling herself for the blow. But she held her ground, even though everyone could see her whole body trembled. When the blow didn't come, she spoke again.

"How many more children am I going to lose, Jack?" She patted the silent baby on her shoulder. "He's almost gone, he's so weak. The only reason he's lasted so long is because of the witches. My milk's gone dry. My body just can't make any more. But Deirdre brought goat's milk today. Maybe we can save him." She choked on a sob. She whispered, "I've lost so many. Please don't make him the next."

Jack lowered his fist. He blinked tears from his eyes. "I'm not a monster," he whispered.

He turned to the witches with rage in his eyes. He stabbed his finger back up the trail. "Go on, go away! Leave here and don't come back!" he barked.

Arabella and the rest didn't need any more encouragement. They scampered up the edge of the path, trying to give the angry field workers as wide a berth as possible.

"If I ever see you here again, I *will* kill you!" Jack howled at their backs.

CHAPTER XVII

Wherein Arabella Catches Julian in a Well-Meant Falsehood

I T WAS STILL RAINING THE NEXT MORNING. ARABELLA FROWNED AT THE dreary grey day outside her window. There would be no getting samples today. The loss of time made her teeth itch. Her feet were finally on the right path past the impediments that had hung over her head for so long—the famine, the local distrust of witches, her own political position with the Council—and now she was confounded by a rainy day. And just when she believed the solution to deliver the samples to Henry faster than she could take them there herself was at hand, thanks to Julian's messenger birds. Or so she assumed. There was no knowing without samples to send, and she had yet to solve the riddle of making the birds fly to the correct person.

A timid knock sounded at the door. Arabella shook her head to clear her thoughts.

"Who is it?" she called out.

"It's Sally, mum," one of the housemaids replied from behind the closed door. "Lord Plunkett-Nelson was wondering if you would be joining the table for breakfast or if you were still feeling poorly?"

Arabella sighed. The evening before, the rain began in earnest shortly after they had hiked back to the small open chaise. They'd arrived back from their experience at Molly's cottage soaked to the skin and deeply shaken. She and the other ladies had excused themselves from dinner and took soup, bread, and tea in their rooms. But there was only so long she could avoid Lord Plunkett-Nelson. Sooner or later, she would have to face the baron and the reckoning over raiding his larder.

"I'll be down in a moment," Arabella replied. "Is there anyone else at the table?"

"Your sister has promised to come along in a moment. Your…" Sally paused. "Helpers? Are here at the door. Lord Plunkett-Nelson and Master Julian are at the table. They said they would wait for the ladies to eat."

Arabella cringed. She briefly considered claiming a sudden new headache. Then she straightened her shoulders and drew up her courage, leaving the shelter of the bedroom for whatever awaited her at the breakfast table. It was not as if she had not faced down dangerous men before.

Rowena joined her as she strode down the hall. Eliza and Sarah followed in silence, keeping their own council.

"How bad do you think it will be?" Rowena murmured as they descended the stairs.

"He's waiting for us to begin eating," Arabella said.

Rowena winced.

When they entered the breakfast room, they discovered Lord Plunkett-Nelson and Julian perusing folios of papers while they sipped tea in what appeared to be companionable silence. Arabella and Rowena exchanged nervous glances as they took their seats. The sounds of Eliza and Sarah moving their chairs to sit seemed unbearably loud in the stillness. Arabella laid her napkin in her lap. She accepted tea from the maid as she scrutinized Julian and his uncle, looking for any clue about what was to come. Finally, Lord Plunkett-Nelson straightened his papers and handed them off to a taciturn fellow hovering behind him, while Julian did the same. Arabella did not recognize the dour-faced man.

"My apologies, ladies," Lord Plunkett-Nelson said with a jolly smile. "My Emmeline used to scold me so when I brought papers to the table. But there is just so much to be done." He chuckled.

"I imagine it is quite a job to manage an estate of this size," Arabella said. Could it be possible that the Lord of the Manor was not upset over the kitchen raid? She caught Julian's eye. He winked at her, but he said nothing.

"Very much so," Lord Plunkett-Nelson said. He gestured to the servants to bring the breakfast dishes. "And there are my lands in England, as well. Something always needs tending to." He spooned beans onto his plate with obvious relish.

"What happened?" Arabella mouthed to Julian while Lord Plunkett-Nelson was distracted with the beans.

"No need to be so secretive." Lord Plunkett-Nelson winked at Arabella. "Julian told me exactly what you rascals were up to." Arabella let out a startled gasp then swallowed hard.

"He did?" She crumpled her napkin in her lap under the table.

"I can't say that I was thrilled initially when I heard about you raiding my kitchen," Lord Plunkett-Nelson said. "But after Julian explained the whole plan to me, I saw the wisdom of the action."

"The wisdom of the action?" Arabella looked to Rowena, who shrugged.

Lord Plunkett-Nelson favored Arabella with a fond smile. "You poor thing, you must still be exhausted from your efforts yesterday. Have some more tea." He gestured for the maid to refill Arabella's cup. "Don't forget to clean your plate!" He wagged his fork at her. "You'll need your energy to finish the experiments."

"Finish the experiments?" Arabella threw a helpless look at Julian.

Julian cleared his throat. "I had to tell Uncle everything, Arabella. Having such a well-connected man on our side is a must if we are going to succeed."

Arabella tamped down her frustration at Julian. "How much of everything is everything?"

"Well, of course, I didn't bore him with the details of the chemistry or the mechanics," Julian chortled.

"I would have listened," Lord Plunkett-Nelson murmured with another fond smile for his nephew.

"But I told Uncle Sas all about the encouraging results you've had working with your brother to solve the potato blight and the strides we've made with the messenger birds so we can get the samples to him faster. How this will be the proof of concept for our messenger business." Julian paused. He locked gazes with Arabella, his eyes pleading for understanding, but for what, Arabella wasn't sure.

Julian swallowed hard. "And I told him about our plans to wed if we're able to establish our messenger business so we can support ourselves and not be a burden to the family."

Her fork clattered onto her plate.

"Plans to wed?" she choked. Arabella felt as if the world dipped and swayed around her. She clutched the edge of the table with one hand. While she'd tentatively touched on the topic of matrimony with her sisters and her imagination, she'd never dared do so with Julian.

"I must say," Lord Plunkett-Nelson said, seemingly oblivious to the blood leaving Arabella's face. "I am quite impressed with your practicality, my dear. It's a laudable quality so often absent in young ladies."

"But you would forgive her even if she were rash, wouldn't you, Uncle Sas?" Julian said. He locked eyes with Arabella again. "Uncle Sas is always more forgiving of family," he said firmly.

"Ah, I… suddenly…" Arabella stammered. She'd never quite imagined being proposed to in such a way. It was intoxicating to feel wanted but infuriating to not have her opinion considered. "Lord Plunkett-Nelson, if you'll excuse me…" she began to rise.

"No, my dear, you must call me Uncle Sas now." He waved her back into her seat. "After all, we're to be family! I can understand you're upset that Julian spilled your little secret. But there's only a few of us here. I'm sure we can all hold our tongues." He reached across the breakfast table and patted Arabella's hand. "I promise we'll have a grand party to present this blessing to society. For now, it will just be between us, the family."

"You're too kind, Lord… Uncle Sas," Arabella murmured as she sank back into her seat.

Rowena leaned over and whispered into her ear, "I can't wait until Mother hears about this."

"Mother will hear about nothing," Arabella hissed back.

"But before we may be wed," Julian cut in. "We must finish the blight cure and establish the messenger service."

"Indeed, indeed," Lord Plunkett-Nelson rumbled. "What do you need from me?"

"First, we need samples of the soil and of every part of the blighted plants." Arabella pushed aside her own feelings for the good of the mission at hand, frowning as she glanced out the window. "But clearly, we cannot secure them today."

"Couldn't we send someone to fetch them for us?" Lord Plunkett-Nelson asked. He sopped up egg yolk with his bread.

"Who would you trust with such a task?" Julian asked.

Lord Plunkett-Nelson shrugged. "Mr. Yates, most likely."

"No." Arabella snapped. "Out of the question. I do not trust him in the slightest."

"Nor do I," Eliza agreed. Rowena and Sarah murmured likewise.

Lord Plunkett-Nelson furrowed his brow in puzzlement. "What's wrong with Mr. Yates?"

"He hates witches, for one," Sarah said. "Not to mention his lack of charity. He tried to stop us from taking the food to the cottars."

"He's been terribly rude to all of us since we got here." Arabella resisted blurting out Eliza's suspicions that he might lack a soul. "I wouldn't put it past him to attempt sabotage on our work." Her eyes flashed as she lifted her chin.

"Oh, surely it can't be that bad," Lord Plunkett-Nelson huffed. "Mr. Yates has been with me for years, very loyal. His father served my father. He's quite nearly family."

"And how many witches have you had in Louth Hall while Mr. Yates has been in your employ?" Eliza asked.

Lord Plunkett-Nelson frowned. "You would be the first."

Eliza sipped her tea and raised her eyebrow.

"We'll gather our own samples, thank you," Arabella said. "Hopefully, tomorrow will be dry."

"In the meantime, we need to refine the messenger birds further," Julian said. "I've already implemented your earlier suggestions, but I haven't been able to run any trials yet."

"We may not have time for long test flights," Arabella said, shaking her head. "We can't take days and days assessing how quickly the springs will run out. We must get the samples to Henry as soon as possible."

Julian nodded. "I don't like sending them out without being absolutely sure of how they will perform, but..." He sighed. "We do still need to resolve the issue of making sure the bird gets to the right person. It doesn't matter how far the bird can fly if it won't reach Henry in the end."

"We'll work on that today," Arabella said with a sharp nod. "We haven't a moment to waste."

After breakfast, Lord Plunkett-Nelson disappeared into his office, and Julian led the ladies back to his workshop. He went right to his workbench and lifted up a new bird with both hands for Arabella to see. It was larger than the one he showed her upon her arrival. It was almost the size of a gull, with a wingspan to match.

"As you can see," he said. "I've put together a larger carrying cavity to accommodate the samples, longer wings for gliding to conserve spring energy, and changed out the gem eyes for etching to lighten the weight. Now, if we can just…"

Arabella cut him off, crossing her arms across her chest. "Before any of that happens, we must discuss precisely what you told your uncle. In great detail." When Julian didn't start speaking immediately, she began tapping her foot.

"Ah yes, well…" Julian blushed and stared at his shoes. "I had rather hoped that would blow over."

"What do you mean, *blow over*?" Arabella snapped. The frustration she'd forced down swiftly grew into anger. "This is not some silly argument about whether to serve guests chicken or fish at dinner. You told your uncle we are getting married!"

Eliza and Sarah settled onto the settee while Rowena perched herself on the battered armchair.

"This is almost as good as a play," Rowena stage-whispered to the Guardians. Sarah snickered.

"I had a good reason!" Julian blurted.

"Oh really? And what would that be, pray tell?" Arabella pursed her lips.

"Uncle Sas is very forgiving of family members. Family is very important to him." Julian ran his thumb down one of the bird's seams. "So, if he thought you were family or about to *become* family, he would forgive or overlook anything… bizarre you might do in pursuit of curing the blight and helping the cottars. If he didn't think you might be family, he could ask you to leave. I didn't know if you had anywhere else safe to go." Julian's voice dropped to a whisper. "And I didn't want you to leave."

Arabella rubbed her temples. It was indeed a sensible plan. She just wished she hadn't been caught unawares. "As good a reason as that is, you should have warned me! A gentleman would have sent a note with one of the maids!"

Julian looked up through his lashes with a twinkle in his eye. "I promise to do better next time."

"Next time?" Arabella huffed. "What makes you think there will be a next time?"

"Well, if we are to be wed…" Julian spread his hands out.

"Oh! You are impossible!" Arabella stamped her foot. Behind her, Sarah, Eliza, and Rowena tried unsuccessfully to contain their laughter. Arabella whirled on her sister and the Guardians. "This is not funny!" she snapped.

"I beg to differ," Sarah said as she tried to catch her breath. "This is highly entertaining."

Arabella pinched her lips together. "I'm so glad I can be a source of amusement for you."

"Yes, thank you," Rowena giggled. "It is very kind of you to provide entertainment. Things can be quite dull in the country."

At that, Rowena and the Guardians broke out into raucous guffaws.

"I am surrounded by impossible people," Arabella muttered to herself.

"I really am sorry, Arabella," Julian said softly as the laughter died down. "I truly only meant to protect and help you."

"For one, I don't need protecting. I have a Guardian for that," Arabella sniffed. "For the other, it would have been better if you had discussed your plans with me first. You could have spoiled something I had planned."

Julian paled. "Did I? Did I ruin anything for you?"

Arabella lifted her chin. "That remains to be seen. I may be able to work with the position you have left me in, but I must know everything you told your uncle."

"Yes, so…" Julian blew out his breath. "I told Uncle Sas that you and your brother had been working on a cure for the blight and that you've had some promising results. Uncle Sas was very impressed with how levelheaded you are, working with a mundane person rather than prolonging a problem trying to demonstrate the superiority of magic."

"But Henry and I have not conducted any experiments, Julian," Arabella said, exasperated. "He only suggested that he might be able to try something, perhaps draw in some of his more horticulturally inclined friends."

"Yes, yes, I know," Julian went on. "But you don't know Uncle Sas like I do. I'm trying to make him feel more kindly toward you so that you wouldn't have any more trouble than necessary. I've always found him easier to deal with if I soothe his ego and play to his bias."

"You mean, you get what you want if you manipulate him?" Rowena put in. She leaned forward on her elbows and frowned.

"I'm sure he didn't mean it like that…" Arabella said, her ire at Julian already fading. He was only trying to help. Given their budding romance, marriage would not be out of the question in due course of time. She was sure he'd make a proper proposal when the time was right.

"No. No, Rowena's right," Julian said. His brow puckered. "It just sounds a bit more malicious the way she put it." He looked over at Rowena, his eyes pleading. "Yes, I do manipulate my uncle, but I would never try to hurt him or make him do anything that was truly against his morals or ethics. I love my uncle, and I respect him deeply."

Rowena narrowed her eyes as she leaned back in the chair. "I'm having my doubts. Do you always manipulate the people you claim to care for? Or should I be wary for my sister?"

Julian paled and swallowed hard.

"Rowena!" Arabella said sharply. "I'm sure Julian would never do anything to hurt me." She turned back to Julian before Rowena could say anything in reply. "Was that everything? Is there anything else you told your uncle?"

"I told him that you were trying to be sensible about finances and that you did not want to wed without our business being on sure footing so we could support ourselves." He glanced at Rowena, his face miserable. "Because you have so many sisters, and you're the youngest. I said, there's not much family money for you."

Rowena drew herself up straight, her face full of fury. Arabella held out her palm to forestall the explosion. Julian would face her umbrage first.

"The Sortilege family of Blackstone House is in no way financially embarrassed. Our House can support all of her daughters and support them well." Arabella informed him, her voice taut with her own reawakened anger. "Further, I am my own witch, and I can make my own way in the world. I have no need for my mother or a husband to care for me. I am not a mundane woman." She lifted her chin a notch, her eyes blazing.

"There is nothing mundane about you, Arabella," Julian murmured. "Even without magical powers, you are far from ordinary."

Arabella's shoulders relaxed a little.

"I'm sorry if I offended your independence," Julian said. "As I said, I was only trying to put you in the best possible light with my uncle, and he does have certain expectations about the fairer sex."

Arabella waved off his apology. Holding on to her anger over how mundane men perceived the fragility of women was not practical. "Done is done. At least I know what the playing field is now." She looked thoughtful for a moment. "And you may have given us an out from our sham engagement. If we don't show financial success rather quickly, you can always tell your uncle we broke it off."

"Sham engagement?" Julian looked stricken.

"Well, I can't consider it a real engagement when you've never asked me, now can I?" Arabella said. She felt her heart soften. There was no reason to hold on to her ill will when he hadn't meant any harm, and marriage sounded like a charming possibility so long as he asked first. "And there's no ring! How am I supposed to brag about my engagement in society without a ring?"

"A ring, of course," Julian smiled. "You should always have a ring."

Rowena glared at Julian, her jaw tight. She seemed on the verge of saying something, but there was a knock at the workroom door. Sally let herself in when Julian called for her to enter.

"Master Julian, Ladies." Sally bobbed a curtsy. "There's a visitor for Miss Arabella and Miss Rowena. She said she needs to see you right away."

The witches all exchanged glances. "Is it Deirdre?" Arabella asked.

"No, ma'am," Sally said. She blushed. "I'm sorry, but I've forgotten her name. It just went clear out of my head."

"That's alright," Arabella said kindly. "I'm sure she'll introduce herself properly when we meet her. Will you lead the way?"

"But the birds!" Julian sputtered. "We need to work on the birds!"

"And we will, Julian," Arabella soothed. "But we can't leave a visitor waiting when she's been out in such awful weather." Arabella gestured to the grey day outside.

"Find a place to put another one of those power springs while we're gone," murmured Arabella as she patted his shoulder. "The bird has to go all the way to London."

CHAPTER XVIII

*An Unexpected Guest Arrives
Bearing Gifts and Promises of Aid*

ARABELLA AND ROWENA FOLLOWED SALLY DOWN THE HALL. THE MAID chattered to them the whole way to the kitchen. Eliza and Sarah followed quietly at their heels, like ghosts.

"Usually, Mr. Yates would be the one to handle a caller for a guest, but he's in the Lord's office. Has been for a while. They usually don't stay locked up together that long. Bonnie said she heard raised voices, though, while she was dusting the banisters near his office. His Lordship must be upset about something. So, anyway, I let the young lady in, but Cook was passing through the grand foyer, and she said she, the young lady that is, was her cousin, so she took her off to the kitchen so she could get warm and have a spot of tea in comfort. I hope you don't mind seeing her in the kitchen. You ladies strike me as sensible and not needing high airs at all. And here we are." Sally led the way into the kitchen.

"Did she take a breath at all the whole way here?" Rowena murmured.

Arabella blinked. "I don't think she did."

Perched on a stool next to the high stone-topped table where Cook rolled out dough sat a plump little witch with deep red curls peeking out of the edges of her cap. She was just lifting a steaming cup of tea to her lips when they walked in.

"Oh! There you are!" She set her cup down and hopped down off her stool. She bobbed a curtsy. "The daughters of the Grande Dame," she said in a voice full of wonder. "You're just as lovely as Deirdre said you were."

"You are too kind," Arabella said. "Please, do sit. You came a long way in the rain. You must be chilled through, you poor thing!"

"Ah, yes, 'tis lovely to rest my feet." She settled back onto the stool, then hopped right back up. "Oh! But I haven't properly introduced myself!" She bobbed another curtsey. "Aurienne Healy, if you please, of House Realta and cousin to Deirdre on my father's side."

"And cousin to me on her mother's side," Cook said with a smile as she laid out four more cups of tea. "It's lovely to be around people I can be open about my kin with." She gave a contented sigh as she turned back to the stove.

Aurienne took in Eliza and Sarah. Her mouth formed a little o. "And Guardians... I've never seen a Guardian with my own eyes. We did have one of our House picked up by your lot about ten years ago. I was away that day. Poor little Mary, her first manifestation of power was quite upsetting. She frightened everyone near out of their wits, especially herself. I've always hoped she's done well, but we've barely heard a word from her since."

"Mary Healy?" Eliza asked as she stirred sugar into her cup.

"Yes, ma'am," Aurienne said.

"She is quite strong," Eliza said. "And her power came on young for her type of expertise. Her training has been rather intense." She smiled at Aurienne. "But that's no excuse to ignore her family. I'll encourage her to write more when I get back to London."

"Thank you, that would be lovely," Aurienne said. "Her mother worries about her so."

Sally pulled up two more stools to the table. Eliza and Sarah leaned against the counter next to the sink to enjoy their tea and observe.

"I'd best be off to my other duties," Sally said with a little wave as she hustled out of the kitchen.

Arabella and Rowena settled themselves onto the stools Sally had brought.

Arabella inhaled the fragrant steam rising from her cup. "Oh my, but this smells just delightful!"

Cook smiled as she laid a plate of scones and a pot of gooseberry jam in front of them as well. "The Master insists on Ceylon, but Darjeeling seems so much richer to me. It's nice to see someone else appreciate it. Shall I make sure we always have a stock?" she asked with a twinkle in her eye.

Arabella blushed and dropped her eyes. It seemed word of Julian's marriage scheme had already escaped the breakfast table. "You don't have to make a special effort just for me."

Cook patted her hand. "I may not have to, but it's a pleasure to do for someone who appreciates your efforts." She slipped Arabella a wink. "And for someone who keeps the true old ways to care for the land and her people."

She fixed herself a cup and nodded toward the battered armchair in the corner by the door into the kitchen. "I'll just give you ladies some privacy. I'll let you know if anyone is coming."

"Well, that's an unexpected blessing," Rowena murmured as she sipped her tea.

Aurienne nodded. "Margaret gets a hard time from the rest of the mundane family for keeping in touch with me, and of course, she can't say a word about me in front of Mr. Yates." She shuddered.

"Yes," Arabella said. "We gathered that Mr. Yates is… difficult about witches."

"That's an understatement," Aurienne muttered. She plucked a scone from the plate.

"He may be more than just a difficult mundane man," Eliza cautioned. "We have recent reason to believe that preternatural forces may be involved with his hateful manner."

"You've seen something amiss with his aura as well?" Aurienne turned to Eliza sharply.

Eliza nodded. "Auras are part of my specialty. But even with my additional training, I can't quite figure why his aura isn't clear. I'm certain he's dangerous, but I'm not quite sure how and casting false accusations when the Lord of the Manor trusts him may cause more harm than good."

Aurienne sighed. "I'm relieved that it's not just me that sees it. My skills in that area aren't strong, but I can see enough to know he's more trouble than an average man. We are watching him carefully." Aurienne turned back to the table.

Arabella waited until their guest had enjoyed a bite of her scone before she spoke of the business that brought Aurienne through the rain.

"I suppose since you know Deirdre that the message you bear hails from her?" Arabella asked.

Aurienne nodded. "Yes, messages and a gift." She nudged a basket on the floor by her feet with her toe.

"We should probably send back word about the business yesterday to Deirdre," Rowena said. "It wouldn't do for her to have no warning."

"You mean about the business with Molly's husband, Jack? Him threatening you and all?" Aurienne asked. "Deirdre knows. She spoke to Molly after Jack went to bed. He's more bark than bite, but he's still a beast, so we're careful about him."

Arabella blinked, startled. "Yes. It just happened yesterday, before it started raining. And it's been raining ever since. How do you know already?"

Aurienne chuckled. "I suppose we're a bit more used to hardships here in the countryside. City witches are a bit soft, especially English city witches."

Arabella frowned as she swirled her tea in her cup.

"I meant no offense," Aurienne said quickly. "Just that me and Deirdre went out in the rain during the night to gather the samples of dirt and plants you said you needed to find a cure for the blight. And I didn't think you would be able..." She half-smiled and shrugged.

Arabella gasped. "Digging in the dirt in the dark in the middle of that horrid rainstorm!"

"And with *that man* sleeping just a few yards away!" Rowena gulped.

"It was just a little rain. We're not made of sugar. We won't melt." Aurienne shook her head, waving away their alarm. "And Jack is a heavy sleeper. You could run a four-in-hand down the lane outside his house and he'd not rouse."

"So, you have the samples we need?" Arabella said eagerly.

"Indeed, I do," Aurienne said. "That's one of the presents I mentioned." She gave a firm nod.

"That is an immense help. Thank you, Aurienne." Arabella turned to Rowena. "Now we just have to get the messenger birds settled, and we can get the samples to Henry!"

Rowena frowned over her tea. "Assuming those contraptions work."

"I'm sure they will." Arabella waved Rowena's negativity away. "Julian is brilliant."

Rowena rolled her eyes.

"I don't know what messenger birds you're talking about," Aurienne said. "But Deirdre said that she and Kiera found two half-wild ravens who would be willing to carry a message for you as far as your ancestral home in Boscastle. But they'll not go as far as London. Oh, and Tilly is willing to loan you her jackdaw if he could be of any use. He can't go as far, but he's fully witch-trained, so he is reliable. Deirdre said she'd send them over as soon as the rain stops."

"The ravens could carry messages and samples to Vivienne and Mother," Arabella said thoughtfully, tapping her fingertip on her lower lip. "If we have enough samples to spare, that is. And we need to tell them we're coming home. I must convince Mother we need to take more action here. We can't continue to abandon our Sisters."

"Vivienne may be able to perceive something other witches have missed," Rowena agreed. "Her earth talents are considerable." She sipped her tea.

"Thank you so much, Aurienne," Arabella burbled. "You've been such an enormous help, and we can't thank you enough."

"I do have one more thing for you," Aurienne said. She reached into a pocket under her cloak and produced two grimy envelopes. She slid them across the table to Arabella and Rowena. "As Kiera promised, here are the letters that arrived for your mother and your aunts after the... unfortunate incident."

Arabella stared down with wide eyes at the grubby envelopes on the table. They might have once been ivory, but thirty years had yellowed them. Streaks of grime from their travels crisscrossed the thick, heavy paper. They were addressed in an elegant, looping hand, one to her mother and one collectively to her aunts. Arabella picked up the one addressed to her aunts with inquisitive fingers, gently turning it over. There was no return address. But there was a black wax seal on the flap. The seal was chipped on one side, but it still adhered well to the paper showing that it had not been tampered with in the intervening years. Curiosity fluttered in her belly. She squinted at it, trying to read the crest, but the light in the kitchen was just not good enough to make out what it was pressed into the dark wax.

"Thank you," Arabella breathed, turning the letter over and over in her hands. Rowena picked up the one addressed to their mother.

"I wonder what it says…"

"We'll have to wait to find out, I guess." Arabella sighed. As much as she wanted to know their contents, neither letter was addressed to her.

"Why?" Rowena frowned.

"They're not our letters, silly," Arabella laughed. "We can't just go poking around into someone else's private correspondence."

"Really, Ari." Rowena pursed her lips. "Aunt Lenore and Aunt Lorena are dead. I hardly think they'll object to us opening their letter."

Arabella nodded slowly. What Rowena said made sense, but she still felt hesitant. "Mother, however, would no doubt object to us snooping in her correspondence, or theirs, even if it is older than we are."

"True," Rowena said. "So, we'll leave her letter alone and open the other. I'm positively perishing of curiosity."

"Later, when we have some privacy," Arabella murmured as she tucked the letter into the pocket of her skirts. She plucked Mother's letter from Rowena's fingers and tucked it into her pocket with its sister.

CHAPTER XIX

*A Truce Is Made, and Arabella Learns
the Secret of Talking to Birds*

ROWENA TROTTED DOWN THE HALL IN ARABELLA'S WAKE. "I DON'T SEE why you want to delay reading the letter. It's very selfish of you." Eliza and Sarah followed after, Sarah with the basket of samples on her hip.

Arabella stopped and put her hands on her hips. "I'm being selfish? Is there a reason you want to read the letter, beyond your own entertainment?"

Rowena had the good grace to flush. "Well, I…" She blew out a deep breath and stared down at her shoes.

"Exactly," Arabella said. She started down the hall again. "We'll look at the seal on Lenore and Lorena's letter after dinner tonight, I promise. It may offer us some clues. But we have to get those birds off with the samples as soon as possible."

Arabella, Rowena, and their Guardians found Julian still in his workshop, hunched over a worktable with magnifying goggles protruding from his face. He did not raise his head when he heard the sound of footsteps.

"It's too early for luncheon, Sally," he said without lifting his head. "And I'm not hungry even if it were time. I've almost got this third spring fitted. I'm near certain it will go all the way to London!"

"All the way to London?" Arabella asked, her eyes sparkling with amusement. "That is good news, indeed."

Julian's head jerked up. He almost fell off his stool as he startled backward at a suddenly magnified Arabella. He fumbled the goggles off his face, nearly dropping them several times.

"Arabella! Oh! I didn't know it was you," Julian said. "So sorry. Did you have a pleasant conversation with your visitor?"

"We certainly did. It was most productive," Arabella enthused. "Deirdre and Kiera collected all the samples we need last night, in the rain." She gestured for Sarah to put the heavy basket containing the samples onto a clear corner of the workbench. "And as soon as the rain clears, we'll have two ravens and a jackdaw at our disposal."

"Why would we need them?" Julian muttered absently as he peeled back the cloth cover on the basket. He frowned down at the crockery filled with damp earth nestled to thick handfuls of mottled greenery that covered half a dozen wizened diseased potatoes at the bottom. He wrinkled his nose. "I didn't know diseased potatoes had such a stench. We will have to transfer the soil into something else. Crockery is far too heavy and fragile, even if these containers were of an appropriate size."

Rowena leaned over Julian's bench and sniffed, considering the mass of brass and wire with a cold eye. "We need the living birds because your contraptions might fail."

Julian's face fell as he turned to Rowena. "You expect me to fail?" He turned to Arabella, desperately searching her face. "Do you expect me to fail?"

Arabella gasped. "Of course not!"

Rowena crossed her arms over her chest. Pursing her lips, she said, "Just a moment ago when you thought we were Sally come to fetch you to luncheon, you said you weren't completely certain the bird would make it to London. And if it falls out of the sky into a patch of heather in the countryside, how will it finish the trip? Do you think some shepherd will find it and know to deliver it to Henry Leyden in London?"

"I said I was *near* certain it would make it." Julian pressed his lips together. "Don't misrepresent me."

Rowena threw her hands into the air. "Ugh! Twist the words all you want, but it means the same thing. You do not know for certain this thing," Rowena jabbed her finger at the workbench, "Will make it all the way to London."

"Then send your precious ravens," Julian retorted.

Rowena deflated. "They definitely won't go as far as London." She grimaced. "Deirdre and Kiera could only get them to agree to go as far as Boscastle."

"Hah! The unreliability of the flesh rears its ugly head again!" He took a breath to continue.

"Enough!" Arabella shouted. "Enough from both of you!" She put her fists on her hips. "It has become painfully obvious that the two of you don't get along. But we don't have time for such childish behavior. We have work to do, and the two of you will make an effort to be civil until that work is done." She gave both of them a stern look. Neither would meet her gaze. "Have I made myself clear?"

Rowena blinked. "My goodness, you sound like Mother."

Arabella tilted her head to the side, her face humorless.

"Fine, fine," Rowena sighed. "I'll hold my tongue."

"I apologize for my rudeness," Julian said. "I will endeavor to not let my emotions get the best of me again."

Eliza called out from the window. "It looks like the rain is beginning to ease. Perhaps Rowena and I should go outside to wait for Deirdre and Kiera's friends?" She gave Rowena and Julian a severe look. "It will be most difficult for you to argue with one another if you're not in the same room."

"Arabella, would you be so kind as to examine the inner workings before I close the cavity up?" Julian said. "Perhaps you could confirm that it will make it to London."

"Julian…" There was a note of warning in Arabella's voice. Rowena and Eliza swept out of the room. Rowena's jaw was tight, but she did not say a word.

Scarcely half an hour later, Eliza and Rowena returned to the workshop with two ravens and the promised jackdaw, the latter perched primly on Rowena's left shoulder. On his left leg, he had a jaunty bow of bright blue ribbon. The ravens, on the other hand, seemed determined to remind everyone present that they were not fully tamed. Eliza entered the workshop with one raven on each shoulder, but in the space of a breath, they launched themselves into the air. They swooped around the high ceiling, examining the workbenches below them as they flew. They alighted on a disused workbench holding a variety of glassware and proceeded to hop about, cawing at their reflections in the glass.

"Oh dear, oh dear." Julian raced to the workbench with his hands outstretched. He stopped cold when one of the ravens lowered its head, extended its wings, and clacked its beak at him. Julian swallowed hard and turned his pale face to the witches in the room. "What do I do? How do I tell them not to damage my experiments?"

"I've been led to believe that speaking is the usual way for humans to communicate intentions and wishes," Rowena said airily as she glided by.

Julian narrowed his eyes. "Yes, yes, of course. But how do I make them understand that?" He gestured to the raven, who was delicately tapping its beak against the tapered neck of a laboratory flask.

"Darlings," Rowena sang as she approached the workbench. The two ravens immediately turned to her and tilted their heads to the side. "This human," she gestured to Julian, "is protective of his things. Please be dears and don't damage them." One of the ravens let out a gurgling croak, rising in pitch.

"Yes," Rowena responded. "I promise there will be food soon."

The two ravens followed her, hopping from workbench to workbench as she made her way to the seating area at the far end of the room. They did not break or even disturb anything. Rowena settled herself gracefully in the battered armchair.

"Julian," she said, a forced smile on her face. "Perhaps you can make some arrangements for food for our guests? They are about to embark on difficult flights after all."

"What do they eat?" Julian looked perplexed.

"Almost anything, they are omnivorous," Rowena said. One of the ravens croaked at her from the arm of the settee. She nodded. "Some bread and meat would be lovely, and perhaps some berries if they are available. His mate loves berries." The raven perched on the back of the armchair ruffled her wings and cawed softly.

Arabella settled next to the raven on the settee arm. "Do they have names?"

"Not that we can pronounce," Rowena said. "If a bird is fully bonded to and trained by a witch, she usually gives them a human name." She gestured with her open hand to the jackdaw pacing the edge of the small carpet in the sitting area. Every few steps, he plunged his beak into the knotted fringe, hunting for something the humans couldn't see. "This is James." At the sound of his human name, the jackdaw looked up and made a cackling noise.

"Should we give names to the ravens?" Arabella asked.

Sarah shook her head. "That would be rude. If they wanted a human name, they would have bonded with a witch by now. Best to respect their independence, or you'll get bit." The raven next to Arabella clacked its beak and croaked in a way that almost sounded like laughter.

"Right then," Arabella said. Her eyes widened. "No human names for the ravens. What do we do with them now?"

"I thought first we'd send James with a message for Bathsheba," Rowena said. "We'll need to get home as quickly as possible so we can consult with Henry on his research. And since we don't know where she is and when she and the *Kittiwake* might be available, the sooner we find a place in their schedule, the better."

"Indeed," Arabella murmured.

"Then we need to rig the ravens up for the long flight to Boscastle," Rowena continued. "They'll need some sort of carrying pouch for the samples. We can't just strap them to their legs like we would with a paper message."

"My father taught me some leatherwork before I attempted the Trials," Sarah revealed. "Said he wanted me to have honest work." She looked to Julian. "If you have leatherworking tools and scraps of leather, I think I could put something together."

Julian nodded and motioned for Sarah to follow him to an old armoire tucked in a dusty corner of the workshop. They put their heads together, talking quietly as they rummaged through the contents for the things Sarah needed.

"Julian?" Arabella called out. "Where might I find paper and ink? We need to write out the note to Bathsheba."

"The writing desk behind the settee. You should be able to find what you need in the cubby holes," Julian called back over his shoulder. He muttered to himself, "I don't think the ink is dried out... Can't remember when I used it last."

By the time Sally brought a small tray of food for the birds, Arabella and Rowena had settled on the message for Bathsheba, blotted the ink dry, and curled the paper into the tiniest roll they could manage, sealed with a smear of red wax. They waited until James had had his fill of bread and berries before they tied the note to his leg.

"Alright," Eliza said. She patted her lap. James hopped up, looking at her expectantly. "Arabella, pay attention. This is how I instruct a messenger bird. First, you need physical contact." She gently cupped her hands around James's head. "Then I pull energy from the ether as I construct a clear picture of the recipient in my mind's eye."

Arabella felt a tug on her metaphysical senses as Eliza started drawing the energy to herself. She stifled a gasp, not wanting to distract the Guardian. It felt exactly like the magic she used to unstick watches, to move the gears in Julian's owl at the Club. How was this possible? There were no machines involved. Arabella forced herself to breathe.

"This is where it gets more difficult," Eliza whispered as she closed her eyes. The very air around her throbbed with energy. Arabella clapped her hand over her mouth. She could see the sparkling energy she saw with machines gathering around Eliza's hands and in the middle of her forehead, right where her third eye would be. Rowena sat up straight in the armchair, concern for Arabella written all over her face.

"How a witch gets the image from her mind to the bird can be as individual as the witch herself," Eliza went on. "You might have to try different things when you work with the mechanical birds. For me, I imagine opening the bird's third eye very gently." James grew very still in her lap. He didn't even seem like he was breathing. "Then I place the image I created in my own mind's eye in his." A shudder ran down the length of the jackdaw's body. Arabella saw his whole head suddenly sparkle with the glow of magic.

Eliza opened her eyes. She blew out a big breath, and her hands dropped away from James. She sagged back on the settee. The jackdaw fluffed his feathers and flapped his wings. He shook his head in an almost human gesture as if to clear it.

"And that's it," Eliza said with a small smile. She looked down at James. She softly caressed his back. "I hope that wasn't too hard on you. Do you know who to find?"

James bobbed his head up and down, clicking his beak together.

"Alright then, we'd best get you on your way." Eliza held out her hand and helped James onto her shoulder. "I'll be right back. I have to get him to an open window or door," she said to Arabella. "We can discuss any questions you have after you've had a moment to think." Arabella nodded dumbly as she watched Eliza walk away.

Rowena shifted from the armchair to the settee. "Are you alright?" She whispered in Arabella's ear. "What happened?"

Arabella blinked and shook her head. She lifted her fingertips to her temples and massaged them. "I'm not sure. Let me catch my breath and we can talk."

By the time Eliza returned, Arabella had recovered herself a bit. She still felt shaken, but she could put coherent words together again.

"Remind me again what magic looks like to you?" Arabella asked Rowena.

"We've been over this before when you first saw the machines," Rowena said with a sigh. "Everything sparkles. It's golden."

Arabella turned to Eliza. "And you? What do you see?"

"Golden sparkles, just like Rowena does. Every witch sees that," Eliza said.

"I saw it again." Arabella whirled back to Rowena. "I saw it in Eliza's hands, then her mind's eye, then around James's head."

Rowena's brow furrowed in thought, then her eyebrows shot up. "After a witch experiences her first power, it opens her up, and sometimes she can start accessing other kinds of magic that were closed to her before."

Eliza leaned forward on her elbows on her knees. "Yes, it's something we try to stimulate in Guardians during their training. Sometimes we're out in the field with little assistance, so having more types of magic at our disposal can save our lives."

"You mean, you could do something completely outside of your bailiwick?" Arabella asked. "Could you manipulate the wind like Bathsheba does?"

Eliza chuckled. "Not nearly as well, I'm afraid. But I have studied the principles, so if I were stuck on a very small boat on a windless day, I could, very slowly, push us to land. Eventually. It would exhaust me, but that's better than dying of thirst in the middle of the sea."

Rowena leaned forward and snatched up Arabella's hands. "You have more abilities awakening! This is wonderful!"

"I suppose…" Arabella murmured, a shocked look on her face.

"Have you had any other manifestations?" Eliza asked softly. "Or is this the first time you've experienced magic outside of machines?"

Arabella knit her brow. She squeezed Rowena's hand, then her eyes flew wide open. "After the spell sickness… no, during."

"Do you mean after you made the clock work at the Manor?" Rowena asked.

"Yes, yes," Arabella's words came in a rushing torrent. "It was at night. Grandmother came to give me a potion to help me recover. While she was mixing it, she grabbed my forehead and said I shouldn't go roaming. Not yet." Arabella looked back and forth between Rowena and Eliza. Her lips trembled. "Is that bad?"

Eliza looked thoughtful. "Not bad, just something you have to be careful about."

Rowena nodded. "It seems that you started to spontaneously astral project. It is a good skill to have, but if you're not in control of it, you could have problems." Rowena patted Arabella's hand. "We can start working on lessons right away. The good thing here is that it's known territory. We know how to teach you."

Arabella's body relaxed, then she stiffened again, jumping up from the settee.

"What's wrong?" Rowena gasped.

"I don't have time for lessons just yet," Arabella said. "We have to get the samples sent. We have to find our way home."

"But if you accidentally start to project again…"

Arabella cut Rowena off. "It hasn't happened since that night. I won't let myself get spell sick and have Grandmother feeding me potions again, not until I know what I'm doing."

By the middle of the afternoon, Arabella's back was sore, her clothes were soaked with sweat, and her stomach rebelled over missing luncheon. She gnawed at a heel of bread she snatched from the ravens' plate, giving the brass starling on the workbench in front of her an accusatory glare.

"Do you want to try one of the other birds again?" Julian asked. "The starling was my first prototype. I've made so many improvements that might make it easier."

"Perhaps we should try again tomorrow? You said you didn't want to risk spell sickness." Rowena squeezed her shoulder.

Arabella shrugged off her sister's hand. "I can do it. I won't make myself sick," she grumbled. She started pacing back and forth in front of the workbench.

"Are you sure…" Eliza began.

"I'm sure!" Arabella said with a scowl. She stopped pacing. She took a deep breath in and blew it out. "I'm sorry. I shouldn't have snapped at you. I know all of you are just trying to help."

"Yes, we are, Ari," Rowena said. "Will you take the help, please? Perhaps a hot meal and a good night's sleep will make everything clearer in the morning."

Arabella shook her head. She took a vicious bite of the bread. "I feel like I'm on the verge of solving it," she mumbled around her mouthful. She swallowed hard and looked around. "Could we get some tea? I'm parched."

"I can take care of that." Julian hurried to the door and called out to a passing housemaid.

Arabella resumed glaring at the starling. "It feels like it's right on the tip of my tongue."

Rowena joined her in glaring at the bird. She chewed her thumbnail, lost in thought. After a moment, she mumbled, "Do you want to walk me through what you've tried?"

Arabella sighed. "It's the same every time. The power feels like it's building, everything seems to be going just like it should, and then… fizzle. I can't find a mind's eye to put the picture in."

Rowena pursed her lips. "Maybe that's the problem."

Arabella rolled her eyes. "Your grasp of the obvious is phenomenal, sister dear."

"No, no," Rowena said. "Think about it. Living creatures have mind's eyes. This," she gestured to the shiny thing on the workbench, "is not a living creature. Of course, it doesn't have a mind's eye. And how can you put a picture into something that doesn't exist?"

"So, what's the solution?" Arabella said with an exasperated sigh.

"I don't know," Rowena said with a shrug. "Machines are not my field of expertise."

Sarah spoke up from the settee behind them. "But machines are *your* field of expertise, aren't they, Arabella?"

Arabella snorted. "If expertise can be considered an inexperienced blind woman trying to navigate the streets of London for the first time.

Alone." She shook her head. "I've only been around machines for a few months. What I don't know far outweighs what I do."

"But you still know more about machines than any witch on Earth, yes?" Sarah persisted.

"I suppose..."

"You made Westerfeld's machine dance. You stopped his braces from working. And you did that right as you were discovering your power," Sarah said. "You know more now than you did then. How did you do those things?"

Arabella furrowed her brow. "I just reached out into the machine and felt the magic within. I followed it and bent it."

Sarah shrugged and threw her hands up. "Have you tried that yet?"

Arabella turned back to the workbench, murmuring to herself. "No, I haven't. I kept focusing on the picture in the mind's eye."

Arabella cupped her hand on the starling's head. She let her physical eyes flutter shut and reached into the intricate inner workings of the starling with her magic. It would have been easy to lose herself in the elaborate functional art Julian had created. The beautiful light seemed to dance in each coil and spring. She felt safe, warm, and at ease. But how to help this little bird find its way? That's when she felt a tug, just a gentle pull toward the head of the bird. The compass. There was a tiny magnetic compass where a living starling's brain would be. Arabella prodded it, pushed it. She had a feeling the answer to the riddle lay there if only she could see it.

She sighed and counseled herself to be patient. She was closer to the answer now than she'd been all afternoon. She heard the scuff of a footstep behind her and caught a whiff of Julian's cologne. The corners of her mouth began to curve up just a bit as she thought of him.

The compass trembled.

Arabella's heart beat faster. She constructed a clear picture of Julian in her mind. Then she pushed that thought form toward the compass. The compass absorbed it like a sponge. Arabella's eyes flew open just in time to see the starling twirl on the workbench. Its beak pointed to where Julian fumbled through the armoire, searching for some thinner, more flexible leather for Sarah. Arabella snatched the bird up from the workbench. She clutched it to her breast.

"Julian?" Arabella's voice trembled.

"*Hhhmm*, yes?" he said absently without turning around.

"I need you to leave."

He popped around the open armoire door, his confusion evident. "I'm sorry?"

"I mean, I need you to leave the room," Arabella said. "I think I may have figured something out, and I need to test it. I need you to go somewhere else in the house that I would never guess."

A grin spread across Julian's face. "Oh, this is exciting," he said as he trotted from the room.

Arabella waited for a slow count of twenty-five, holding the starling to her breast. She could feel it quivering against her hands, insistently pulling for the door where Julian had disappeared. When she couldn't wait a moment longer, Arabella wound the starling up and let it go.

The mechanical bird sprang from her hand, tiny wings whirring. It streaked out the door. Arabella held her breath and waited.

She heard Julian before she saw him. His excited whoops echoed off the stone walls of Louth Hall, getting louder as he approached. He burst into the workroom, the quiescent brass starling in his hands.

"It found me! It found me!" he shouted. "It even chased me when I tried to fool it and walk away."

Gently depositing the motionless little bird onto the workbench, he wrapped his arms around Arabella, lifting her off her feet and twirling her.

"You did it! You did it, you brilliant, beautiful woman!" he cheered. He set her back on her feet, but he didn't let her go. Arabella trembled as they locked gazes, then her knees started to give way.

"I think I need to sit down," she gasped.

"It must be the excitement," Julian said as he guided her to the settee. "I always feel a little lightheaded when I make a discovery." He looked thoughtful for a moment. "Or it could be because I often forget to eat when I'm on the verge of a breakthrough."

Rowena knelt in front of Arabella and snatched up her sister's hands. "You're trembling!" Arabella felt warmth as Rowena close her eyes and focused her healing skills. A soft golden glow suffused their entwined fingers.

"You're not spell sick, not yet. But you're close." Rowena said as she opened her eyes. Fumbling with the tea service, she poured Arabella a fresh cup and dumped two heaping spoonfuls of sugar in. "Drink this."

Arabella's thoughts were sluggish as she forced her quivering fingers around the cup Rowena pressed into her hands. The tea sloshed as Arabella brought it to her mouth. She gulped down half the tea gratefully. "Thank you," she said in a hoarse voice.

"How could you?" Rowena hissed. "How could you do this? You promised me you wouldn't allow yourself to get spell sick!"

"I'll be fine," Arabella groaned. "Please don't be angry with me."

"There's no way you can perform this spell on the larger birds to get the samples to Henry." Rowena shook her head. "We'll just have to carry the samples ourselves when we can arrange passage on the *Kittiwake*."

"No, Ro, I'm fine." Arabella patted her sister's hand. "The final spell, the one that worked, wasn't a strain at all. I could send a whole flock all over the world without any trouble, now that I know *how* to do it. I just used so much energy trying to do it the wrong way before I figured it out. A good hot meal and some rest and I'll be ready."

"You mustn't do any more magic today," Rowena insisted. "As your older sister, I forbid it."

Arabella raised her eyebrow. "Oh, really?"

"Yes, really. If you won't take care, I'll just have to protect you from yourself."

Arabella smiled fondly at her sister. "As you wish, my sweet Rowena. We'll send the samples tomorrow."

CHAPTER XX

Wherein Hopeful Witches Cast Messages to the Wind

THE NEXT DAY DAWNED BRIGHT AND WARM, WITH ONLY A FEW FLUFFY white clouds decorating the bright blue sky. Julian was missing from the breakfast table.

"Lord Plunkett-Nelson…" Arabella began.

The lord in question chuckled and wagged his finger at her. His eyes twinkled playfully.

"Ah, yes." Arabella cleared her throat. "Uncle Sas, do you know where Julian is?"

Lord Plunkett-Nelson smiled and nodded as she spoke. He forked another thick sausage onto his plate.

"I'd imagine he's in his workshop, my dear," Lord Plunkett-Nelson said. "I learned a long time ago that when he is enmeshed in a project that it's useless to try to get him to the table. Even if you do manage it, he'll be surly the whole time. Not good company at all." He winked at Arabella. "But I imagine that is something you'll learn for yourself as time goes on."

Arabella blushed. "I suppose so." She changed the subject. "We will be releasing our first mechanical messenger birds today, Uncle Sas. We are quite excited."

"Are you sure you're ready?" Rowena asked, her brows knit with concern. "You were shaking so after that last test flight yesterday."

"I'm fine, Ro." Arabella held her hand out flat, palm down. "See? Steady as a rock."

Lord Plunkett-Nelson frowned. "You were shaking yesterday after an experiment? Do I need to call for a physician?"

"Not at all, Uncle Sas," Arabella soothed. "I was just having a bit of trouble getting the directional spell right. I was a bit overtired at the time, but I'm fine now."

"Good. It's quite agreeable to see a strong woman of sound, hardy stock," Lord Plunkett-Nelson said as he dug into his beans. "Too many delicate wilting lilies these days, I say. It does not make for strong children."

"Children?" Arabella said in a strangled voice. She'd only just become acclimated to her imaginary engagement, and now Lord Plunkett-Nelson was suggesting children.

"Yes, children," Lord Plunkett-Nelson continued as if he hadn't heard the discomfort in her voice. "It's the next logical event after a wedding."

Arabella stammered, trying to think of an appropriate way to respond. Eliza cleared her throat.

"I believe we've all had enough to eat, haven't we?" she said in an overly cheerful voice. "We wouldn't want to be weighed down right before launching such an important flight. Shall we join Julian in the workroom?"

"Yes, indeed," Sarah agreed. "I must do a fitting of the harness on the ravens before we send them off. I think I have the straps set right, but we should make sure."

The witches excused themselves from the table, thanking Lord Plunkett-Nelson for the lovely meal as they hastened from the room.

"Thank you," Arabella whispered to Eliza as they spilled into the hall. The Guardian merely winked at her.

"I'll meet you there," Rowena said. "I have to fetch the letters from my chambers to send with the samples. And don't think I've forgotten about reading Aunt Lenore and Aunt Lorena's letter. Your near spell sickness only gets you a one-night reprieve."

"I'll call the ravens down from outside," Eliza said. "And meet you in the workroom."

Arabella and Sarah did indeed find Julian hunched over his workbench, wearing his magnifying goggles, and muttering to himself. Sarah went right to the coffee table in front of the settee and set to fiddling with the straps on the leather carry pouches she'd sewed for the ravens the day before.

"We missed you at breakfast," Arabella said after she stood at Julian's shoulder for a moment. "I thought the birds were ready before dinner last night?"

"I couldn't sleep," Julian mumbled as he reached deeper into the chest cavity to tweak a spring. "I kept thinking about what Rowena said… about the bird falling out of the sky into a patch of heather and never making it to Henry." He slipped his goggles off and looked up at Arabella. "I've made sure we have two birds ready to fly. If something should happen to one, then the other can complete the delivery. I've also installed a fourth power spring in each of them to work in sequence. I am now quite confident they could fly past London if need be."

"Oh, Julian! How wonderful!" Arabella clapped her hands in delight. "You've thought of everything, haven't you?"

Julian turned back to the bench with a frown. "Probably not. This is the fastest I've ever tried to push a project to completion. I'm concerned something will go wrong."

"Everything will be fine, I'm sure of it." Arabella squeezed Julian's shoulder.

As Rowena breezed into the workroom with the letters, Arabella dropped her hand from Julian's shoulder.

"I have a letter for Mother and one for Vivienne, one for each of the ravens, then another one for Henry to tuck in with the mechanical bird," Rowena said, holding the letters up. "Do you think we should dash off a quick note for Father so he doesn't feel left out?"

Eliza entered with the ravens on her shoulders just in time to hear Rowena's question. "Do we have the time to waste to soothe an ego?" she asked.

"It wouldn't be about ego now," Arabella said. "We have two mechanical birds ready to fly to the gentlemen in London, so we'll need a letter for each bird. It only makes sense for one of them to be addressed to Father."

Rowena tapped the edge of the folded paper on her lip. "And what if Henry is away? If one of the birds can reach Father, then he can find Henry."

"Your hand is fairer than mine, Rowena," Arabella said. "Would you mind writing out the one to Father? You could copy most of Henry's letter." With a nod, Rowena scurried over to the dusty writing desk and set to work.

"Sounds like you won't be able to get the mechanical birds up for a bit," Eliza said. She turned her head and called to Sarah. "Are the pouches ready?"

Sarah looked up from the tangle of leather straps and buckles spread out in the table before her. "I think so," she said. "We need to put these on them to see if I need to make any adjustments."

The ravens took off from Eliza's shoulders and flew across the workshop to the seating area. They alighted on the table. With careful beaks and claws, they examined Sarah's handiwork. They croaked and cawed to her, and she responded in a soft voice explaining which strap went where and how the pouch would hang.

"It's rather amazing to see an animal interacting with a human as if they were intelligent," Julian said, his voice filled with wonderment.

"They *are* intelligent," Arabella huffed. "Ravens and crows are just as intelligent as most children."

"Even untamed corvids in the wild use tools and play games," Eliza added.

Julian shook his head in astonishment. "So many things to learn…"

"If you want to turn your sham engagement into a real one, you better start studying," Eliza said with a wink as she headed across the workshop to help Sarah dress the ravens for flight. "That is, if you want to fit in with her world."

Julian and Arabella both blushed.

"How soon will the mechanical birds be able to fly?" Arabella asked, quickly changing the subject.

"We really should come up with a better name for them…" he muttered to himself as he turned back to the bench. "In any case, they can fly as soon as their cargo is ready. I parceled out the samples last night." He pointed to a small pile of glass vials filled with soil and waxed canvas packets of diseased leaves and potatoes. "So as soon as

Rowena is done with the letter and you're ready to cast the spell, they can fly."

"I'm ready," Arabella said quickly. "I can't wait to see them in flight." She called over her shoulder. "Rowena…"

"I heard, you're waiting on me," Rowena said without lifting her head from her task. "I'm almost finished with the writing itself. Then I need to blot the ink. I won't be long."

"Success!" Eliza crowed. On the table between her and Sarah, one of the ravens stood fully kitted out in its flying gear. A small pouch about the size of a large man's hand nestled snugly against the bird's chest. Thin leather straps crisscrossed around his body to hold everything secure without impeding flight. The raven spread his wings for a few experimental flaps. He hopped and fluttered across the table, then turned his head to caw to his mate. She stepped forward and held her wings out slightly to make dressing her easier.

As Sarah worked the buckles, she said, "It looks like I need to nip off a bit on the ends of the straps, so we don't have excess length flopping about. But otherwise, they seem to be a perfect fit."

"If you weren't a witch, you could have a fine career as a leather worker," Arabella said with a smile.

"I'd rather be a witch, thank you," Sarah murmured as she examined the fit on both birds.

Eliza leaned over the pile of samples on the workbench. "The raven pouches are more limited in capacity than your mechanical birds. One vial of soil each, and the smallest potato packets, I would think." She rifled through the packets.

Julian leaned past her and plucked two from the pile. "These each only have one small potato; they are the lightest."

"All done!" Rowena called from the writing desk.

Arabella took a deep breath. She turned to Julian, her eyes sparkling. "Let's load them up and get these birds in the air."

Arabella ignored Mr. Yates' scowls as the high-spirited group trooped through the halls. She was not going to let his gloomy face spoil the most marvelous thing to happen to her in a long time. They tumbled out the door and onto the lawn, laughing. Arabella waved to Sally and one of the other housemaids who watched from the doorway, curious.

Eliza shaded her eyes with her hand as she looked up to the clear blue expanse. "Well, we've certainly been blessed by the weather for our endeavor."

"We should probably send the ravens first," Rowena said thoughtfully. "They might be spooked by the mechanical birds."

Sarah nodded. "Best for you to give them directions. You know your mother and sister better than we do."

Sarah and Eliza cradled the ravens against their chests like babies while Rowena cast her directional spell with each bird. They both shivered and cawed when it was done.

"You understand who to look for, darlings?" Rowena asked as she caressed their heads one last time. "You'll be careful?"

The ravens croaked their assurances to Rowena then launched themselves from Sarah and Eliza's arms. The whole group watched the ravens fly east until they lost sight of the two specks in the sky.

"I guess it's my turn," Arabella said. She blew out a deep breath. Nerves fluttered in her stomach like a whole flock of birds.

"Wind them up first, or after you've done the spell?" Julian asked.

"First, I guess?" Arabella pursed her lips. "The starling was desperate to move when I did the spell before the winding yesterday. We might not be able to contain these larger birds. I wouldn't want anyone to get hurt."

They wound the mechanical birds, then Julian and Sarah held the vibrating brass beasts, the energy of their coils barely contained. Arabella slipped the image of Henry into the compass of the bird Julian held and the image of her father into the compass of the bird Sarah held. She tried to be quick, mindful of the strain she saw in their arms.

"Done," she said softly, stepping back.

Julian and Sarah released the now-straining birds. The sun flashed on their brass wings as they leapt into the sky. Julian cried out. His hand flew to his face. When he drew it away, there was blood on his fingers.

Arabella gasped. "Julian! You're hurt!" She went to him and examined the shallow cut on his jawbone.

"It's nothing," he insisted. "One of the feather edges caught me as it launched." He pressed his hand to his jaw again. "I've been hurt worse. I almost lost a hand when I tried to build a steam horse when I was twelve." Julian laughed.

"That's not funny! Let me see it again," Arabella said.

"It's shallow. It's nothing," Julian said. But he obligingly lifted his fingers so Arabella could get a better look.

"A blood sacrifice," Sarah grunted. "Maybe this experiment will be blessed after all."

Rowena shaded her eyes. "I can't see them," she murmured. "They're already gone."

Having satisfied herself that Julian wasn't grievously injured, Arabella sighed. "What do we do now?"

"Nothing to do but wait for someone to respond to our letters," Rowena said. "We can't leave until we find Bathsheba and book passage on the *Kittiwake*."

"Perhaps now you can actually read one of those novels you brought with you." Sarah nudged Eliza with her shoulder. "I saw half your bag is full of books."

"Reading soothes me." Eliza chuckled ruefully. "I like escaping into other lives."

Everyone was quiet for a moment, looking up into the empty, brilliant sky.

"Luncheon?" Julian suggested.

"Yes, luncheon would be lovely," Arabella said. She slipped her arm through his, and they all trooped inside.

After dinner, Rowena followed Arabella to her room. They settled into the plush armchairs arranged in front of the empty fireplace.

"I hope we're gone before it's cold enough for Sally to light this for us," Arabella said with a sigh.

"I'm sure Bathsheba will get back to us at the earliest possible moment," Rowena said.

"How can you be so certain?"

"Well, if she's not interested in ingratiating herself to the newest breed of witch..." Rowena gestured to Arabella. "And she's uninterested in helping downtrodden people in distress..." She gestured broadly to the lands outside the window. "I'm fairly certain that Blackstone House money will encourage her."

Arabella frowned. "I don't like to think of her as that venal. She... Life has been cruel to her."

Rowena shrugged. "Difficult circumstances don't make you a good person. We'll see how she responds to our letter."

"You don't know..." Arabella trailed off.

"Don't know what?" Rowena furrowed her brow.

Arabella took a centering breath. "She used to be a slave in America," she said. "Her situation was horrific. Since the American Witches Council procured her passage here as a child, she's been trying to…" Arabella swallowed hard. "Purchase her relatives so she can bring them here to freedom."

Rowena gasped. "That's appalling! When did you find this out?"

"On the ship. We talked during the night after I woke from a nightmare." Arabella put her chin in her hand and stared off into the distance.

"Well, I can certainly see why you don't want to think ill of her," Rowena murmured as she smoothed the front of her skirt.

"Is the whole world this horrifying?" Arabella whispered after several long moments of silence. "Are people always taking advantage of each other? Hurting those who can't fight back just because they can? Slaves in America… The cottars here… It's all just beyond dreadful."

Rowena thought for a while. "I don't have a good answer for you, Ari. I wish I did." Her voice barely rose over the hush of the room. "It certainly seems that way sometimes. And it's all very overwhelming." Rowena leaned forward and caught Arabella in an intense stare. "But there are things we can do. We can be good people ourselves, and when we see a chance to help, we seize it."

"Like feeding people… and finding the cure for the blight?"

"Yes, precisely. And talking to Mother about protecting the Irish witches."

"Is it enough?" Arabella's voice trembled. Tears gathered in her eyes.

Rowena sighed and sank back into her chair. "It has to be. One can only do so much, and if you let yourself get paralyzed by all the wickedness of the world, then you can't even do that."

"It's like trying to stop the tide."

"Sometimes, yes."

"And I have yet to exhibit any water magic," Arabella grumped. She gave Rowena a sly look through her eyelashes.

Rowena snorted, covering a laugh with her fingers. "Perhaps we can convince Josephine to intervene."

"Oh yes, because our half-mad sister absolutely wouldn't make things worse by throwing the world into complete chaos." Arabella rolled her eyes and giggled.

"She'd march crabs and lobsters through the city streets demanding fair wages for the cottars and an end to slavery around the world." Rowena shook her fist as if in an imaginary protest in the streets.

"Talking crustaceans, my, my..." Arabella's eyes sparkled. "That would be quite a feat, even for a Sortilege witch."

"Well then, perhaps she'd convince a leviathan or two to blockade key ports until our demands are met." Rowena clapped her hands together. "They will work for squid, and of course, Josephine would convince those squid to swim right into their great maws."

"I see..." Arabella tapped her chin with her index finger, as if seriously considering the proposition. "Josephine *can* be quite persuasive."

Rowena and Arabella stared at each other for a moment, struggling to keep their faces straight, then they burst into laughter.

When her mirth slowed, Arabella wiped the tears from her eyes and said, "That was utterly inappropriate and completely ridiculous."

"Do you feel better?" Rowena asked, wiping her own tears.

Arabella looked thoughtful for a moment. "Yes. Yes, I do."

"Then imagining our sister gleefully throwing the world into turmoil was absolutely the right thing to do," Rowena said. "Laughter lifts some of the weight on your shoulders so you can get on with the work to be done. By necessity, sometimes that laughter is dark..."

"You are a wise woman, Ro." Arabella smiled fondly at her sister.

Rowena tented her fingers under her chin. "...A wise woman who knows you've kept the old letters gifted by dear Magistra Walsh from me." She gripped the arms of her chair and leaned forward. "Come now, surely even you can't think of any more reasons to delay. We're stuck here waiting on word from Mother or Bathsheba with nothing better to do."

Arabella frowned. "I still don't feel right about opening correspondence meant for someone else, even if it is decades old."

Rowena threw her hands up. "Arabella! You are absolutely impossible! Where would historians be if they were squeamish about reading letters written to long-dead people?"

"Mother isn't dead," Arabella pointed out.

"I already agreed that we wouldn't read Mother's letter," Rowena groaned, dropping her head into her hands. She sighed deeply and looked up. "Really, Arabella, you promised."

Arabella pinched her lips together. She closed her eyes and blew out a deep breath. "Fine." She bit off the word and rose, crossing the room to her bedside table. Opening a small box tucked back behind the oil lamp, she withdrew the two letters and turned. Arabella held the well-worn envelopes up.

"For the record," she said. "I don't think this is a good idea. I have a feeling this is going to lead us to trouble."

Rowena raised an eyebrow. "Precognitive feeling or mundane unfounded anxiety? There is precognitive magic in our bloodline, and if you're opening new abilities…"

"I don't know," Arabella grumbled. She dropped her arm and stamped back to her chair. "How can you tell the difference?" she huffed as she dropped back in her seat.

Rowena shrugged. "Practice. But even that isn't foolproof. Remember how Grandmother kept us away from every stream and river one summer? Wouldn't let us so much as dangle our toes in?"

Arabella chuckled. "Yes, she swore that one of us was going to drown."

"And yet, years later, we all remain un-drowned."

"But she insisted that was because of her vigilance." Arabella's brow furrowed.

"Of course." Rowena shook her head. "It couldn't have had anything to do with Theodosia losing a grandniece to drowning the week before she forbade us to go near the water. Even one of the great precognitive witches of her generation can fall victim to unfounded fears."

Arabella pulled a face. "Can we go back to discussing crustaceans mounting protests in the streets instead of the fallibility of our family?"

"We could discuss the letters instead," Rowena said as she snatched them from Arabella's grip.

"Only the one to Aunt Lorena and Aunt Lenore!" Arabella insisted. "We have to leave the seal on Mother's letter intact."

Rowena rolled her eyes. "It's like you don't trust me."

"Of course, I trust you, Ro." Arabella placated her sister. "I just want us to be careful. You know how cross Mother will be if we accidentally open her letter."

Rowena passed the letters back to Arabella. Then she crossed her eyes and stuck out her tongue.

"Don't be a child," Arabella chided as she set their mother's letter to the side. She turned the letter addressed to her aunts over in her hands.

"Make up your mind," Rowena grumbled. "One moment, you want me to be silly to cheer you up, and the next, you scold me for that very behavior."

"I'm sorry, Ro." Arabella didn't look up from the letter, her voice distracted. She squinted at the dark blob of wax that sealed the letter. It might have been any of the darker shades originally, deep green, navy blue, or even burgundy. But the grime of time had turned it black. "It seems like there's something pressed into the wax, a crest maybe? Perhaps some kind of spell? I can't make it out." She looked up and frowned at the room at large. "There's simply not enough light. I don't want to break the seal until we see what it is. It might offer a clue about who it came from."

"Oh, no, you don't," Rowena growled. With a flick of her wrist, she conjured a small ball of golden witchlight, about the size of an apple. "You've made me wait this long, and I'm not letting you make me wait longer." She stood and positioned the light just over Arabella's shoulder. "Does that help?"

"Yes, very much," Arabella murmured. She tilted the letter this way and that to get a better look at the shape pressed into the misshapen bead of wax. "But it still doesn't make any sense."

Rowena leaned over her shoulder and squinted at the seal. "What do you see?"

"Wings… What looks like a big cat body… a lion, maybe? But I can't tell because there's a snake where the tail should be." Arabella bit her lip and tilted the letter again. Rowena touched her fingertips to Arabella's wrist and nudged it back.

"The impression is muddled where the head should be," Rowena muttered to herself.

"I know," Arabella griped in annoyance. "I told you that it makes no sense."

"We could stare at this seal for hours and it won't make any more sense," Rowena said. "The letter inside has more information. It must."

Arabella gently worked her thumbnail under the wax seal. "I'll try not to break it. Maybe Mother or Grandmother will know what it means." The seal cracked in half. Arabella gasped.

"Don't blame yourself. The wax is very old. It was bound to break," Rowena said. "Now open it before I pass out from anticipation!"

The thick, creamy paper has been folded so long, it at first resisted Arabella's gentle fingers as she spread it open. The interior was a velvety ecru, showing the high quality of the paper and why it held up against the years. Deep black ink swept across the page in a sure hand:

Dearest Lenore, or Lorena, whomever decides to open this first,

We hope this letter finds you well and that Mother's little mission to that Goddess-forsaken Isle is not too taxing. Tell Minerva we said hello and that we expect the baby is growing well. We hope little Vivienne will enjoy her new sister. Or brother, but as always, we wish for a girl. Please come see us on the Continent. We miss you so much it's quite nearly unbearable. House Cagliostro has been unarguably welcoming, but it's not like home.

(I can prepare Louisa to be away from the Chapterhouse for a few days. I can handle it. We could meet halfway. Perhaps somewhere in France? Please say you'll come.)

In the meantime, Louisa wrote this letter for our niece. Please see that she gets it. (She won't tell me what's in it, secretive little mouse.)

Please tell the rest of the family we love them and miss them.

All our love,
Susannah and Louisa

Cradled in the stiff outer paper was another piece of the same rich paper folded tight on another message. The sealing wax on this letter held no curious non-sensical figure, just a fingerprint. Arabella flipped it over. The letter A carved deep into the thick paper, bold and stark. The paper rattled as Arabella's hand trembled. A feeling of dread stole over her, and she could not say whether it was a silly mundane worry or if it was an awakening of precognitive ability. Rowena pulled the open letter from her fingers and let the smaller sealed one tumble into Arabella's lap.

Her eyes flicked over the page, taking it in. "Susannah? Louisa?" Her hand crept up to her mouth. Arabella looked up at her.

"Mother's older sisters? The aunts we've never met?"

Rowena nodded dumbly as she read the letter again.

"Mother always made it sound like they were never close, that it was a relief when they were no longer in the House. But this letter sounds so familiar, loving." Arabella shook her head. "Why did they leave? Where did they go?"

Rowena looked up from the letter. "I've only been able to put together bits and pieces because I went into the Archive to look for what they were assigned to, right after my own Investiture. I was so curious!" Her eyes drifted back down to the letter.

"Well?" Arabella prompted. Curiosity burned through her.

Rowena's head jerked up. "Louisa had a very strong precognitive ability, and she was also very strong-willed. She would sneak out of the house at odd hours, refused to dress in acceptable clothing… Jessamine and Josephine are paragons of stability compared to the accounts of her behavior. Susannah was the only person she would listen to. But even she had trouble controlling Louisa, which interfered with the development of her own skills. Grandmother sent them to the great House Cagliostro in Italy in hopes that they could help tame Louisa, or at least teach Susannah a few tricks to control her better."

"You knew this since right after your Investiture?" Arabella's voice rose a notch. "Why didn't you tell me?"

Rowena blinked. "I'm not sure. There must have been something going on…" Her voice trailed off as her eyes returned to the letter once more.

"When did they come back?" Arabella asked.

"They didn't," Rowena murmured without looking up. She traced the letters with her fingertips. "Louisa and Susannah never came back. The falling out happened sometime after Mother returned from Ireland. They must still be there. There was never another mention of them in the Archives again."

"How strange." Arabella frowned. "Why would they never come home?"

"Which niece?" Rowena breathed, her eyes trained on the letter. "Only Vivienne was born at that point. Mother was pregnant with Amelia on her trip to Ireland."

"The A must be for Amelia then. It only makes sense," Arabella said. "If Louisa was such a strong precog, she had to know that Mother would name her next child Amelia."

Rowena's head snapped up. "Or that she would name her seventh daughter Arabella! The letter could be for you!"

"No!" Arabella shook her head. "Rowena, no! It can't be." She picked up the smaller letter from her lap. "Can it?" Fear and excitement both flickered through her.

Rowena shook Susannah's letter at Arabella. "Aunt Susannah only said to give it to their niece. We're both their nieces. We can open it. We must open it!" She took a deep breath. "If it turns out it was truly only meant for Amelia, we'll apologize. You know she'll forgive us."

Arabella didn't need any further encouragement. She broke the messy wax seal without another thought. With trembling fingers, she spread the creased paper open.

The contents were not quite a letter in the traditional sense. A drawing dominated the center of the paper. What words there were skittered all over in every direction, following no rhyme or reason. Arabella smoothed the paper flat as best as she could over her knees. Rowena leaned in and pulled the witchlight closer.

The drawing at the center showed a creature possessing the body of a lion with huge wings flaring from its back. As with the broken seal on the original letter, there was a snake where the tail should be. But where the wax had refused to give up the details about the head of the creature, Arabella and Rowena could see it clearly now. It was the face of a handsome man with a fine, straight nose. Perched on his head was an elaborate headdress.

Cramped handwriting next to the strange beast's front paws said, *he's going to be angry when he finds out.* Hard, stiff letters marched across the top of the page, *You Must Come.* Arabella had to turn the page to read a smaller cluster of words crawling sideways up the left margin. *Please come. You are needed. Perhaps Calais? Maybe Paris? Definitely France.* France was underlined twice.

"It makes no sense," Arabella murmured. She smoothed the paper again as if the touch of her hand could bring order and understanding.

"Aunt Louisa obviously wanted someone to come to France," Rowena said.

"So did Aunt Susannah," Arabella replied absently as she scanned over the words again.

Rowena pointed to the lower right-hand corner of the paper. "What's that? Under your thumb…"

Arabella lifted her hand and peered down at the paper. The letters Rowena had caught peeping out from under her hand were tiny, narrow things. They looked like they had been written with a pin dipped in ink rather than a pen. Arabella felt a wave of cold pass through her like someone dumped a bucket of icy water over her head.

"Is it…" Rowena gasped.

"It's my name," Arabella whispered.

Rowena straightened up. "Well, the letter was definitely not meant for Amelia."

Arabella looked up at Rowena. "How could she know? When she wrote this," Arabella waved the letter at Rowena. "I wouldn't be born for another twelve years!"

"I told you Louisa's precognitive ability was significant," Rowena said softly.

Arabella and Rowena retreated into their own thoughts. It was Arabella who broke the silence.

"What do we do now?" she whispered.

"We go home to deliver Mother's letter and find out if Aunt Susannah and Aunt Louisa gave her any more information in their message to her," Rowena said. "Then we go to France to find Aunt Louisa."

Arabella raised her eyebrow. "We?" Then she shook her head. "Dragging you along on my first assignment is quite enough. Aunt Louisa only asked for me. I'm going alone."

"Absolutely not! I won't hear of you going alone." Rowena lifted her chin. "You must be accompanied by a Guardian at a minimum. You haven't the combat skills to protect yourself yet." Her voice took on a wheedling tone. "It's such a long journey. You'll want company you actually enjoy."

Arabella's face softened, and she sighed deeply.

"Besides," Rowena continued with a twinkle in her eye. "I have to find out how this mystery ends. You owe me that at least for coming to this Goddess-forsaken Isle with you." Rowena winked and rose to say goodnight.

Arabella gathered the letters together to return them to their box, fear and excitement warring in her breast. She couldn't imagine how she would be able to sleep tonight, knowing that some mysterious destiny awaited her in France.

In the quiet lull in their conversation, the squeak of the loose floorboard outside their rooms sounded like a scream. Sarah's shout rang out in the hallway, and the sound of heavy, booted feet pounded away. Arabella and Rowena scurried to the door and pressed their ears to the wood. They could hear nothing. Cautiously, Arabella eased the door open and peered out.

Eliza stood with her back to them, stance wide, blocking the way into the room.

"Get back inside and shut the door," Eliza growled.

Arabella looked over Eliza's shoulder to see Sarah at the top of the staircase scowling down. "Yates!" the Guardian called out. "Who ran past you? Were they armed?"

"I said, inside," Eliza hissed to Arabella and Rowena.

But Arabella couldn't move a muscle. Panic froze her in place as she watched Sarah step back from the head of the staircase, her hands going to the weapons on her belt. Yates climbed the stairs, fist balled at his sides, his face creased in rage.

"You will address me with respect, witch!" he spat. "My Lord's sympathies for you can only cause me to hold my tongue so long."

Sarah's hand tightened on her dirk. "*Mr.* Yates, who ran past you? Were they armed?"

"No one ran past me, you hysterical woman," Yates hissed.

"The loose board creaked. I heard boots. I saw someone, someone large, fleeing down the stairs," Sarah insisted.

"No one passed me," Yates fiercely clipped off each word.

"But I saw…"

"Are you calling me a liar?" Yates hissed and as he raised a fist. Sarah bared her teeth and held her ground.

"Perhaps we had better wake his Lordship?" Eliza called out. "If some brigand has breached the Hall, then all of us could be in danger."

"The only people in this Hall who shouldn't be here are you four." Yates regarded them all haughtily. "Lord Plunkett-Nelson will not be roused as the imaginations of hysterical women are not worthy of waking him. Stay in your rooms, witch," he snarled as he turned on his heel and stomped back down the stairs.

Sarah backed down the hallway. Together she and Eliza bundled Arabella and Rowena into the bedroom.

"Damnit, girls," Eliza barked. "You have to listen to me. If you don't listen, you put us all in danger!"

"Eliza is right," Sarah said as she checked all the windows. "If you don't do as we say, we can't protect you."

Arabella's heart beat a frantic rhythm. "What happened? *Who* was that?"

Sarah shook her head. "I'd gone down to the end of the hallway to check a noise at the window. I thought it might be a crow message from Kiera or Dierdre. That loose floorboard saved us. Whoever it was, he was large, and I don't think he meant us any kindness."

"We all stay in here tonight," Eliza said. "I can't be sure that Yates isn't gathering forces against us right now. We'll talk to the Baron once it's light. The darkness hides too much."

The Guardians worked together to drag a heavy blanket chest in front of the door, then they each drank a potion designed to keep them awake and alert. Arabella crawled into the bed beside her sister and pretended to sleep while Eliza and Sarah kept watch. At some point in the wee hours, Arabella did fall into a brief and fretful doze. Hulking shadows menaced her dreams.

CHAPTER XXI

Wherein the Witches Wonder if the Danger has Truly Passed

RABELLA FLINCHED AT THE SIGHT OF HERSELF IN THE MIRROR THE next morning. Her gaze looked haunted and dark circles had formed beneath her eyes. Rowena looked no better. Their Guardians, while alert and efficient, still showed their tension in every taut motion.

"We know Lord Plunkett-Nelson will be at the breakfast table at this hour," Eliza said crisply. "We must broach the subject of safety with him immediately."

Arabella nodded dumbly. She felt drained, completely emptied out. Silently, she chided herself for having the temerity to think her troubles would all go away simply because she'd managed to put some letters and a few bits of vegetation and soil into the wind. Even if the samples made it to Henry, even if he managed to cajole his friends into helping, there was no guarantee the blight would be solved. And even if it was, the hatred of witches still ran deep in Irish soil, possibly tended by the shadowy new menace Kiera spoke of, the *Ilhexerai*. And what would Mother think of all this? Arabella's shoulders sagged as she imagined the displeasure on her mother's face when she found out that Arabella had disobeyed her. She'd not just quietly ensconced herself in some discreet corner and read novels until summoned home. Everything

Arabella had done and discovered since she'd set foot on Irish soil would cause her mother heartache and strife. Each trouble weighed her down like another stone. Arabella felt as if she waded through thick mud as they all headed down to breakfast, she and her sister tucked between their two very tense Guardians.

They did indeed find Lord Plunkett-Nelson already at the breakfast table, head down in his customary paperwork while Julian perused a newspaper. Mr. Yates hovered at the servant's entrance like a noxious fog, glowering at the witches.

The Baron raised his head, about to speak, when he saw their severe expressions. His jolly demeanor dropped away. "...Oh, my... Has something happened? Did you receive an upsetting message?"

"There was an intruder last night..." Eliza began in a tight, clipped voice.

"Lies!" Mr. Yates snarled. "The Hall was peaceful until these hysterical creatures started baying about figments of their imagination. Fortunately, I was able to keep them from waking you over nothing."

"It wasn't nothing," Sarah said through gritted teeth. "I saw a large man heading for Arabella's room until I frightened him off. He had to have run past Yates to escape. Who is lying now?"

"My Lord!" Mr. Yates put his hand on his chest theatrically. "Do you hear the way these foul creatures speak to me?"

Julian sprang to his feet. "Now, see here! I will not hear you insult these ladies so."

"Ladies..." Mr. Yates scoffed.

"Enough!" Lord Plunkett-Nelson roared as he rose to his feet. "I will not have my household brawling like common ruffians!" Tense silence descended on the room. The Baron straightened his waistcoat. He first turned to Sarah. "Could you have been mistaken about what you saw? Perhaps one of our larger girls going about the business of the house. I imagine it was very dark..."

Sarah pressed her lips together and snorted. "Only if one of your maids is suddenly twice as wide at the shoulders and wearing hob nail boots."

Lord Plunkett-Nelson furrowed his brow and turned to Mr. Yates. "Could you have been mistaken, Yates? Perhaps someone did run past you while your back was turned? Were all the doors locked tight last night?"

"I am shocked that you would even hint that I was lax with my duties and allowed some prowler to trespass in these halls that have been my home since I was a boy," Yates exclaimed indignantly.

Cold certainty trickled down Arabella's spine. Mr. Yates never said he hadn't left a door unlocked or let someone in, only that he was insulted to be accused.

Lord Plunkett-Nelson spread his hands. "You must see my conundrum…" He sighed. "On the one hand, I have my esteemed guests and the lovely young lady who is betrothed to my beloved nephew, and on the other, I have my valued retainer who, along with his father, has served me well for years. I want to believe you both, but I cannot reconcile the stories."

Eliza lifted her chin, eyes blazing. "If Louth Hall is no longer a safe refuge, then we shall have to leave and find another place to rest."

"Good," Mr. Yates spat.

"Uncle Sas!" Julian cried. "You can't mean this! Guardian Gardner has no reason to lie, and Yates has been absolutely horrid to the ladies since they arrived. His prejudice against witches is obvious!"

"Well, yes," Lord Plunkett-Nelson allowed. "Even I can't ignore his less than proper behavior…"

"Less than proper!" Arabella blurted out. Heat rose in her cheeks. "His malice has been barely checked since we crossed the threshold! It's obvious he's hiding the truth. Why, he wouldn't even say clearly that all the doors were locked last night. He only said he was insulted to be accused."

Lord Plunkett-Nelson scowled and turned on Mr. Yates. "Tell me plainly, now. Were all the doors secure last night? Did you have a hand in letting anyone in?"

"You'd believe that bloody parasite," Yates jabbed his finger at Arabella. "Over me? I never…"

"Tell me plainly!" Lord-Plunkett Nelson bellowed.

Mr. Yates shrank back for a moment, his face full of confusion. Then he drew himself up and crossed his arms over his chest, his expression haughty. "I do not have to dignify the accusations of a foul-mouthed witch with a response."

"If you wish to remain in my employ, you *will* dignify my question with a truthful answer." Lord Plunkett-Nelson's voice rumbled with quiet menace. Shock stole over Mr. Yates's face as the blood drained from his cheeks.

"You… you can't…" Yates stuttered. "For *them*?" He waved his hand at the witches.

"Oh, Yates…." The anger fled Lord Plunkett-Nelson's countenance, replaced mournful sorrow. "Go pack your things. Louth Hall is no longer your home. I'll give you a month's wages in recognition of your service, but you must leave today."

Mr. Yates narrowed his eyes, his gaze flickered all around the room, taking in the Baron's sadness, Julian's shock, and the witches' fury. "Your decision is firm, my Lord?" Yates's voice was soft.

"It is." Lord Plunkett-Nelson gave Mr. Yates an almost tender look. "Please don't make this any more difficult than it has to be."

Mr. Yates bowed his head for a moment. His head snapped up, eyes burning with rage as he fixed his gaze on Arabella and her entourage. He spat and crooked his fingers in the gesture against the evil eye. "I hope the Devil uses your spine for a ladder in Hell." With his back stiff, Mr. Yates turned on his heel and disappeared through the servant's door.

Arabella's knees turned to water, and she sank into the nearest chair. The distress plain on his face, Lord Plunkett-Nelson called for a housemaid.

"Some fresh, hot tea, that's what we all need after such a disquieting episode," he murmured as he returned to his seat.

"I'm afraid we need more than tea," Eliza retorted. "We need the carriage prepared immediately. We are departing."

The Baron frowned. "But I've removed the danger. Mr. Yates won't bother you any longer. Surely you are all safe now?"

"No," Arabella said. "No, I don't feel safe. Who's to say that someone else wasn't working with the intruder to distract Sarah with the noise at the window? Only that loose floorboard saved us, and now *they* know about it. Yates is obviously in league with someone, or even several someones. Who else was out there in the darkness waiting for Yates to let them in?" Arabella's voice began to rise to a hysterical pitch.

"And if he was confident enough in your support," she gestured to the Baron. "To have me… us… attacked under your very roof, what else might he think he can get away with?"

Lord Plunkett-Nelson's jaw dropped open. "I'm wounded…"

"Arabella, wait…" Julian sank to his knees next to her chair and took her hand in both of his. "You are understandably upset. It's logical to lose your trust in a person you don't know after an event like this. But you know me, yes?" He brought her hand to his lips and kissed her knuckles. "You can trust me, can't you? Please, trust me when I tell you that Uncle Sas would never hurt you, and he would never allow anyone to hurt you if it were in his power. I've known him since the day I was born. He is an honorable man."

Arabella took a trembling breath and gripped Julian's hand back.

"Please," Julian pleaded. "Stay. We'll keep you safe." He kissed her hand again. The tension in Arabella's shoulders began to ease. She took a deep breath and looked up at Sarah and Eliza.

"What do you think?" Arabella asked. "I want to stay, but I know I'm not thinking clearly."

"No, you're not," Rowena said as she glared at Julian. "No one who truly cared for you would ask you to stay where you feel unsafe." Julian ignored her barb and kept his gaze resolutely on Arabella. The Guardians exchanged glances.

Sarah shrugged. "Where would we go? From what we saw in the city, the anti-witch sentiment is even stronger there. It would take us time to find another rural Lord with a witch-friendly view."

Eliza grimaced as she rubbed her hand across her face. She looked deep in thought for a moment, then said, "We can stay until we have somewhere else to go, but we treat this house as hostile territory until it is proven otherwise."

Sarah nodded sharply. "I'll talk to Margaret in the kitchen to see about the herbs we need for more vigilance potion. We'll not be sleeping for the duration, eh?"

"Anything you need, it is yours," Lord Plunkett-Nelson broke in. "My nephew is right. I could never allow harm to come to you ladies if it were in my power. I will check the doors myself, every night."

"We shall see, my Lord," Eliza said crisply. "Deeds, not words."

After an anxious day spent at loose ends, the first night after the aborted attack was quiet. Rowena stayed with Arabella in her bed again. Eliza and Sarah once more moved the blanket chest in front of the bedroom door, just in case. True to his word, Lord Plunkett-Nelson checked all the doors and took Mr. Yates's old ring of keys to bed with him. The hoot of an owl near the witching hour was the only sound to break the hush.

The next day dawned bright and clear, and Arabella wondered if Uncle Sas really had spoken true, that she could feel safe. Her appetite started to return. She helped Julian putter about his workshop. But after dinner, under the veil of night, Rowena still shared her bed. Eliza and Sarah still shifted the blanket chest. The owl returned to mark off the witching hour outside the still and peaceful Hall.

A week after the attack, Arabella strolled with Rowena through the kitchen garden under the watchful eyes of their Guardians, where they enjoyed mild autumn temperatures a month before they would see them in London. The vines and branches of the garden hung heavy with the first fruits of the harvest.

"We've missed Lughnasa with being cooped up in the Hall, haven't we?" Arabella asked with a sigh. The oversight left her feeling anxious and incomplete.

"We could still celebrate. The moon isn't quite full yet," Rowena responded. "I know Mother was always particular about keeping the household celebration on the first of the month, but you know how Grandmother would let us come with her for her own little celebration on the following full moon."

Arabella chuckled. "Mother has always been a bit rigid about her calendar… and everything else! Grandmother's fluidity seems to infuriate her."

Arabella stopped and turned to the Guardians. "Please, can we celebrate Lughnasa? The moon will be full in two days."

Eliza started to shake her head, but Rowena spoke before she could say anything.

"It's been peaceful for a week, no sign of trouble at all. Surely that means something?"

The Guardian grunted. "It could mean that Yates is biding his time, trying to lull us into a false sense of security."

"But perhaps Uncle Sas is right?" Arabella cajoled the grim-faced Guardians. "Yates wouldn't dare go against such a powerful Lord, would he?"

Sarah's expression softened after a moment, and she gave Eliza a sideways look. "Arabella may have a point…"

Eliza groaned. "Not you too! We agreed to treat this house as hostile territory until we leave."

"Or until it proved to be safe," Sarah said.

Eliza raised her eyebrow. "Has it proved safe? Or are you just too eager to celebrate Lughnasa?"

Arabella bit her lip in thought. Yes, the traditional light-hearted Lughnasa celebration might not be worth the risk, and Lugh would surely forgive them their lapse in reverence so they would still be alive to honor him in the next season. But Lugh was also a protector, especially against blighted crops.

"I never…" Sarah gasped.

"But what if we asked Lugh for his favor? To protect us and bless our efforts to end the potato blight?" Arabella chimed in, trying to head off an argument between the Guardians.

Sarah rubbed her chin thoughtfully. "There has to be a sacred spring nearby. Kiera would need one for ceremonies."

"Hang it all!" Eliza growled. "It's too dangerous!"

"But, Eliza," Arabella said. "I think we *need* to do this. What if we go to all of this effort only to fail because we tried to do it all on our own? We need Lugh's blessing…"

Eliza kept her face impassive, but Arabella noticed her worrying her thumb against her forefinger surreptitiously. They all watched her. Eliza pursed her lips, then finally and blew out her breath.

"Fine, yes." She frowned deeply. "You're right that our efforts could benefit from the ritual. But we need to be safe."

"Of course, we'll be safe!" Arabella said. "I'm sure we can get some candles from Margaret that we can consecrate in time."

The frown never quite left Eliza's face, but she offered no more protests.

CHAPTER XXII

Wherein Faith Is Misplaced and a Ritual Is Interrupted

ARABELLA FINISHED TYING THE LAST RIBBONS AND PLACED THE PURE bees wax candles into her basket. Margaret had pulled them from the back of the pantry with a wink and a smile. These were the same fine candles the Baron saved for holiday celebrations with guests. Last night, after dinner, each of the witches took a candle and carved the symbols for one of the cardinal directions as they whispered their consecrating prayers. Arabella ran her hand over the graceful whorls and swirls of her carving with pride, finer than Eliza and Sara's simple, crisp lines. As for Rowena's wax work, for once, Arabella outshone her sister in an element of the arcane, the sole benefit of years of drudgery preparing for her sisters' rituals. The candles weren't the proper colors for calling the elements, but the ribbons she and Rowena had managed to scavenge from their own wardrobe, coupled with pure intention, would make up for that. Preparing for a ceremonial circle without her mother's meticulously curated supplies both excited and frightened Arabella. It felt closer to the bone of things.

Sarah closed the door softly behind her as she slipped into Arabella's bedroom, where the rest of them waited. "The house is almost settled," she murmured. "We'll be able to leave shortly."

Eliza looked out the window at the sky. "Good. We don't want the moon too much farther up before we start the ritual."

"You're sure you remember the way to the spring?" Arabella asked.

Sarah nodded. "Jacqueline gave me good directions, and I scouted it out earlier today. It's not far."

Eliza raised an eyebrow. "Jacqueline is an unusual name for an Irish lass."

Sarah shrugged. "She came over from France to nurse a distant uncle who was in poor health. She said she liked it here better, so she found work after he died instead of going back home."

Arabella sighed. "Can we leave now?"

Sarah poked her head back into the hallway and listened. She straightened and motioned for the other women to come. "It's quiet. We can slip out by the kitchens. Hopefully, we'll be done and back before anyone notices we've gone."

Creeping through the dark and silent Hall added a frisson of excitement for Arabella. She'd never had to hide away the Pagan celebrations of the Sisterhood of Witches before. Was this what her Sisters in Ireland experienced every time they wished to practice their faith? She frowned to herself as she crossed over the threshold and into the kitchen garden. Probably not. Sneaking about was thrilling when you knew you could go safely back to where you were welcome, but to live constantly with those who wished you ill couldn't really be described as exciting or thrilling.

Eliza kept watch as they paused in the garden to quickly harvest the last of what they needed for the ritual. Arabella plucked ripe blueberries and strawberries while Sarah dug up a couple of early carrots.

The spring was indeed not far. Clear, crisp water flowed from a narrow little cleft in some rock nestled between two hillocks. The water gathered in a small pool before feeding a stream that meandered off into the distance. A sessile oak stood sentry at the crown of one of the hillocks, like the Oak King keeping watch over his lands.

As they climbed to the bare crown of the opposite hillock, the energy of the place tingled against Arabella's skin. "Are you sure this isn't the sacred well Keira uses? It certainly feels like it could be."

"Whether it is or it isn't, it's a fine place for our ritual," Eliza said as she pulled the candles out of the basket.

Sarah drew her dirk and began sketching the circle in the rich, dark brown soil. Rowena followed behind her, laying consecrated salt into the line. Arabella gathered water from the spring and laid it out with the harvest they'd brought from the garden. Eliza set the candles at the cardinal points, pushing their ends deep in the dirt to ensure they would not fall. After they laid all the necessary ceremonial ingredients in their proper places, each witch took her place behind the candle she carved runes into. The full moon shone brightly upon them, near as bright as day.

Sarah, in the position of North and the Earth, raised her arms to the sky. Her voice rang out clear. "I call upon the…"

A large stone whizzed out of the shadows. The sharp edge cut across Sarah's forehead, and she fell to the ground. Her blood glistened vividly crimson against the muted colors in the moonlight. The air around them filled with the shouts of angry men. All turned to chaos.

Strong arms clamped around Arabella from behind.

In her ear, a low voice growled, "We'll show you damn witches your place." His breath stank of onion and cabbage.

Arabella heard Eliza's voice calling out above the men's shouting, but Arabella's mind refused to parse the words. A sharp knife of wind blew past her cheek, and suddenly the arms that clutched her were gone.

"Get to the Hall!" Eliza shouted.

Arabella gathered up her skirts and ran. *Get to the Hall. Get to the Hall.* The terror blazing through her allowed only that one thought to beat in time with her pulse. *Get to the Hall.*

A rock caught her foot. Arabella sprawled, the wind knocked out of her. Before she could catch her breath, strong fingers dug into her hair and dragged her to her feet. Arabella cried out as the powerful fist yanked her around, revealing her captor.

Molly's burly, bearded husband stared hard at her, his eyes glittering with fury. With one hand, he held her hair tight. In the other hand, a naked blade gleamed.

"And there you are again, little snooty witch bitch," he spat. "Perhaps you'll regret sticking your nose where it don't belong now?"

Arabella gasped. "Jack!"

"Don't you say my name!" he shouted as he shook her head from side to side. "I know what you damn witches do with names!"

Arabella's head spun with dizziness. Her scalp stung. She searched her thoughts for something, anything, that might convince the enraged field worker to not use the knife in his fist on her. Her mind remained blank.

"Please, don't hurt me," Arabella squeaked.

Jack put his face down into hers. "And why shouldn't I?"

Arabella's mind raced and lighted on the first thought it found. "Your boy, your son. How is he?"

Jack fell still for a moment.

"He cried this morning," he whispered. "For the first time in weeks." His grip on her hair loosened slightly.

"That's good! That's good!" Arabella stammered. "He's drinking the goat's milk, then? He'll be alright. He'll be alright."

"What do you know about my boy's future?" Jack hissed.

"I don't know anything. Please!" Arabella's voice shook.

"Then how do you know he'll be alright?"

"If he eats, he lives, he grows. The goat's milk from Deirdre will keep him alive."

"That witch is casting a spell on my son?" His voice rose, and his grip tightened again.

"No! No!" Arabella held out her palms in front of her. "Nothing like that at all."

"Then what?" he growled, shaking her as a hound might shake a rabbit.

Arabella clenched her teeth to keep from crying out. "Deirdre just wants to help." Arabella sobbed. "She only wants to help. All of us want to help. My mother sent me here to find anything that might help us cure the blight." Tears began to trickle down her cheeks. "We just want to help."

Jack stilled once more, but his grip did not relax. Soft and low, he said, "Why would the likes of you want to do anything for us?"

Arabella gazed up at Jack through tear-soaked lashes. She watched his face twisting through anger, hurt, and confusion.

"We're not evil," Arabella whispered. "We don't want to see the people of our lands suffer."

Jack's voice hardened. "So, we belong to you? I've had enough of belonging to other people!"

"No! No!" Arabella gasped. She closed her eyes and cringed back as far as his grip on her hair allowed her. "We all belong to the land. We are the people of the land. You are the people of the land. We want to help you, as our brothers and sisters."

"I'm not your brother," Jack snapped, but something in his stance softened.

"Maybe not mine," Arabella soothed, seeing her opening. "But Deirdre considers you one of her own, quite nearly kin. She wants Molly's boy, your boy, to grow up big and strong. That's why she brought the milk. She starves herself for a chance to help your boy."

Jack's brow furrowed in thought. He glanced back over his shoulder. Cries and shouts echoed in the darkness.

"I couldn't be seen taking help from a witch."

"Dierdre understands that. That's why she came in the daytime while you were in the fields." Hope began to bloom in Arabella's breast.

"If I let you go, would you make her bring more milk?" Soft desperation entered his voice.

"I wouldn't have to make her," Arabella said, fighting to keep the tremor out of her voice. "But yes, I'll make sure she knows to keep bringing the milk."

"I won't let Molly lose another one, not if I can help it. It would break her." He choked back a sob. "Losing her would break me," he whispered.

Jack pulled his fingers out of Arabella's hair and stepped back. He glanced over his shoulder at the sound of fighting again. It was closer this time.

"You better run, girl," he growled softly. "If you're to keep your promise, you better run."

Arabella didn't need any more encouragement. She ran.

Wind howled at Arabella's back. She couldn't be sure if it was natural phenomenon or if one of the other witches whipped it up through a spell. Clouds in the grip of the wind flooded across the face of the moon. Arabella raced through near pitch-black darkness, hoping that she was headed in the right direction. The unfamiliar terrain looked all the same to her. She could very well be fleeing away from Louth Hall and the safety she might find there. But the shouting faded behind her. At least she moved away from the men attacking them.

A body slammed into Arabella from her right and knocked her to the ground. She shrieked. Scrabbling on her hands and knees, groping for a rock she might throw, Arabella worked to put distance between her and whoever had hit her. The wind finally dropped away.

A sob came from the darkness. "Arabella?"

Rowena. Arabella dropped the rock in her hand and went to her sister. They clutched each other in the dark, sobbing.

"What happened? Who are they?" Rowena snuffled into Arabella's shoulder.

"Some of the anti-witch field workers, I think." Arabella's voice trembled. "Jack caught me. But he let me go when I promised I'd have Deirdre keep bringing his boy more milk."

Rowena sat back on her heels, wiping the back of her hand across her face. "But how would they know we were here?"

Arabella stood and offered Rowena her hand. "Someone in the Hall is telling tales beyond the walls. It has to be Jacqueline. Margaret wouldn't betray us. She's been protecting her magical kin too long. And they were the only ones who had any idea where we might be tonight."

Arabella tugged on Rowena's hand. "Come on, we need to get to the Hall. Eliza said get to the Hall." She paused, looking around in confusion. "Do you know the right direction?"

Rowena considered the sky, with tattered clouds drifting past the moon and stars. "North," she said, her voice firm. "We need to go north." She took a step in a different direction than Arabella had been running. She hissed and drew up her right foot in pain.

"What's wrong?" Arabella asked.

"My ankle," Rowena said with a gasp. "I think I twisted it when we ran into each other."

Arabella offered her shoulder. "Lean on me."

The girls limped north, their ears trained on the sounds of fighting in the distance. It seemed that Eliza and Sarah were giving the men a good fight.

"Does it sound like they are getting closer?" Rowena asked with an edge of barely contained hysteria. "I think they're getting closer." She gasped. "What if they're between the Hall and us?"

"Can you manage a shield? Something to cover both of us?" Arabella asked.

Rowena nodded, her face pale.

"Then do it," Arabella said. "You pay attention to our shield. I'll guide us back to the Hall."

They continued on in silence. The sounds of the fighting indeed drew closer. Arabella bit her lip and hoped they would be able to make it to the Hall before the battle swallowed them up. Then all at once, the terrain began to look familiar again. They were at the edge of the field just outside the Hall, where the sheep grazed and where they'd released the birds nearly two weeks before. Arabella moved faster. Rowena whimpered but did her best to keep up. They rounded a hill and saw the dark outline of Louth Hall hulking against the night sky. It was still quiet and dark. There were only a few small lights in the kitchen windows where Margaret was no doubt already awake and tending to the pre-dawn baking.

A stone flew out of the darkness and bounced off Rowena's shield. Both girls cried out, but the shield held.

"We need to run. Can you run?" Arabella asked her sister.

Rowena stumbled a few steps, then fell to her knees with a cry. "No, no. I can't."

Arabella hauled her sister to her feet, slinging Rowena's arm over her shoulder again. "Then hold the shield," Arabella said through gritted teeth. The girls stumbled on, eyes focused on the flickering lamp light in the kitchen windows.

A figure swathed in a dark cloak swerved into their path and brought them up short. The figure reached out his hand, brushing his fingertips against Rowena's shield. Dark mist wreathed around his hand, and the shield shuddered. Rowena cried out in pain. He chuckled. "Too easy."

Arabella pushed Rowena behind her, hoping she'd have the good sense to get herself out of the way. With a furious roar, Arabella leaped forward and shoved both hands against the man's chest as hard as she could. She might not have the skills and training of a Guardian witch, but she would be damned if a daughter of Blackstone House would go down without a fight. Her leap caught the overconfident man unawares and he stumbled back. His heel caught on a stone, and he sprawled out in an ungainly heap. His hood fell aside to revealed Arabella's attacker.

It was Yates.

Hate glittered in his eyes. "Foul creature…" he growled.

Arabella didn't wait for him to complete his statement. She dodged around him and sprinted for the Hall. She saw Rowena just up ahead, limping along, whimpering with every step. She'd made good progress in light of her injury, but Arabella caught up with her quickly. She wrapped her arm around her sister's waist, trying to take weight from her ankle, half-carrying her across the field. Arabella scanned the horizon, searching for something, anything that could help them escape Yates. Her gaze landed on the windows of Julian's workshop at the far end of the Hall full of the banked golden glow of technomancy potential. She reached out with her magical senses and felt all the power at her beck and call if she could just get it out of the workshop.

Heavy footsteps sounded behind them.

Arabella gathered her will and forced the simple lever locks on the windows open.

The footsteps drew closer.

"Can you call up enough wind to blow open Julian's windows?" Arabella grunted to Rowena. "I have a plan."

Rowena screwed up her face and screeched as she poured out the effort to call the wind in the still air by the Hall. Julian's windows flew open.

"Keep going, get to Margaret," Arabella hissed to her sister, pushing her toward the safe harbor of the kitchen.

Arabella whirled around, sending out her magic call as she did so. Yates was almost on top of her.

He knocked her to the ground as he plowed into her. The touch of his hands burned like cold fire through the fabric of her sleeves.

Yates pulled back his fist. Arabella covered her head with her arms.

A metal gull slammed into Yates's chest and knocked him back. Close after it came the rest of the flock of mechanical carrier birds Julian had been busy building since the launch of the prototypes to Boscastle. They descended on Yates at Arabella's command. Sharp wing edges slashed. Beaks pecked and jabbed. Even the half-built birds threw themselves at him like sentient rocks. Yates flailed and screeched, trying to bat the metal birds away without success.

Arabella scrambled to her feet just in time to see Julian's original prototype sparrow land on Yates's forehead and dig its claws in his brow for purchase. Yates howled. Its amethyst eyes gleaming in the moonlight, the bird pecked down viciously, again and again. Yates shrieked and clasped his eye. Blood poured between his fingers.

Arabella turned and ran. She could apologize to Julian later for borrowing his birds without permission.

Her breath coming in painful gasps, Arabella finally made it to the kitchen door and fell right into Margaret's arms. The moment she reached safety, she used her magic to command the birds back to the workshop, praying she hadn't done too much damage to them.

"Oh dear, oh dear, oh dear..." Margaret murmured as she helped Arabella over to a kitchen chair beside Rowena, who hunched over in

Margaret's battered armchair by the fire, her ankle propped on a footstool. She clutched a housemaid's shawl around her shoulders with trembling fingers.

"Where are Eliza and Sarah? Have they come back?" Arabella's voice rode the razor edge of hysteria.

"Not yet, darling, not yet," Margaret said, wringing her hands. She darted back to the door to the garden and peered into the darkness. "How far behind you were they?"

"I don't know," Arabella sobbed. "We lost them in all the chaos. These men attacked us…"

The kitchen door leading into the house flew open. Julian charged through, a groggy housemaid on his heels. "Who attacked you?" Fury and concern warred on his face. He went straight to Arabella. He cupped her face in both hands. "Are you hurt?"

Arabella looked up into Julian's eyes, full of concern and care. All the terror and fear she'd been holding back to get to safety crashed down on her like a wave. Tears poured down her face. With a hiccupping sob, she threw herself into Julian's arms. He wrapped them tight around her and held her gently as she wept against his chest. Stroking her hair, he murmured into her ear, "It will be alright, you're safe now. I promise."

"Miss Arabella!" Margaret called from the door.

Arabella jerked her head up just in time to see Eliza and Sarah limp in, their clothes ripped and torn, streaked with dirt and blood. One of Eliza's eyes had nearly swelled shut, and her lips were swollen and bloody. Sarah could hardly keep her feet. Blood covered her face, and more kept oozing from the ragged gash on her forehead. Eliza helped her to another kitchen stool.

Arabella abandoned Julian and went to Sarah. "Sweet Goddess, you're bleeding!"

"Of course, I'm bleeding," Sarah grumbled. "Head wounds bleed."

Eliza turned to Margaret. "I was able to reach Deirdre with telepathy. She's coming with Kiera and the healing herbs we need. But we'll need clean water and soft cloths to help cleanse the wounds."

"Of course, ma'am." Margaret bobbed a curtsey and set to work.

Eliza looked Arabella over. "You seem to have come out alright."

"I'm fine. Rowena's hurt her ankle and can hardly walk," Arabella said.

Eliza leaned against the counter, exhaustion written on her face, and nodded. "I'm sure either Deirdre or Kiera can fix her right up. I just don't have the strength for the spell right now."

Margaret bustled over and helped Sarah press a clean cloth to her head wound, then helped Eliza onto a stool of her own.

"What can I do to help?" Arabella asked.

"You don't know even the most basic healing spells, do you?" Eliza asked.

Arabella shook her head. "That hasn't awakened in me yet."

"I thought so," Eliza sighed. "How are your energy reserves? Can you lend energy to the healing spells? We can walk you through that."

"I only called Julian's birds from his workroom to attack Yates. I can help."

"My birds? Attacked Yates?" Julian interjected.

Arabella blushed. "Yes, I'm afraid I had to call on them when Mr. Yates attacked me. I've returned them. Some of them may be bloody. Or broken. I'm terribly sorry."

Julian gently squeezed her shoulder. "I only wish I'd built more, my darling."

The servants' door opened again. "What's this Emma is telling me about wounded women in my kitchen?" Lord Plunkett-Nelson boomed.

He stopped short as he saw Eliza and Sarah.

"Good Lord...." He whispered. "Who did this?"

Eliza winced as she shifted on her stool. "Apparently, Yates still has ways of gathering information from this household. He ambushed us as we were about to enact a ritual at a sacred spring."

The Baron gasped. "The fiend! But I didn't even know you were leaving the house. Who could have told him?"

"We have reason to believe the downstairs maid Jacqueline may have passed him the information," Arabella said crisply.

Lord Plunkett-Nelson turned to Emma. "Go find that girl and bring her to me immediately." He turned his attention back to the witches in his kitchen. "I'll send the stable lad for the physician immediately. I daresay it looks like you need one, and a month's rest."

Eliza shook her head. "We have our own ways of healing. Deirdre and Keira are on their way already. And we can't stay here any longer. We leave at dawn."

CHAPTER XXIII

On Secrets Borne by Missives Old and New

ARABELLA COULD HARDLY SEE WHERE ELIZA HAD BEEN WOUNDED the night before. Keira was indeed a talented healing witch. Even the nasty gash on Sarah's forehead had left only the whisper of a scar. Rowena's ankle was fixed as good as new. Kiera and Dierdre had also pressed more healing and vitality potions on them for their journey, for which Arabella was glad. There was no telling what could happen or who they might meet on the way back to the safety of Blackstone Manor. The sun had barely cleared the horizon when Lord Plunkett-Nelson had the carriage drawn up to the door, ready to take the ladies wherever they wished.

"Again, I cannot convey how utterly mortified I am that such a horrendous thing happened to you under my roof," he said. "You must know that Yates had me wholly deceived about his honor and his intentions. I had no idea that anti-witch sentiment ran so deeply…"

Eliza held up her hand to stop him. "You do not have to keep apologizing, My Lord. We believe that you had nothing to do with the attack last night. We just cannot stay any longer."

He turned his pleading eyes to Arabella. "I do hope that this doesn't change things between you and Julian."

Arabella favored him with a wan smile. "My feelings for Julian are unchanged for the moment."

A sharp caw sounded from the sky above, and James the jackdaw swooped over their heads. He banked on a wingtip over the roofline above them and sailed back to land on the gravel driveway at their feet. James croaked and hopped in excited agitation.

Arabella knelt, reaching out to get the pieces of paper tied to James's leg with the same bit of bright blue ribbon they'd sent him with.

"Did you find her? Is that from Bathsheba?" Rowena asked breathlessly.

Arabella stopped and slapped her palms against the tops of her thighs. "If you don't hold still, I won't be able to retrieve the message. I know it's important! Hold. Still."

James stopped hopping. He extended the leg with the message tied to it to Arabella. With trembling fingers, she undid the knot and pulled the tiny bit of rolled-up paper from his leg. Her hands shook so hard she dropped the paper twice as she tried to unroll it. The second time Eliza snatched it up from the stone.

"Here, let me," she said. "You'll tear it before we can find out what it says." Eliza quickly smoothed out the palm-sized bit of paper. Her eyes flicked over the lines. James squawked and chirped as he danced around her feet. "Yes, yes, you've done a fine job. You'll get something good to eat."

"What does it say?" Arabella burst out, rising to her feet. She twisted her fingers together.

Eliza tucked the paper into her trouser pocket. "Bathsheba is waiting for us in the harbor. She's been in contact with your mother, and we must get you back to Boscastle as soon as possible." Eliza held her hand out to James and helped him up onto her shoulder. Catching a footman, she transferred James to his shoulder and asked him to deliver the jackdaw to Margret in the kitchen. The man tottered off stiffly with a stunned look on his face, but he did as was requested.

"Does it say anything else? Why Mother wants us home so quickly?" Arabella asked.

"You can read the full message in the carriage on the way to the harbor," Eliza said. "We have no time to waste."

Arabella sighed as she watched the servants load the last of their luggage onto the carriage.

"I wish you didn't have to go," Julian murmured. "It's been so lovely working with you in the workshop."

Arabella shook her head. "After last night and now the summons from Mother... We must go now, although I've not seen the summons from my mother yet."

"I said, you can read it in the carriage," Eliza said as she strode past to mount the step into the carriage. She turned in the doorway. "Say your goodbyes. We have to go."

Arabella turned to Julian and gave him a weak smile. "You'll still write to me?"

"Of course, I will," Julian said. He leaned in close and whispered in Arabella's ear. "I confess, I have hopes that our sham engagement will become a real one someday soon."

Arabella's eyes widened, and a flush crept into her cheeks. "I..."

Rowena leaned her head out of the carriage window. "Arabella, we must go!"

"Come back to England as soon as you can," Arabella said in a whisper.

As she turned to leave, Julian caught her hand. He brought her hand up and lightly brushed her knuckles with his lips. They locked eyes.

"Nothing could keep me away," Julian said.

Arabella squeezed his hand and then turned to the carriage with a visible effort of will. The carriage door nearly clipped her heel as Eliza pulled it shut. Sarah rapped on the roof to tell the driver to go. The carriage lurched forward and threw Arabella back into her seat.

"I hardly think that was necessary," Arabella said with a frown.

"We've had enough of you dilly-dallying." Sarah clenched her jaw.

Eliza pulled the palm-sized scrap of paper from her trouser pocket and handed it over to Arabella without saying a word. Arabella unrolled the curled paper. Rowena leaned over her shoulder to read it at the same time. The brief missive swirled across the page in a highly embellished but sure script.

The Grande Dame wants her little witchlings home immediately.
The cure to the blight is at hand.
We wait for you in Dublin harbor. Come without delay.

Arabella's and Rowena's eyes met as they looked up from the note.

"They got through," Rowena breathed.

"They found a cure," Arabella gasped. The girls broke into peals of laughter. Arabella turned to Eliza. "Why didn't you just tell us? Why all the secrecy?"

Eliza straightened the seam on her trousers. "This isn't a casual summons home. If the Grande Dame wants you home immediately, it's for your safety. Something has changed."

"What aren't you telling us?" Arabella whispered. "You said there wouldn't be any more secrets."

Sarah and Eliza exchanged glances. Eliza cleared her throat.

"We can't be sure," Eliza said. "Both Sarah and I have been having unsettling dreams since the intruder came, and we thought the attack at the spring explained them. Then this comes, and your mother wants you home immediately. Something is in the air."

"But those dreams could have been nothing?" Arabella nodded to Eliza, raising her eyebrows and trying to sound encouraging. "You said yourself on the *Kittiwake* when I had that awful nightmare that sometimes dreams are just dreams. Witches are capable of having mundane and meaningless dreams."

"Perhaps." Sarah pressed her lips together and clenched her hands in her lap. "But the haste won't hurt us if there is no reason to fear." She paused. "And it could save our lives if there is…" Her voice trailed off.

Arabella swallowed hard. "Right, then. Well, we're on our way now. We'll be alright, won't we?"

Eliza looked at her quietly for a moment. "You'll be alright. I'll make sure of it. I made a promise to your mother." Arabella bit her lip and cast her gaze down to her lap. The carriage remained quiet for a long time.

Arabella looked out the window and sighed. "I wonder why Mother didn't send the ravens back with her summons if it was so important. Why did we have to hear through Bathsheba and James?"

Sarah looked up from examining her fingernails. "We were lucky enough to get a wild pair all the way to Boscastle. Getting them to fly back would be dicey at best. They probably took off as soon as your mother emptied the carry pouches."

Eliza crossed her arms across her chest and snorted. "I wasn't sure they'd complete the flight at all."

Rowena frowned at her. "Well, you're in a fine mood, aren't you?"

Eliza narrowed her eyes and glared at Rowena, but she said nothing.

Arabella patted Rowena's hand. "We're all a bit on edge," she murmured. "Perhaps a bit of grace is called for." Rowena blew out her breath and nodded.

"In any case," Arabella continued. "It will be easier to make arrangements to get to France from Boscastle than it would be from Louth Hall. It's better that we get there as soon as possible."

"France?" Eliza straightened in her seat. "What's this about France?"

Arabella glanced at her sister. "I don't think it's anything you need to worry about. We have some family business to take care of."

Eliza groaned to herself and sank deep into her seat. She covered her eyes with her hand. "It's not bloody likely the threat to your life has ebbed so much that your mother will allow you to leave the country without a Guardian escort."

"And we'll likely get the assignment since we've already been attached to you." Sarah rolled her eyes.

Rowena frowned. "I really don't understand why the both of you are suddenly so antagonistic toward us. I thought we had an amicable relationship. Didn't we?"

Eliza rubbed her temples with her fingertips. "Sleep deprivation. Residual soreness from the beating that a spell won't take care of..." She sighed. "I apologize for being so snappish."

"Me as well," Sarah grunted. "You don't deserve the short end of our tempers."

"Is there anything we can do to help?" Arabella cocked her head to the side.

"Wait a few days to book your passage to France so we can get a few nights of decent sleep before we're off again?" Sarah groaned.

"A little more information about why we're headed to the Continent wouldn't go amiss either." Eliza fixed Arabella with a pointed gaze.

Arabella looked to Rowena. "Should I?" she asked.

"The letter was addressed to you," Rowena said. "It's your decision."

Arabella looked thoughtful for a moment. "Magistra Walsh was in possession of two letters sent thirty years ago, one to our Aunts Lorena and Lenore and one to our mother. She gave them to us as an enticement to plead the cause of the Irish witches to the Grande Dame."

"I hardly think your mother will appreciate you reading her mail," Sarah scoffed.

"We didn't read her letter," Rowena piped up.

"We only read the one addressed to Lorena and Lenore." Arabella paused. "And wrapped in the letter to them was a letter to me."

Eliza raised an eyebrow. "A letter written to you more than a decade before you were born?"

Arabella nodded. "Yes, I know. It's all very odd. But our Aunt Susannah wrote to Aunt Lenore and Lorena to ask them for two things. One, to come visit her and Louisa in France because she missed her sisters, and two, deliver a letter from Aunt Louisa to me."

"Didn't know I'd need to study your family tree to make sense of things…" Sarah mumbled.

"You're sure the letter was for you?" Eliza asked.

"I am. At first, I thought it might be for Amelia because the outside was addressed to "A." But then when I opened the letter my name was clearly written inside. Aunt Louisa asked me to come to France, just as Aunt Susannah asked her sisters."

"Aunt Louisa is a strong precog," Rowena added.

"Clearly," Sarah grunted. She leaned forward, resting her elbows on her knees. She looked sideways at Eliza. "What do you think?"

Eliza did not take her eyes off Arabella. "I think I'd like to see the letters."

Arabella nodded, then she dug into her reticule. She handed Eliza all three letters, one to her aunts, one to her, and one to her mother. Eliza handed the one addressed to her mother back to Arabella immediately.

"I don't want to risk the Grande Dame's wrath by cracking the seal, even accidentally," Eliza said. She scanned over the letter to Lorena and Lenore quickly, then passed it to Sarah. "Nothing unusual," she murmured. Sarah concurred and passed the letter back to Arabella.

Eliza's gaze fell on Louisa's letter to Arabella. Her eyes widened. Her skin paled. She tilted the letter toward Sarah. Sarah blanched and swallowed hard.

Eliza's voice came out in a hoarse whisper. "You're certain this letter is authentic? That there is no manipulation?"

Arabella frowned. "As certain as I can be." She exchanged glances with Rowena. "The paper seems old enough, and Magistra Walsh knew details about Mother and our aunts. Magistra Walsh doesn't have any reason to lie."

"Doesn't she?" Eliza murmured. She rubbed her chin and returned her attention to the letter. "Your mother has left the Irish witches in a bad position for quite some time. And Magistra Walsh is very dedicated to the witches in her care. She might try anything to keep them safe." Eliza looked up to Arabella again. "I ask again, are you certain the letter is authentic?"

"Now that you put it that way," Arabella said. "Not at all certain."

Eliza nodded to herself. "There are certain spells we can perform once we're home to ascertain the authenticity."

"Those spell ingredients are rare," Sarah said. "We might be better served by asking the Grande Dame if she recognizes the handwriting, if the voice matches her sister's."

Eliza shook her head. "That could be faked by someone who knew them well enough. We should cast the spell to be sure."

Sarah pressed her lips together in a white line and nodded. "But we still need to notify the Grande Dame."

"Indeed." Eliza held up the letter so that Arabella and Rowena could see the drawing that dominated the paper. "What do you know about this… drawing?"

Rowena and Arabella exchanged glances.

"Almost nothing," Rowena said. "It's the first time either one of us has seen anything like it."

"It's more accurate to say we know nothing for certain and that we've tried to guess a few things since we opened the letter," Arabella corrected her sister.

Nodding, Eliza handed the letter back to Arabella. "What have you speculated?"

Arabella shrugged and ran her thumb along the edge of the paper. "The only thing that seems to make sense is that Aunt Louisa is suffering from the insanity that so many precogs suffer from, that seeing so many conflicting fragments of the future has driven her mad. Nothing about this figure makes sense."

Eliza sighed deeply. "That would be much more comforting than what I suspect."

"Our aunt's madness would be comforting?" Rowena said sharply.

"Not that her illness of the mind is comforting in and of itself," Eliza said. "But that it is more comforting than the alternative." Sarah patted her shoulder.

"What's the alternative?" Arabella whispered.

"That drawing has many of the characteristics common to the Egyptian Gods," Eliza said.

"A mix of animal traits with a human head is commonplace in that pantheon," Sarah added.

"And there is something about this Egyptian god that makes you nervous?" Arabella prompted.

Eliza chuckled. "The whole Egyptian pantheon is not one to be treated lightly. They are formidable, and they have strong opinions."

"But do you recognize *him*?" Arabella pressed.

"Not right off, no," Eliza said. "But your mother has an extensive library. We may be able to find a name after we get to Boscastle."

"This troubles me," Sarah said, resting her chin on her fist. "We don't know if the letter is authentic. If it is not, it could be a part of some elaborate game designed to lure Arabella to France for nefarious reasons. The maid who betrayed us came from France, and Kiera said the Ilhexerai have a strong base there as well. However, if it is truly a letter from her precog aunt, she may have drawn the attention of an Egyptian god."

Arabella gulped. "Neither option sounds very appealing."

A bitter laugh bubbled up from Eliza's lips. "They aren't, are they?" She shook her head. "Appealing or not, we have to deal with it."

Fear and sorrow warred on Arabella's face. "I know Mother will insist I have some kind of protection, but it doesn't need to be you." Arabella looked from Sarah to Eliza and back again. "I'm sure the Chapterhouse could send fresh Guardians, and you can wash your hands of me."

Sarah barked a sour laugh. "You don't understand, do you?"

Arabella frowned. "I'm afraid not."

Eliza sighed. "Sarah and I swore to protect the both of you from all harm until we returned you home and your mother releases us."

"Then Mother will just release you as soon as we get to Boscastle," Rowena said. "I don't see what the problem is."

Eliza shook her head. "The blood oath we swear at the start of a body Guardian assignment says that we will protect you from all threats that arise during our care. That," she jabbed her finger at the letter that lay in Arabella's hands, "is a new threat arising during our care. We cannot stand down until that threat is gone or we are dead, even if your mother tries to release us. The magic that binds us will not allow anything less."

"You're stuck with us as much as we are stuck with you," Sarah said with a smirk.

"Well, then," Arabella murmured, shock plain on her face. "Perhaps we should try to find ways to be more amiable travelling companions."

CHAPTER XXIV

On Puzzling Prophesies and an Old Witch's Mutterings

THE CARRIAGE RATTLED TO A STOP AT THE HEAD OF THE DOCK WHERE the *Kittiwake* berthed. The strong stench of fish struck Arabella as she stepped down from the carriage.

"Ugh!" She wrinkled her nose.

"The fishing fleet's just in," Sarah remarked. She caught her satchel as the driver tossed it to her from the roof of the carriage. Eliza frowned.

"If the fishing fleet is just coming in, then it means the tide will be against us," Eliza said. "We'll have to wait for the tide to go out again."

"You don't have to wait on my watch," Bathsheba called as she strode down the dock toward them. Deckhands from the *Kittiwake* trotted after her. They gathered up the luggage without a word. "I can bend the wind well enough to get us out of the harbor without any trouble." She winked at Eliza.

"Did my mother say anything about why she wants me home so quickly?" Arabella asked.

Bathsheba laughed. "As if the Grande Dame would trust me, a lowly wind witch, with the secrets of the kingdom." She shook her head. "No, little witchling, your mother did not share her reasons with me. All I know is that the faster I get you home, the larger my reward will be. Let's get you aboard!" Bathsheba clucked her tongue and began herding them down the dock.

Sarah was the last one on board. The moment her feet touched the deck, the men cast off the lines. The gentle creak of wood sounded as the sailors pushed away from the dock with boat hooks. Bathsheba began to fill the sails with wind. They slipped serenely through the water past the fishing boats and cargo ships. Sailors on the other vessels stood slack-jawed as Bathsheba pushed them out of the harbor against the tide. As they glided past the mouth of the harbor, Bathsheba called out, "Hold on to your stockings, ladies!"

The wind witch bent low at the waist as if gathering something from her feet. Her chin tucked to her chest, she slowly rolled up to stand, straight and tall, arms round before her holding the sparkling gold of magical power. The words that tumbled from her lips in a torrent tickled the edges of Arabella's hearing. She couldn't quite make them out. Bathsheba tilted her head back and threw her arms up wide to the sky. The sails suddenly bellied out to full capacity. The deck jerked under their feet, then the Kittiwake skimmed over the waves, almost flying.

Bathsheba drooped. She bent over, hands braced on her knees, panting. Beads of sweat stood out on her forehead. Captain Midstock hovered at her side, one hand raised as if he wished to comfort her, but he wasn't sure his touch would be welcome. Concern creased his face.

"Bathsheba?"

"I'm fine, Harry," she croaked. She shook her head and stood up straight. She took a deep breath and blew it out again. Her voice was stronger but still hoarse. "Getting that first gust off right after the delicate work of getting out of the harbor is taxing, but I'll be fine. Maintaining the speed isn't as hard as getting us started."

Captain Midstock clasped his hands behind his back, rocking heel to toe. "As long as you're alright."

Bathsheba chuckled as she patted his shoulder. "Right as rain."

The captain smiled. He gave the other witches a nod and turned to go about his work. Eliza stepped close to Bathsheba's shoulder with a fake smile fixed to her face. She murmured softly enough that her words did not carry beyond the small knot of witches.

"You're not going to tell him how much that hurt you, are you?"

"Would you?" Bathsheba murmured back without turning her head. "He's a kind enough man for his place and his time, but showing him that much weakness wouldn't do."

Eliza nodded. "We have some vigilance potions. We could shore you up if you think it would help."

Bathsheba inclined her head slightly. "That would be much appreciated. Perhaps during the night watch would be best."

"Indeed," Eliza said with a small dip of her head.

The *Kittiwake* slid into Liverpool harbor just as the sun passed noontime the next day. Every witch on board was exhausted and jittery. Bathsheba pressed her hands against the small of her back and arched a bit.

"The comfort of my bed will be sweet indeed after this long night," she groaned. She rolled her shoulders as she winked at Eliza. "But it would have been worse without you, and for that, you have my thanks."

Sarah looked pointedly over Bathsheba's shoulder and coughed. Captain Midstock strolled up to the witches with his hands clasped behind his back.

"That is the fastest I've ever made the passage from Dublin to Liverpool," he said. "I'm certain I could find paying customers if you'd consider doing it again, Bathsheba."

Bathsheba kept her countenance neutral, but Arabella noticed her hand clench in the folds of her skirt by her side. Bathsheba's eyes flicked to Eliza and Sarah. She forced a chuckle.

"Stirring up that much wind is not an easy task," she said. "I'd not do it again unless the pay is quite high… But I'll always at least consider an offer."

The captain inclined his head. "You are prudent and wise, as always, Bathsheba."

The deck shuddered lightly as the men drew the lines tight and tied up the *Kittiwake*. Eliza shaded her eyes with her hand as she looked up the dock.

"Jeannette is already waiting for us," Eliza said.

"We'd best be going," Sarah said with a nod.

"Thank you for your great service, Captain." Arabella curtseyed. "You have been most helpful. Blackstone House will never forget that."

The captain gave her a small bow. "It was my honor, Miss Leyden. I'd be happy to serve Blackstone House again."

Bathsheba nudged him with her elbow. "You mean your wallet would be happy."

Captain Midstock flushed and coughed. "Well, yes, a man does need to eat. But I'm certainly loyal to the witches of the Isles as well."

Nearly the entire population of the boat trooped up the dock toward Jeanette and the waiting carriage. The deckhands carried the luggage while the captain and Bathsheba made pleasant conversation about the weather with their departing passengers. As they approached, Jeanette dug into a satchel at her side.

"Captain Midstock, Bathsheba Mabushaedig," Jeanette boomed as she hopped down off the box. "Blackstone House is honored by your service. I am sure the Grande Dame will be exceptionally pleased with your haste." She presented each of them with a fine leather pouch full of gold guineas.

Bathsheba curtseyed and inclined her head. "It is my honor to serve the Grande Dame."

The captain bowed low. "I am ever at the service of Blackstone House."

Jeanette turned her attention to Arabella, Rowena, Eliza, and Sarah. "Now that the formalities are over, get in the carriage, ladies. We've miles to go, and the Grande Dame wants you home yesterday."

"Can you tell us why Mother is in such a hurry?" Arabella asked.

Jeanette shook her head as she climbed back on the box. "It's best to let her explain it."

Jeanette pushed the horses and the enchantments on the carriage as much as she dared. The sun hovered at the horizon as she pulled the carriage up in front of the manor. A footman who had been waiting under the portico hustled down to the carriage to open the door and hand out the ladies. The horses panted, their heads drooping. Jeanette hopped off the box and petted them, crooning promises of carrots and sugar lumps and fresh water.

Arabella rubbed her neck and groaned. "I want one of Mrs. Holly's meat pies, a hot bath, and my own bed."

"That sounds like a bit of paradise," Rowena agreed with a smile.

The sound of the front door slamming open startled them all. Minerva hustled down the front steps with indecorous haste, her gaze fixed on her youngest daughter. Ignoring everyone else, her eyes bored into Arabella as she cupped her face in both hands.

"No difference? Is there a difference?" Minerva whispered to herself. She turned her head and shouted over her shoulder, "Mother!"

"I'm almost there," Eleanor grumbled as she hurried across the gravel drive, one hand on her low back and the other on her cane. "You have to give these old bones some time."

Eleanor stopped in front of Arabella. She cocked her head to the side, like a bird, and gave her a smile. Minerva let go of Arabella and stepped out of the way. She rubbed her hands nervously together, her brow deeply furrowed. Eliza and Sarah exchanged nervous glances and frowns.

"Did you have a pleasant trip, child?" Eleanor asked.

"It was... mostly lovely," Arabella said carefully. Her eyes narrowed. Caution held her tongue, and some inner voice whispered to her to smooth over the story just for now. "There were only a few uncomfortable moments. But Eliza and Sarah handled everything admirably."

Eleanor nodded. "And your young man, he is well?"

"Julian?" Arabella tittered. "I'm not sure I'd call him *my* young man yet, although there is a story there to tell over tea..."

"Mother!" Minerva's voice cracked. "We don't have time for useless pleasantries. You told me that yourself."

Eleanor blinked owlishly at Minerva. "Did I now?" She shook her head as if to clear it. "Perhaps I did..."

Eleanor snatched up Arabella's hand and turned it palm up. She leaned in close to examine the creases. She traced the lifeline, then the heartline with the tip of her middle finger. Then she leaned in close, her nose nearly touching Arabella's skin, and she inhaled deeply. Everyone else stood absolutely still, staring as Eleanor straightened up, her eyes closed.

Her eyes popped open. "She's fine," she chirped. She patted Arabella's hand before she let go.

"Fine? Just *fine*? I need more detail than that, Mother," Minerva said in a strangled voice. "You woke me in the wee hours of the morning with a dire warning about my child, then you say everything is fine, and that's it?"

"Oh no, dear," Eleanor said with a grin. "She's fine right now. He hasn't touched her yet. She may not be fine soon, though. But for right now… yes. Fine. Perfectly fine."

Minerva closed her eyes and shook her head with a sigh.

"Who hasn't touched me?" Arabella asked. "Julian? He was a perfect gentleman."

Eleanor leaned closer to Arabella and winked. "Oh no, sweetling, not a living man. A living man is not your problem."

Eliza cleared her throat. "Grande Dame, there are things we need to discuss. A troubling incident at Louth Hall and a concern that revealed itself as we were travelling to the port yesterday."

"The letter…" Arabella nodded.

"Perhaps and perhaps not," Eliza said. "But we all need to gather somewhere a bit more comfortable and speak plainly with one another. It seems there may be a greater puzzle to solve, and we each hold a different piece."

Minerva's jaw tightened. "Mother, how much time?"

Eleanor looked thoughtful for a moment. "We have some time while he sleeps."

"How long?"

Eleanor shrugged. "His time runs contrarily to ours. He might just be having a rejuvenating nap that lasts for years." She paused, and Minerva's shoulders loosened. "Or it could be a refreshing night's sleep that lasts but an hour." Minerva's fists clenched.

"I wish you would just speak plainly for once!" Minerva hissed through gritted teeth.

"If I could, I would, sweetling," Eleanor said. Her face fell, tears gathered in the corners of her eyes.

Minerva sighed and straightened her shoulders. "Come then, into the house and the protection of the wards." Minerva gestured for them to follow her as she glided serenely across the pea gravel. "We have time to look in on the progress your brother and sister have made before we sit down to dinner."

CHAPTER XXV

*Wherein the Harmony of Disparate Chords
Reveals the Solution*

VIVIENNE AND HENRY HAD COMPLETELY TAKEN OVER THEIR MOTHER'S workroom. Arabella's eyes roved the chamber. She was aghast at the arcane tomes and ephemera pushed aside for beakers and brass scales. But Vivienne's mark was clearly there as well in the bundles of herbs and vials of tinctures.

Vivienne and Henry stood side by side at the largest central worktable staring into a tin pail. They each bore deep frowns on their faces. A nanny stood two paces behind Vivienne, bouncing little Adella on her hip. They didn't seem to notice Minerva enter with all the new arrivals trailing behind her.

"I think this may be the best we can do," Henry said as he rubbed his chin.

"That's unacceptable," Vivienne said in a clipped tone. All of her siblings winced. She sounded exactly like their mother. "We set out to find a cure and find a cure we shall."

Henry groaned and ran his hand through his hair. "We've hardly slept for a week, Viv. A preventative may be all we can manage for now. I don't know what else to do."

Mother cleared her throat.

"Hello, Mother," Vivienne and Henry chorused without taking their eyes from the bucket.

"Perhaps some fresh minds may be able to help?" Mother said primly.

Vivienne's head snapped up.

"Arabella! Rowena!" She rushed over and embraced her sisters. "Are you alright?"

"I don't know why everyone seems to be expecting me to be hurt," Arabella said.

Vivienne glanced at their mother, who shook her head slightly. "Yes, I suppose Mother hasn't had time to talk to you yet." She tugged on Arabella's elbow. "Come see what we've done. Your samples were so very helpful."

"Hello, Henry," Arabella said as she stepped up to the table. Henry grunted, still staring into the bucket. Rowena and Arabella leaned in a little to see just what he was staring at. The bucket was filled with a milky, blue liquid.

"It's so… blue!" Rowena burst out.

"That's mostly because of the copper sulphate," Henry muttered.

"Does it work?" Arabella asked. "Mother's message through Bathsheba said the cure was in sight."

"Yes and no," Vivienne said with a sigh.

"Bah!" Henry threw his hands into the air and stomped away from the worktable to the window overlooking the rose garden.

"It works as a preventative," Vivienne said. "If you spread it over the young potato plants before they are infected, they won't become infected when exposed to the blight. If they've already been exposed to the blight before treatment, it's much less effective."

"It's not effective at all!" Henry called from his place at the window.

"You must be precise, brother dear," Vivienne chided. Henry rolled his eyes. Vivienne turned back to her sisters. "If the blight hasn't gotten a firm hold, if there are only a few infected plants in the crop and they are only mildly infected, the blight can be arrested and most of the crop saved."

"I thought the potato growth cycle was much longer than a couple of weeks," Sarah said as she took her turn to peer into the bucket. "I'm amazed you've made so much progress when you've had so little time with the samples."

Vivienne shrugged. "There are spells to push a plant through its growth cycle much faster. It's made iterating the formula much easier."

"Huh, too bad there isn't a spell to reverse the growth cycle," Sarah said.

"But this is still wonderful!" Arabella enthused. "This is so much more than the people of Ireland had before. The cottars won't have to starve!"

"In the future, yes," Vivienne said. "But what about now? What about the blighted crops in the field that should be feeding them now?"

"What did you say?" Henry stomped up to the table, his eyes fastened on Sarah.

"I said, what about…" Vivienne began.

"Not you," Henry interrupted. He stabbed his finger at Sarah. "What did you say?"

Sarah frowned. "That it's too bad there's not a spell to reverse the growth cycle?"

Henry whirled around to Vivienne, his eyes wild. "Is there? Is there a spell to reverse the growth of plant life?"

A faraway look stole over Vivienne's face. "I don't think so…"

But at the same time, Arabella felt excitement building within her and cut her sister off. The long years of dusting her mother's study and reshelving books to "learn responsibility" might finally serve a good purpose.

"Maybe…!" She turned and sprinted to one of her mother's bookshelves. Her fingers danced along the spines as she muttered to herself. "Aha!" She snatched a volume off the shelf. Making her way back to the worktable, she rifled to the pages. She dropped the open book onto the table in triumph.

"There!" she jabbed her finger at a handwritten spell. "A spell to arrest plant growth and allowing it to restart later. I can see why you didn't think about it because its application has always been so frivolous. Most witches use it to delay blooms so that their garden is particularly lush for a specific event, like a garden party."

"Can you alter it to reverse the plant growth?" Henry asked breathlessly.

Vivienne set her hands on either side of the book, leaning in close. "I think so…" she said in a distant voice. "It doesn't seem that difficult."

"But how does that help?" Rowena interjected. "Won't the plants just be younger and still as overwhelmed with blight?"

Henry pounded his fist into his palm. "This is an important part of the puzzle. I know it! We're so close…"

Arabella remembered being on the edge of a breakthrough in Julien's lab not so long ago and felt her siblings' frustration. "What about the blight itself?" she asked. "If you can reverse the growth of the potato, can you also reverse the growth of the blight?"

Vivienne and Henry stared at each other, wide-eyed, frozen for a moment as Arabella's idea sank in.

"Where's the blight sample?" Vivienne said in a breathy rush, flapping her hand at her brother. "Get me the blight sample! I need to confirm something."

Henry tossed papers and notes willy nilly, crowing as he came up with a small rectangle of glass. He handed it to his sister. She slid it into a contraption Arabella did not recognize, then bent to look in one end of a tube pointed to the bit of glass.

"What is that?" Arabella asked.

"It's a microscope," Henry responded. "It magnifies things so we can get a proper look at aspects too small to see with the naked eye."

"It's been quite useful in this whole process," Vivienne said as she adjusted a small knob without looking up from the eyepiece. Then she gasped.

"What is it?" Henry cried.

"I don't know why we didn't think of this before…" Vivienne murmured.

"Don't keep me in suspense, woman!"

Vivienne looked up from the microscope with a twinkle in her eye and a wide grin on her face. "The blight is a tiny fungus. It's a plant! I can arrest the growth with the spell Arabella found, or if I can adjust the spell—reverse the growth!"

Henry whooped and clapped his hands. Vivienne smiled at her brother.

Another thought flickered across Henry's face, and he dropped his arms. The smile faded from his face. "But the people will still need witches to cast those spells." He whipped his head around, eyes searching for his mother. "How many witches do we have in Ireland who would be capable of casting this?"

"Not enough, I'm afraid," Mother said with a frown.

"That's only one way to do it," Vivienne interjected. "I can bespell the mixture like we do with any potion, and it would still work for the most mundane person."

"But can you target the growth retardation to only affect the blight and not the potato plant?" Henry jabbed the air.

Vivienne smirked. "Of course, I can."

Henry swept his sister into a tight embrace, lifting her off her feet. He swung her around in circles as they both laughed.

"The harmony of the minds can solve more problems than the instrument of a single intellect." Grandmother beamed. "Can we have dinner now? I'm starving."

"We're so close with this breakthrough," Vivienne said. At that moment, Adella began to fuss.

"I think the baby is hungry as well, ma'am," the nanny said.

Vivienne reached for her daughter. "Dinner it is, then."

Henry gazed over the worktable longingly. He sighed. "Yes, I suppose we must feed the body as well as the mind." He squeezed his sister's shoulder. "We've almost done it."

Vivienne smiled up at her brother.

"Perhaps we can work on other projects when this is done? I must confess, I'm quite excited about the possibilities now that I see what magic and science can do together," Henry said.

Vivienne laughed. "Let's finish this project first, Henry. Then we can discuss the future." She began walking to the door of the workroom. "For now, we eat."

"Mother, I need to talk to you," Arabella called out. "We all do." She gestured to Rowena, Eliza, and Sarah.

"It can wait until after dinner," Minerva replied airily, waving away the concern in Arabella's voice.

"No, it can't." Arabella's voice was firm. "We need to discuss this now."

Mother glanced at the door to the workroom as Henry followed the last lady out. "Fine," she huffed. "Let's make this quick."

"We need to know what you and Grandmother were talking about when you greeted us," Arabella said. "Who hasn't touched me yet? Did Grandmother get a vision? What has you so concerned?"

Mother tilted her head to the side and sighed. "Your grandmother woke me out of a dead sleep a week ago. She was quite agitated and insisted she saw some sort of man-beast stalking you. Nothing would calm her until I promised to bring you home straight away. I sent a message to Bathsheba Mabushaedig, hiring her to bring you home as quickly as possible." She sighed dramatically. "Can we get ready for dinner now?"

Arabella paled and looked to Rowena and then Eliza. Her voice trembled. "A man-beast? Grandmother said I was stalked by a man-beast?"

Mother threw up her hands. "You know your grandmother's visions aren't always accurate, and they've been getting less so as she ages. She probably just overindulged in her sweets and had a bad dream."

Arabella's gaze sharpened. "When I arrived, you seemed more worried than a case of dyspepsia would call for."

"What of it?" Mother said. "I've seen you with my own eyes and confirmed that no man-beast is chasing you. Is there anything else?"

Arabella pulled out the worn and sealed letter she'd carried all the way from Ireland and held it out to her without a word. Mother frowned as she took it.

"What is this?" She turned the grubby letter over in her hands. It only bore her name and no return address. "It's filthy."

"It's a letter from Aunt Susannah and Aunt Louisa," Arabella said. "It was supposed to find you in Ireland. But then the... unfortunate incident... happened. Magistra Walsh has been trying to return it to you for almost thirty years now."

Mother kept her face stony still, but her widened eyes betrayed her shock. The letter stilled in her hands. "Is that all?" Her voice had a brittle edge.

"There was a letter to Aunt Lenore and Aunt Lorena too," Arabella said.

"Give it to me," Mother demanded. She stretched out her hand. Arabella handed her the opened outer letter. "You already opened it?" Mother's voice rose. Her eyes blazed.

"We did," Arabella responded calmly. She swallowed hard. "There was another letter inside it." She paused. "A letter addressed to me."

"That's ridiculous," Mother snapped. "You weren't even a gleam in my eye thirty years ago."

"It shocked me as well." Arabella kept her voice soft. "But Aunt Louisa clearly wrote my name in the letter. It was meant for me."

Mother scowled. "Are you going to tell me what she wrote, or are you going to keep it a secret?"

"She wants me to come to France..." Arabella began.

"Out of the question!" Mother cut her off. "You've only just come home, and there have been visions about danger to your person."

"You just said Grandmother's dream was nothing but a bellyache!" Arabella protested.

"There's no reason for you to go to France," Mother snapped. "It's been thirty years. There's no telling where Louisa is now."

"We could scry and find out," Rowena suggested. "Do we have any of her personal items stored away?"

Mother glared at Rowena, then shifted her gaze to the Guardians. "You allowed this to happen?" she growled.

Eliza straightened her shoulders. "Your daughters are grown witches, Grande Dame. We were there to protect them, not control them."

"Grande Dame, there may be a connection between your mother's vision and the letter within the letter," Sarah said. "There is a drawing of what we think is an Egyptian god. He could be interpreted as a man-beast."

Mother blanched. "How do you know so much about this and I don't?"

"We're trying to talk to you about it now, Mother." Arabella winced at the whine that crept into her voice. "Please. We think your letter might contain more clues."

"Alright." Mother ripped open the seal with trembling hands. As she scanned the lines, her face grew even paler. Her hands began to shake so hard the paper rattled. She put a hand to her mouth and started to keen. She sank to the floor and crumpled the letter into her midsection. Arabella rushed to her. She dropped to the floor and tried to put a comforting hand on her shoulder.

"Don't touch me!" Mother shrieked. Tears rolled down her cheeks. She bent forward almost double. "Leave me, please leave me alone," she moaned.

"But..." Arabella protested.

Rowena grabbed her arm and pulled her up from the floor. "We'll tell Vivienne," Rowena whispered in her ear. "We'll let her have a moment and send Mrs. Holly in with a hot toddy."

"But..."

"Your sister's right," Eliza murmured as she helped Rowena lead her to the door, Sarah at their heels. "She needs a moment to gather herself."

"But it's cruel to leave her alone when she's obviously in pain," Arabella dissented.

"It's also suicidal to stay in firing range of a powerful witch when she's not in her right mind," Sarah hissed. "Now move!"

Arabella let them guide her away, but she looked over her shoulder the whole way at her mother weeping on the floor.

CODA

ARABELLA COULD NOT SLEEP. AS THE ENTRY HALL CLOCK STRUCK midnight, she wrapped a shawl around herself, then crept from her room and out into the gardens. The dew-soaked grass soothed her feet. The soft night air caressed her cheeks.

She found her mother sitting in a grassy patch at the center of the rose garden. She wore the same dress as earlier in the evening, her skirts pooled around her on the ground. Arabella settled next to her. Even in the dim moonlight, she could see Mother's eyes rimmed red from crying. They sat in silence for a long while.

"I want to stop you from going to France," Mother said finally. Her voice was hoarse.

"I know," Arabella said in a small voice. "I'd rather not go, but I think I have to."

"You do." Mother's voice cracked.

"Your letter…" Arabella's voice trailed off.

Mother nodded. "I'll share it with you someday, but not now. There are some things you're better off not knowing."

Arabella sighed. "Secrets, Mother? Still?"

Mother shook her head. "When something is fated, and you try to avoid it, sometimes it makes things worse. And the thing you were trying to avoid happens anyway." She gazed at her daughter with pleading eyes. "I'm only trying to soften the blow," she whispered.

Arabella held her mother's gaze for a moment, then nodded. "Alright." She paused. "So, what do we do now?"

"I prepare you and your sister as well as I can, and I send you both to France," Mother said with a sigh. "And then I pray to any god or goddess who will listen for you to come home whole."

ABOUT THE AUTHOR

M ICHELLE D. SONNIER WRITES DARK URBAN FANTASY, STEAMPUNK, AND anything else that lets her combine the weird and the fantastic in unexpected ways. She even writes horror, although it took her a long time to admit that since she prefers the existential scare over blood and gore. She is the author of *The Clockwork Witch* and *Death's Embrace* and has published short stories in a variety of print and online venues. She lives in Maryland with her husband, son, and a variable number of cats.

PATRONS OF THE CLOCKWORK ARTS

Adam H Zerance
Amanda Cavanagh
Anita Morris
Anne Frates
Annie Allen
Anonymous
Apotheosis Studios
April Walters
Ashley VanMeter
Aysha Rehm
Beth Sparks-Jacques
Beverly Bambury
Bradon Jurn
Butch Howard
C.A. Rowland
Carol Jones
Cat Hunter
Charissa D. Jones
Chris Cooke
Christopher J. Burke
Craig "Stevo" Stephenson
Curtis & Maryrita Steinhour
Dale A Russell
Dan Nolan
Daniel Lin
Danielle Ackley-McPhail

David Perkins
David Sherman
David Stolarz
Debbie Cairo
Debra Lieven
Dee Sauerwein
Dex Greenbright
Dino Hicks
Dr Douglas Vaughan
Ed Washburn
Eric S. Schaefer
Eric W. Stephenson
Felicia Browell
Gary Phillips
Gav
Gordon Horne
Greg Levick
H Lynnea Johnson
Howard J. Bampton
IndolentCin
Isaac 'Will It Work' Dansicker
Jakub Narębski
Jay Targaryen
JC Kang
JDN
Jeanne Talbourdet

Jenn Whitworth
Jennifer Della'Zanna
Jennifer L. Pierce
Jeremy Audet
Johanna Sachs
John Green
John Idlor
John L. French
John Monahan
Judith Waidlich
Julian White
Julie Giles Cooke
Keith R.A. DeCandido
Keith Rohrer
Ken Brandt
Kierin Fox
L.E. Custodio
Lark Cunningham
Leokii
Leon W Fairley
Lewis Phillips
Lisa1200
Lori B.
Lorraine Anderson
maileguy
Marc W.
Margaret Bumby
Margaret St. John
Margie Martinson-Brezina
Maria T
Maria V. Arnold
Mark Lukens
Megan Mackie
Melissa Phelps
Mia Naeyaert
Michael Brooker
Mishee Kearney
Museworthy Inc.
Nanci Moy & Dave Bean
NIna Amaya
Oren Truitt

Otter Libris
Paul May
Paul van Oven
Pete Niedzielski
Peter D Engebos
pjk
Rich Riley
Richard Clark
Rick Heinz
Rob in AUS
Robert C Flipse
Robert Claney
Robin Lynn
Russell Ventimeglia
Ryan Harron
Sasquatch
Scherrix
Scott Elson
Scott Schaper
Shane "Asharon" Sylvia
Shell S.
Shervyn
Sheryl R. Hayes
STEAMPUNK Chef James
Stephen Ballentine
Stephen Lesnik
Steve Locke
Tad L. J. Pierson
Taia Hartman
Tasha Turner
The Creative Fund
Thomas Karwacki
Tim DuBois
Tina Noe Good
Tom B.
ToniAnn Marini
Tony C
V Hartman DiSanto
Wil Bastion
Yes